FLAMES REKINDLED

"How are you holding up, Beth Ann? Really?"

She shrugged, unwilling or unable to explain how the last few weeks felt like a long slog through the chest-deep water of an icy lake, how every now and then she stepped into an unseen hole which plunged her far beneath the surface. How even the thought of the intruder in her dark house made her stomach lurch with the sensation of that sickening drop.

"I'm all right if I don't think about things too much," she finally told him. Whenever she did, she couldn't help wondering if the sheriff had been wrong about the man who'd hurt her—if she really had encountered the vicious bastard who had killed her mother instead of a garden-variety thief.

Mark nodded, his brown eyes as warm as a fireside in winter. Comprehension was written in his features, a first-hand acquaintance with the deepest grief.

"You shouldn't be here." Her words spilled out too quickly. "I appreciate the thought, but there's already so much loose talk."

"Do you care what people think?"

"Hell yes. Unlike you, I have to live here."

HEAD ON

COLLEEN THOMPSON

LOVE SPELL NEW YORK CITY

This one is for Connie, with love and gratitude.

LOVE SPELL®

July 2007

Published by

Dorchester Publishing Co., Inc.
200 Madison Avenue
New York, NY 10016

ISBN-10: 0-505-52713-8
ISBN-13: 978-0-505-52713-4

Printed in the United States of America.

Visit us on the web at www.dorchesterpub.com.

ACKNOWLEDGMENTS

So many people were instrumental in *Head On*'s journey from an idea to a finished product. First, I'd like to thank my agent, Helen Breitwieser and my editor, Alicia Condon, for their enthusiasm and support from the start.

Several people provided critical assistance in researching this book. My sister, Connie Swartz, a registered nurse with South Jersey Healthcare HospiceCare, not only inspired me but answered scores of questions about the lives of traveling hospice nurses. Houston trial lawyer Chris Samuelson kindly shared his expertise regarding the legal repercussions of fatality accidents. I also very much appreciate the assistance of Wichita Falls author Linda Broday with details about the area as well as a memorable visit to the charming town of Electra, Texas. Thanks to all of you.

Thanks as well to my early readers, the best network of writing friends any author could have. This talented ensemble includes Patricia Kay and Jo Anne Banker and the members of my critique group, the Midwives: Barbara Taylor Sissel, Joni Rodgers, Wanda Dionne, Linda Helman, and Anna Slade.

One final individual I'd like to thank is Ingrid Hill, a reader who shared with me her devotion to a beloved pet named Maia, a dog who became very real to me during the writing of this book.

Chapter 1

Ask anyone in emergency services—rescue crews or deputies, even the staff of a rural Texas hospital known to area residents as Jackrabbit General. They'll all swear it's true, what you hear about the full moon bringing out the crazies. Friday the thirteenth, too, draws its share of bad luck. Accidents, assaults, attempted suicides: regardless of how the skeptics or the statisticians spin them, the unluckiest events take place on this unlucky day. But every now and then, in a rare alignment of misfortune, Friday the thirteenth coincides with a full moon. On this strangest of strange days, all bets are off and anything can happen.

Including the return of a small community's most hated prodigal, a shock too soon eclipsed by the sort of murder that shatters country-safe complacency and sends sales of alarms and handguns soaring. A murder rooted in a tragedy so painful, it formed fault lines in the bedrock far beneath the time-worn prairie and the clear, unblinking sky.

*　*　*

"I love you like a sister, but don't be telling me which patients I can and cannot handle," Beth Ann Decker warned from the office doorway. She had already pulled on a jacket over her white scrubs and picked up her nursing bag. In ultra-conservative Hatcher County, residents expected a medical professional to look the part—even if she was caring for them in their homes.

Flushing to the tinted roots of her strawberry-blond hair, Cheryl Riker peered up from a cluttered desk in the center of an office crammed with file cabinets. Beth Ann saw that she'd moved her computer—which must have crashed again—into a corner on the floor to make room for still more charts. These past few years, revenue had skidded downhill like bald tires on a patch of ice-slick asphalt. But even in the best of times, the visiting nurse and hospice program was the red-headed stepchild of the system.

The chair creaked as the plump Cheryl struggled to her feet in an attempt to look authoritative. Though she was technically the director of the program, she had never been much good at the bossing side of the equation. "Look, I'm sorry. I don't think it's a good idea for you to take this particular patient, that's all. Let me call in Vickie, cancel her vacation."

Beth Ann shook her head. "You can't do that. That poor woman's been carrying on about this anniversary cruise for months—and when was the last time she had two weeks off anyway?"

Cheryl frowned, her face creasing into lines reminiscent of her mother's. Since her fortieth birthday earlier this autumn, Cheryl had been fretting about ending up looking like a Texas road map—a worry that only made her frown more. "If we had any other nurse available . . ."

It wasn't a discussion worth repeating. With Emmaline Stutz out with a bad back and the current hiring freeze, there was no one else available—and both women knew it.

Cheryl shook her head, concern in her hazel eyes. "You can't go out there, Beth Ann. Hiram Jessup's daughter *died* in that wreck. And his son—well, you know what happened with Mark."

"Oh, for cryin' in a bucket. Three years in hospitals and rehab centers, and you think it's possible I've forgotten any of the details?" How could she with people reminding her every time she turned around?

At her friend's stricken look, Beth Ann added, "Come on, Cheryl. It's been sixteen years. Mr. Jessup and I have long since made our peace."

Not that they'd ever come out and discussed it, but at least Hiram didn't storm out of the town's only grocery store during their infrequent, chance encounters. He nodded almost amiably in church, too, when both showed up for Christmas services and Easter.

"What about that lawsuit?" Cheryl asked.

Beth Ann shrugged. "That's old business between him and my mama. It's nothing to do with me."

This wasn't exactly true, since her mother had filed suit on account of Beth Ann's injuries—or her medical bills, to be specific. But Cheryl, bless her heart, didn't argue the point.

"Maybe I should take care of this one . . . brush up on my field experience." Cheryl fingered the tiny gold cross pinned to the lapel of her wine-colored blazer. She had once confessed to Beth Ann that she had only taken the supervisory position, with its long hours and myriad headaches, so she could wear "grown-up clothes." Scrubs, she complained, made her rear end look wider than a school bus.

"When was the last time you did patient care?" Beth Ann crossed her arms, banging her cane against the doorframe in the process. The stick was one more thing that kept her—and everyone else—from forgetting.

"I handled Mr. Jessup's intake after Emmaline went home with that back strain. Did all the paperwork myself—"

"*Paperwork*." Beth Ann shook her head. "Just let me take care of this. Please."

"Why? Why would you do this to yourself?" Cheryl demanded. "Why's it so important to you?"

"Because for sixteen years, I've been fighting an uphill battle trying to convince everyone in Hatcher County that my first name damned well isn't 'Poor.' I'm tired of it, Cheryl, sick to death of my mother having a better social life than I do—and most people don't even *like* the woman. This is it for me. If I can't prove I'm a competent professional with a *future* and not just a past, I'm pulling up stakes and starting over somewhere new. Somewhere no one ever heard of the Hatcher Red Hawks or some old car crash."

Cheryl sighed, then dropped back into her desk chair, which gave a squeal of protest. "And you think that nursing Hiram Jessup's going to prove to anybody you've moved on?"

"It'll prove it to *me*," Beth Ann said quietly, a little embarrassed by her eruption. The outburst had been coming for months, she realized. Since she'd moved into the new place with her mother—now known as "Lucky Lilly" in light of last year's miracle—Beth Ann had been thinking a lot about her life. Or almost total lack thereof. She hoped to God it wasn't too late to step up to the counter and claim her share. "Maybe that's all I need."

Cheryl glanced toward the Bible-verse-a-day calendar on her desk, then tore off yesterday's page to expose the big, black *13* that lurked between the words *Friday* and *October*. Looking up again, she asked, "You're sure about this?"

Beth Ann nodded. What did she care about some silly superstition? She attended deaths year round and had recently concluded that the failure to live fully was the only true misfortune.

Cheryl nodded. "All right. If that's the way you feel about it. But there's one thing you'd better know first. My sister figured out about Hiram Jessup going on home hospice. And before you start lecturing me about patient confidentiality, I didn't say a word to her about it. She spotted my Tahoe over at his place when I did the intake, and she was talking to Norma Nederhoffer, that woman who does transcription for the doctors. Norma didn't tell her either, but she has this sort of grave nod."

Beth Ann understood. In Eudena, a town of just over four thousand, the combination of Norma Nederhoffer's grave nods and the sighting of a hospice worker's vehicle at a person's house had the authority of gospel, or at least the *Wichita Falls Times Record*. Besides that, Cheryl's younger sister Aimee—now Aimee Gustavsen—had been an infamous blabbermouth since Beth Ann first met her back in kindergarten. That girl could whip a rumor out of less substance than it took a prairie wind to spin up a dust devil.

"You know how Aimee's been lately," Cheryl continued. "Sort of disillusioned with this marriage business."

At thirty-three, the same age as Beth Ann, former Hatcher High Homecoming Queen Aimee was already on her second go-round. Like her sister, she had chosen a deputy this time out, although big, blond Ted Gustavsen was both younger and better looking than Cheryl's Pete. Still, not even the good-natured Ted could hold a candle to his wife's nostalgia for the days she'd put out for pretty much every boy her Baptist parents bad-mouthed. Mark Jessup chief among them.

Beth Ann made the connection. "She called him, didn't she? Told him about his daddy?"

Cheryl nodded and twisted her plain, gold wedding band around her finger. "You know Aimee. Once she decided it was Mark's duty to come back home, wasn't anything going to stop her. A few days ago, she looked him up on her computer, found a number for that *company* of his in Pittsburgh." Her lip curled in a look of disapproval. "Then she called him, bold as brass, and told him it's his place to come and take care of his daddy."

Beth Ann shook her head. "Mark Jessup won't be back. Not after his father turned on him like he did. Besides, people around here won't give two hoots about how rich he is now. All they'll think about is the boy they called Hell on Wheels and three dead cheerleaders, one for each year he served."

A more disturbing thought struck. "And then they'll think of *Poor* Beth Ann—oh, damn it. I'll bury him myself if he doesn't have the sense to stay away."

About an hour later that same October morning, Beth Ann was stunned to realize her words were more than bluster. She really did harbor homicidal instincts.

Previously, she would have admitted she could pull the trigger of a shotgun to save herself from some psycho rapist, or to protect her mama—though some of Eudena's population might fault her for the latter choice. But no matter how tough she talked, or how many people she had watched die these past few years, she couldn't imagine taking a life in cold blood.

Until she saw the big grille of the Ford pickup backed into the driveway of the lonely little house tucked among the scrub mesquites on Lost Buffalo Road. With pinpoints of light exploding across her vision, she gripped her steering wheel and dragged in multiple deep breaths.

"No way is that the same truck," she told herself. "No damned way."

Like the shiny black Camaro she had been driving that Homecoming Friday, the pickup truck of memory had to be long gone now, crushed flat and pancake-stacked behind the fence surrounding Culpepper's Junkyard. Beth Ann's job took her all over Hatcher County, but she'd drive ten miles out of her way to avoid both that stretch of highway and the one on Mustang Road.

With all her flesh-and-blood reminders, she didn't need or want one as immutable as steel.

As her vision cleared, she realized that the pickup's paint was a darker blue, that its bright chrome wheels and fancy mud flaps decked out a vehicle far newer and nicer than the one wrecked sixteen years before. Still, both intuition and the Pennsylvania plates assured her that the truck belonged to *him*.

That reckless son of a bitch, Mark Jessup. "Jess" to all his friends, back in the days when he'd still had some.

Why hadn't he just taken the easy way out—hiring a private health care aide or two to supplement the county's offering? That's what a lot of men did when their mama or daddy's final illness threatened to part them from their important, out-of-town jobs. Most of the women came back, then tied themselves into tight knots trying to juggle the needs of their kids back home along with those of the ailing parent, but the men . . . Beth Ann wondered if in the high-school shop classes, the guys spent time soldering guilt-proof armor around each soft and naked conscience.

But evidently, Mark Jessup's shielding had a crack. Maybe on account of what he'd done to his sister Jordan.

At the thought, Beth Ann considered putting her Subaru, a peeling, red station wagon as homely as it was indestructible, back in gear and cruising past Hiram Jessup's place. Once she made it out of sight—a drawn-out process, considering the flatness of this stretch of prairie and the crisp brilliance of the cobalt sky—she could call the old man to say she'd had car trouble. Anyone who'd ever seen the War Wagon would believe it.

Then she could phone Cheryl and tell her that maybe it was time to trot out those mothballed patient-care skills of hers after all.

But Beth Ann hesitated, convinced that sooner or later—probably sooner, considering her supervisor's penchant for easing her job stress by yakking with her little sister—Aimee would learn that Beth Ann had turned tail. And word would hit this county like hail stones bouncing off tin roofs.

She gritted her teeth as she pictured dings and dents. *Did you hear what happened to Poor Beth Ann? Would've been kinder to whack her upside the head with a two-by-four than showin' up the way he did. Always the nervy one, that Jessup boy. Nervier than a rabid coyote.*

Facing Mark Jessup couldn't be half as painful as losing her toehold on what passed for respect here in

Eudena. Damned hard-won respect, for a never-married female on the wrong side of thirty, a woman who had chosen to ease the passing of the dying instead of working with—or having—babies. A woman who had once been pulled alive from a smashed Chevy ringed with dead cheerleaders.

Maybe Beth Ann would have gone inside, or maybe she would have chickened out and driven north to Oklahoma and straight through to parts unknown. But she never knew the answer because at that moment, the house's front storm door creaked open, and a tall figure descended the wooden steps that led down from the front porch.

A man and not a boy. And still every bit as handsome as store-bought sin.

Beth Ann felt her stomach drop through the floorboards, felt every molecule of air leave her lungs. All these years later, she still knew him, though time had filled out the gangly promise of once awkwardly long limbs, though the king-of-the-world grin that had won so many conquests had given way to an expression so grave and guarded it was hard to imagine he was the same person.

But she'd heard that prison could do that to a man.

There were other changes, too. His once-tawny hair had darkened to a rich brown. He wore it thick and wavy and a little on the long side. Reluctantly, she admitted to herself it suited him, as did the faded jeans and denim jacket thrown over a navy sweatshirt. Heavy stubble darkened his cheeks, as if he'd missed a couple of appointments with his razor. Which made sense, for he must have moved fast to get here so quickly after Aimee's phone call.

But the suddenness of Mark Jessup's arrival meant

nothing, Beth Ann figured as she pulled her car into the driveway. It was just a pretense of devotion, an act to show his hometown he wasn't some kind of monster, after all.

Pretty ballsy, considering how people felt about him. If she didn't have so much cause to hate him, she might even admire his nerve.

He didn't appear to notice her as he opened the truck's front door and pulled a suitcase from the narrow backseat. A big suitcase and a duffel, as if he planned on staying a while.

As if he had that right.

Of course he does, the nurse in her insisted. *He's the only family.* No one but his father was entitled to run Mark off at this point. As Hiram had before, on account of Jordan. As—dying or not—the old man might again.

Out of pure selfishness, Beth Ann hoped he'd do exactly that. But as she climbed out of her wagon and went for her supplies, she decided she had earned the right to peevish thoughts.

She hesitated, frowning down at the cane she'd left tucked behind her nursing bag. A glimmer of her mother's vanity flashed through her, and she thought of leaving the stick, so Mark's first impression of her would not be one of weakness.

Anger flared, and Beth Ann snatched up the thing. Other than the lackeys who worked for him in Pittsburgh, who cared what a murdering ex-con thought? She needed the cane for stability as she carried supplies in for her patient, so she would damned well use it.

Besides, that indignity beat the hell out of letting him see her fall on her rear while she struggled up the porch steps.

Leaving the hatch open—she'd need to make a second trip—she heard the crunch of footsteps on the gravel just behind her.

"Can I give you a hand with tha—?"

He stopped speaking as she turned, and Beth Ann felt perverse satisfaction as she watched the color seep from his face, heard the sharp catch of his breath.

"Beth Ann—you . . ." he tried, but he could get no further. Though the duffel remained slung over one shoulder, his suitcase landed on the gravel with a thunk.

Once more, tiny lights burst across her field of vision, but she faked a smile anyway. Or at least she hoped that's what it looked like.

Professional, she ordered herself. *You're his father's nurse, that's all. Top of your class at Midwestern State.*

She leaned her cane against the bumper and stuck out her right hand. "Yes, and the last name's still Decker. I'm the traveling RN assigned to Mr. Jessup."

Before taking her hand, Mark stared at her a beat too long. Looking for damage, she supposed, telltale remnants of the collision that had forever altered both their lives.

A chill wind rattled the dry leaves of the front yard's single, stunted live oak. The wind stirred the grasses of the lost Jessup acreage across the street, whistling through a trio of oil well pump jacks and peeling more white paint from the old ranch house and its outbuildings.

Beth Ann stared right back at Mark, daring him to comment on her reconstructed nose and cheekbones. They looked good, everyone assured her, with scars so faint as to be invisible beneath her makeup, yet her features weren't the same. She would never have the face she had been born with, or the healthy spine, left leg, or pelvis. By comparison, the one scar she noticed—an inch-long, reddish curve beneath his left eye—seemed like nothing: fate's hand slap for his guilt.

"And he's . . ." Mark hesitated, clearly searching for the right words. "My dad's okay with having you here?"

"It won't be a problem," she said simply. Hiram had never broached the subject with her, had never reminded her that she had been the one to tell his only daughter, *Better hurry or we're going.* Sixteen-year-old Jordan had had a shy girl's terror of being bumped from the fragile fringe of popularity. Even after all these years, Beth Ann saw the blond girl hesitate, then turn and wave to her father instead of kissing him goodbye.

Beth Ann had replayed that moment endlessly, since it was the last intact memory she had B.C.—Before the Crash.

"Your father's a forgiving man," she added. "He's never once blamed me."

"Why should he," Mark asked sharply, "when he had me for that?"

She looked away, troubled by that glimpse of anger and raw pain. Her gaze sought the solace of the nearest pump jack, the only one still rocking gently back and forth. The oil men called the things mosquitoes, for the way they sucked life—and cash—from this dry prairie.

Yet all around the county, the jacks were going still. Mama had been smart to insist on a monetary settlement instead of mineral rights. But unlike her recent stroke of fortune, that prize was gone now, given over to the hospitals and the doctors: a long, long list of them.

"Let's go inside," Beth Ann suggested as she brushed a flutter of red bangs from her eyes. When loose, her hair's soft waves tumbled past her shoulders. Her best feature, people told her. She had clipped it back this morning, but the wind was making steady progress pulling it free, strand by strand. Her nose was probably red, too, and she could use a tissue.

She must look a mess, she thought, then gave herself a mental kick. She wasn't some simpering fool—*like Mama,* a traitorous voice whispered—she was a nurse, here with a job.

And she meant to prove that she could do it, even with Hiram Jessup as her patient. For Larinda, Heidi, even Jordan . . . but mostly, for her own self-respect.

Rosario Gutierrez had the key to the columned white house called The Lucky Pull in honor of the day Lilly Decker walked into an Oklahoma Indian casino with the goal of meeting an oil-rich good time and walked out the winner of the largest progressive slot jackpot in that state's history. Though the wind blew cold beneath the hem of Rosario's black-and-white uniform, the fifty-three-year-old woman buzzed again and waited.

Rosario knocked, too, but no luck. Still, the maid hesitated instead of letting herself inside. *The señora's* daughter, poor Beth Ann, didn't know it, but her *madre* had a lover. Maybe two of them, from the comings and goings that Rosario was too discreet to mention. But discreet or not, Rosario had been upset—*mortificado*—that day last June when she had taken her mop into the huge, new kitchen.

It still astonished Rosario, what she'd seen them doing on that hard countertop. And at Lilly Decker's age—*híjole!* Who would have believed it? So *this,* and not the fit of her silk blouses, explained the disgraceful woman's visit to the doctor for a pert new set of *chichis.*

Still no answer. Rubbing a chilled arm, Rosario thought of going home, where her daughter Carmelita had brought the baby for a visit. But Rosario took her obligations—and her paycheck—seriously, so instead she walked around to the attached garage and stood on tiptoe to peer into the window of the left bay. Señora's big, new silver Mercedes was still inside, and the right bay—where Poor Beth Ann parked every evening—remained empty.

Rosario nodded to herself, satisfied that this afternoon, no strange man's car was hidden in the daughter's spot. Maybe after all these months, one of the neighbors had forgiven the señora for building a palace that dwarfed their fine homes. Rosario smiled as she pictured blond ladies together in a fussy parlor, eating tiny sandwiches with their pinkie fingers delicately crooked.

She drew the key out of her pocket, certain it would be safe to go inside now.

Not guessing that it wasn't. And that what Rosario saw would scar far more deeply than a summer afternoon's tryst on a cool, custom granite slab.

Chapter 2

Mark picked up one of Beth Ann's two cases and said, "You're right. Better head in. Wind's getting colder by the minute."

He said that to excuse his shaking. After more than twenty hours on the road, his eyes were bloodshot and his nerves overloaded with a combination of caffeine, exhaustion, and the residue of the shocking news he had received three days before. Mark might have mentioned the hurried trip and his discomfort, might have offered them as proof of his loyalty, his virtue.

But this was Beth Ann Decker, so instead he fell back on prison habits to camouflage emotion with a lie about the cold.

In truth, he barely felt the chill, maybe as a result of his relocation years before from Bible Belt to Snow Belt. But more likely, he was still numbed by the sight of his father, so reduced by age and illness, and by the man's reaction when Mark had walked through his unlocked door.

"You shouldn't have come." In his threadbare bath-

robe and pajamas that probably dated from the Reagan Administration, Hiram Jessup had not risen from his recliner. *"The county people are taking care of me just fine. And the church's pitched in, too—even though I haven't been real regular with my attendance."*

That was all he'd said, after a nearly sixteen-year separation. And his father hadn't even glanced at the burden his son carried. Grimacing, Mark bent down by the sofa, a worn, plaid hulk his folks had bought when he was ten, and laid down the sleeping boy. Kissing the soft curve of Eli's cheek, Mark tucked a familiar, dark green afghan over the small form. That done, he went to get the suitcase from his truck.

Where he'd run into the only one of Jordan's friends still breathing. Beth Ann Decker, in the flesh . . . .

As she closed the wagon's hatch, he couldn't stop staring, noting subtle changes. As he'd supposed, her face looked different, with the features subtly shifted and a couple of faint scars, too, from all the surgeries. She wasn't fat, but she carried more weight than the nubile figure he'd once lusted after in vain. Hard to tell, since she was wearing a beige jacket over white scrubs instead of the cheerleader's uniform of his old fantasies, but he had a hunch she had filled out the way a woman ought to, with generous breasts offsetting gently rounded hips—

Horrified, Mark choked off the thought. He didn't give a damn about Beth Ann's curves, only that she had matured. In his mind, all four girls—including the survivor—had been locked inside a time warp, stuck forever in their teens.

Cane in hand, Beth Ann waited, and something in her eyes—still that startling blue he remembered—told him she was hoping he would precede her to the house. *She doesn't want me to watch her walk,* he decided, so he went first, since it would also prevent him from checking out her ass.

He reached around to get the door for her, his nostrils filling with the sweetly subtle fragrance of her shampoo. That was when a memory of the hair obsession hit him, the hours he'd spent wondering whether the shade was closer to the color of an Irish setter or a chestnut horse. Not that she would have appreciated either comparison. Beth Ann Decker had always made it plain that she was hell-bent on going places that a boy up to his elbows in engine grease and horse shit couldn't take her.

Funny, how life had made a mockery of both their plans. And consigned his little sister's to the grave.

With the curtains drawn against the brilliant sunshine, the house's interior lay in shadow. Once Mark put down the heavy suitcase, he and Beth Ann navigated their way into the living room by the flickering glow from the TV set. His father was watching some shopping channel, or pretending to, as a plastic-looking hostess waxed orgasmic over cookware. He tucked his left hand behind a thin leg, but not before Mark was jolted by the realization that the thumb was missing.

Once his initial shock passed, Mark took the opportunity to study the man more closely, still amazed that a father who loomed so large in memory could look so small and frail. What hair remained—once thick with only a smattering of silver at the temples—now formed a translucent cloud of white fuzz atop an odd-shaped, spotted head. With his face so shrunken, his ears and nose looked outsized, and his brown eyes bulged. Mark would not have known him had his father not been sitting in this house, that chair.

A pang shot through Mark at the thought that his mother must have changed like this as her disease consumed her. For the first time, he wondered if it might have been a mercy he'd been imprisoned at the time.

He looked at Beth Ann, asked her, "Where would you like this?"

She nodded toward the coffee table, where he put down the plastic case. As she set the other one beside it, she spoke brightly to his father. "How are you this fine day, Mr. Jessup?"

When he didn't answer, she took the remote off his chair's arm and muted the TV's blare. She turned on the lamp beside him, bathing the room in yellow light.

"Mr. Jessup, can you say hello? I've come to see how you are—and I'll need to be able to hear so I can check that blood pressure."

"I was listening to that," he sulked, and Mark thought how he sounded like Eli when he was taken from his cartoons.

But right now the poor kid was still out cold, exhausted from the long ride. Overall, he'd done pretty well, excited by the scenery, the night driving, and the normally forbidden fast-food stops off freeway exits. The boy was oblivious to whatever odd stares the two of them received.

But it was Mark's father's turn to stare now as he appeared to notice the blanket-covered child for the first time.

"What the hell is that?" asked Hiram, glancing up toward his son's face.

"Appears to be a little boy, almost five years old," Mark answered, deliberately ignoring the man's bewilderment.

Hiram sneered. "Looks like—goddamn—that kid looks like a ni—"

"A *Jessup*, that's what he is." Mark felt his own eyes narrow, felt his right fist knot reflexively. "My son and your grandson. And he'd better damned well never hear that word you were about to say. I hadn't better hear it—or any of those others either."

Beth Ann pursed her lips as she looked from one man to the other. Then she smiled at the boy, her blue eyes lighting with something that looked real.

"He has such a sweet face," she said. "That silky hair and those dark lashes—lots of girls around here would give their eyeteeth to have those."

Mark was grateful for her kindness and even more grateful when she went to work, checking his dad's vitals and asking him about his pain and medications.

And giving Hiram a chance to come to grips with the existence of a mixed-race grandson in a place where the only Asian family ran the China Lotus Buffet, and where sightings of African-Americans were reported as infrequently as those of UFOs.

Deputy Damon Stillwater wasn't due to go on duty for another three hours, but when the call came over the scanner he kept in the living room, he nearly tripped over his feet racing to the laundry room to see if his mom had washed his uniform.

She had, but hadn't gotten around to pinning on his badge and name tag. But maybe her hands were bad today, as they often were during a flare-up.

In his hurry to take care of the missing hardware, Damon stuck his thumb, getting a tiny smudge of blood on one corner of the pocket.

"Goddammit," he said, even as he pulled on the tan shirt and fumbled with the buttons.

"*Damon*," Mama called out from the kitchen, the inflection warning of her thoughts on taking the Lord's name in vain.

Even on her sickest day, the woman had ears like a jackrabbit.

"It's a *murder*, Mama." Damon felt his ears redden as his voice slid up an octave in his excitement. "My first ever real live murder."

"A murder?" she called back, distracted from giving a lecture on the Third Commandment. For the moment, anyway. "Not here in Eudena, I hope. Tell me it was over across the county, near one of them Mexican encampments."

"Right here in Eudena," Damon said happily. "First one in . . . I don't know. Since before I was born at least."

His mother emerged from the kitchen, half-moon glasses perched precariously on a ski-slope of a nose and her icy blond hair in the same dome-shaped bouffant she had stuck with since her high-school graduation photos. Though some days her lupus made her so weak, she could barely stay on her feet for fifteen minutes, she never missed her standing Friday morning appointment at Margie's Klip N' Kurl. "There was a killing about thirty years back, I remember. Drifters from somewhere up north. Knife-fighting on the Sabbath, if you can imagine. And *gambling.*"

She added a tongue cluck of disapproval, but Damon shrugged. As far as he was concerned, any event dating back farther than his twenty-two years might as well have taken place in the days of covered wagons. The important thing was that today, he was about to join the big leagues, right up there with those TV CSI teams he admired. He'd been watching the shows since he could work a remote, and he'd paid close attention. Even taken a few notes on the real-life cases that ran on Court TV.

"Don't forget your belt, son, and your shirttail's out in back," his mama told him.

He hurried to tuck it around his skinny hips before she took it in her head to try to help him. Sometimes, the woman had no notion that he was a grown man who carried a gun and locked up drunks and everything. He'd been in the department for six whole months now, but as far as she and his daddy and his married sister were concerned, he might as well still be frying tater tots down at the Dairy Queen. And Sheriff Morrell called him Kid, as if Damon were of too little consequence to have earned a name.

He was pretty sure all that would change after he solved his first murder. Not that he was hoping there would be more. Well, maybe he was, as long as it happened to vagrants and troublemakers instead of his relatives or any members of their church congregation.

"Did they say who it was got killed?" A note of anxiety had crept into his mama's voice.

Damon shook his head, then finger-combed what little there was of his flyaway blond hair. Sheriff Morrell expected his men to be role models for the community's young people. "No, ma'am. They just gave the address. Somewhere over on Mill Pond Bend."

"*O-o-oh.*" Mama drew out the word, her tone rising and falling as it did when she was speaking of what she called the hoity-toity people. Both of the town's doctors lived on Mill Pond, as well as the county judge, and a handful of wildcatters who'd cashed in their chips at the right moment, along with that tacky jack-pot woman, Lilly Decker. Though everyone agreed Poor Beth Ann, who had been so kind when Damon's Great Aunt Estelle got sick, was an angel-on-this-earth, in spite of her spotty church attendance. Which just went to show that sometimes, the apple did roll far from the tree. As well as uphill, in this particular case.

"Well, you be sure to call me if it's anyone we know, so I can get working on a casserole," Damon's mother said, although she didn't sound particularly married to the prospect. The Stillwaters, who ran the sole surviving hardware and lumber outlet, weren't exactly on the same social plane as the residents of Mill Pond Bend.

Damon could almost hear his mama thinking how those women would likely turn up their noses at her good potato chip–tuna casserole. Since he had suffered through years of this despised dish, Damon decided on the spot that he had something in common with those rich folks. And once he solved the murder of one of their own, there was no telling where good taste and detective skills might lead him.

Excitement zinging through his veins, Damon daydreamed about his future all the way to the scene, while he drove his father's hand-me-down Ford pickup along central Eudena's redbrick roads. He'd forgotten the exact address, but he had no problem finding the location, not with two sheriff's department cars there plus an ambulance. The latter seemed to have far more volunteers clustered around than usual, all probably as eager as Damon to get in on the action.

And they weren't the only ones. A dozen or so on-lookers had gathered on the street outside the biggest house in Hatcher County—a house named for a Lucky Pull, an unheard-of stroke of fortune.

But as he hurried to get inside, the irony of the thought passed Damon Stillwater in both lanes.

"I'll need your permission to discuss the details of your care with your son," Beth Ann told Hiram Jessup after she had checked his vitals and finally gotten answers regarding pain management, appetite, evacuation, medication. Hiram had refused to say a word until his son had carried the little boy into the spare room to put him into his pajamas and make up a bed with fresh sheets.

Even after Mark had left, the old man had seemed shell-shocked. Not altered in his level of consciousness, as a man in his condition would be later, but worried and distracted.

"I didn't ask him here," he told her. "Didn't even want him to know. Wish I had an idea what busybody thought it was his place to call."

Her place, Beth Ann mentally corrected, but no good could come of ratting out the culprit. Nothing short of a nuclear holocaust would change Aimee Gustavsen's spots.

"The way I see it," Beth Ann said, "that genie's already out of the bottle. Your son's come back, and I don't think you're gonna change his mind about it."

An unforgiving hardness settled over the old man's thin features. "Jordan should've been here, or his mama. What he did back then, it killed them both."

The collective wisdom of Hatcher County agreed it was grief that buried Letty Jessup in the wake of her daughter's death and Mark's term in state prison. The doctors called it kidney failure, but that hadn't swayed opinion. Beth Ann's daddy had also died eight months after the head-on collision. Though his heart had been failing long before the crash, his death, too, was chalked up by locals as another casualty and laid at the feet of the boy called Hell on Wheels.

"I could send for the chaplain or the social worker to say this, Mr. Jessup, or I could just tell you how I see it."

He eyed her warily.

Taking his look as permission, she continued. "Mark and that boy are what you're left with. Unless you'd rather die in the company of strangers. Or worse yet, alone."

The ticking of an ancient Regulator wall clock swelled to fill the dingy confines of a room that could stand painting. Finally, the old man stretched his one whole hand to reclaim the remote. As he clicked the shopping network back on, he said, "Tell him whatever you like, anything he wants to know. But I already died alone, girl. Sixteen years ago, like you."

A mute protest roared through her, leaving in its wake a shudder of revulsion. When she heard Mark in the hallway, she turned and nodded to indicate she would meet him in the kitchen.

Neither sat, though a quartet of captain's chairs clustered around an old maple table. A reminder of the family that had been.

"Did he wake up when you moved him?" Beth Ann asked of the child.

Mark shook his head, and she saw affection warm his brown eyes. "Barely, but he went right back to sleep."

"What's his name?" Her curiosity surprised her. She'd expected to feel nothing for this man but unyielding hatred. Except in some mysterious way, the past bound them together: the only two survivors. *Do you remember that night? Do you remember the things I can't?*

"Eli—Elijah, really," Mark said. "His mother and I— She's a fine woman, whip-smart, funny, beautiful . . . but we're not together anymore. And when she started med school in Ohio, we both came to the conclusion Eli would be better off with me."

Medical school. Beth Ann's initial surprise was dragged down by something dark and ugly, as if Mark Jessup's ex had stolen *her* life and *her* dream.

Mark shrugged. "I'm glad things worked out this way. I'm still on decent terms with Rachel—and I'm absolutely crazy about our kid."

Beth Ann didn't know how to answer such a declaration. Was he trying to convince her that his life after the crash had merit? Was playing Martyred Son and Gushing Father supposed to earn him cosmic points?

She hated to tell him that in her book, he was still down by a million. That a handsome smile and a pretense of devotion wouldn't buy forgiveness for the deaths of three girls, or the wreckage of her body and her plans.

Time to haul this conversation back on track, she decided. "Your father's given me permission to explain to you what's happening and answer any questions."

A look of surprise flashed over Mark's face. Perhaps he had expected Hiram to demand that he leave. Or maybe he'd caught the sudden chill in her voice.

"I'm not sure if you noticed his left hand," she began.

"I did. What happened to his thumb?"

She nodded. "It was a malignant melanoma, beneath the surface of the nail. Quite an unusual location. When he finally went in for treatment, they thought it was a fungus. But it wouldn't have much mattered. It was already too late."

"So they amputated?" he guessed. "Then they found out it had spread already?"

She nodded. "Melanoma likes to metastasize to the brain. It has in this case. He went to Wichita Falls for treatment, but it wasn't making any difference, so he stopped it."

Mark looked stricken. "How—do they know how long?"

She figured he was trying to guess how long it would take him to get back to his real life, to the thriving company he had built on ruin. Beth Ann had read an article about it. Aimee the Insensitive had e-mailed her the link.

"To qualify for hospice, the diagnosis has to be less than six months." Beth Ann struggled to keep her tone professional. "In his case, I'd guess less than half that, but there are a lot of variables. Dying doesn't stick to a timetable."

"What about pain? Is he suffering?"

"He's fairly comfortable right now, and we'll work hard to keep him that way." Mechanically, she went on to talk about medications to control pain and others to counteract the constipating opiates. They spoke of plastic gloves and pads and diapers, of challenges with feedings: the matter-of-fact indignities that dominated the end of life. He paid close attention, and she realized he meant to tend to these things himself instead of hiring help to do it. Was it possible this wasn't about putting on a show after all? Was Mark Jessup doing penance, or could he still feel something for the father who'd disowned him?

Before she could decide, she heard a wailing swell above the canned voice of the preternaturally cheerful cookware woman. She recognized it as a siren's blare a moment before it died outside the house.

A few steps took her to the kitchen window, where she twitched aside the faded curtain. She glanced back at Mark Jessup in confusion.

"It's a deputy from the sheriff's office," she told him. "Why would he be here?"

Mark's head jerked toward the sound of the car door thunking closed. His pulse thundered, and his vision blurred. He thought of racing to the bedroom, gathering up his son, and slipping out through the back window to hide among the mesquite and the scrubby cedars near the draw.

He would take Eli beyond the barbed noose that was Hatcher County, beyond its cages and its courtrooms, its grief and its bitter shame. He would run and never come back—except his legs had turned to stone.

On the day the sheriff had come for him, he'd been sitting in this kitchen. Brooding over a cup of Mama's tar-black coffee and struggling to fathom that his sister was really dead.

Though his mother couldn't look at him and his father wouldn't speak, it hadn't yet occurred to Mark that he'd killed Jordan. Still seventeen—just fourteen months older than his sister—Mark remained too stunned by the warped jigsaw of mangled vehicles and bodies to make any headway on the abstract imagery of blame.

When Sheriff Morrell had walked into the kitchen with his handcuffs ready, Mark couldn't have been more stunned had he been held accountable for a twister hitting Dallas or a volcano wiping out some island village half a world away.

But that was sixteen years ago. What were they blaming him for this time? What atrocity had he committed that he had yet to comprehend?

The knock at the front door came, more tentative than he remembered. Still, he could not move.

Beth Ann gave him a strange look, then shrugged her shoulders. "Guess I can get that this time." The words trailed behind her as she walked past his father in the living room. "But don't start thinking I'm your maid."

Her reproach snapped Mark back to the present, though the bitter taste of ancient coffee lingered on his tongue. Shaking off his déjà vu, he joined her by the door as she opened it.

A painfully young deputy held his broad-brimmed brown hat in his hands. Sorrow filled his green eyes; his face was nearly the same shade.

"Miz Decker, Sheriff Morrell's sent me here to fetch you." The words were steeped in misery.

Mark moved closer, caught a whiff of bile. Was the deputy as sick as he looked?

"Fetch me?" Beth Ann sounded thoroughly confused. "Why would— Look, if this is about that overdue inspection sticker on my wagon, I was fixing to take care of it, as soon as I finish here."

The greenish tint of the deputy's face gave way to a flush. "No, ma'am. It's about your mama. Why don't you let me drive you home?"

"What about my—" After a long pause, she reached toward the deputy's nametag. *Deputy E. Damon Stillwater*, it read.

The young lawman stepped back, out of range. But Beth Ann pointed out a tiny red splotch on the pocket's corner.

"That—that's *blood*. And there, too." Her voice went high and tight as she gestured toward a dark streak at the calf level of his tan pants. "Tell me, please. Has something happened to my mother?"

"If you'll just let me help you to the car, ma'am. The sheriff will explain it—"

"*You* explain it. Right now," she demanded, once more surging toward the deputy. "Is that my mama's blood?"

Reflexively, Mark grabbed her elbow. She had no idea how quickly this type of situation could turn, how a person could cross the line between victim and suspect in an instant. How there was no turning back.

Misunderstanding, she tried to tug her arm free. "Mark Jessup—get your hands off me."

Mark saw the deputy's hard blink, saw him put the name together with the story undoubtedly told to kids by parents, teachers, and Sunday school volunteers ever since that fall sixteen years back. Though it would have begun as a cautionary tale about the dangers of speed and teenaged drinking, the tragedy would hold the gory appeal of a horror movie. Did the students whisper shivery cautions about ghosts that roamed the halls of the consolidated high school each homecoming? Did they shudder whenever they caught sight of Beth Ann Decker's cane or spit each time his own name was mentioned?

It would be a game to them, but for Mark, the game was over. He saw it in the blink—and the suspicion—flashing through Damon Stillwater's green eyes.

Chapter 3

How simple it was, to go through the expected motions as if nothing different had occurred. How glorious, to lift free of the paralyzing blood and horror only hours in the past.

So complete was the transformation that it was easy to look back on the moments leading up to it, those moments when the water from the faucet spilled cold enough to make hands ache.

"Her fault, her fault, her fault. I. Am not. That monster."

Yet the lost soul who'd stood there trembling saw a torrent—saw the whole world—painted in the shades of blood. Felt the hot spurt of scarlet and the splash of crimson, the spatter bright as rubies. Heard the pulsing, wet and shocking, as pure as the fury of a wrathful God.

And twice as horrifying. Images ripped through consciousness: the slash and flail and shriek of it, the gape of a cherry mouth resembling a wound in its own right.

Shove the vision down deep, even deeper than the gore-slicked sack crammed down her throat to stop the screaming. Yet as if to mock the effort, the memory bobbed back to the surface like a plastic doll's head to stare with fixed, blue nightmare eyes.

"*Of course I have the proof still,*" she'd sneered before the red wave of fury broke through the last traces of control. *"A lady likes to keep insurance."*

It was just another dream, came a whisper. More vivid and more horrible than any of the others, but no more real, for all that. Yet in dreams, such unholy strength had never taken over. In dreams, there were no shoes and clothing buried by a lonely prairie road, no stripping down and shivering, no washing until the skin stung and reddened.

The plastic bristles of the scrub brush tore back each cuticle and dug deep beneath each nail. The temptation swelled to keep at it, to scour and scrub until the skin peeled from hands that seemed like a stranger's. *The hands of Cain,* a cold voice whispered. *Hands that sliced and mutilated . . . murdered.* Totally detached from the core of good within.

Terror flapped great vulture's wings, beating against ribs and chest wall, fanning sparks of panic. The brush was stowed, the water turned off. Hands were blotted with the caution one would use to dry an animal that might turn tooth and claw to rend flesh at any moment.

And not only mine. Innocents would be wounded, no, destroyed, should today's actions be discovered. An idea formed, as stark and clear as the cross atop the steeple of the Fundamental News Church, the county's tallest structure.

I was meant—no, I was appointed *to deliver the fate the whore deserved. The punishment that fit her sins so perfectly, a higher power surely ordained it.*

A higher power who would never want blameless souls to suffer. Who would, of a certainty, condone anything done to protect them.

Anything at all.

The thought lifted the heavy yoke of guilt. The shaking ceased and the One Appointed went on about the day's business with a soul scrubbed as clean as the hands that did God's bidding.

During the fifteen-minute drive to Eudena's Mill Pond neighborhood, Beth Ann wondered if she could be having a heart attack. Her chest felt like one big squeeze, and pain radiated through her limbs like shock waves from an interior explosion.

Under different circumstances, she would have pried some answers out of Damon Stillwater. She knew his mother, Ginny, who volunteered for the hospice program whenever her own health allowed it; she could use the relationship to her advantage. But since climbing into the passenger seat of the patrol car, it was all Beth Ann could do to keep upright and breathe, to survive what felt like the longest car ride of her life.

Besides, she felt sorry for the deputy, who was clutching the steering wheel for dear life in an attempt to keep his hands from shaking. He wasn't much more than a boy, she thought, with healing nicks along his jawline where shaving had abraded acne. Whatever waited at her mama's house, Beth Ann sensed that it had been his introduction to certain brutal truths of this world.

Truths she had first glimpsed in a pair of bright, on-coming headlights at the age of seventeen. Not that she remembered on a conscious level, yet she sensed that the knowledge lurked beneath the surface, an unseen facet in a prism that colored every day that followed.

As they turned onto the street that encircled sparkling Mill Pond, Beth Ann saw the neighborhood had taken on the mood of a block party. Despite the chill breeze, the neighbors had come out in jogging suits and jackets. Some walked yappy dog-lets or pushed infants in strollers. Others struggled to herd toddlers more interested in chasing fat white ducks than staying with the adults who had gathered near a locked bank of steel boxes, though the mail would not arrive for hours. Outsiders had shown up, too, as evidenced by the ragtag collection of pickup trucks and the presence of plaid flannels and denim, a handful of cowboy hats. This last group didn't bother to disguise its gawking, but clustered hungrily beside the ambulance and sheriff's department vehicles, with their lights flashing like a carnival attraction.

"What the—?" Beth Ann's throat clamped down around the question as a snub-nosed man with a scruffy black mustache pointed her out to the crowd. She stared back blankly, unable to make sense of the childlike excitement painted on his face. Yet she read the lips of the small woman standing at his elbow, saw her mouth three syllables. *Poor Beth Ann . . .*

Damon pulled past the onlookers and into the gray brick driveway that flanked her mother's palace. Beth Ann didn't move until he shut off the car, then came around and opened the door for her. He offered her a hand, but she refused it.

Leaning more heavily than ever on her cane, she followed Damon to the front entrance. She hesitated when he opened this door for her as well, convinced that once she crossed the threshold, her life would change forever.

"I'm real sorry, Miz Decker," he told her. Moisture glimmered in his green eyes, and a fresh flush spread over his fair skin.

She stepped through, if only to escape the gawking presence of those at the edge of the front lawn. Once inside, it took several moments for her eyes to adjust to the sudden absence of bright sunshine. In that brief span, she heard a woman weeping.

Mama? Relief swept over her, so strong it buckled her knees. But as the deputy grabbed her arm to steady her, she recognized the maid, Rosario, sitting on one of a matched pair of rich, gold-embroidered sofas in the formal living room. Hunched over in a rounded lump, she was sobbing into a linen dishtowel, with Sheriff Morrell patting her hand.

"Where's my mother?" Beth Ann's gaze snapped to the sitting area at the opposite end of the long room, where Lilly so often curled up in a striped overstuffed chair to read. But the chair beside the secretary desk was empty, save for a historical romance novel left lying open and facedown on the cushion. An expensive world globe loomed atop its walnut base above the steamy cover, as if in disapproval of Lilly's reading habits. "Has she been hurt?"

Surely, that explained the waiting ambulance. And the fact that she wasn't out here hollering about everybody walking on her living room's white carpet without first taking off their shoes.

Sheriff Morrell pushed himself up from the sofa with

a grunt of effort. A former local football hero who had traded on that reputation for four decades, Big Jim Morrell still had the powerful frame of an all-star lineman, though the years since graduation had added bulldog jowls and a beach ball of a belly to go with his salt-and-pepper flattop haircut. Once on his feet, however, he composed himself with the solemn dignity of an undertaker.

"How 'bout if we step into the study, Beth Ann?"

He nodded toward the closed door, but a crinkling sound drew Beth Ann's gaze to the staircase. A deputy—it was Cheryl Riker's husband, Pete—headed downstairs, a camera in his hands. Plastic covers, the source of the crinkling, protected his shoes, and he breathed noisily through his mouth. His skin was as pale as a catfish belly.

As she gaped in his direction, his look softened into pity. At the same moment, Sheriff Morrell put an arm around her and steered her into the study, a room she used to do her nursing paperwork. He paused to close the door behind them, which abruptly cut off the sounds of Rosario's weeping.

Beth Ann's gaze touched on rich, wine-colored walls that Mama's decorator—some snooty anorexic out of Dallas—had insisted would complement the golden built-in bookshelves and the tasteful antique desk. Beth Ann had lobbied for a color that didn't call to mind fresh blood. But the decorator's haughty, raised brows had turned Mama against Beth Ann in a heartbeat, a precedent so often repeated that she gave up arguing and started strategically placing tacky knickknacks around the house just to puncture their pretensions.

It seemed so childish now and petty, as did her refusal to let her mama buy her the new Escalade to replace "that horrible rust-heap that drips oil on my designer garage floor."

Her heart brimming with remorse, she stared up into Morrell's face. "Take me to my mother."

He gestured toward one of a pair of leather chairs in front of the desk she had claimed as her own. Ignoring the unspoken suggestion, she insisted, "I need to see her right now."

He looked down at the desktop, frowning at a trio of rubber ducks displayed there, the last survivors of her mama's War on Kitsch. They were done up like a mariachi band, complete with mustaches, fringed sombreros and tiny instruments.

Sheriff Morrell leaned forward, looking Beth Ann directly in the eyes, filling her vision with his grave face and her ears with the same deep voice that sang bass in the church choir.

"This is a hard thing, but you've got to know it. Your mama's upstairs dead."

Inside her chest, another cold shock detonated. But he went on, relentless as the most aggressive cancer.

"Somebody's killed her, in her bedroom. Mrs. Gutierrez found the—found the body."

"We don't have murders here," Beth Ann said, and something in her lightened. The sheriff was obviously mistaken. This was one of Mama's misguided bids for male attention. Everybody in the county knew of Lucky Lilly's cravings. And Morrell's wife, Evelyn, had left him last spring, so he was probably too distracted to pick up on Mama's prank.

Sheriff Morrell shook his head. "We didn't used to have murders. But we—I hope you'll forgive my language—we sure as hell have one today. Your mother's gone, Beth Ann. You have to accept that."

She shook her head and used her cane to help her stand. "Of course she isn't. Let me see her. I'm sorry she's caused all this commotion, but we'll straighten this up right now."

Beth Ann apologized for her mother reflexively, as she had for years uncounted. But this time, her shame was almost impossible to swallow. *This is the last time ever,* she swore to herself.

The sheriff rose, his head still shaking. If he didn't slow down, it was going to come unscrewed.

"You don't want to see that. You don't want to remember her the way this sonofabitch left her."

Alarm smashed through Beth Ann's fragile calm. "What—how *who* left her?"

"We don't know yet, but I swear to you, we're going to find out. And if I have a single thing to say about it, the animal who did this is gonna end up on death row."

Beth Ann spun toward the door, and—cane or no cane—beat the sheriff to it. The bloodred walls were closing in on her, and his lies throbbed through her brain like a world-class migraine. Maybe it was true, the rumor that Evelyn had left Morrell over his drinking. Maybe he was drunk now, even if Beth Ann couldn't smell any liquor on his breath. One thing was certain, though: She wasn't about to stand here listening to another second of his wild talk.

She opened the door just in time to see young Deputy Stillwater escorting Cheryl Riker inside. When Cheryl spotted Beth Ann, the older woman hurried toward her as fast as her short legs could carry her, her arms widening to enfold Beth Ann in an embrace.

"I'm so, so sorry, sweetie. I got here as quick as I could."

That was the moment it hit Beth Ann. This was all real, not some elaborate hoax or the sheriff's alcohol-soaked nightmare. Her face felt hot and wet, and her nose stopped up. She drew in great gulps of air, only to expel them in a series of mute sobs that wracked her body.

As Cheryl stroked her hair and back and made soft hushing noises, Sheriff Morrell touched her shoulder.

"We'll find this person," he repeated, his voice undeniably sober. "If we have to work night and day for ten years and scour every corner of this county."

As Cheryl's little cross pin pressed into Beth Ann's cheek, Damon Stillwater cleared his throat loudly. Out of the corner of her eye, she saw him straighten his spine to look the larger man square in the face.

"I don't think it'll take us years, sir, only hours." The young deputy's voice was earnestly insistent. " 'Cause I've got a pretty doggone good idea of just where we need to look."

Chapter 4

"You want to leave, leave." Though Hiram Jessup never took his eyes from the TV screen, he was clearly speaking to his son, who had just come back into the room. "Surprised you haven't already lit out, the way your face looked when that deputy showed up."

Mark glanced down at his father and resisted the impulse to lay a comforting hand atop that fuzzed and spotted head. The old man reminded him of a newly hatched bird of prey, screeching out its hunger—and an equally fierce determination to take wing.

"I'm not going anywhere," Mark said. He wanted to argue that he wasn't that same scared seventeen-year-old he'd been sixteen years back. He kept his peace, though, for the shell-shocked kid remained huddled inside him, trembling and uncertain. Even so, it hadn't taken Mark five minutes from the time Deputy Stillwater left with Beth Ann to decide he damned well wasn't running from anything Hatcher County could dish out.

What *had* happened at the Decker place? At the

memory of Stillwater's greenish cast and the splotches of dried blood on his clothing, an aftershock of horror rippled through Mark, an ancient echo from the collision that had altered both Beth Ann's life and his.

Swallowing back the taste of bile, he changed the subject. "I've been working on your kitchen, taking stock and organizing. I wanted to know how you felt about the chicken tenderloins I found in the freezer for this evening. I can make some rice to go with them, maybe steam some carrots."

To Mark, this sounded easy on the stomach. Plus, Eli needed something healthier than the fast food they'd been living on for the past two days.

One bone-thin shoulder rose and fell. Though he still wouldn't look at his son, Hiram's mouth tightened in a grimace. "I don't give a damn what you do. I'm not hungry. If I want anything later, I'll have one of them shakes or some such. Just get up out of my chair my own damn self and get it from the kitchen—I can do that much yet."

"Beth Ann—Miz Decker—says it's important for you to eat as much real food as you can." Mark left the *while you can* unspoken. "Small, frequent meals. You don't have to eat a lot at one time, but—"

His father whipped around in his chair to shoot a peevish look in Mark's direction. "I don't *have to* do a damned thing. What do you think, that you're the daddy all of a sudden? That you can waltz back in here—"

"He is a daddy. He's *my* daddy," said a small voice from the hallway. Eli yawned, his black hair sticking up in the back, where he had the same cowlick Mark had fought since his own childhood. Tall for his age—as Mark had always been—Eli wore a pair of light blue pajamas with dark blue cuffs and neckband and held a stuffed blue bunny much like the one his father had dragged around for years.

Yet as Mark watched his father stare, he knew for certain Hiram wasn't seeing the cute kid who would turn five inside of two weeks any more than he was noticing the Jessup cowlick or the Jessup height. Instead, the old man was cataloguing Eli's differences, the light golden-brown complexion, the broader nose and darker hair and the slightly sloped eyes that bespoke his mother's Afro-Asian features. Beautiful features, Mark thought with pride, inherited from a bright, ambitious woman . . . a woman who, despite their differences, had given him the greatest gift he'd ever known.

He waited, every nerve taut as a bowstring, to hear how his father would respond. And to know whether he and Eli could stay here after all. For Mark was ready to take on his father's attitude and whatever suspicions the town had regarding his return, but he'd be damned if he'd sit back and let anyone hurt Eli.

"He may be your daddy—" distaste simmered just beneath the surface of Hiram's words "—but I'm *his* father. And that damn—that darn well means he doesn't get to tell me what and when I have to eat."

Eli's dark gaze went from the old man to Mark's face, and the boy's mouth pinched, as it did when he was deep in thought. With a look of intense concentration, he moved closer to Hiram's chair, then broke into a smile. "If you're my daddy's daddy, then you're my *grandpa*, aren't you?"

Mark's breath hitched as his father's brown eyes narrowed. Instinctively, Mark moved close behind his son.

"You can call me Hiram," the old man said.

Mark exhaled. It wasn't the open-armed embrace he might have hoped for, but at least his father hadn't said something unforgivable.

"Why don't you come out to the kitchen, Eli?" Mark suggested. "You can have a snack while I make dinner, maybe help me get things ready."

Eli straightened. "I can set the table. I know all the places."

Mark smiled at him, though he ached to hear his son trying to win over a man whose heart was as hard and shriveled as a prune pit. How long had Mark strived for his father's approval? Was he doing it still, by coming back here?

"I know you do, champ," he told Eli. "You're a big help. Can't imagine what I'd do without you."

He lured his son into the kitchen, where he gave him milk and oatmeal cookies from a surprisingly well-stocked pantry. It seemed strange to see the kitchen arranged differently from the way his mother had always kept it, but it was clear enough that someone had been helping Hiram with the shopping and the cleaning. Maybe hospice volunteers or some of the ladies from the church. Mark figured his father must really feel like hell to have allowed it. After Jordan's death, he'd bolted the door against the well-meaning sympathizers with their casseroles . . . .

Only to unlock it for the sheriff when he'd come to arrest Mark for intoxicated manslaughter.

An hour and a half later, after eating four bites from the small plate carried to his TV tray when he'd refused to join his family in the kitchen, the old man repeated history. Struggling up from his recliner, he walked to the front door, and unlocked it to let in Sheriff Morrell.

* * *

Big Jim Morrell was shaking Hiram's hand as Mark poked his head out of the kitchen. Behind Morrell stood a deputy Mark would always recognize, despite the way the years had grayed and thinned the man's hair and thickened his waistline. Pete Riker had been first on the scene after the crash, and he'd been with his boss when Mark had been arrested, too.

"How're you doing, Mr. Jessup?" the sheriff asked in a voice as deep as ever, though he, too, was heavier than the last time Mark had seen him. Must have been some big-time chicken-fried-steak lunches at the sheriff's office over the past years.

"Been better," Hiram answered. Illness had slumped his back and shoulders, making him look far shorter than his one-time height of six feet.

"Why don't you just have a seat then," the sheriff told him. He glanced up, in tandem with Riker, and caught Mark's eye. "It's your boy I came to speak with."

Mark felt time fold back upon itself, but the spell shattered when Eli slipped a small hand into his. In the tightness of the child's grip, Mark knew his son's fear. Both men were imposing, in particular Jim Morrell, whose deep voice, badge, and uniform surely loomed large to a four-year-old in unfamiliar territory.

"It's okay, Eli," he said. "These men aren't here about you."

"That Decker girl," Hiram interrupted, still looking at the sheriff. "Is she all right?"

Morrell nodded, his face grim and older-looking than the version in Mark's nightmares. "She's had a shock, but she'll get through it, God willing."

"What happened?" Hiram pressed.

Instead of answering, Morrell took a few steps toward Mark, then squatted down and smiled at Eli.

"Hey, there, partner." He stuck out a big hand and added, "I'm Sheriff Morrell, and I make it a point to welcome visitors to Hatcher County."

Pete Riker crossed thick arms in front of his chest and stared down at the spectacle. Judging from the man's expression, he was either stunned at the sight of Eli or had a bad case of indigestion.

Eli glanced at Mark and waited for a reassuring nod before shaking Morrell's hand. "I'm Elijah Jessup, and my birthday is in ten days."

When Riker's expression soured, Mark hated the man more than ever.

"That's good to know," the sheriff told him. "How old will you be? Six?"

"Five," Eli corrected.

"That's real lucky. I have some special honorary deputy's badges out in my car, but I only give 'em to boys and girls on their fifth birthdays. If you were six or only four, you would've clean missed out on your chance, Elijah."

The boy grinned, clearly warming to the sheriff. "You can call me Eli. Everybody does."

"Okay, Deputy Eli. Mind if I take a walk with your daddy here? You can stay inside and keep an eye on your grandpa."

Hiram opened his mouth as if to protest, but Morrell shot him a sharp look and added, "Why don't you show him what kind of cartoons we get here in Texas, Hiram? My grandkids like the ones on—is it Channel Twenty-Two, Pete? You've got daughters."

Riker shrugged and avoided eye contact with Eli. Racist bastard.

Hiram grumbled a little—possibly at the idea of being referred to as Eli's grandpa—but in the end, he settled back in his chair and turned on something that made Eli exclaim, "You have this one here, too? Those guys are my favorite."

Mark excused himself to grab his jacket. He made a point of keeping his movements unhurried, despite the tension coiled in his gut.

Once they stepped out the back door and down the wooden steps, Morrell told his deputy, "How 'bout you meet me back at the car, Pete? And see if you can dig out one of them extra-shiny little badges from the glove box. This young man's about to get himself an early birthday present."

Riker walked away, his stride stiff as his neck.

Mark told Sheriff Morrell, "Thanks for putting Eli at ease. He's a little nervous—new place and all. And Hiram . . ."

Their feet crunched on the gravel driveway as they meandered in the direction of the garage.

"So. Your daddy know about him? Before you got here, I mean."

Mark shook his head. "Didn't seem like the kind of news to scribble on a postcard. I tried a letter or two a while back, but they were returned unopened. The one time I called—well, I'll bet you can guess how long that conversation lasted."

It still hurt to remember his father slamming down the phone the instant he recognized his son's voice.

Morrell nodded, the pursing of his mouth making his jowls look more pronounced. "I figured that was how it was. Suffering hardens a man—and I guess you and I both know being a father isn't easy, even in the best of times. And doing it on your own, that's tougher still."

Mark stopped walking to turn toward him. He

damned well didn't want to hear Morrell wax poetic over his relationship with his daughter, or with Scotty. Mark particularly didn't want to hear the things he knew already: that Morrell's pride and joy—who had at one time dated Beth Ann Decker—was now practicing law and running for state senate up in Amarillo. It had made the front page as a "Local Boy Makes Good" piece in Hatcher County's weekly news rag, which Hiram had left lying on the kitchen table. "Let's get to the point, Sheriff. What's going on with Beth Ann Decker?"

Morrell flinched. Though he recovered quickly, Mark could see that his directness had surprised the older man. Good. The sheriff needed to know he wasn't dealing with a teenager this time.

"Somebody up and killed her mama."

"Mrs. Decker?" Mark tried to recall what the woman looked like and came up with the fuzzy image of a red-head like Beth Ann who had worn her hair in some kind of sleek upsweep. Mostly, though, he remembered his mother fuming about Lilly "prancing around" church socials and meetings of the PTA in her skimpy dresses. Mark had never really noticed her appearance, but back then, he'd spent far more time sneaking glances at Beth Ann than looking at anybody's mama. "Poor Beth Ann. Why would anybody want to hurt Mrs. Decker?"

Sheriff Morrell grimaced. "Can't say yet, but this is a hell of a thing. Worst I've seen in forty years of law enforcement."

In spite of the chill breeze, heat rode over Mark's face. Head shaking, he blurted out, "It's not right, not with all Beth Ann's been through. Is there—does she have anybody with her?"

Morrell nodded. "She's got friends and plenty of 'em. People around here think the world of Miz Beth Ann."

"And you have no idea—no idea who could have done this?" Mark couldn't keep the bitterness from washing through his words. "So you and your favorite goon have come out here looking—what was that line from *Casablanca*? Looking to 'round up the usual suspects.' Or *suspect,* meaning me."

Morrell held his gaze. "Now, Mark. You know we've got to check out anybody with a motive—"

"*What* motive?"

"One of my deputies seems to think revenge could be an issue."

Mark thought of the way the deputy who came to pick up Beth Ann had looked him over. "You mean that kid you sent here earlier? He thinks I'd want revenge against Mrs. Decker? Revenge for what?"

The sheriff turned and gestured toward the rusting pump jacks across the road. "All that was Jessup land at one time. And all the land around this little postage stamp your daddy's got left. Jessups ranched this spread for generations—"

"All the years I lived at home, my father worked part time at the post office, drove a delivery truck when he could get a job. Even at their highest, the oil royalties never covered the expenses, and the ranching business is no living for the small operator—hasn't been for decades."

"It was the Jessup legacy, and Mrs. Decker sued your father for it." Morrell spared the house a rueful look.

Mark saw the old place as the sheriff must, with its flaking paint and missing shingles, its sad collection of sagging outbuildings. Like the garage ahead, with its missing door, its clutter of odds and ends, and his father's old green Chrysler. Next to Mark's loaded new pickup, it looked ancient. "I can take care of my dad. I can more than take care of myself and my son, too. And this *legacy*—this whole damned county—doesn't mean a thing to me."

Once more, Morrell's gaze bored into him. "Doesn't it?"

Self-righteous son of a bitch. "This is bullshit, Morrell. I'm back in town half a day and here you are, hoping I'll just stand around dumbfounded while you screw me over one more time? Has it occurred to you I learned my lesson from the last go-round?"

Morrell laid one hand on the butt of his gun. "I don't think you want to take that tone with me, Mark."

"It's *Mister* Jessup to you," he corrected. "And I don't think you want to take this one step further. Not unless you're ready for a lawsuit that will rock your world—and bury you up to your neck in more old shit than you can shovel."

"I've heard about your little enterprise." Morrell's blue eyes went stern. "I know that you've got money. But if you think for one minute I'm going to let that stand between me and the bastard who carved up Lilly Decker—"

Mark flinched, unable to imagine such a crime taking place in Hatcher County—and became abruptly aware of the more recent connection that an investigation might find between the murder victim and himself. Could such a link be used against him?

Sheriff Morrell must have noticed his reaction, for he stopped in mid-sentence.

"Do you honestly believe," Mark asked, deliberately keeping his voice low, "that I stopped by Bowie Road on my way to my dying father's house and did a thing like that while my four-year-old sat waiting in the truck?"

"Bowie Road . . ." Morrell said. "You expect me to be-lieve you haven't heard about the Lucky Pull?"

"The Lucky *what?*"

"The Deckers live over on Mill Pond Bend these days. On account of Lilly Decker's slots jackpot—biggest one they've ever had in Oklahoma. It was in all the papers, made the news clear across the country. Up in Pennsylvania, too, I imagine."

"News to me," Mark told him. He hadn't paid atten-tion to the address on the return envelope she'd en-closed, and since he'd had custody of Eli, he paid less attention to the evening news than ever. He put in a lot of hours at work, and he didn't like spending those he shared with his son in front of a TV.

Mark's jacket rattled with the chill wind as the two once more locked gazes. It was clear as glass that the sheriff figured he had heard of Lilly Decker's newfound fortune and had come back home to settle some kind of blood feud. Or at least that was the theory the law-man was trying to fit into his image of the kid he'd once called Hell on Wheels. Too bad it was bullshit, even further from the truth than the story Morrell and his deputy had concocted sixteen years before.

For what seemed like an eternity, the two men faced each other, staring, like the moment before a made-for-TV gunfight.

Morrell looked away first, turning toward his patrol car, which was parked behind Mark's pickup. "Let me get that badge for your boy. Eli, is it?"

When Mark did not respond, Morrell added, "So, you're married?"

"Not lately." In reality, the answer was "not ever," since Rachel had refused his repeated offers after they'd learned she was pregnant. But Mark already knew the rumor would spread quickly that he'd shown up with a child in tow—and a mixed-race child at that. He couldn't stand the thought of the word "bastard" being thrown into the mix, couldn't predict how he would respond if someone used it in his hearing. "He's a great kid, though. I'm glad to have him with me."

There was a slight hesitation before Morrell nodded and then headed toward his sedan. As promised, he got a wrapped "Junior Deputy" badge from Riker and handed it to Mark.

"You'll be around, then, for a while?" he asked, that sonorous voice rumbling like thunder on the horizon. His gray eyes seemed to darken just before he added, *"Mark."*

Mark nodded. "As long as my dad needs me, I'm not going anywhere . . . *Jim.* And that's one thing you can damned well count on."

Chapter 5

Six days later

"I hope you'll understand, Mr. Lipscomb, but I'm in no mood for lawyer talk this afternoon." Beth Ann wasn't trying to be rude to her mother's long-time attorney, but the funeral had been a hell of an ordeal, and she'd only just now shooed the last of the well meaning—save for Cheryl—and the curious out of the Lucky Pull, where people had picked over finger sandwiches and macaroni salad while waiting to offer their condolences. It would have gone on forever had Pastor Timmon's wife, Helene, not caught a couple of the notoriously light-fingered Snyder kids trying to pocket silver serving forks. Two deputies arrived in short order to haul off the shrieking, swearing teenagers, but the ugliness of the incident had served as a disquieting reminder that brutality had visited Eudena, a brutality that had ended Lilly Decker's life.

"I'm terribly sorry, but this can't wait," Stan Lipscomb murmured, looking up at her from beneath a gel-lacquered wing of hair suspiciously dark for a man who had to be in his mid-sixties. Since she'd first met him as a little girl, Mr. Lipscomb—one of the county's handful of practicing attorneys—had reminded Beth Ann of a basset hound, with his sorrowful, brown eyes and drooping facial features. Her mother loved to tease him, often with scandalous suggestions, just to see if she could prompt the man to "get the stick out of his ass and smile for once in his life."

Today, however, Mr. Lipscomb looked sadder than ever, prompting Beth Ann to relent and lead him down the length of the formal living room, thick with funeral flowers, to the sitting area her mother had favored. From the kitchen, she heard the comforting clink of plates as Cheryl busied herself putting away food and cleaning.

"You should have a seat," he told her, gesturing toward the striped chair by the globe on its stand. "Can I bring you anything?"

Shaking her head, she sank into the huge chair and laid her cane on the floor beside her. "So what is it? I know all about the will situation. Mama went over it with me in detail. Probably figured I'd cut her a little more slack on her shenanigans if I knew I'd inherit everything one day."

To her surprise, Mr. Lipscomb *did* smile, though he quickly moved his hand to cover a mouthful of crowded and discolored teeth. "That sounds like your mother, all right. So tell me, did it work?"

"Lord, no," Beth Ann said. "First of all, as far as I can see, that damned money's stirred up more trouble than it's worth."

When word first got out about the multi-million-dollar jackpot, her mother had had no end of people coming to her with their hands out, even people she didn't know from Adam. She'd lost friends over it, too, when she got smart and put it into the hands of pros so she couldn't be pressured or tempted to go along with every harebrained scheme someone suggested. Worse yet, she'd been forced to change phone numbers and have an alarm system installed when she'd received anonymous threats. But those had long since died down, and she'd gotten lazy about setting the alarm during daylight hours. Beth Ann wondered, had her mother left a door unlocked, too? Or had she invited her killer inside and upstairs to her room last Friday? Could it really have been someone she knew? Even someone who'd come to the funeral or stopped by to offer condolences?

Mr. Lipscomb pulled out the chair from the secretary desk and took a seat across from Beth Ann. "Miss Decker? Are you all right?"

She snapped to and quickly said. "Oh, sorry. You were asking if the idea of inheritance got me off my mother's case. Afraid not. The two of us stuck with our assigned roles. Mama played the wild but lovable teenaged daughter, which left me with the part of parental spoilsport. But we made it work for us. Most days."

Except on October thirteenth, the day some bastard had killed her. Beth Ann's gut knotted, and her hands clenched with a desperate need to rip someone to pieces. But who? For all Morrell's promises and Deputy Stillwater's bold claim on that awful afternoon, the sheriff's department hadn't named a single suspect. With frustration pounding at her temples, she felt the threat of fresh tears.

"What can't wait, Mr. Lipscomb?" she asked. "If it's about the will—"

"No, no. There's a ten-day posting period required before a hearing can be scheduled, so there's time enough to talk about it when you're ready." He pulled a plain white envelope out of the breast pocket of his frumpy, dark brown suit jacket. "But your mother insisted that upon her death, I was to deliver this to you following the services. She made me swear it with my right hand on the Bible."

A prickling sensation curled around Beth Ann's middle. "What on earth?"

He placed the envelope in her hand. Her name, she saw, was written on the front. In her mother's girlish script.

"It's not terribly uncommon for a parent to leave a private message with an attorney, especially one who is also acting as executor for her estate. I wasn't privy to what's inside," he said earnestly, "but I can assure you, your mother didn't plan on dying while she was so young and so vibrant. The day she gave this to me last year, she was grumbling that she'd probably have to go through 'this last-will-and-testament bull all over' when I kicked off ahead of her."

"Thanks, Mr. Lipscomb." Beth Ann managed a shaky smile. Her mother, who had turned fifty-six in August, would have been thrilled to be recalled as "young and vibrant." Aging gracefully had never been a part of Lilly Decker's plans.

He shook Beth Ann's free hand before standing. "It's Stan, please. I'll be in touch in a few days, or you can call me when you're ready or if you need anything at all. Otherwise, I'll leave you to your privacy."

She saw him out, her fingers quick to turn the deadbolt in his wake. Afterward, she locked herself inside the red-walled study and dropped into the chair behind the desk, where she pulled a letter opener from the top drawer.

Her hands shook in her hurry to slit open the envelope. Would it hold answers? Questions? The goodbye she'd thought had been forever lost?

Blinking away tears, she read:

> *My dear, dear, dear Beth Ann,*
> *In truth, the world is yours, should you be bright and bold enough to claim it.*
> *I love you always and I'm sorry. Forgive me, baby? Please?*
>
> > *Hugs & smooches,*
> > *Mama*

Beth Ann turned the note over and blinked in confusion at the blank back of the page, then flipped it once more and read it over, out loud.

"What the hell?" she asked when she had finished. The message was inane, nonsensical. What did her mother mean, forgive her? Beth Ann had expected to feel overwhelmed or tearful. Instead, she felt wounded, even annoyed, that rather than easing her heartbreak, her mother's last words sounded more like some sort of childish game.

Beth Ann took the letter to the kitchen, where Cheryl was carefully counting out the serving pieces.

"I think one of those Snyder kids made off with the slotted spoon from the melon balls. Those snot-nosed little heathens."

Beth Ann shrugged. "If they want to polish the damned things, I'll gladly give 'em the whole set. Look at what my mama left me. It's a letter she'd arranged for Mr. Lipscomb to deliver."

Shock registered in Cheryl's hazel eyes, and she hesitated before accepting the page from her friend. She held it by its edges, as if the paper might burst into flames at any second.

She squinted, then said, "Doggone it, I can't see this. I left my reading glasses in my purse up in your bedroom. If those Satan's spawn haven't made off with that, too."

"Never mind. I'll read it to you." Maybe the third try would bring some sense to it.

But once she'd finished, Cheryl looked as confused as she felt.

"Sorry for what?" she asked. "I don't get it."

"I was afraid it was just me." Beth Ann frowned down at the words. "What the devil does she mean about the world being mine if I'm 'bright and bold enough'?"

Cheryl's lips bunched and drifted slightly to the left as she considered. Finally, she nodded. "Maybe she means that you should quit being such a tightwad and have fun with the money."

Beth Ann grimaced. "Or maybe she was on her third margarita when she wrote this."

There was a subtle shift in her friend's expression as her gaze retreated to the silver she'd been counting. "That could be true, too. Your mama always did get kinda maudlin when the tequila started talkin'."

Beth Ann closed her eyes. "Right about now, I wish I *liked* tequila. I'd drink a damned bathtub full of margaritas if I could forget this past week ever happened."

But Beth Ann couldn't take a sip of alcohol without getting dog sick. And she was well aware that she had already forgotten more than she should sixteen years before.

Chapter 6

Two weeks later

Boarded-up old storefronts lined the bloodred, bricked streets of Eudena's downtown, an occasional surviving business lingering among the dead. Even those sported CLOSED signs on a Sunday morning, with the controversial exception of the county's sole remaining grocery store.

As she glided past the cars parked around the Fundamental News Church in her mama's silver sedan, Beth Ann felt the disapproving stares of late arrivals to the service. She cranked up the Dixie Chicks in an attempt to silence the malignant whispers her fear conjured, but paranoia drowned out the song's lyrics.

Didn't take Beth Ann Decker long to change. Look at her, driving that high-dollar Mercedes, lording it over all of us now she's the richest woman in all of Hatcher County.

Defiantly, Beth Ann turned the song—the raucous

"Sin Wagon"—even louder as she pulled into the lot of Barty's One-Stop. Her old Subaru had refused to start this morning, and she needed coffee in the worst way. And tissues—heaven help her, these past few weeks she'd gone through more Kleenex than an asthmatic Brownie troop on a campout in cedar-fever season.

She could have asked Cheryl to pick up groceries— or any of the friends and neighbors who had practically begged her to call and let them know what they could do. But after three weeks of being coddled and consoled and protected from out-of-town reporters scavenging for exclusives, Beth Ann had finally had enough. She'd tied back her hair, pulled on jeans, a dark green sweater, and a pair of clogs and grabbed her mother's key ring before she lost her nerve.

After shutting off the car, Beth Ann climbed out from behind the tinted windows and blinked in the bright sunshine. Her eyes adjusted to take in the crape myrtle trees planted along the lot's edge to hide the decay of a service station boarded and abandoned since the sixties. Among the crape myrtles' peeling, half-bare branches, she caught the flutter of disintegrating red-and-black streamers, remnants of the Hatcher Hawks' homecoming that had taken place only seven days after the atrocity at the Lucky Pull.

Beth Ann aimed and punched the remote to lock the Mercedes. At the alarm system's chirp, a shopper loading groceries into a dusty hatchback glanced in her direction. With the wind tousling her short, prematurely white hair, the slightly built woman hugged herself reflexively, then nodded. But it was the pity in her expression that had Beth Ann gritting her teeth and making for the store entrance as fast as she could manage.

Resentment of her money was one thing, but the

Poor-Beth-Ann routine was more intolerable than ever. *What about Poor Lilly?* Beth Ann wanted to shriek to the heavens. *What about my mama?*

To hell with grief, with its choking tears and clogging nose and crippling helplessness. *Rage* was what she needed—a fury that flared so hot, it not only incinerated the animal who'd killed her mother but scorched Jim Morrell, his incompetent department, the slavering reporters, and this whole damned county's useless pity.

Her anger propelled her through the aisles with her fists clenching the grocery cart, her glare daring anyone to make eye contact. But the trouble with rage was it took too much energy to maintain. By the time she reached the deli counter—she wanted some sliced pepper-jack for grilled cheese sandwiches—Beth Ann was shaking with the effort. And worse yet, the impulse to punch open one of the tissue boxes and blow her nose was nearly overwhelming.

If she let herself do that, she knew she'd lose it. So she bit down on her inner lip and focused on the knowledge that if anyone spotted so much as a trace of moisture on her face, the rumor that she'd been bawling inside Barty's would be all over Hatcher County before sundown.

Though the store was close to empty—with five still-viable churches, this was a town that took its Sabbath seriously—and no one else was waiting, the two employees behind the counter were so engrossed in their conversation, they kept their backs turned to her, even after Beth Ann cleared her throat. She was about to try a more direct approach when, to her horror, she caught her mama's name among their words.

"That Lilly Decker was just asking for trouble, the

way she acted," dried-up old Gertrude Pederson—who had been Lilly's best friend until Lilly refused to continue doling out cash to her last winter—croaked in her cigarette-rough voice. "Bad enough she'd been flaunting her body all over town as long as she did, tempting other people's husbands. But once the likes of her got money—"

"Lilly's been Lilly for years on end," Sid Talley, the butcher, interrupted. His white apron barely covered his expansive belly. "And she'd been rich more'n a year now. The only thing that's different is that Jessup boy's come back to town."

Beth Ann knew she should say something—or at the very least, should get the hell out of there before she had a meltdown. But she remained rooted to the spot.

"Hell on Wheels . . ." Gertrude nodded. "Can't believe he had the nerve to come back. I think it's a damned shame he ain't in jail still, good-for-nothing trash like him killing all those sweet girls. And ruining Poor Beth Ann the way he done—it's tragic."

Beth Ann wished she could dissolve into a puddle on the store's white tiles. . . . In her mind, the loudspeaker buzzed the message: *Cleanup at the deli counter. Better bring two mops and the big bucket.*

"What I can't understand is why it's taking Sheriff Morrell and that half-assed crew of his so long to figure this out," Talley went on. "Did they all come down with group amnesia, or is that boy throwing his weight around, now he's got his blood money—or maybe buying off the sons of bitches. Billy Hyatt won't be bought, though, not for all the gold in—"

Loosened by her trembling, Beth Ann's cane slid off the cart where she had it balanced, then clattered to the floor.

The pair behind the counter turned as one, their eyes widening and faces reddening in unison.

Gertrude recovered first, slapping on a tobacco-stained smile to mask the desperation in her eyes. "I'm sorry we didn't see you, sweetie. May I help you?"

Beth Ann stood, still speechless for a moment. Then she snapped, "My mama's dead, murdered in her own home, and you *dare* insinuate that she deserved it?"

"I—I never meant—" Gertrude tried.

"We're sorry. We're both sorry," Talley interjected. "We didn't mean for you to hear us. Never imagined anyone could slip up on us like that."

"I'm not exactly known to tiptoe, Mr. Talley. And if you have one lick of evidence as to who—who *butchered* my mama—" Beth Ann ignored the shaking of his head "—you should haul that carcass of yours over to the sheriff and report it instead of standing around here flapping your gums like a damned fool."

Holding on to the cart with one hand for balance, Beth Ann scooped up her cane and managed to rise in a halfway graceful manner. It was a good thing, too, because she'd hate to spoil her exit—and the most notable tirade of her life—by falling flat on her face. As she stormed over to the only open register and glowered her way through checkout, it occurred to her that despite years of working in the market's meat department, Sid Talley and Gertrude Pederson might never recover from hearing the words "butchered" and "carcass" used in that particular context.

Served those gossips right, Beth Ann decided as she tossed the bag containing the tissues and the coffee into the sedan's trunk. She'd been planning to go home and brew a half-pot, but the confrontation in the grocery store made caffeine beside the point.

Instead, she started the big car and revved its engine, her blood thrumming with the feeling of its power. *Her* power, refueled by a fresh surge of righteous fury.

She wasn't going home at all. Sunday morning or not, she was going to find the sheriff—even if she had to drag Jim Morrell out of the choir box at church.

After three weeks of shock and grief and horror, it was high time to get some answers. And she damned well meant to hear them now.

She had nearly reached the Fundamental News Church when Beth Ann missed the stop sign at the intersection of Travis Street and Second Avenue, a junction as familiar to her as her own face in the mirror. At the sharp blare of a horn—a minivan leaving the church parking lot was bearing down on her left—she slammed on her brakes and twisted the steering wheel. The big sedan fishtailed, its rear end swinging wide. One of the squealing back tires jumped the curve, and with a solid thunk, the corner stop sign toppled over.

"Oh, my Lord," Beth Ann breathed as she put the Mercedes into Park and killed the engine.

The van honked once more before disappearing.

But Beth Ann barely noticed, fixated on the dim figures lying broken all around the car. In the sudden darkness, headlights lit the bodies of her three friends. Larinda Hyatt, Heidi Brown, and Jordan Jessup, all wearing stained cheerleading uniforms.

"No, no, no," Beth Ann cried, squeezing her eyes shut against the awful vision. She shrieked at a tap on her window.

"You all right, Beth Ann?"

The voice was muffled by the glass, but at least it

served to yank her back to the present. Opening her eyes, she glanced first at Big Jim Morrell, dressed in a suit and tie for the service, and then into the street around her. The mirage-corpses were gone.

Jerking to attention, she swallowed past a hard lump, then opened her door. "I'm sorry, Sheriff. I—I was completely in the wrong."

Her attorney—actually, Mama's attorney—would surely have a fit to hear her make such an admission, but Beth Ann was far too shaken to do anything but blurt out the truth, not only to the sheriff, but to the crowd of congregants still spilling from the church. Only a few were in earshot, but more were hustling her way.

She could almost hear the Poor-Beth-Anns already. Damn it.

"I overheard some people over at Barty's running down my mama," she went on, "and I was so upset I took off. Didn't see the stop sign 'til it was almost too late."

"You're lucky you didn't kill somebody." Morrell looked stern, with his freshly buzzed flattop and his lawman's expression, but his words were steeped in sympathy.

Beth Ann shuddered at the ghostly images of her vision. After all these years, could it have been a memory—her first real memory of the head-on collision that had wrecked so many lives?

"I know," she told him, completely forgetting why she'd raced this way in the first place. "Believe me when I say I know."

Half turning, Morrell waved off the approaching churchgoers. "Everybody's just fine," he called, "so y'all can go on home and enjoy your Sunday."

Beth Ann caught the look of disappointment on a few faces—the chance to act concerned while scoping out the newly rich daughter of the town murder victim was a powerful draw—but no one disobeyed the command that lurked beneath the sheriff's neighborly suggestion.

Beth Ann reached for her cane, only to find it had fallen into the narrow space between the passenger seat and door.

"Let me get that for you." Morrell went around to the opposite door and opened it. By the time he came back with her cane, she had climbed out of the Mercedes.

"The car's not too banged up," he told her, "just a little dented where the rear fender popped that stop sign."

Cane in hand, she went to see the small crease. Her stomach dropped at the thought of damaging her mama's pride and joy. Why hadn't she called AAA this morning and asked them to come check the battery on her car?

"I'll have the sign fixed this afternoon," Morrell said, "and I'm sure Red Hawk Body and Motor can put your car right in no time. Nephew of mine runs it—I guess you remember Gene from school."

Back in the day, "Mean Gene" Calvert had been the Red Hawks' starting quarterback, an honor that had gone to his head and, in Beth Ann's opinion, wedged there permanently. She'd make the two-hour drive to the Wichita Falls dealership before she'd let him touch the car.

Good time for a change of subject, she decided. Carefully avoiding any mention of his estranged wife, who had moved into their daughter Sandi's bed and breakfast, Beth Ann went for the one safe member of the family. "I heard your boy's the frontrunner for the state senate election next week. Hope it goes well for him. Scotty was always a good guy."

She meant it, even though they'd broken up two weeks before her accident. They'd had fun during the six months they had dated, and everyone had said they'd looked good together, the handsome wide receiver and the captain of the cheerleading squad. At the time, such ridiculous factors had counted for something in Beth Ann's mind, but eventually, Scott got a little too serious and a lot too horny for her liking. Yet even though she'd dumped him, Scotty Morrell had been one of the few who had visited and written to her during her years in hospitals and rehab. He still sent her a Christmas card each year, with a picture of himself, handsome and well-dressed, beside his pretty, teacher wife and their toddler daughter.

When Morrell beamed and thanked her, she dared to hope that, unlike her effort after last month's speeding episode—he'd clocked her doing eighty-four on an empty stretch of highway as she'd hurried to a patient's home—this bit of sucking up might get her off the hook. Mindful that any more points against her license could pose a huge problem for her, she looked up at him. "So, am I . . . am I free to go?"

He shook his head. "No ticket today, Beth Ann. No one's hurt here. And we've got more important crimes to deal with in this county."

Their gazes locked, and in the sheriff's, she saw a promise. Whatever his own problems might be, he wasn't about to give up on finding justice for her mother.

Beth Ann jolted, abruptly remembering Sid Talley's gossip, along with the question that had sent her racing over here.

"I have to know," she blurted, not caring if he changed his mind and issued her the ticket after all. "Is it true?"

His brow furrowed. "What do you mean? Has something happened?"

She stared up into his face, her every atom screaming, *Hell, yes, something's happened. My mama's lying in the cold ground in a coffin and you haven't done a thing about it.*

"Is it true," she demanded, "that you're not looking at Mark Jessup as a suspect because the man has money?"

His expression hardened, his look of sympathy evaporating in an instant. He grasped the back of her arm, and half guided, half marched her around the corner of the church, away from the prying eyes of those still watching from a distance. She had trouble keeping pace with his long strides.

"Beth Ann Decker, where on God's green earth did you come up with such nonsense?" Despite the harshness of his voice, he kept his tone low. Clearly, he didn't want anyone to overhear this conversation.

"I told you, Sheriff, people are talking. Gossips who've already tried and convicted Mark Jessup. And you, for being too slow on the uptake."

"Damned armchair detectives. They all think these cases get solved in an hour, like on their TV shows." Morrell shook his head. "I spoke to Mark the same day your mother was . . . found. There's no way he was involved. He didn't even know where you and Lilly lived or anything about the jackpot."

"Is that what he told you?" Beth Ann pressed.

Morrell nodded. "And the timing was all wrong, too. Mark had just arrived in town with his kid. Judging from the way old Hiram was acting, he wouldn't have exactly volunteered to babysit while his son went out to run an errand. And no way do I buy that Mark would—would do what was done to your mama with his boy around. It's plain as can be he loves that little fella."

A knot inside Beth Ann loosened with his words. Yes, she thought. Mark Jessup does love Eli, just as he cared about his father. How could she have allowed herself to be persuaded, even for a moment, a man like that would carry the kind of rage in his heart that had clearly gone into her mother's killing?

In spite of the accident so many years before, she held on to that thought.

Her vision blurring with hot tears, Beth Ann wiped at her eyes. "I shouldn't have gone off like that. It's just—every time I think about those fools and their talk, I go a little crazy.

"I'm sorry," she went on. "I know you're doing your best, you and your men, too. But it's—it's been three weeks now. And it's so damned hard to be alone in her house, to know what happened in her bedroom."

"I wish I could have spared you that autopsy report," he murmured.

"I was the one who insisted," she said, shaking her head. "And it was right that I should know—how she—how my mother died. What that piece of filth did to—"

Her throat closed around the images, and her head sagged forward. Which was how Beth Ann came to find herself sobbing against Jim Morrell's chest, his big arms wrapped around her as if she were a child.

Though the body froze in its tracks, the heart of the One Appointed throbbed wildly at the sight of the whore's daughter. What was *she* doing here this morning? And what had so upset her that she'd nearly plowed straight through the intersection?

Did she see me? Does this mean she's found the proof?

Terror dug in, with self-loathing snapping at its heels. On the Day of Reckoning, the One Appointed had been so stunned by the sudden surge of fury, so horrified by the dripping blood and staring, dead eyes, that there had been no thought of searching the place. No thought of anything but cleaning off the blood and getting out before someone came.

Sheriff Morrell spoke to Beth Ann for a minute—before abruptly towing her around the corner of the recently repainted, white church.

Trouble, the One Appointed figured, yet the sense of panic eased. Surely, she would have stopped and stared if she had found the evidence. She would have pointed and screamed the ugliest of accusations.

And that would have been the end. With a chill breeze, a shudder rippled beneath a growing slick of perspiration.

"Are you coming?"

The question startled, as did the warmth of the Companion's words. After nodding in answer, they walked on as the One Appointed made a silent vow that the Maker's warning would not go unheeded.

I'll go to Lilly Decker's mansion. I'll lay waste to room after room until I find what the whore hid. And if Poor Beth Ann interferes—well, then, I'll know that I have also been appointed to end her suffering.

Thy will be done, my Lord the Terrible, the Almighty. Thy will be done.

Chapter 7

The back door banged shut. *Eli.* He must have slipped outside again, going for another great escape. Too bad he couldn't seem to stay clear of trouble out there. Last week, he'd climbed into the hayloft looking for the half-wild cat that hung around the barn. Mark had nearly passed out, seeing his son so high—and knowing that the loft floor was nowhere near as solid as it should be.

Mark grimaced, then glanced at his father, who was dozing in the hospital bed that had been delivered and put in the living room two weeks before. They'd been watching football for the past hour, but Hiram's eyes were closed, his breathing even.

In case he was awake, Mark whispered, "I'll be right back. Have to check on Eli for a minute."

After Mark grabbed his jacket and ran outside, he shouted his son's name. Eli—the little turkey—couldn't have gotten far, but he didn't answer. On purpose, Mark was sure.

He took a deep breath and reminded himself his son had good reason to act up. Normally an active kid, he had spent most of the past few weeks—including a pathetically low-key fifth birthday and then Halloween—cooped up in the old house. Sometimes he drew pictures at the kitchen table or watched TV with the man he still had not been invited to call grandpa. Other times he played with his toy cars and action figures.

"Hi there, kitty." Eli's voice floated, sweet and earnest, from behind the well house. "I can be your friend, see? I brought a piece of cheese for you."

Clearly not persuaded, the silver tabby burst out of the tall grass and bolted toward the barn. Mark expected his son to follow, since Eli had yet to figure out that chasing the animal only made it warier. When he didn't appear, Mark went back to see what he was doing.

He found his son within striking distance of a three-and-a-half-foot prairie rattler. Clearly fascinated by the snare-drum vibration of the snake's tail, Eli bent forward, his face painted with a soft smile. In the space of the single heartbeat before Mark could react, the boy's hand stretched in the direction of the quivering rattle that transfixed him.

"*Shit*," Mark hissed as he swooped in behind Eli, wrapped an arm around the boy's waist, and jerked him backward, out of harm's way.

Eli yelped in surprise as Mark demanded, "Don't you know that's dangerous? Didn't I tell you if you ever saw a snake here, you needed to come get me? *Especially* a rattler."

He clutched his son—who'd started crying—tight to his chest and blinked back moisture. "I'm sorry. I know I scared you, but you took ten years off my life."

An hour later, with the snake quietly dispatched to serpent heaven and Eli still sulking in his room, Mark stood before the open kitchen cabinet, harbor to a vast fleet of prescription bottles. A glance at the medication log he'd been keeping told him it was nearly time for his father to have a pain pill, along with another tablet meant to control his restlessness.

By now, Hiram would be measuring the minutes until the doses—and probably working up a couple of nasty accusations in the process. Time had done little to blunt his hostility, but the last two weeks had added suspicion. Mark decided he'd better ask the new nurse about it when she came tomorrow. Was this part of the progression of his father's illness, or was it proof that dragging Eli down here had been a fool's quest?

"Are you still mad at me?" Eli's voice was tentative, as quiet as his approach.

As he turned, Mark saw that moisture clumped the boy's long lashes, and his nose was dripping. Mark grabbed a tissue from the box on the counter, squatted down, and wiped his son's face clean.

"I'm not mad at you," he said. "I was just scared because I love you so much. I couldn't stand to see you get hurt. Mad's how that comes out sometimes."

He thought back to his own father yelling, in the months before the crash. Hiram had raged about Mark's recklessness, his poor grades. Could there have been love there, too, buried deep beneath the anger?

When Eli hugged him, Mark squeezed his son tight. "I frightened you, too, didn't I? I'm sorry about that. Let's try not to scare each other again for a long time. Deal?"

Eli nodded, and Mark decided he needed to find someplace, perhaps a preschool or a daycare, where his son could interact with other children. Preferably an active program that would burn off all that banked-up energy.

But how would Eudena be for Eli? Little kids, Mark had noticed, weren't as hung up on differences as adults. At least not until their parents passed down their biases. But his greatest fear was a different prejudice altogether, one that would taint Eli with his father's sins.

If the accident were not enough, Mark understood that now there would be plenty of talk connecting his reappearance with Lilly Decker's murder. Resentment hammered at his temples, and he wished he'd never heard the Decker name.

"After Hiram's medication," Mark told Eli, "we'll start the spaghetti. I'll show you how to do meatballs with the ice cream scoop. You can help if you—"

"Oooookay." Eli drew the word out, cornering the market on long-suffering. "If I can't go out and see the kitty."

Before he could go further, someone rapped at the back door. Strange, a visitor showing up now. None of the hospice people or volunteers was expected on a Sunday, and Mark hadn't heard a car.

Anxiety tightened his stomach. Had the sheriff—still clueless about the murder, according to the news reports—decided to come back for him after all?

"Just a minute, Eli," he said as he walked past the washer and dryer in the mud room and looked through the small window near the top of the back door.

He swore under his breath. What was *she* doing here? But instead of ignoring Beth Ann Decker, he opened the door to tell her they didn't need her help, that they were making out just fine without her.

Despite his resolution, when he saw her struggling to balance the bags and platter she carried, he reached out instinctively to help her.

"Let me get that," he said. The bags were heavier than he'd expected. "What's all this, Beth Ann?"

She smiled. "A spiral-sliced ham. There's some macaroni salad, a green-bean casserole, buttermilk rolls, and cookies, too. Half the county—even that dried-up pack of hypocrites who wouldn't let my mama join their precious revitalization committee—has shown up at my doorstep with more food than I could eat in two lifetimes. I figured you could use some over here."

Part of him wanted to hand back the food and tell her no thanks, but Mark could almost hear his mother insisting that he invite their guest inside.

Before he could say anything, Eli had squeezed in beside him to ask, "What kind of cookies?"

Beth Ann smiled at him. "Sandi Sawyer's famous chocolate-chip oatmeal. So good, they'll make you wanta slap your mama."

Eli jerked and made a face that had Mark grinning. He couldn't recall the last time he'd heard that expression. Before he'd left the South, for sure.

"She doesn't really mean it, Eli," he said. "It's one of those things people say, like 'raining cats and dogs.'"

"Oh," the boy said, though Mark could tell he didn't really understand. Some parts of Texas culture had to be absorbed rather than explained.

"Please, come on in, Beth Ann." He stepped back to give her room. "Eli, this is Ms. Decker. You were asleep when she was here before."

Beth Ann nodded on her way in. "Good to meet you," she said. "And you can call me Miz Beth Ann. Everybody around here does."

The tap of her cane on the linoleum attracted Eli's sharp gaze. "What's that for?"

Mark bit back a curse. Would Beth Ann tell a five-year-old that his father was the reason she would never walk unaided?

But no tension rippled the calm of her demeanor. "Some people need glasses to see better—"

"My mommy wears them."

Mark made a mental note to work on his son's tendency to interrupt.

Beth Ann nodded once more as she added, "And I need my cane to walk better."

Eli started to say something else, but a digital timer in the kitchen beeped, and a strained voice called from the living room, "Boy? I need them pills now. Unless you're takin' them yourself or sellin' 'em off to the dope fiends."

Mark shut off the timer, then took a deep breath before answering his father. "I'll be there in a minute."

As he set the food on the counter and placed some cookies on a plate for Eli, Mark wished he could disguise the sear of shame, too. It was bad enough that his father still refused to use his name, but to accuse him of stealing pills with Beth Ann listening . . . Would she think he'd picked up a drug habit in prison?

Turning to Eli, Mark held the plate just out of his reach. "You know, you shouldn't really eat sweets until after dinner, but why don't you take these to your room? And maybe you can draw Miz Decker some racecars. All right?"

Eli looked inclined to argue—he hated being left

out of adult conversations—but his interest in the cookies won.

"I'll make you a real nice picture," he promised Beth Ann as he made a beeline for the room Mark still thought of as Jordan's.

Beth Ann laid a hand on his arm. "Don't worry over what your dad said about the medication. Paranoia's not uncommon in hospice patients. The stress and physical changes do that to people sometimes."

Mark looked down to where she touched him and felt swallowed whole by her compassion—and ashamed of his earlier impulse to send her packing. He was more aware than ever, too, of the reason she'd been showered with so many gifts of food.

"I'm so sorry about your mother," he said.

She flinched, the color draining from her face as if he'd said something—

Oh, God. Had Beth Ann's true mission in coming here been to check out the rumors of his involvement in the murder?

"Sheriff Morrell told me what happened," Mark explained, "when he and Deputy Riker came to get your car. It—it must have come as a terrible shock. I still can't imagine anything like that happening in Eudena."

He busied himself putting his father's pills in a paper cup and recording the times and dosages on his chart. As he worked, he felt more heat rise to his face. Despite her smiles, the food, and the kind words, her silence told him she clearly saw him as an ex-con—the same loser who had already screwed up her life once.

So what did you expect? he asked himself. In Pittsburgh, people treated him well enough, even sucked up to him. When he spoke about his product, about his firsthand knowledge of the tragic results of reckless teenage driving, he had earned respect—along with enough money to pursue his philanthropic goals.

But he'd damned well known things wouldn't play out that way in Hatcher County. And even if he had decades to convince some residents to accept him, he couldn't imagine Beth Ann numbering among them.

"I'm sorry," she said quietly. "Sorry I looked at you like that. I never should have come—"

He looked up sharply, wondering if she'd read his mind. "How could you know what I was—"

She shrugged. "Your neck and ears flush when you're upset. They've always given you away—even back in the days when Mrs. McLendon called on you to read aloud in second grade."

Remembering that humiliation, Mark picked up the cup of pills. He'd worried that Eli would inherit his dyslexia—until the kid stunned him a few months earlier by picking out words from the storybooks they read together, then pointing them out and reading them on road signs later.

Even so, Mark couldn't help wincing at the thought of himself turning beet red as a boy. Huffing out a sigh, he said, "So much for my carefully cultivated, Billy Bad-Ass image."

She laughed. "Don't worry. You fooled plenty in your day. Including all those girls you had drooling over you in high school."

But not you, he thought, and for some reason he felt grateful. Not because he hadn't wanted her—not by a long shot—but because she'd been perceptive enough to see through his tough-guy act in a way that no one else had. "I—uh—I'd better take my dad his medication before he starts up again."

She followed him into the living room. As usual, the curtains were drawn and the TV blared. When Mark turned on the table lamp, Hiram blinked and grumbled, looking thinner and more drawn than ever beneath his pile of blankets.

If her patient's decline surprised her, Beth Ann didn't show it. As Mark shut off the television, she said, "It's good to see you, Mr. Jessup. How are you doing?"

Taking both the pills and the cup of water from the bedside tray Mark handed him, Hiram swallowed before answering. "I'm dying, that's how I am."

Instead of his usual anger, his words held a sadness Mark had rarely heard.

Beth Ann reached out to touch the bony arm, her fingers sliding up Hiram's wrist in a near-caress before finding his pulse. She glanced down at the sweep second hand of her watch.

"You don't gotta do that," Hiram told her. "Miz Stutz'll be back tomorrow. She comes out twice a week since your mama passed, rest her soul."

Beth Ann looked up and their gazes touched. Mark would swear he saw unspoken words pass in that glance.

"No reason I shouldn't check up on you while I'm here," she finally said. "Wouldn't want my nursing skills to get rusty."

"I was real sorry to hear about what happened." Hiram hadn't taken his eyes off her. "That Lilly was a spitfire, she was. They broke the mold when they made her."

Beth Ann smiled. "A lot of folks would say 'thank

goodness.' And I appreciate your telling me that. Of all people, after—"

Hiram's hand flapped weakly to wave off her concern. "Water under the bridge, that lawsuit. Your mama didn't do no more than she had to to get you fixed up. I didn't understand it for a long while, but I heard about those bills she had. And I know Lilly had a living daughter to take care of."

Mark could almost hear the words he left unspoken. *Not like me. All I had was one fuck-up of a son.*

Probably, Hiram would not have put it quite so bluntly. But he'd made his feelings clear enough in other ways.

Beth Ann said, "That's very understanding of you, Mr. Jessup. Especially in light of your own losses."

When she looked at Mark, he fought the urge to shudder. Was she counting him among his father's losses? Had Hiram ever done the same, or had he written off his only son even before the accident, when Jordan's stellar grades, blond beauty, and sunny disposition eclipsed the disappointments of an elder brother better known for his poor schoolwork and troublemaking than anything of merit?

Changing the subject, Beth Ann asked Hiram the usual questions as she checked on everything from his vitals to his skin condition.

"When I'm not hurtin', I'm sleeping," Hiram told her, "leastways, I'm trying to sleep—when the boy ain't pestering me to eat—"

"You mean Mark," Beth Ann corrected. "Eli's the only boy here."

"Yeah, of course I mean *him.*"

"Mark," she repeated, "appears to be taking very

good care of you. And the house, too. I've noticed the back door's fixed, and the kitchen's been repainted. The old place is looking good."

Shrugging, Hiram turned his head away. "It's no more than he ought to do."

Mark felt his stomach clench. He'd be damned if he'd listen to any more of this. "I'll be out putting that ham and stuff in the refrigerator."

He put away the food more noisily than necessary, partly due to his banging dishes and partly due to his swearing under his breath. Why the hell was he doing this to himself? It was obvious his father hated his presence, considered Eli's existence a slap in the face, and bore not the slightest regret for turning his back on Mark after the crash.

The only damned thing that cantankerous old man was sorry about was that Mark had survived.

"I think you need to talk to your father. Soon."

Mark turned to find Beth Ann behind him. Standing too close for his comfort and speaking in quiet tones that brought to mind the intimacy that followed the most private acts between a man and woman.

But then, his thoughts were never too far from the bedroom when he was near her. Old fantasies died hard, he supposed.

"What do you mean?" he asked. "I talk to my father every day."

Her head shook. "I mean discuss what stands between you. The way I did, when the two of us spoke about my mother and the lawsuit."

He blew out a hard breath. "What's the point of bringing up that bullshit? It's not like we can turn back time. Jordan's gone—and Heidi and Larinda. And you—no matter what I do, you're not the same and never will be."

She straightened to her full height with some emotion—either pride or anger—flashing in those blue eyes. "No, I won't."

"Does it help to hear I'm sorry? Does it make it any better? Because as hollow as it sounds, I am." As badly as he wanted to look away, he refused to allow himself to do so. He'd written her a letter once, during the time he spent in prison. He'd written Heidi's and Larinda's parents, too. But saying the words to Beth Ann was far harder. "From the bottom of my heart, I *am* sorry, Beth Ann. All these years, I have been. Every day of my life since that night."

She stared at him until his lungs ached—letting him know he held his breath in anticipation of her answer. Of the families he had written, he had only heard back from Larinda's. It had been her father, county tax assessor Billy Hyatt, saying he would hunt down and kill Mark if he ever had the balls to try to contact them again.

Finally, she cleared her throat, then asked, "If you can tell me, then why not him?"

Mark shook his head, disappointment settling in his gut. *Of course, she can't forgive me.* "He doesn't want to hear it. Besides, he—what's the point?"

"The point is, time's running out. Remember what I said about his cancer spreading to the brain?"

Panic sliced through the sense of futility that gripped him. "You think the end will come soon? How much longer?"

"I can't know that. No human being can say exactly when. Sometimes it's fairly quick once they start sliding downhill this way. Other times, the patient hangs on past anything you'd think human endurance could withstand. Especially when something this important's unresolved."

Mark felt crowded by her nearness. Crowded by the weight of expectation and her fifty-cent psychology.

"I was seventeen when I was arrested," he said bluntly. "On my eighteenth birthday, they sent me to a grown man's prison.

"I'm not telling you I didn't have it coming. I'm not saying people didn't suffer because of my mistakes. But it would have mattered, having my old man there for me. And I know damned well—my lawyer told me—he was the one who put his foot down. Who kept my mother away, too. And then she—she was gone before my sentence ended. Because of him, I lost my chance to make things right with her."

Beth Ann went to the sink and took a clean glass from the dish drainer, poured from the pitcher of water in the refrigerator. But instead of drinking, she handed him the full glass.

"You have one last chance with this man. Here and now," she told him. "And why did you come back here, if you didn't need to make this right?"

He set the glass on the counter with a hard clunk. He didn't want her sympathy, didn't want her caretaking to spill over onto him.

"You tell me, why are *you* here?" Infused with pain, his words came out like an accusation. "To prove you're Superwoman? Or to find out if I could still be a killer, after all these years?"

She turned away from him, but not before he glimpsed the raw pain in her eyes. He'd been right, that she'd come here harboring a few suspicions.

But neither had his motives in coming home been

purely altruistic, no matter what he'd told himself during the long drive from Pittsburgh. Catching her by the wrist, he said, "It's all right. I don't blame you. Everyone in Hatcher County knows I did hard time for killing those girls. Everybody knows I wasn't worth much before that."

She jerked her hand free and glared up at him. "Don't lump me in with 'everybody.' You don't have a clue what I think. Never did, as far as I could tell."

As he watched her rub the spot where he had grabbed her, he felt a chasm tear open inside him. A need closer to starvation than a simple case of hunger. It was the raw desire to touch her, the same craving he had felt the night he'd watched her cheer at that ill-fated homecoming football game. He'd told himself he'd shown up only to keep an eye on Jordan, to make sure that asshole quarterback, Gene Calvert, didn't make another run at convincing her to lay her virginity at the altar of eternal popularity. But it was the bounce of Beth Ann's ponytail that lived inside his memory, the flip of her short skirt and the perfection of those long legs as she performed her gravity-defying aerials. At the outset of that final, glorious night, the girl had flown.

At its conclusion, she lay broken in a smoking, wrecked Camaro with her friends—and his sister—dead around her.

Yet she stood here now, in this kitchen, when she had more cause to hate him than almost anybody in the town that shunned him.

"So what *do* you think?" he asked quietly.

She drew in a deep breath before saying, "That you're a damned sight better man than most folks realize. Yourself, especially."

He took a step closer, allowing himself to be drawn in by her words, her warmth, and the unexpected gift he glimpsed in her eyes. Allowing himself to resurrect an old fantasy, to tip back her chin with one finger and plant the softest kiss on her mouth.

A kiss that tasted of redemption, or at least its possibility. For a time he measured in the space of heartbeats, she leaned into it, a shift that sent awareness ricocheting through his body. His free hand skimmed down her back, then settled along the curve of her hip. As in dreams uncounted, a sweet murmur rose from her throat.

But in one nightmare instant, she jerked away and stared at him as if he'd lost his mind. Or she had.

"No." She shook her head rapidly. "That isn't what I meant, Mark."

"I think you might have," he said. "I think there's something here. Between us. I think maybe it's been there all along."

"It's stress," she assured him. "I'm certainly dealing with my share, for one thing. And it's not all that uncommon for patients' families to mistake a nurse's professional concern for—for something more personal."

"You kissed me back, Beth Ann, and I'm not likely to forget it." He smiled at her in thanks for the surge of hope she'd brought him. "It's the nicest thing I've felt in a long time."

Her cane's tip smacked the linoleum floor, and she took a step backward. "I was an idiot to come here."

Her side-swept bangs had fallen into her eyes. Mark longed to smooth back her hair, ached for any excuse to reach out to her once more.

"I wish you would stay," he said. "Why not have dinner with us? Thanks to you, there's plenty."

She shook her head, avoiding his gaze. "Sorry. I'm sorry if I gave you the wrong impression. I—I'll phone your father's new nurse, let her know how he's doing."

"Don't run off like this, Beth Ann. At least let me get you something. Coke or water—I have some iced tea made." He stepped into her line of sight, tried another smile. "If you want, I'll call in Eli. He can chaperone."

She didn't smile back. Instead she moved toward the door, the stiffness of her body all but shouting her discomfort. "No thanks. Say goodbye to your son for me. He seems like a sweet kid. Really."

As if on cue, Eli trotted in from the hallway, a sheet of paper from his art pad clutched in one small hand. "I made this for you, Miz Beth Ann," he told her as he gave up his offering. "The red one's yours, the blue one's Daddy's."

Mark peered over her shoulder at the pair of race-cars his son had drawn freehand. Those cookies must have hit the spot because it was one of his better efforts, with what Mark thought was an amazing amount of detail for someone barely five years old. His son had included headlights, bumpers, and door handles, everything but drivers. In typical Eli fashion, flames were shooting out from beneath the tires—and this time he'd added a few puffs of silver smoke.

"This is *really* good." Beth Ann sounded startled. "Thanks, Eli. But I guess I shouldn't be surprised. I remember your dad was a terrific artist. Liked to draw fast cars, too."

His claim to fame, Mark recalled—at least until he figured out that the odds on surviving the sixth grade were far better for a hell-raiser than a kid who sat around and drew because he couldn't read the assignments in the textbook. He was surprised that anyone remembered. Especially a girl who'd made it so clear that she had bigger plans than Hatcher County.

"Thanks," Eli said. He dropped his gaze, and Mark noticed his ears reddening.

Poor kid. It seemed he'd inherited at least one of his father's curses.

"What are the cars doing?" Beth Ann asked. "Are they racing?"

Eli shook his head. "Nah. See how they're facing each other? They're at a fancy car show like the one my daddy took me to. They're waiting for all the people to come and look and pick the best one."

But Mark's pulse quickened as saw something different in the drawing: two cars hurtling toward each other, about to strike head on.

Chapter 8

"I have half a mind to call that Sheriff Morrell myself and ask him what he's thinking, sending a half-grown—"

"*Mo-om*," Damon Stillwater interrupted. Already he felt queasy at the memory of his boss's recent lecture. And Ginny Stillwater, with her hand on the hip of the pink robe he'd bought her last Mother's Day, hadn't even properly warmed up yet.

"All right," she amended, "an inexperienced *young man*. The point is, the sheriff's got no business sending you out on night patrol all by your lonesome. Especially with a murderer on the loose."

Anger slashed through him at the unfairness of Morrell's decision, but Damon would cut out his own tongue before he'd whine about it to his mama. Instead, he said, "You don't want to get overly excited, Mama. You know what the doctor said about that."

Her face reddened, and he winced, expecting her to accuse him of using her illness to his advantage.

But before she could say a word, Damon's father muted the TV and turned from the ten o'clock news, which had just gone to a commercial. "Did you ever stop to think Jim Morrell might have a damned good reason for moving Damon to the graveyard shift? He *is* the boss, you know."

Both Damon and his mom were startled by the unexpected comment. After a long day's work at the hardware store, Earl Stillwater didn't normally expend energy involving himself in minor family squabbles. More evenings than not, he could be found as he was at the moment: dressed in a pair of faded, navy sweats that strained against his paunch and ensconced in his beloved La-Z-Boy recliner, where he either hid out behind the *Wichita Falls Times Record* or watched newscasts so stodgy, they put Damon to sleep.

"What reason?" Ginny asked. "Unless you mean it's because that complainer, Evelyn, is bad-mouthing him around town about a little harmless drinking. But terrible a thing as divorce is, it's no excuse for risking Damon's safety."

Staring into his father's eyes, Damon shook his head quickly. It was humiliating enough, being relegated to Siberia, as the deputies called the late-night detail. But having his mom know the true reason would be far worse, not least of all because she might get it into her hair-netted head to call Sheriff Morrell and give him a piece of her mind.

If that happened, he might as well quit the department and haul ass to the *real* Siberia, because he'd be stuck on graveyard duty—and with the name Kid— until he was an old man.

But if Earl Stillwater took note of his son's head-shaking, it didn't stop him. "From what I hear, our Damon's been putting his nose where it's not wanted."

Oh, hell, thought Damon. He should have known

better than to hope word wouldn't hit his father's hardware store. "I was only trying to help out with the investigation."

It went without saying that he meant the investigation into Lilly Decker's murder. Weeks after the fact, it remained all the talk around town.

Resentment burrowed deeper into Damon's gut. He was almost positive the case would have been solved by now, if Morrell hadn't dismissed the "new kid's" instincts.

"Were you *asked* to help?" His father looked at him gravely over the black rims of a pair of reading glasses.

"I *should* have been." Damon fiddled with his badge, trying to flash the message that *he* was the only member of this family working in law enforcement. "It's a waste of resources putting me on barking-dog and candy-pinching calls when the case of the century still needs solving."

"Did it ever occur to you that the routine calls might need handling to free up the more experienced investigators?" Earl shook his head and frowned. "That was always the trouble with you, son. You never *listen* to authority. You're always too convinced that you know *better*."

Damon raked his fingers through his hair. Good thing it was so short, or he might just tear it out. "This *isn't* about when I worked down at the hardware store with you when I was back in high school. And it isn't about my troubles with that bossy Jo-Ellen Baxter over the size of ice cream cones down at the DQ. This is about a woman's life."

He stuck out his chest, struck by the importance of his statement.

"About Lilly Decker's life," Earl said, shaking his head.

"That woman." His mother's hand fluttered up to

clutch the collar of her bathrobe. "She was trouble alive, and she's trouble dead. People don't want you stirring up this ugliness and making them feel like common *suspects.*"

So she'd heard some of the complaints, too, probably during her standing appointment at the beauty shop. God forbid the Blond-O-Dome should ever falter.

"Well, they *are* suspects," Damon insisted, "as long as they hold some kind of grudge against the victim. We call that 'motive' in the business. Whether it was because she built that big new house where it blocked their view of Mill Pond or she wanted to elbow her way onto their committee or because she snubbed 'em after she got money or made cow eyes at their husbands—"

His mom sniffed. "I cannot *believe* you would bring up such things to some of my own friends. Why, Norma Nederhoffer was beside herself, with you insinuatin' a respectable person like her could—"

"We can't automatically discount someone because they look regular or act regular," Damon told her, though he had trouble imagining Old Lady Nederhoffer getting mad enough to do the kind of violence that had been done to Lilly Decker.

Damon's mother crossed her arms over a sagging bosom. "If you ask me, you'd be better off checking out that Mexican encampment if you absolutely *have* to stick your nose into this dirty business. You know how those people like their knives. And they like their drinking, too—tequila and what have you."

"We don't figure her killer was a stranger to her." With no sign of forced entry and the personal nature of the attack, Damon had concluded this himself— though he'd been increasingly cut off from inside information.

"A little too much gumption, too soon. Sort of reminds me of my own son, Scotty, back before he took on law school." Sheriff Morrell had laid a huge paw on Damon's shoulder as he'd said it. *"Let me give you some free advice, Kid. Folks around here don't take kindly to being called to account by a fella barely old enough to shave regular. These are our friends and neighbors— you've got to learn to handle 'em real smooth-like or they start squawkin'. Best we keep you out of sight a spell 'til they get over it."*

And he had flat forbidden Damon from bringing up Mark Jessup again. *"He's been excluded as a suspect,"* was all Morrell would tell him.

"You just do what the boss says for once," Damon's dad insisted, "and you'll be fine. Just learn to follow orders and you'll go far in this life."

The commercial break had ended, and Earl Stillwater turned up the volume, his signal that the conversation was officially closed for the evening.

"I still don't think that man ought to make you ride alone," Damon's mom said in a stage whisper. "Everybody knows the kind of people that run around by moonlight. Dangerous people. Like Mexicans . . . and worse."

Damon didn't bother pointing out to her that the bloodiest, most sadistic crime in the county's history had, according to the coroner, happened in broad daylight. Or that good and evil were nowhere near as well ordered as the spray-lacquered blond bouffant beneath her net.

Two-forty-nine A.M. The town of Eudena would be sleeping, all the watchers and the talkers—and Beth Ann Decker, too.

A cold prairie wind was blowing, drawing a curtain of clouds across the starry sky. With a rushing noise to mask the sounds of movement and thick darkness to conceal an intruder, the storm was clearly wrought by the Almighty to mask His servant's work. Or perhaps it was a warning, a message that His matters must no longer be delayed.

Chilled, the One Appointed shivered. Perhaps with the anticipation that came of doing God's will. Not fear, no certainly not that, for with every moment's prayer, it grew clearer that the plan unfolding must be preordained.

The whore had been meant to die as just punishment for her sins. And any shred of evidence that might cause the innocent to suffer must be sought out and destroyed as well, before it was too late.

Near the mansion's back door, the echoes of screams and a vision bright with blood struck like a closed fist. Hands trembled as the kit was opened, a kit packed with the tools needed to sever the electrical and phone lines before entering.

A pair of pliers clattered on the back deck. At the sound—the metal end had struck a flowerpot—the One Appointed froze and blessed the howling wind.

Even as the tool was lifted, one last prayer rose to the heavens: *Lord, grant me the guidance to find that letter and the strength to do whatever must be done.* After giving over all worry, the One Appointed felt a quiet power flowing, felt body and will guided, as if by a greater hand.

In spite of the gusting chill, a surge of heat melted the final vestiges of mortal conscience and seared away the last, faint indecision.

Time to go about His work now, with thoughts free of dread and pity, with a soul cleansed of guilt.

Chapter 9

Beth Ann dreamed the kiss a dozen times, her mind embellishing upon each touch until Mark's lips blazed a tingling trail along her neck and over her breasts and his hands ignited a touch point even lower.

"Jess . . ." She murmured the nickname, only to wake, heart racing, her body moist in places that had too long gone untended.

Groaning, she sat up in the darkness and punched one of the spare pillows she used to prop herself into a halfway-comfortable position. Damn it, she had Mark Jessup to blame for sixteen years of restless nights—but never one that had disturbed her on this level.

Outside, she heard the rush of wind, as if the night mirrored her body's agitation. And not only her body's. Her mind, too, was relentless, dredging up ancient memories of her friend Jordan's hell-raiser of a brother, a boy she'd been all too aware of for as long as she could remember. A boy she'd warned herself would mean big trouble, for instinct told her that falling for him would put an end to her grand plans.

Funny, how he'd managed to derail them with five thousand pounds of steel instead of the explorations she'd imagined in such vivid detail throughout their high-school years. An image flashed through her mind—not of the fevered coupling of their bodies but of the sudden veer of headlights into her path through the darkness.

Swallowing back bile, she pulled the covers higher against a sick chill. And flinched at a dull thud from somewhere in the house.

What the hell was that? Fear uncoiled in her belly, then slithered up the pathway of her spine.

Then she remembered how, on coming home, she'd been so unnerved by her encounter with Mark Jessup, she'd paced the Lucky Pull from one end to the other, stopping to spin the stodgy globe or rearrange her mariachi ducks, then move on to the next room as if it might be the one to hold her lost sanity.

Though she had avoided it for three weeks, some-how she had found herself standing in her mother's bedroom, staring at the new carpeting and bedding and the freshly painted, white walls. The cleaners, a trauma scene outfit from Wichita Falls, had done a good job, but the room smelled wrong to Beth Ann, too antiseptic. Certainly nothing like her mama, who, since her jackpot win, had all but bathed in the frou-frou fragrances she could finally afford.

Figuring a good airing couldn't hurt things, Beth Ann had thrown open two large windows in the back-corner bedroom. Since she couldn't remember clos-ing them, she figured that one of her mama's fussy knick-knacks must have toppled in the wind.

Beth Ann clicked the switch on her nightstand lamp, but nothing happened. Grimacing, she cursed the rural electric cooperative, whose half-assed power grid failed nearly every time a blue norther rolled in off the Great Plains.

She groped in the darkness for both the flashlight in her drawer and the cane she always left in easy reach. Yet she hesitated, heart still thumping, imagining her mother splayed across her mattress, her room awash in blood.

Beth Ann didn't know for certain that the bed was where her mama had died. She thanked God every night that the sheriff hadn't let her look. But that hadn't stopped her imagination from painting gruesome pictures, and the horror of the autopsy report supplied details she never would have thought of in a lifetime.

But Mama isn't there now. You saw that yourself. She isn't lying there, hacked open, her mouth gaping, and her throat stuffed with—

Beth Ann gasped and cursed her own stubborn insistence on knowing the details. For three nights afterward, she'd stayed with Cheryl and Pete, who kept sneaking out to his woodshop rather than helping his wife with the house or their three daughters, until the couple's bickering had driven her back home. She could have simply locked up the Lucky Pull, switched on the alarm, and rented a room at Sandi Sawyer's bed and breakfast until she found a smaller place to buy on her own. But the idea grated, especially the thought of another damned chorus of Poor Beth Anns rising all around the county.

She'd rather tough it out than face that, and she certainly didn't want her mama's bedroom getting soaked with the rain that had been forecast. Gritting her teeth, Beth Ann switched on the flashlight and climbed from her bed, then walked into the hallway.

Some ten yards down, her mother's bedroom door was shut tight, though Beth Ann was all but certain she had blocked it open with a grapefruit-sized chunk of rose quartz, a last remnant of her late father's rock collection. Had the wind been strong enough to nudge the door past the impediment, freeing it to slam shut?

Remembering the noise she'd heard, she thought it a likely explanation. Still, her hand lingered on the doorknob as blood-soaked imagery filled her mind.

Drawing in another deep breath, she told herself, "Damn it, Beth Ann, suck it up and do this. Your mama's *not* inside that room."

She turned the knob and pushed before stepping— and then *flying*—forward.

Chapter 10

So fast, so hard and unexpected, the attack struck like a bolt of lightning from a clear blue sky.

Beth Ann was tumbling, her head slamming into the hard corner of a dresser before her mind registered the hands that had grabbed her neck and arm and slung her forward as she stepped into the room. As her flashlight struck the floor, it cut out, plunging the room into terrifying blackness.

She sprawled there moaning, pain arcing over her skull and her palms pressing her bleeding scalp, when the adrenaline kicked in. Words from the autopsy report flashed through her mind, words like *mutilation, exsanguination,* and *asphyxiation.*

Damned if she would die as horribly as her mama.

She swung her cane like a baseball bat at God-only-knew-what target and heard a sharp cry as she slammed something hard at shin level. With panic ripping through her, she struck again and again, and horror mixed with satisfaction when she heard another grunt, followed by the heavy shudder of the dresser as a body fell against it, flinging a hail of knick-knacks to the carpet, including one item that bounced off Beth Ann's shoulder.

She barely felt it as she blindly swung—yet this time, she heard only the wooden crack of the cane against both the dresser and the doorway, and then the heavy breaths of her attacker receding into the hall.

Her sticky hands bumped objects on the carpet—a silky scrap of cloth, one of Mama's paperbacks, perhaps a set of bracelets—as she crawled for the door to close it. As it swung shut, she heard feet pounding down the staircase. Seconds later, the front door slammed open, banging hard against the entryway wall.

Had she really scared off her attacker, or was the intruder coming back, this time with a weapon like the knife that had killed her mother?

Nausea assailed Beth Ann, and the dark room spun around her. Hot liquid dripped through her hair, and her skull felt as if an axe blow had split the top in two. *Concussion,* her nurse's training told her, even as sparkling dots materialized before her.

Don't you dare pass out, or throw up either. She couldn't afford to lose control now. In an act of will, she pushed back the shimmering confetti and the awful pain.

Reaching up, she locked herself inside the room. Still keeping low—she couldn't imagine climbing to her feet—Beth Ann made her way to the nightstand by her mama's bed. As she felt around its top, she knocked the lamp against the wall, but she didn't stop until she found the cordless phone.

She couldn't make the thing work, no matter what she pushed. That was when she realized that her power outage was most likely man-made and not caused by the storm.

Groaning, she resisted the temptation to drag herself inside the walk-in closet and hide behind her mother's clothing. She needed help, but the idea of unlocking the bedroom door and crawling to her room, where she'd left her cell phone, scared the hell out of her.

For several minutes she sat dead still, pain cleaving her skull as her ears strained for the slightest sound. The rush of wind was all she heard at first, until—what was that? Like popcorn, a few kernels bursting at a time and then—

It's raining. Only raining. With tears sliding down her face, she gritted her teeth and used the bed beside her to struggle upright. It took everything she had to stay on her feet as the sparkling dots resurfaced, then swirled around her.

She forced herself into motion, lurching forward, then slumping against the bedroom door.

Did she dare open it? Or was the lock her last defense against a brutal killer?

From downstairs, she heard pounding, followed by shouted words she couldn't make out. Her heart thrashed, and her insides turned hot and liquid.

"Please, God, no," she whispered.

That was when she heard him coming up the stairs.

With brilliant flashes exploding in her vision, Beth Ann barely registered her slow slide down the closed door. By the time she hit the carpet, she was already out cold.

Chapter 11

Damon Stillwater was at the front door, his whole body trembling miserably as the sheriff's car swung in behind the ambulance parked along the curb. Big Jim Morrell unfolded himself from the Crown Victoria and trotted through the rain to the Lucky Pull's front porch.

"How bad?" The big man puffed with exertion, though the distance covered hadn't been far.

Damon shook his head, still aching in the shoulder he had used to pop open the bedroom door, still reeling at the dark sheen of blood that had glistened in his flashlight's beam. The thought took him back to the dread that had balled up in his stomach as he'd seen Lilly Decker's fixed eyes, her face a garish mask of crimson, her jaws forced open by what he'd later learned was a gouged-out breast implant the killer had shoved down her throat.

His gut heaved, and two steps later, he was puking into the shrubs that lined the front porch. *Again*—only this time he was doing it in front of the sheriff.

Maybe he wasn't cut out for this work, after all.

Jim Morrell patted his shoulder. "It's all right, Kid. I spewed, too, my first bad one. But I have to know, how's Beth Ann?"

Damon spat, then told him, "Bloody. There's a nasty cut on top of her head, but she's conscious and talking. Or at least she was when Pete Riker sent me down to wait for you. He's up there with the rescue workers and his big flashlight. Power's been cut to the house. Phone line, too."

"Tell me what the scene's like. Tell me everything from the beginning."

Damon took a deep breath, which cleared his head a little. "One of the Winfield boys—I think it was Matthias—called it in. He spotted the front door open as he drove past on his way home from a friend's party. Got worried about Miz Beth Ann, but he was too spooked to go in on his own."

"Smart boy. Intruder could've still been inside."

"I rolled in, lights and sirens off, and saw the door still open. I knocked and hollered, 'Sheriff's department,' but there was no response. So I went in to check things out."

"You should have waited for your backup," Morrell said sternly. "You'll get yourself shot, playing cowboy like that."

"I know, and I'm sorry. It's just—I kept thinkin' about how we found Mrs. Decker. I kept thinking about Poor Beth Ann, and—"

"I know what you were thinking, and I know it turned out right this time. But you charge into an unsecured scene alone like that again, and I'll have your badge. You understand that?"

"Yes, sir. And I'm sorry, sir." Damon wondered if his old job frying tater tots was still available.

"Not half as sorry as I'd be if I had to explain to Earl and Ginny Stillwater why I let their only son get himself killed. Now go ahead with your story."

"I looked around some with my flashlight, saw the office, or whatever they call it, torn to pieces—and that secretary desk out in the sitting room was tossed, too. Papers strewn all over, files pulled out, that big globe stand beside it knocked down. Then I heard this thump from upstairs, so I went looking."

"What did you see?" Morrell asked.

"Mostly, everything in order. Except one bedroom—I think it's Beth Ann's—was empty, the bedding messed up like someone had been sleeping. Then I saw the door to *Mrs.* Decker's room was shut tight.

"It was locked, too," Damon continued, "and I heard moaning inside when I tried it. So I hit it two or three times, 'til something splintered and the lock gave."

He rubbed his throbbing shoulder. Popping open doors looked so much easier on TV.

"And that's when you found Beth Ann?"

He nodded. "Yes, sir, but it was still tough getting inside. She'd fallen up against the door, and it took a while before she could roll out of the way."

"When you went inside, what did you see?" With one big hand, Morrell made a rolling motion, encouraging him to get down to it. "I want to get your impression of how the scene looked before those rescue fellas and Pete and all tromped over everything. Then I'll go check it out myself."

"I saw the blood first. Some had run down her face, and her hair's matted with it. There were bloody handprints on the carpet and the bedspread, too, beside the nightstand. But not nearly as much blood as with Lilly—Mrs. Decker."

"Forget about the blood for right now. What else?"

Damon pictured the spotlight of his beam as it swung around the room. He'd held his gun in one hand, half terrified and half hoping that Beth Ann's attacker was still inside, that he'd be forced to shoot down the monster. Then Sheriff Morrell would probably pin a medal onto his uniform instead of calling him "Kid" and threatening to fire him.

But instead of catching a crazed killer, his light had touched on chaos. "Room was pretty torn up. Drawers pulled out and those little bookshelves emptied. Lamp knocked over, too, and shattered. Looked like somebody dumped out a jewelry box on top of the bed."

"Could be we have a burglar, not Lilly Decker's killer, after all. Although that cut phone line makes me wonder," Morrell mused before abruptly switching focus. "What about Beth Ann? What did she have to say?"

Voices distracted Damon from the conversation. As he peered inside the open door, he saw the EMTs carrying a stretcher down the staircase. Deputy Pete Riker was guiding them with a flashlight big enough to spotlight a chorus line.

"Well?" the sheriff prompted.

"She was checking out a noise in the master bedroom when somebody grabbed her by the arm and neck and yanked her right off her feet. Said there was a struggle and she hit her head on something—she thought it was the dresser—but whoever did it ran off."

"She recognize a face? A voice?"

"Too dark to see, she told me. And I—I forgot to ask her if the guy said anything. By that time Pete had got there, and I was rendering first aid."

Or trying anyway. At Beth Ann's direction, he'd wadded up a pillowcase so he could apply direct pressure to the cut. But it must have been sore as anything, because she'd jerked away, breath hissing through her teeth, and told him, *"Touch my head again and I swear I'll rip your lips off."*

"Poor Beth Ann," Morrell muttered as Riker and the EMTs approached the doorway.

"Don't call me that." Beth Ann glared up from the stretcher, determination cutting straight through the mess of blood on her face. "Don't anyone call me that. Or I'll rip your lips off, too."

"I still cannot believe you threatened half of the department," Cheryl Riker said as she walked into one of Jackrabbit General's semi-private rooms. Her younger sister, Aimee Gustavsen, waltzed in after her and immediately plopped down on the room's second bed. It had been unoccupied since yesterday morning, when its tenant had decided gallstones were less risky than a roommate whose attacker might show up any minute to "finish off both of us."

"My feet are killing me." After tucking a bobbed, platinum-blond strand behind one ear, Aimee pulled off a pointy-toed horror of a high-heeled shoe. The pair was royal blue, to match the jacket she wore over a trendy, tiered skirt. "Why I torment myself like this, I can't guess."

Since Beth Ann felt no sympathy for any woman who insisted upon crippling herself, she ignored Aimee to focus on the used grocery bag in Cheryl's hand. "Tell me those are my clothes. Real clothes."

Unlike the former homecoming queen, Beth Ann had long since lost any interest in fashion, but she drew the line at butt-baring hospital gowns.

"First, you have to tell me," Cheryl said, grinning,

"did you honestly threaten Big Jim Morrell to his face? And why didn't I hear about this when I came to see you yesterday?"

Beth Ann huffed out a sigh. "I had other things on my mind, not to mention the headache from hell. And I confess, I wasn't exactly at my Mitzi Margate–CharmSchool finest the other night with Sheriff Morrell and the others."

Cheryl laughed. "I only wish I'd seen the look on Big Jim's face. Sweet Pete told me it was priceless."

Beth Ann was always amazed that a woman who called her husband by such an affectionate nickname could spend so much time arguing with the man. Must be one of those inexplicable married-people things.

"I apologized," she told her friend. Though Beth Ann wasn't all that sorry, she appreciated what the authorities were doing enough to scrape together a white lie. Even if their investigation so far hadn't turned up anything in the way of solid evidence. As she understood it, Morrell and company figured she had surprised a thief who'd heard the idiotic rumor that Lilly Decker had hidden her money in the mansion because she didn't hold with banks.

"How about handing me my clothes so I can get out of this hellhole?" she asked.

"Young lady, did I just hear you call my hospital a hellhole?" demanded Henry Crabtree, who had delivered all three of them, along with a good percentage of the county's inhabitants. Tucked beneath the snowy fringe that wreathed an otherwise bare head, his hearing aid whistled so loudly, Beth Ann was surprised he'd caught her remark.

"Sorry, Doctor—"

"This hospital was good enough the other night, when you needed stitches—"

"Yes, sir." Beth Ann silently prayed she wouldn't find a huge bald spot beneath her bandage, where Dr. Crabtree's nurse had prepped her.

"And good enough to offer you employment." His wrinkled face scowled. "Good enough when you were brought into this world, too—"

"It's a veritable Mayo Clinic, sir," she said, despite the fact that everyone seriously ill or injured tried like hell to make the two-hour trip to Wichita Falls or even Fort Worth. If they couldn't, they were transferred as soon as possible.

Dr. Crabtree narrowed a pair of blue eyes, still sharp for a man in his early eighties. "Let's not push it, Beth Ann. I still think you could stand another day of observation. A concussion's nothing to fool around with."

"It's been more than thirty-six hours already. I need to get on with my life." First order of business: escape Jackrabbit General, preferably in real clothes. Second: buy the best alarm system available, one with a backup power source. And then she was going to get the biggest, meanest guard dog she could find. The jury might still be out on whether she'd tangled with a burglar or her mother's killer, but either way, she wasn't taking any chances. Every time she thought of what had happened to her—and what could have happened— Beth Ann's hands grew slick with perspiration, and her mouth went dry as sand.

"I swear, Doctor, I'll look after her." Cheryl held up one hand in the Brownie Promise salute. "Pete and I won't let her out of our sight."

Beth Ann winced. Cheryl might be a great friend,

but she and Pete together were best reserved for short visits. A barbecue, maybe, or a birthday party for one of their daughters. Longer than that and the couple's recreational squabbling was enough to make a saint cuss. And contrary to all the "angel of this earth" stuff she'd been hearing since she went to work with the hospice program, Beth Ann Decker had never claimed to be a saint.

Dr. Crabtree gave her a cursory examination before signing her discharge orders. "You listen to your friends, you hear?" he said on his way out.

Beth Ann dumped out the shopping bag and took inventory. She sighed at the sight of her favorite pair of jeans; a soft, blue sweater; socks and underwear; a well-worn pair of tennis shoes. "Thanks, Cheryl. I'll feel a whole lot better in my own things . . . and my own place, too."

She had to establish right away that she intended to get back to the Lucky Pull as soon as it was made safe and cleaned up.

"You can't possibly mean to go on living there," Aimee protested, just as she had after Beth Ann's mother's death. "Not after everything that's happened."

Beth Ann simply stared at her. *Wait for it . . .*

"I'm absolutely certain I could sell it just like that." Aimee snapped her fingers, the tips of which were painted bloody crimson. "I've got a couple of live ones—a pair of out-of-town bounce-backs with money in their pockets, and they're just itchin' to show their old cronies how they made it big in Houston."

Though fewer young people than ever were putting down roots in Eudena, a number of those who had grown up here were coming back home to retire, an influx that had boosted hopes that a nursing home or senior center might be on the horizon. The flow ensured the already overburdened hospice employees some measure of job security as well, along with workers at the town's sole funeral home. Unlike the days when life had bubbled from beneath the windblown prairie, death and dying were the only growth industries left to Hatcher County.

"I haven't decided about the house yet," Beth Ann told her, mostly to be contrary. Though she wasn't ready to set a date—or commit to any Realtor—she knew she'd feel like a ball bearing in a tin can rattling around that huge place on her own. Worse still, every room was filled to overflowing with the tastes, the voice, the memory of her larger-than-life mother.

As well as with the echoes of her dying screams.

With her eyes stinging, Beth Ann said, "I can't imagine anybody wanting it now anyway. Not with it being on the news the way it was." Or so she'd heard. She hadn't turned on a TV or read a newspaper in weeks, for fear of what she might see. Cheryl had warned her, in a halting stammer that touched Beth Ann, that without a viable suspect in the murder, reporters had chosen to focus instead on Lilly's reputation. As well as on the nature of the attack against her.

Someone, Cheryl had reluctantly admitted, had leaked the news about the breast implants a few days earlier. And the way the killer had hacked one out of . . .

While Beth Ann squeezed her eyes closed, Aimee babbled on that some buyers wouldn't at all mind the idea of the house's fame, that Beth Ann could probably get out without much of a loss. She went on to point out, quite truthfully, that she was the only full-time Realtor in the county, as well as the most competent by far. Aimee also mentioned—in a voice darkened by resentment—that if Lilly had seen fit to listen to the expert real-estate advice Aimee had offered, the place would have much better resale value. "I told her and told her she should've put the master bed and bathroom on the ground floor, and heaven only knows why she wanted to put in a heart-shaped pool. But your mama had to listen to that snooty crowd from Dallas."

"Not about the pool," Beth Ann remembered with a grimace. "That one was all Mama."

"The local talent wasn't good enough. Neither were the local workers and suppliers. Who certainly could have used the—"

"Aimee Lynn Baker Johnson Gustavsen." The way Cheryl said her younger sister's full name warned of certain violence if she didn't shut up. "Leave Beth Ann alone. Now."

Beth Ann glanced up in time to see Aimee's hand flutter to her throat and her artificially blue eyes well with an equally fake show of emotion . . . .

"I only meant to help." She sounded positively wounded. "Tell me honestly, Beth Ann. Am I upsetting you?"

"Yes." Beth Ann had long ago learned that tact was lost on Aimee. "Now, could I have a little privacy? I'd like to get dressed and get out of here."

A pout soured Aimee's pretty features. "Fine. I can take a hint."

She poked her feet back into the heels before moving toward the door. Beth Ann watched, hands folded across her chest, and waited for Aimee's self interest to kick in. *Three, two, one . . .*

On cue, Aimee turned, her smile as sheepish as it was contrived. "I do hope you'll forgive my insensitivity,

Beth Ann. I know this is a difficult time for you, and I hope that whenever you feel ready, you won't hesitate to consider an old friend—a friend who loves you dearly—as your personal Realtor."

Without waiting for an answer, she swept out of the room, leaving Beth Ann to roll her eyes and Cheryl to mumble, "I can't believe that girl is swimmin' in my gene pool."

Beth Ann laughed. "Don't worry about it, Cheryl. I don't hold her against you."

"Thank God for small mercies." Cheryl sighed. "I know she could really use a fat commission, but still—"

"Aimee and Ted are having money troubles?"

"Those shopping trips to Dallas don't come cheap, and that girl always did like her credit cards way too well. Besides, a few fat cat retirees may be scouting out the newer, nicer places, but a lot of the older homes are sitting for so long on the market that people abandon them to go off somewhere else and look for work."

Beth Ann nodded. She'd seen the profusion of FOR SALE signs tattered by the ceaseless prairie wind.

"I'll be outside the room waiting," Cheryl told her. "If you need any help, just holler."

She began opening the door, but froze as she looked through the crack.

"What?" Beth Ann asked.

Turning toward her, Cheryl mouthed two words. Though Beth Ann had never been good at reading lips, this time, she understood perfectly.

Mark Jessup.

"What's he doing—" she began until Cheryl pressed an index finger to her mouth for silence and opened the door a little wider.

Beth Ann strained her ears and made out a feminine murmur. Mark's deeper voice carried much better, echoing in the narrow hall.

"Sorry, Aimee. I've appreciated your calls and visits, but the flowers are for Beth Ann. I heard about what happened. And she's been awfully good to my dad, so I thought I'd stop by while a couple of the volunteers were at the house."

"You're here to see *Beth Ann?*" This time, Aimee's voice was clearly audible. "You're kidding. Of all the people in the world—"

"Have a good day, Aimee."

It was an unmistakable dismissal. Beth Ann smiled, imagining the look on Aimee's face. Married or not, she didn't suffer rejection lightly. And she'd especially hate it from such a mouthwatering man.

Cheryl backed away from the door just before he tapped at it. She glanced at Beth Ann and waited for her friend's nod before saying, "Come on in. I'm Cheryl Riker, from the hospice program. We've spoken on the phone."

Beth Ann's heart picked up speed as he stepped into view. Tall, lean, and clad in denim, he filled the room with his presence, squeezing the air out of her lungs. *Quit being a damned idiot,* she told herself. He was just a man, like any other—okay, a great-looking man, but still, she wasn't some besotted teenager taping celebrity photos to her bedroom wall. The fact that she was zeroing in on the tiny dimple in his left cheek, just below the scar, was evidence that the knock to the head she'd taken had rattled loose her good sense. How could she have forgotten—even for a second—that this was the same man who'd killed her friends and nearly put her in the ground, too?

He carried a spray of yellow roses, a couple of dozen long-stems that must have set him back a pretty penny. There would be talk about it, from the town florist to the nurses to the queen mother of all gossips, Aimee Gustavsen herself. Beth Ann cringed inwardly, imagining the malicious spin Aimee might put on her version of the story. *Would* put, since she'd clearly had hopes of another fling with the notorious prodigal.

Mark shook Cheryl's hand. "I want to thank you for everything that's being done on my father's behalf. And I especially wanted to thank Beth Ann here for her kindness."

He turned to look at her. "When I heard some son of a bitch had hurt you—"

"The flowers are beautiful." She did her best to disguise a sudden case of dry-mouth. "But they're really too much."

"Gorgeous," Cheryl purred as she took them. "Let me put these in some water."

"Eli said you'd like them," Mark told Beth Ann as Cheryl disappeared into the bathroom. "He's the one who picked them out."

"You tell him he has a good eye. Where is Eli?"

"I just dropped him off at Mrs. Minton's. He needs something—someplace he can learn and play and maybe even make some friends." There was a note of doubt in Mark's voice, as if he found the last possibility remote.

"Good choice—Cheryl tells me she's great," Beth Ann said. Tired of waiting for her only son to make her a grandmother, Margaret Minton had opened a home daycare a few years back. A retired teacher, she was known to have a waiting list a half mile long. Beth Ann wondered whether Mark had charmed or bought his way to the top of it. And how much other locals would resent that.

An awkward silence settled before Mark asked, "How are you holding up, Beth Ann? Really?"

She shrugged, unwilling or unable to explain how the last few weeks felt like a long slog through chest-deep water of an icy lake, how every now and then she stepped into an unseen hole that plunged her far beneath the surface. How the thought of the intruder in her dark house made her stomach lurch with the sensation of that sickening drop.

"I'm all right if I don't think about things too much," she finally told him. "Instead, I try to plan out what I'm going to do. The next step—that's all. I can't get too far ahead."

Whatever she did, she couldn't help wondering if the sheriff had been wrong about the man who'd hurt her—if she really had encountered the vicious bastard who had killed her mother instead of a garden-variety thief.

Mark nodded, his brown eyes as warm as a fireside in winter. Comprehension was written in his features, a firsthand acquaintance with the deepest grief.

"You shouldn't be here." Her words spilled out too quickly. "I appreciate the thought, but there's already so much loose talk."

"Do you care what people think?"

"Hell, yes. Unlike you, I have to live here."

"Do you?" he asked.

Cheryl came back into the room, the yellow roses arranged in a hospital water pitcher. One of the blooms, older than the others, spilled a few soft petals, which fluttered to the floor.

"My work is here," Beth Ann told him. To avoid his

gaze, she fixed hers on his reddish scar. "I'm going back to it soon."

"You take as much time as you need," said Cheryl. "Vickie's back from vacation, and we can borrow Lou Ann from the nursery for a few more weeks. It's not like there's much in the way of babies bein' born here lately."

"You could do anything." Mark looked straight at Beth Ann. "Anywhere you wanted."

He wasn't the first to point that out. How she could resettle in the mountains or the tropics—buy two or three homes if she wanted. Get fancy cars and fine clothes and travel all she liked, using her mother's fortune. She could even pursue her long-lost dream of medical school if that was what she wanted. Money was no object, and no family obligations remained to tie her down.

Choices yawned before her, a vast, unbridgeable chasm between who she'd been and who she would be, without the boundaries that had always defined her. She thought of the many ways the money had changed her mother, of old friendships shattered and new resentments kindled, of the plague of vampires intent on sucking dry her sudden wealth. For all her weaknesses, Lilly Decker had been surprisingly smart about her money, shrewd and tough and brave enough to listen to the financial pros she'd hired and to ride out the resulting storm. Though in the end, it might have killed her. Beth Ann's chest tightened, and panic pulsed in time to a swift heartbeat. It was too much, far too much to consider.

"Beth Ann?" Mark asked.

"Are you feeling all right, honey?" Cheryl sounded worried. "You want me to get the doctor?"

Beth Ann shook her head to clear it. "All I want is to get out of here. Thanks for coming by, Mark. And thanks again for the roses. They're incredible."

She struggled to make the dismissal in her voice as clear as his had been with Aimee. To pull it off, Beth Ann summoned the memory of that glimpse of his truck's headlights as they'd swung into her path.

Whether real or imagined, the image was indistinct compared to what she'd seen of Mark with his father and his child, what she'd felt unfurl inside when they had kissed.

Jess, she thought, harking back to his old nickname.

He nodded, and his eyes told her he was remembering that kiss, too. And hoping to repeat it. A thrill of awareness ignited her nerve endings. She pulled the sheet higher, to cover breasts that felt all too exposed by the thin gown.

The tilt of his smile said he knew what she was thinking, and the wicked glint in his eyes promised that the two of them weren't through. A spark had caught back in his father's kitchen. A spark that Beth Ann meant to stamp out right now, before any real harm could come of it.

But before she could say anything, he told her, "See you later, Beth Ann. Take care of yourself."

He turned and in an instant, he was gone, the door closing firmly in his wake.

Cheryl stared after him, saying only, "Wowza, Beth Ann. You? And him?"

Beth Ann frowned at her. "Don't even start with me. That kind of aggravation's the last damned thing I need."

Cheryl winked. "I don't see that, sugar. I think maybe it's what you've needed all along."

Chapter 12

As Mark made for the nearest exit, he felt the stares acutely. The tall custodial worker with the jug ears who was mopping near the entrance. The nurse who stopped mid-stride, her eyes goggling behind her glasses before slitting in a catlike glare. The blue-haired volunteer with the bad dentures who crossed her arms and scowled from behind the "Welcome" desk.

People recognized him, and they knew he had come back. The news had rolled over Hatcher County like the recent cold front. If some—Cheryl Riker and Mrs. Minton among them—seemed not to hold his past against him, most didn't bother with even the pretense of civility. Their icy regard followed him at the pharmacy and the hardware store, when he stopped to fill up his truck's gas tank.

He told himself it didn't matter, that as Beth Ann had pointed out, he would soon leave this town, this county, and this state, never to return.

So why come to the hospital with a parade float's worth of roses instead of leaving well enough alone?

As grateful as he was for Beth Ann's kindness, as physically attractive as he found her, Mark reluctantly admitted that he had come for the same reason he had heeded Aimee Gustavsen's call to him in Pittsburgh. To prove something to his hometown. To prove something to himself.

But what? Was he trying to show people he was human—or that he didn't give a damn if they thought he was a monster?

After buttoning his faded denim jacket, he made his way to the sunny lot, where he noticed a mud-caked, red tow truck backed up to an old Buick. The driver, a man whose bullish neck and shoulders threatened to split the seams of his blue coveralls, was hooking the sedan's bumper to his rig.

Mark stiffened, his body recognizing the dark stubble of the buzz cut and the huge hands an instant before his mind put a name to the wrecker operator: Gene Calvert, the former Hatcher Red Hawks quarterback.

Heart pounding, Mark gritted his teeth and—for the first time since prison—literally saw red. His hand fisted, and before he knew what he was doing, he took three long steps toward the tow truck.

He hesitated at a woman's cry behind him. "Oh, nonono. You *can't.*"

She rushed past him, despite the burden of the towheaded toddler in her arms. A sandy-colored ponytail slapped her back: straight hair in need of washing. Her sweater had once been a rich purple, but it had faded to pale lavender in spots.

"Stop. Please stop it," she begged the wrecker driver.

Calvert barely looked up. "Can't do that, Lori. Not unless you've got cash to pay me for that alternator."

She turned, offering Mark a glimpse of terrified blue eyes and round cheeks flushed with desperation. Young—no more than twenty-one or -two—with her scant share of prettiness already fading. Her child curled against her chest, his thumb stuck in his mouth and his eyes enormous in his thin face.

"But I paid. I wrote a check," she pleaded.

"You gotta have money in your account or those things bounce." Calvert's voice was anvil-flat.

The tiny boy whimpered, squirming in his mother's arms.

"It did? Oh, damn it. Jay's child support check must've been bad again, or it would've sailed right through. Come on, Mr. Calvert. I've got to have this car, or I can't work to pay you. And Jimmy here's sick. I have to pick up his prescription."

Calvert finally looked at her. Hard. "My shop's not a charity. Four hundred and the car's yours. Plus, another sixty for the tow."

Bullying bastard hadn't changed a bit. Mark eased his way closer. Calvert either didn't see him or ignored him.

"Four?" The woman rubbed the toddler's back to soothe him. She shifted his weight, revealing the bulge of another pregnancy, perhaps six months along. "But the bill was only three-fifty."

"Got a returned-check fee to deal with now. And like I said, the tow, once I'm done here. Four-sixty altogether."

"Oh, God. But I can't possibly— Could I pay you over time? I'm supposed to get a raise next month, and—"

"If you'd paid *on* time, we wouldn't have this situation." Calvert checked the connection to the bumper

117

of the Buick, then made his way to his truck's lift controls. "And don't bother offering to take it out in trade. You ain't got what it takes to tempt me."

"*What?*" She jerked back, causing the child to stiffen and cry out, wet thumb popping loose from his mouth.

"Four hundred?" Mark interrupted.

He fought back a grin as Calvert whipped around. So, the asshole hadn't seen him, after all. Good. Because it was rewarding as all hell to see the beefy face darken and the massive shoulders tense.

"Jessup," Gene said when he'd recovered. "Heard you'd come crawling back to Eudena."

"I asked you, was her bill four hundred?"

"What the hell is it to you?"

Mark reached into an inside pocket of his jacket, where he'd tucked the cash he'd picked up from the savings and loan before he'd stopped for the flowers. Four hundred was nearly all he had left, but what the hell? He could always get more, and it was more than worth the price to count out a raft of twenties and watch Calvert's face contort.

For a moment, Mark thought he wouldn't take the cash. But when one big hand shot toward him, Mark jerked the money out of reach and said, "Unhook her car first."

A muscle twitched in an overshot jaw, and a fat vein throbbed in Calvert's temple. Mark waited a full minute, half expecting the guy to stroke out on the spot. He knew Calvert wouldn't hit him. Big and tough as the bastard was, he'd never had the guts without his backups waiting.

Calvert stomped back to the Buick's bumper. "Fucking loser. Jerk-off. Hope you took it up the ass in prison."

Grinning—he couldn't hold it back now—Mark waved off Lori's thanks.

"I'll pay you back. I swear it," the young woman continued, tears gleaming in her eyes. "My name's Lori Fuller, and I'll pay you back the minute I can."

"Don't worry about it," Mark said. "I would've dropped a thousand just to see this show. We go way back, me and Gene here. Old friends, you might say."

She shushed the child, but she was smiling. "I'm not sure Mr. Calvert shares the love, but you're *my* friend as of this moment, Mr. Jessup. And I don't give a flip what anybody says about you."

"Just let's not add this story to the mix, okay?" Mark had enough ill will without people suspecting he was flashing his money around town in an attempt to buy his way into their good graces.

She shrugged. "If that's what you want. But stop by the Blue Coyote—that's where I wait tables every evening. Least I can do is treat you to a cup of coffee. We have great pie, too."

Since she had called him "Mr." Jessup, he didn't take it as a come on. "I might do that," he said as Calvert stalked back toward them.

Gene stuck his hand out flat. "Ready now, or were you just talkin'?"

Mark handed him the folded bills, which Gene made a big production of counting.

"All here," he admitted before shooting a scornful look at Lori. "Seems to me you could've bought a *quality* piece of ass with your blood money."

As he turned away, Mark snagged the collar of

Gene's coveralls. He spun around so fast, the fabric tore.

"What the—"

"You owe the young lady an apology." Mark ground out the demand through clenched teeth, but part of him was hoping Calvert would refuse. He'd love to lay the bastard out right here on the concrete. For Jordan. For himself.

Surprise flashed over Gene's expression, and his thin lips pressed together. He took a step back, followed by a deep breath. And then he did the last thing Mark would have expected.

"I'm real sorry, Lori. My mama raised me better than to take out my attitude toward a worthless piece of shit on a woman. What I said—I didn't mean it. I hope you'll forgive me." He cleared his throat against encroaching hoarseness. "And I hope you'll come back to Red Hawk Body and Motor soon."

"Not likely," she muttered.

"For a ten percent—make that *fifteen* percent discount on any labor." He shot her a repentant look that didn't fool Mark for a minute. "I'd like the chance to show you—"

"I'll think about it." Her voice radiated a chill far deeper than the crisp, fall morning.

Mark could almost smell the man's humiliation as Calvert climbed back into the muddy tow truck and rolled out of the lot. It was a deeply satisfying moment, one that stayed with Mark through his last few errands.

And ended abruptly outside Barty's One-Stop, as he pushed his loaded shopping cart back toward his pickup.

At least Mark *thought* it was his pickup. Tough to say, with a gallon of fresh bloodred paint dripping off the hood and windshield, and the shape of a huge footprint denting the driver's side door.

An old man sidled up to stare. After hawking up a wad of phlegm and spitting on the asphalt, he said, "Might want to have it towed to Red Hawk's. Calvert's a good man for paint and body work."

"Yeah." Mark couldn't tear his gaze from the destruction. "Sure as hell looks like that to me."

Chapter 13

Nine days later . . .

Above the gold-green sprawl of the autumnal prairie, a layer of featureless, gray clouds bore down, so low that only the support of the pump jacks and church steeples prevented it from smothering the whole of Hatcher County. In contrast to the night Beth Ann had been assaulted, no wind stirred the grasses. No rain soaked the thirsty soil.

Instead, an early-morning silence hovered in the fog bank, waiting with its breath held.

Feeling no less anxious, Beth Ann pulled into the Jessup driveway. For the past few days, she'd been driving a new blue hybrid SUV, which she'd bought after donating the repaired War Wagon to the food bank and trading Lilly's Mercedes in Wichita Falls. While she was in that city, she'd also visited a kennel to check out the fangs on a guard dog for sale by a trainer her co-worker Emmaline Stutz had recommended.

The thought prompted Beth Ann to glance back at the golden form behind her new vehicle's gate divider.

"Hey there, Maia baby." She spoke to the oversized Lab mainly to ease her own misgivings about confronting Mark Jessup with her questions. But partly because, despite the trainer's warning not to "ruin" the dog by making a pet of her, Beth Ann thought it would be best to get the hundred-pound beast on her side so the animal would eat an attacker and not her.

Behind the bars, the yellow Lab beat an otter-thick tail against the SUV's side window hard enough to make Beth Ann wonder if the warranty would cover wag-related cracks. Still, she found herself smiling and hurrying to the back to collect her new companion. Lilly had always claimed to be allergic, so Beth Ann had never owned a pet before.

"Not a pet, a *guard* dog," Beth Ann told herself as she grasped the lead and ran an admiring hand over the broad yellow-and-gold head.

Eye to eye with her new owner, Maia licked the side of Beth Ann's face.

"Maia, no," Beth Ann corrected, as she had been instructed. But inside, she felt a warm glow at the show of affection—assuming the Lab wasn't simply tasting to size her up for a meal.

The dog jumped down and heeled politely as Beth Ann approached the Jessups' back door. Maia was patient as her mistress negotiated the steps, and the Lab sat on command before Beth Ann raised her fist to knock—

She hesitated, the dog-induced calm running out of her like ice water through a colander.

After shifting her cane, Beth Ann pulled a white

business-size envelope from her purse and glanced once more at the hand-printed address. It had been mailed to Mrs. Lilly Decker. The return label had Mark Jessup's name and address, and the postmark, dated September fifteenth, said Pittsburgh as well.

The man who'd installed the new security system had found the envelope on the living room floor, behind her mother's secretary desk, but no matter how much Beth Ann searched, she couldn't locate the letter that had come inside it—or any other evidence that Mark Jessup and her mother had had contact. For the past two days, she'd tried to tell herself there had to be some simple reason Mark would have written her mother nearly a month before he'd reappeared in Hatcher County. Some innocent reason, she prayed.

But two restless nights later, she still had not come up with any explanation. This morning, she had finally decided to take the envelope to Sheriff Morrell. She had nearly reached his office—where she suspected she'd be patronized within an inch of her life—when Beth Ann found herself turning toward Lost Buffalo Road instead. She told herself that Morrell couldn't— or *wouldn't*—give her answers, but Mark surely could.

It had seemed a good idea at the moment, with the memory of his kindness and the kiss they'd shared to prompt her. But as she stood beneath the breathless clouds, Beth Ann wondered if she'd made a terrible mistake. Was going to Mark instead of the authorities a betrayal of her mother? Or was it flat-out dangerous?

"Oh, get a grip," she told herself as she knocked firmly. He was hardly going to morph into a crazed killer with his father and little Eli present.

It took at least a minute for Mark to make it to the door. Though it was only a little after eight, his wired intensity made her suspect that he'd been up for hours—or possibly all night.

"That was quick. Your office said it would be at least an hour before someone could come out, but thank God you're here." He stepped back to let her into the laundry room, his gaze flicking to Maia, then dismissing the dog in an instant. "You have to do something."

"What's wrong?" she asked. "I'm actually not here on hospice business."

She planned to start back to work tomorrow, but her job status didn't stop her from following him toward the living room.

"It's his breathing," Mark said. "It sounds like marbles rattling in his chest. And he feels so damned cold, no matter how many blankets I put on him. Besides, he can't keep still, even though he stopped responding to me last night."

Beth Ann shoved the envelope back inside her handbag. Her questions could wait, at least until she got Mark calmed down.

As they passed into the living room, Hiram's limbs writhed as restlessly as snakes beneath the blankets. Even without a stethoscope, Beth Ann could hear the congestion in his lungs. She called his name, but his deeply shadowed eyes remained closed, his twitching face as pale as skim milk.

After dropping her purse beside the coffee table, she told the Lab to sit and stay.

"I'm here, Mr. Jessup—Beth Ann Decker." She touched Hiram's forehead lightly, smoothed its furrows with the pad of her thumb. "I'll be giving you something to make you more comfortable. Your son's here with me."

She glanced at Mark. "Is Eli here, too?"

"He's in his room, dressing. One of the moms from Mrs. Minton's daycare is picking him up to take him there in about five minutes. Or should I—should I keep him home today?" Mark grimaced as he looked down at his father.

"Let me check your father's medication log and see what we have here that can help him." She canted her head toward the kitchen, a signal for Mark to follow.

He took the hint, trailing her into the other room, where she glanced over the log and then took the comfort pack from the refrigerator.

"You should call the office back. Tell them I'm here, and they won't need to send another nurse. I've got my kit and most of my supplies outside." She was grateful she'd packed the items she'd removed from the old Subaru in anticipation of tomorrow.

"I will, but first I need to know," he said as she took out a bottle containing sublingual drops along with a transdermal patch. "Is this it? And should I keep Eli home? You have to tell me, Beth Ann. You have to help me stop this."

She turned and looked at him. "It's all part of the natural process. You know that."

"I had it in my mind my dad would make it to Thanksgiving. That's just another week, right? A week and a few days?"

"People do that—they set mental deadlines. A birthday or a holiday, a child's graduation. You can't bargain with this thing, Mark. Your father's in the final stages. But this part could take hours, even days. That's a long time for a little boy to wait."

Mark nodded, then sucked in a deep breath, and the red line of his scar stood out against his pallor. He was a grown man, yes, but at the moment he looked so vulnerable, with his rumpled hair and shining brown eyes, that Beth Ann ached to pull him into her arms to offer comfort.

The impulse startled her. She dealt with so much death, guided so many grieving family members through the process. What was it about Mark Jessup that blurred the line between professional concern and all-too-personal compassion?

"I'll—ah—I'll go and make sure Eli's teeth are brushed," he told her. "He likes it there at Mrs. Minton's. I think he even has a girlfriend. He's been drawing pictures for her every evening."

Mark's attempt to smile fell short, but even so, Beth Ann had to steel her heart against it. When her suspicions about the envelope failed to shore up her defenses, she found herself dredging up old memories of her rehabilitation: the years of painful work to recover from her injuries.

The sound of laughter echoed through her consciousness. Boisterous and feminine, the laughter of her dead friends and of her unbroken self.

By the time the memory faded, Mark was using the kitchen phone to call the office. Her equilibrium regained, Beth Ann got her bag from her SUV before returning to check his father's vitals and administer the medications to ease both his breathing and what those in her field referred to as "terminal restlessness." She removed most of the blankets, too, for despite the coolness of Hiram's extremities, his core temperature was high.

As his limbs grew still, she monitored his pulse and listened to his respiration stop and start up several times. Still, awareness prickled behind her neck as Mark passed from the kitchen to the hallway where the bedrooms were located. She tuned out the creak of a door opening and the low murmur of his voice as he spoke to Eli.

"It's all right, Mr. Jessup," she told Hiram quietly. "Your wife's there waiting. And Jordan, too. They'll be so glad to see you."

As his father's breathing evened out, Mark came in, holding Eli by the hand. Neatly dressed and groomed, the boy smiled when he saw her. "Hi, Miz Beth Ann. You got any more of those good cookies? *Hey.*"

His voice rose on the last word and, after freeing himself from Mark, he made a beeline straight for Maia.

"Wait," Beth Ann warned him. "She's a trained guard dog."

Maia jumped up, prancing with excitement. Her thick tail fanned the air, and Beth Ann could swear she smiled. Eli buried his hands in the fur of her neck, and before anyone could stop him, gave the dog a hug.

When Maia lapped at the side of his head, he giggled.

"She's as nice as Beau," the boy declared as he pulled away and wiped a sleeve against his ear. He wore a silver badge printed with the words JUNIOR DEPUTY pinned to his red-checked shirt.

"Beau's our dog," Mark explained. "He's a Lab, too, a big chocolate-colored lug. We have him staying with a friend while we're away. And whoever told you a Labrador retriever would make a decent guard dog must've seen you coming. Or your money, more than likely."

Beth Ann frowned. "But he swore to me . . ."

She let it drop, thinking that the dog guy *had* seemed a little dicey—and he'd had the Stutz cleft in his chin, too. If she did a little digging, she'd probably find out he was one of those down-at-the-heels relatives Emmaline was always going on about before staff meetings.

As Mark rubbed Maia's ears, a little of the tension in his shoulders eased. "That's all right. They're good for lots of other things."

"Can I see Stormy before it's time to go?" Eli asked his father. "I think she might let me pet her this morning."

"I'm not sure that cat's ever going to let you touch her," Mark said.

Before Eli could argue, a car's horn honked outside. He started toward the door, but Mark called after him, "Hold on a second, champ. You should say goodbye to Grandpa."

Something in his father's tone made Eli turn, his little body stiffening.

"It's all right, Eli. See, he's quiet now," Mark said. "But he can hear you, I think."

Eli edged forward, still looking uncertain. "Bye-bye, Hiram. I hope you feel better when I come home. Then we can watch your favorite TV show—even the shopping channel if you want to. And I'll draw you another picture."

His gaze rose to take in Mark and Beth Ann. "See you, Dad. Bye, Miz Beth Ann."

Mark followed him outside. Beth Ann looked after them, the realization dawning that Mark had asked Eli to say goodbye to *Grandpa,* but the child still called the old man Hiram. She felt one corner of her mouth tic downward.

So much unfinished business, father to son, grandfather to grandchild. It bore down on this house as oppressively as the gray mist on the prairie, as the grief that veiled her heart.

Sometimes, God used the natural world to do His sacred bidding. With this morning's clouds, for example, He had dimmed His realm, a miracle that allowed the One Appointed to follow Beth Ann Decker across the flat expanse without attracting notice.

After the failure nine days earlier, it had been tempting to try again to break into the mansion—to make one more attempt to find the letter sent to Lilly Decker, the one she claimed to have kept for sixteen years. But the sheriff's department was closely watching the Lucky Pull, and in spite of inside knowledge, there had been no way to tell who might show up to do a walkthrough at any given moment. And then the security had been upgraded, leaving little option except to watch Beth Ann whenever possible for any sign that she had found that which must be destroyed.

It had been a challenge, monitoring her movements. Difficult to slip away, time and again, without raising suspicions. And seemingly pointless, judging from her activities during these past few days.

Perhaps the whore mother had been bluffing, only taunting as Lilly liked to do so often. And so fatally, that last time. The One Appointed felt the splash of blood, warm and bright and wet against the skin. Felt the first stirring of eagerness to be done with this misfortune, to eliminate the risk once and for all.

To feel God's blessing in the wake of carnage.

This morning, there had been yet another warning—marrow-freezing horror when Beth Ann's new SUV backed from her driveway and headed straight toward Main and Travis. Not thirty yards short of the combined fire and sheriff's department building, she'd made an abrupt turn before leading her pursuer out onto the prairie.

Straight to the Jessup house.

Was she returning to work, despite the fortune she'd inherited? Talk was, she planned to do so, though a fair number of people, unable to imagine staying on a job for any reason except money, said they would believe it when they saw it.

Yet it was the other gossip that sprang to mind this morning, talk of the expensive yellow roses Mark Jessup had brought to the hospital when she'd been injured. Word was that despite the deadly outcome of their senior-year crash, Jessup—of all people—was pursuing her. Was he after a chunk of Lilly's millions, or did he truly see past Beth Ann's limp and cane? Either way, the One Appointed worried that she had decided to trust Jessup with a discovery instead of going to the sheriff. Possible, since Lilly's letter might well alert her as to Morrell's conflict of interest in the matter.

The view from a pair of high-powered binoculars seemed to bear out the suspicion. In the poor light, it had been difficult to see details, but the white rectangle Beth Ann pulled from her purse was the correct size for an envelope. Or a folded letter.

Surely, I was meant to see it. Why else obscure the morning sun to let me follow? Why else guide my hand to focus the binoculars mere seconds before she stepped inside the house?

I understand you, Father. And I know that I have been appointed to end not one more life, but two.

Chapter 14

"Do you think he might wake up again?" Mark asked. Panic needled at his stomach. There was so damned much left unsaid.

Beth Ann lowered herself onto the opposite end of the sofa from the spot where he sat hunched, his elbows resting on his knees and his hands pressed together.

"It *could* happen."

Her tone made him think of other far-fetched possibilities: finding a diamond in the hayloft or stepping out the front door and being struck by lightning. What would a few minutes of his father's consciousness matter anyway? They'd had days and weeks to talk things through, sixteen years, to be truthful—and both of them had blown it.

"There wasn't enough time." He lifted his coffee from the lamp table and sipped, though it had grown cold. Up since three A.M., he was in dire need of caffeine. Turning his head, he said, "God, Dad, I'm so sorry. About everything."

"There's never enough time," Beth Ann said. "It's one of the lessons of this work."

"You tried to warn me earlier. You told me, but I couldn't—I couldn't talk to him about Jordan. About my mother, either, or the years he and I missed in each other's lives."

"I'm sorry."

The simple statement had him wondering how often she told other patients' loved ones the same thing. She'd gotten good at it, at least. She looked at him directly and didn't stammer around the discomfort of his trouble, as so many people would have.

"Do you—do you have to go soon? I—I know you'll have other patients." Over the telephone, Cheryl Riker had carefully explained the heavy workload of the hospice nurses to him. At the same time, he'd been given the numbers of the program chaplain, the same Pastor Timmons from the church his family had once attended, and the tireless volunteers. A home health-care aide came several days a week, too, to help with bathing, changing bedclothes, and a host of other essential tasks. But as kind as all of them had been, he still thought of them as strangers. He didn't want their company. He only wanted Beth Ann.

"I don't have anyone until tomorrow," Beth Ann told him. "And I'd stay a while anyway to make sure he's really settled."

He could almost hear her thinking: *Until* you're *really settled.* Gratitude washed over him, humbling him as nothing had since he'd been led away in handcuffs.

"Why did you come anyway?" he asked her. "You said it wasn't hospice business."

Her lips pursed; then her eyes softened.

"Not now," she said, her quiet voice at odds with the shift in her expression. "We'll talk about it later."

"What?" he pressed.

"I—uh—I heard somebody messed up your truck. Is everything all right there?"

He doubted that was why she'd come, but he was too distracted to push any harder. "I can handle it," he told her.

"You don't want to talk about that right now, do you?"

He shook his head, grateful that she was so perceptive.

"You really should have been a doctor." Patients would line up for one who listened the way she did. "I know it's what you wanted. Everybody figured you were a shoo-in for a scholarship. Before." *Before my pickup smashed through your dad's car.*

Beth Ann shrugged. "I was mad about missing out on med school for a long while. Still am, from time to time. Mad as all hell."

"I'd understand if you hated me. Anybody'd understand it."

"I did hate you. My friends were dead, and I spent years in physical therapy. For a lot of years, it was tough to get around."

"Do you still hurt?"

She shook her head. "I'm not looking for anybody's pity. I deal with what I have. I graduated top of my class at Midwestern—and I graduated from a wheelchair to a walker in those four years, too."

"You're a brave woman."

She rolled her eyes. "Oh, please. No more than I'm some kind of angel. I cried a lot of tears and cussed a lot of blue streaks. Wasted way too much time being pissed that I'd *only* gone to school in Wichita Falls instead of Austin and I'd *only* managed to get my RN and not an MD because of money. Then I was resentful because the only job opening I could find that would hire someone with my physical limitations was home-care hospice—and I sure as hell didn't want to hang around the dead and dying all the rest of my life. I found out fast, not all of them are old. And some have suffered so long . . . It was pretty tough."

"I'm always hearing about nursing shortages, in all the major cities. Why didn't you try somewhere else—"

"And it wasn't like I was going to escape by getting married, either," she went on, as if she hadn't heard him. "Men around here see me and think tragedy, not dating. And rumor has it I'm too busted up inside to give anybody kids."

He wondered if it was true, but Mark couldn't bring himself to ask her. He wasn't sure he could face knowing he had taken that possibility from her as well.

To his surprise, she smiled. "Maybe that's why I've had it up to here with all that 'Poor Beth Ann' bull. Because I damn near drowned in my self-pity."

It was impossible not to smile back at her. He'd never met any woman who looked at herself so honestly. Or any man, for that matter. "I know a thing or two about that."

Her head cocked as she looked at him, and a shiny red wave fell loose from her hair clip. He had to stop himself from reaching up to tuck it behind her ear.

Finally, she nodded. "I hadn't thought about it, but I guess I can see that."

Her gaze flicked to his father, and Mark imagined she was thinking of how the old man had turned his back on his surviving child. At the time, Beth Ann had been in Dallas, in intensive care, but he imagined she'd heard every detail in the intervening years.

"So what turned things around for you?" he asked. "How did you get past the anger and self-pity? Because you're here with me now, and at least so far, you haven't clawed my eyes out."

She smiled again, but it was fleeting. "Believe it or not, it was the work. At first, I thought I'd stick it out for a year or two to get experience. Then I'd find another job or maybe move somewhere else. Physically, I was getting stronger all the time. But when you work with dying people, when you face mortality head on, you start to see things other people miss."

"Like what?" It was taking everything he had to watch his father die, even though the two of them had been estranged for years. He couldn't imagine going through the process again and again with different people. Somebody's spouse, another person's mother—grief after grief in a never-ending cycle.

"You're going to think it's stupid." She spoke over the rim of the mug he'd brought out to the coffee table for her.

"No, I won't," he promised.

She sipped the brew and made a face. "This is pretty strong stuff."

"Sorry—I needed a good jolt to my system. There's milk and sugar in the kitchen."

She shook her head and set down the mug.

"I used to just about gag," she said, "when I heard people—mostly at the church—talk about having a calling to do something. But after I took this job and spent a few months working, I understood the concept. Easing people's passage, helping their families come to grips with the next stage of their own lives—the work felt important to me. Worthy."

"I can't argue with you there." It was the same feeling that had prompted him to take his product to the market in spite of all the roadblocks he'd faced along the way.

"But it wasn't only about giving—though that was satisfying. I found myself understanding how fundamentally unfair death is, how being good or young or loved doesn't make you exempt. And I found myself thinking more and more that facing our limits is the only way to fully appreciate what we have in the moment. Too many people shy away from that knowledge—like some of the professionally bored kids who went through college with me."

Mark laughed. "Yeah. I had this one roommate who always dressed in black and practiced looking listless in the mirror. I went to college a few years later than my peers, too. Makes it a little tough to fit in, doesn't it?"

"Yes, but what about you?" Beth Ann asked, interrupting his train of thought. "What was it that got you to stop feeling mad at the world?"

He hesitated before telling her. "A lot of things. Starting with a couple named Bill and Carol Graff. When I was paroled, I was twenty-one with nothing but a GED between myself and living on the street. But I was still as crazy about cars as ever, and Bill decided to take a chance and hire me to work in his auto shop outside of Dallas. He and Carol had a couple of sons of their own who'd been in trouble in their younger years, so they had a soft spot for guys like me. They'd half pushed, half bullied their boys into college and stability, and for some reason I'll never understand, they saw fit to do the same with me."

"They must have seen potential. About time someone noticed it."

Mark shrugged, struggling to suppress a smile. "Bill thought I had a gift for mechanical design. And one of his and Carol's sons is dyslexic, too, like I am."

It wasn't an admission he'd made to many people. But unlike most, Beth Ann had never treated him as if he were stupid.

She nodded. "So, you reverse letters when you try to read? Or do they look scrambled?"

"A little of both, but I've found ways to compensate. Carol showed me. She helped me fill out applications, too, and find scholarships through different programs. She and Bill gave me a fresh start."

"They sound like amazing people."

"They are." Mark still called them often, sent gifts on holidays, and visited with Eli several times a year. And for their parts, Bill and Carol had been proud as hell when his company went public and investors fell all over themselves to get onboard with his project.

The rattling in Hiram's chest grew louder. Mark sprang to his feet and in three steps was at his father's side. He searched the pale features for signs of distress and took the cool hand in his own. The fingernails looked blue.

"He's suffocating, isn't he?" In desperation, he looked back at Beth Ann, who was rising from the sofa. "Can't you do something? Isn't there some kind of suction thing to help him?"

She approached and took a cloth from the attached bedside table, then gently turned his father's head to one side. "I've already put a patch behind his ear to help dry up the secretions, and this may help a little, too. But the suction would be . . . uncomfortable— and mostly for your benefit, not his. In spite of the way it sounds, this congestion isn't bringing any more pain."

"I just—I need to do something."

"Then tell your father that you love him. Give him your blessing to move on."

"But I don't want him to—"

"Is this the life you'd want for him? Is it what he'd choose for himself?"

Mark turned away and started pacing. He hated the panic that sliced through him, the sense of helplessness. He wanted to rip down the curtains, to put his foot through the TV screen. He wanted to turn back the clock's hands or, better yet, the pages of the feed store calendar out in the kitchen.

When he turned, he saw that Beth Ann had stepped out of the room to give him privacy. So Mark went back to his father and leaned over to kiss him on the temple, a kiss the man would never have allowed if he weren't helpless.

"It's okay, Dad," Mark said, tears welling in his eyes. "You can—you can go on now, to whatever's next. I love you enough to want it for you, too."

He meant to say more, meant to offer his father his forgiveness, but the words lodged hard and thorny in his throat. Mark wanted to let go of his anger, wanted to shed its weight for his own sake as much as Hiram's, but did that mean forgetting the metallic click of handcuffs, the clang of the cell door, the sickening memory of being stranded in the alien world of prison, a place so terrifying and so hopeless that he had prayed each night for death?

Turning away once more, he saw the yellow Lab's solemn eyes following his movement.

"This is Maia," Beth Ann said from the kitchen doorway. "It's a Swedish name, the trainer told me."

Mark sank down beside the animal and ran both hands through her thick fur. As his own Beau would, the Lab looked at him as if she understood what he felt.

"Some killer guard dog," Beth Ann mumbled as her purse began to ring.

"Sorry," she said quickly before moving to the sofa, where she'd left the bag, and pulling out a cell phone. After a quick glance at the screen, she silenced it.

"You could've taken it," Mark told her.

She shrugged before going back to recheck his father's vitals. "It's just my mother's attorney. Probably some estate thing. I'll get back to him later."

"So," she added once she'd finished recording Hiram's temperature and respirations, "what else was it that changed you? Before you told me about Bill and Carol, you said it was a lot of things."

Mark understood she was only trying to distract him, but talking was a hell of a lot easier than waiting for his tension to burst through the fragile shell of his skin.

"I fell in love," he said.

"With—was it Rachel?"

He was surprised she'd recalled the name of Eli's mother. Mark nodded, though the memory of the affair was bittersweet. "She was brilliant, sexy—with the greatest sense of humor. And I couldn't believe she found me interesting."

"You were happy?"

"God, yes. Happier than I'd been since—well, since a long time before the accident. For one thing, dating

Rachel meant I wasn't—that I wasn't the man I had to be in prison."

Beth Ann shook her head, releasing another lock of her red hair. "I don't get what you mean."

"To be eighteen in an adult facility. To be a lily-white kid from a decent family in a little town where not much happened—"

"You had to get tough? Is that what you mean?"

"Tough isn't enough, Beth Ann. You had to get *connected* real quick. And the way it mostly shakes down in state prison is by race."

He saw comprehension dawn in her eyes as she looked his way.

"You mean, like one of those gangs? With the tattoos and—"

"It cost me a fortune to get rid of them. But being with Rachel—her dad's an African-American veteran who met her Vietnamese mother overseas—*loving* Rachel burned away the marks beneath the skin."

"So what happened?" Beth Ann sleeked back the fallen strands and adjusted her hair clip to hold them. "Obviously, you two aren't still together."

"Turned out that I was her rebellion, her way of acting out against her father's expectations. It wasn't about the color of my skin but my prison background and the fact that I was older. By the time we both figured out we'd each been trying to prove something, she was pregnant. I wanted to get married. I asked and asked, but she wouldn't go for it. And her dad was really pissed. He all but forced her to go for an abortion."

At Beth Ann's shocked look—the "A" word wasn't often mentioned in this zip code—Mark shook his head. "She refused, thank God. If she had—well, I can't imagine my life without Eli. He's the other thing, the real kicker, that's helped me learn to live with my past. With all the lives I've wrecked."

"Eli is darling—a real sweetheart," Beth Ann said. "Did your father ever come around with him?"

"No." The admission came out harsh. "I couldn't bring myself to talk to him about the crash or Jordan or what happened after, but I damned well tried as best I could to help him get to know his grandson. That stubborn old man refused to listen—refused to acknowledge my son or even call him by his name. He tolerated Eli, but no more than that."

Mark noticed his father's breathing had grown quieter.

After Beth Ann finished wiping Hiram's mouth, she looked back Mark's way. "The same way he's tolerated having you here."

"Right. Because he wasn't strong enough to kick our asses out," Mark managed. "And I wasn't going anywhere."

"So your business—it allows you to travel for long periods? But I guess that's how things work, when you're the president of your own company."

The curiosity in her voice was edged with disapproval.

"I never set about to make a lot of money on it, Beth Ann. When I started tinkering with my device, I was just thinking how emerging technology could be adapted. Harnessed to save lives by checking the behavior of young drivers."

"It's call EZ-Driver, right? I read some stuff about it on the Internet." As she moved back to the sofa, her frown told him she wasn't a fan of his idea. "The way I understand it, your unit's mostly used by fleet directors—companies employing drivers—to keep track of their speed, acceleration, and braking. They use the GPS to spy on and fire employees who stop home to take a pee or make a quick side trip for cigarettes."

Mark grimaced and shook his head. "I know some critics think it's Big Brother in action, but I swear to you, that's not what we're about. Yes, the EZ-Driver can be set to report on vehicles that stray from a preset route or range, but the device gives two audible warnings first. Our real aim is to teach young or irresponsible drivers to self-correct dangerous behavior so they *won't* have to be managed—or policed. The trouble is, we haven't yet been able to get the cost down low enough to get it into the hands of the families who need it most. So yes, we've marketed to corporations and municipalities."

"Making a fortune in the process."

"Making competitive salaries for the company's employees," he admitted, "and funding a foundation to give units free of charge to the families of at-risk young drivers."

"Really?"

Maia rolled over and pawed at him until he rubbed her chest.

"So far, we've donated five thousand units in the Northeast. I'm hoping to expand and double that number by the end of next year and take the program nationwide," he said. "Guess that information hasn't hit the Hatcher County grapevine."

Beth Ann smiled. "Maybe I'll see that it does. All I'd have to do is mention it to your friend Aimee."

"I'm not sure she's in the mood to give me any good press right this minute."

Emotion flickered in Beth Ann's eyes. "She's a married woman."

Was that jealousy he'd spotted or merely disapproval? "I know that. And I had to be a little more direct than I'd have liked to let her know I'm not interested in taking her on a trip down Memory Lane. I sure as hell don't want to remember anything from those days."

The ticking of the wall clock sounded loud in the long pause.

"I do," Beth Ann said at last.

"You do what?"

"Want to remember. That last night, anyway."

"God, Beth Ann. Why would you?" He shuddered, though the house was overly warm, for Hiram's comfort. If he could erase a single memory from his lifetime, it would be that evening.

After giving the dog a last pat, he rose and paced again to stretch his legs.

"I can remember stopping by your house to pick up Jordan, and then *nothing* about anything that happened for months afterward," Beth Ann said. "I've been told that's not unusual in cases of head trauma."

"How about we change the subject?"

"All these years, it's been a blank spot. Except, since you've been back, I've . . . seen things. Headlights in the darkness. Bodies tossed out on the—"

"Beth Ann."

"I'm sorry, Mark," she said, ignoring his protest as words rushed out in a torrent. "I know it's probably hard for you to talk about it. Just the way it's hard for Sheriff Morrell to talk about *you* for some reason."

"Please just shut up and *listen* to me." He shook with the adrenaline ripping through him. "It's my *father*. He's not breathing."

Chapter 15

When he finally made it home after his graveyard shift, Damon Stillwater found his father at the back door. Damon froze at the sight of him, shocked to find the man at home instead of at his store. He was dressed for work as usual, in the blue polyester slacks and short-sleeved, button-down shirt, and loafers he considered his business uniform, but Damon could never remember him being home at this hour.

Panic jolted through him. "What's wrong? Is it Mama? Has she had a bad spell?"

His mother's lupus had been a factor in their lives for so long, Damon didn't generally pay it much heed. But in the back of his mind, he knew—they all knew—that it might someday take a fatal turn.

His father's shook his head. "Your mother's a little achy today, but she'll be fine. She's over at Barty's picking up a few things."

"Then what's wrong? Why are you home? Are you sick or something?" This last question was a true stab in the dark, for Damon's father didn't believe in allowing anything to distract him from the sacred work of keeping Hatcher County in plywood, paint, and hinges.

"It's you, son. I'm damned worried about your job. You should have come straight home this morning. Didn't Sheriff Morrell tell you to stop bothering people about Lilly Decker? Let bygones be bygones and allow the real professionals to do their work."

"But I haven't—"

"Don't lie to me, Earl Damon."

When his father used his first name like that, Damon knew he was in deep shit. He might have been named for the old man, but he'd been called Damon since he was in diapers.

"Why don't you just tell me what you've heard down at the store?" Better that than confess to something that had not yet reached his father's ears.

"Your mother came in earlier, all upset. Agnes Miller called her. Fit to be tied that you would question her mister about some supposed relationship with that Decker woman."

Hell . . . If she'd complained to his mother, Agnes Miller might call Sheriff Morrell, too. Then he'd be lucky to get off with a suspension.

"Look, Dad," he said carefully. "It's just common sense to check out anybody who might have had a reason to hurt the victim. And that includes anyone who might have been involved with her."

His father's round face grew florid. "*What* did your employer tell you? Have you no notion of the meaning of the term 'chain of command'? And do you have any idea how hard it will be to find another job around here if you lose this one?"

Damon pressed his lips together, in part to keep

from saying something he'd regret. Though he knew
very well it might mean the end of his dreams for a big-
time career in law enforcement, he had firm ideas
about the way the Decker investigation ought to be
run. Ideas that bore little resemblance to the half-assed
"look-see" the case was being given by those assigned
to it in his department. But it was useless to try to explain such things to his father, who insisted on treating
him as if he were twelve.

"Your mother has been friends with Agnes since the
fourth grade," Earl Stillwater said, "and we've both
known Douglas Miller even longer. The man's a rock. A
steady provider for his family. A Christian man who's
never been known to raise a hand in anger—"

"I realize you and Mama like to think that everyone
we know in Eudena's perfect." All the churchgoing
white folks, anyway. "But it's not so."

"Christians aren't perfect," Earl Stillwater quoted Pastor Timmons, "just forgiven."

"Maybe up in heaven," Damon told him. "But down
here in Texas, they've still got to go before a jury for the
crime of murder."

His father gave a sigh of complete exasperation.
"Stop being so damned pompous. Everyone in this
family is sick of listening to you go on like you're
Hatcher County's last hope of justice. Doug Miller's not
a murderer. He's just a man, with a man's weaknesses,
upon occasion—the same as your father."

Damon stared, heart pounding. Was his father saying what he thought? *His* father? Earl Stillwater? No—it
was impossible.

"It happened years ago." His father's gaze slid down
to the door trim, which he'd repeatedly hinted could
stand painting. For a hardware man who often doled

out advice on such things, he piled the household fix-its on his son whenever possible. "You and your sister were still in grade school, and I was—your mother and I were having . . . a few problems."

"Before anybody understood about her lupus." Damon remembered periods of his childhood when his mama did little more than stare vacantly for hours. She'd complained of feeling achy and exhausted, but the doctors in Eudena—and increasingly, her husband—told her the whole thing was in her mind.

His father ignored the reference to the illness Ginny and her Fort Worth specialist had learned to manage over the years with medication. "It had been a long time for us, ah, with your mother feeling so bad. A long time for a man to go without—"

Earl's color deepened, which was not surprising, given that he had never even spoken to his son about the facts of life. Instead, his mother had placed an "Abstinence for Young Believers" pamphlet on Damon's dresser on his thirteenth birthday. Defeated by the cryptic language, Damon had gotten his friends to more or less fill in the details—with varying degrees of accuracy.

"Lilly seemed to notice I was feeling down," Earl said, "and I have to tell you, it was awful flattering having such a pretty woman make a big deal over a fellow like me. Stopping by the store in her short skirts and those low-cut blouses. Making little private jokes with me, and touching—"

"Jesus, Dad, please stop."

His father looked up sharply, but before he could reprimand his son for taking the Lord's name in vain, he seemed to think better of it. Nodding in acknowledgment, he said, "I'm ashamed of what I did, son. I've talked it out with Pastor Timmons, and made my peace with the Lord a lot of years back. But I'm afraid it would kill your mama if she found out. Maybe literally."

Damon exhaled. "So she doesn't know."

His father's head shook, the movement stiff, as if his neck were tight with tension. "And she won't ever have to—or your sister, either—if you'll quit meddling in affairs that aren't any of your business."

Damon winced at his word choice. Affairs, indeed. That cheating dog . . . And yet, tears gleamed in his dad's eyes, the first his son had ever seen there. It must have nearly killed the man to admit his failing, and worse yet, to take his son into his confidence.

But according to the strands of gossip Damon had teased from both the willing and the judgmental, Lilly Decker had done far worse to many families, enticing husbands even while her own was bedridden with a bad heart. The way she'd seen it, *she* wasn't the one dying, so why *shouldn't* she go out and have a little fun?

Damon was abruptly furious with the dead woman, who was blamed for at least two divorces, along with several separations. He felt sick to his stomach, and for the moment he truly longed for the hiss of tater tots sizzling in his basket as he manned the DQ's deep fryer.

"I'm sorry, son," his father said—another first, in Damon's memory. "Sorry for disappointing you and sorry to set such a poor example."

Earl Stillwater stuck out a thick hand and waited, pleading with his eyes for Damon to take it.

Damon hesitated for several moments before pushing past his father's right and giving him the kind of bear hug the two hadn't shared in years.

Three days later . . .

Beth Ann rarely attended patients' funerals. To do her job effectively, she had to maintain some distance. Besides, if she set the precedent, she'd be expected to attend services on a far-too-frequent basis.

But as she walked her new dog on the circular path around Mill Pond, which she was trying to get in the habit of doing every morning, Beth Ann decided to make an exception to attend this afternoon's services for Hiram Jessup. Or rather, for his son, who was now left so alone—with no friends here as far as she knew. And anyway, what real choice did she have? She wasn't about to demand answers regarding the envelope until Mark's father was decently buried, so she had to keep open the lines of communication. Or so she told herself.

But in spite of the nagging questions about Mark's contact with her mother, Beth Ann's mind kept circling back to the fine man a lost teenager had grown into . . . and to what she had reluctantly self-diagnosed as an old-fashioned case of lust.

Still exhausted from a night of tossing and turning, Beth Ann turned her face to the breeze and attempted to inhale the faint warmth of the sunshine.

She wasn't the only one out early this morning. Her next-door neighbors' teenaged sons were tossing back and forth a football on the grassy slope close to the water.

Too close, for a bad throw by the younger of the pair sent their ball sailing out and then splashing into the greenish water.

"Maia, no," Beth Ann shrieked as the big Lab jerked her off balance on the dew-slick grass. The leash was torn from her hand, and Beth Ann went down hard, her bad knee twisting painfully beneath her.

The Winfield boys came running to help as Maia blithely leapt into the pond and paddled toward the floating ball, her splash sending a trio of white ducks flapping with quacks of protest to the far shore.

"We're really sorry, Miz Beth Ann. We swear we didn't mean it," said the older of the brothers, a starting running back for the Red Hawks. The reluctant topic of his father, Dr. Winfield's, endless boasting, the senior was also the target of considerable speculation among Eudena residents. Fast and nimble, though not particularly big, the kid was supposedly attracting interest from college recruiters eager to offer him a full-ride scholarship.

But Beth Ann wouldn't know about his talent first-hand. Though she'd loved the game when she was cheering, she couldn't even watch football on TV since that long-ago homecoming, and she steered well clear of the Friday night lights that would draw most of the town's residents to the high school stadium this evening.

"I'm sure it was an accident," she said. She could never keep the boys' names straight—their parents had inexplicably called the two Matthew and Matthias—but Beth Ann accepted the big, calloused hand that Big Matt offered and stood. When she put weight on her left leg, she winced at its tightness—as well as the smell of duck that she imagined clung to her clothes.

"You're hurt, aren't you?" asked the younger brother, a shorter, broader version of his sibling. Built like a small tank and wearing a Cowboys T-shirt, Little Matt was clearly into football, too, like nearly every able-bodied boy in town. Turning toward his brother, he said, "We can make a chair out of our arms and team-carry her to her house."

At the thought of their linked hands under her butt with all the neighbors peering out their windows, Beth Ann shook her head and tried to pretend she wasn't leaning so heavily on her cane.

"I'll be fine," she insisted, "if you could just catch the dog for me. I have to get cleaned up."

Not only did she have a funeral to attend this afternoon, but she needed to check on several patients and squeeze in a quick visit to Stan Lipscomb's office, a chore she'd put off for days, to go over some of her mother's final bills.

Maia emerged, shaking off the water. The shower of droplets sparkled in the morning sunlight. She trotted toward them, her jaws clamped around the football and her thick tail wagging joyfully. Kibble-for-Brains looked so damned pleased with herself, Beth Ann had to smile, until the dank odor of pond water caught her nose.

"We'll do you one better," the older boy offered. "Since my *brother's* famous passing got her filthy, we'll give her a bath."

"That would be fantastic," Beth Ann said, "but don't the two of you have school?"

"Not today," crowed the younger of the brothers. "We're off for teacher training—"

"At least 'til practice and the game. Maybe you'd like to come tonight? We could get you tickets."

"No. I can't, but I'll be rooting for you—and I'd love to take you up on bathing Maia. Thanks so much."

She'd have to tell their parents that the Matts were really good kids, the kind of teenagers who defied the stereotypes the media preferred to broadcast. "Your mama will skin you both alive if you take her inside

your house, so why don't you clean her up in my backyard? There's a washtub and some old towels in the
shed, and you'll see where the hose is."

She gave the pair the entry code to her backyard
gate, and after limping back home, she brought the
boys her back door key and left off the alarm so they
could put the dog inside when they were finished. After thanking both of them, she went inside for a quick
cleanup and a change of clothes, then headed off to
see her patients.

An hour later, as she was leaving the home of her
first patient, her cell phone vibrated in her pocket. She
fished out the phone, her stomach tightening. What if it
was Mark, calling to tell her that he and Eli were already on their way to Pittsburgh?

But the caller ID said *A.J. Winfield*—the father of
Matthew and Matthias. Assuming it was one of the
boys, she hit a button and asked, "Is everything all right
with Maia?"

"Well, sort of," one of the Matts answered. The older
one, she thought. "We gave her a bath and toweled her
off okay, but she got a little excited. When we let her in
the house, she went barreling through the living room
and knocked over that big floor globe. We're so sorry,
Miz Beth Ann, but one of the wooden stand legs
snapped near the top when it fell."

Beth Ann winced, not because she was especially attached to the stuffy-looking globe, but because she remembered Lilly's delight when it had been delivered.
"Look at that," she had exclaimed. *"It's just like some-
thin' one of them handsome English lords would have in
his library."* Beth Ann would swear the woman had fon-
dled the thing while reading her historical romances.

Something clicked in her subconscious, sending

cold chills rippling through her. But try as she might, she couldn't bring it to the forefront, so she let it be for the moment.

"We carried it over to our garage to try to fix it." Matthew or Matthias's voice cracked, and the poor kid sounded close to tears. "But then our dad said we'd better call you. He said to tell you we'll be glad to pay for it or—"

"It's all right, Matt." She figured that was a safe thing to call him, whichever one it was. "I'm not mad. You were trying to do me a favor, that's all. It's not your fault Maia's being so ornery this morning—and that globe stand was already knocked over once. I'll bet the thing was cracked then and I didn't notice."

She heard his exhalation, a puff of pure relief.

"Thanks, Miz Beth Ann. So, do you want us to try some wood glue on it?"

"Don't bother with it," she said. "I have a friend whose husband lives to work on stuff like that. I'm afraid his feelings will be hurt if I don't ask him."

Beth Ann didn't give a flip about hurting Pete Riker's feelings, but it was kinder to say that than admit she feared the teenaged boys might botch the repair job.

"Should we carry it back to your place?"

"You don't have to do that. If it'll be okay there for the next few hours, I'll ask Deputy Riker to stop by and pick it up as soon as he can."

After ending the conversation, she made a quick call to the Rikers' place, where she caught Pete at home. Afterward, the incident was pushed out of Beth Ann's consciousness by worries about Mark and the pain in her left knee. The one thing that never crossed her mind, however, was the gaping hole she had left that morning in the Lucky Pull's security.

* * *

Arriving late to the service, she nodded at Pete, who was standing in uniform in the back doorway of the funeral home chapel. His and Cheryl's bickering might be annoying, but she had to admit, he was always more than willing to lend a hand where it was needed.

"Thanks again for offering to take care of that globe stand," she whispered as she attempted to slip past on her way inside. But Pete caught her arm, then inclined his head to indicate she should follow him outside. Curious, she moved back out into the sunshine.

"I'm surprised to see you here." Disapproval edged his voice.

"I could say the same," she said. "I had no idea you were friendly with the Jessups."

"Oh, I wouldn't go so far as to call it *friendly*." His frown implied the opposite. "You ought to be careful about heading down that road yourself."

"Why's that, Pete?" Beth Ann asked. In all the years she'd known him, he'd always been quick to give advice on cars or lend a hand with a repair. Still, Beth Ann remained wary of asking him too often, since he seemed to feel that sharing his manly expertise gave him license to tell her how she ought to think or vote. Now, apparently, he thought he was entitled to pick her friends as well. What a Neanderthal.

"You don't want to get mixed up with some ex-con who'll be leaving town before you know it. Any day now, I'd imagine, since his daddy's gone."

"Who says I'm mixed up with Mark?" Beth Ann kept her voice low, but it came out sharp nonetheless.

"My wife, for one."

Beth Ann made a mental note to take her friend to task about the pillow talk. But since Cheryl blabbed to her about the problems Pete—who was ten years his wife's senior—had been having lately in the bedroom, Beth Ann should have realized that her private business would be shared with him as well.

"Well, your *wife* is wrong," Beth Ann said. "Hiram Jessup was a special patient, that's all. That's the only reason I'm here."

He gave her one of those condescending looks she hated, so she turned around and walked back inside Hill Funeral Home without waiting for his reply.

Standing behind the largely empty rows, she spotted Mark and Eli, each dressed in a sport jacket and sitting in the front row. Though Hiram had supposedly been mad enough at God to forbid a regular church service, a handful of Fundamental News regulars had driven out, including the familiar gray and white heads present at all the congregation funerals. Big Jim Morrell was in attendance, wearing an ill-fitting gray suit instead of the more familiar brown and tan of his official getup. She spotted a few local business owners as well: Bart and Kay Lynn Shepherd, of Barty's One-Stop fame; Earl Stillwater from the hardware store, with Ginny, who looked well today; and the widowed Ty Quitman, who ran the county livestock auction. That was about it, though. Never very social, Hiram had become nearly a hermit since first his daughter's and then his wife's deaths.

Losing his land to her mother's lawsuit probably hadn't helped. Beth Ann felt bad about it, but she understood her mother had done what needed doing— even if most people tended to lump Lilly's every action under the headings of trashy or grasping.

Beth Ann took a seat in the chapel's rear pew. Though the funeral director, Arlen Hill, spoke—in mostly generic terms—of Hiram, her mind was full of the mother whose services she'd attended nearly a month ago, a funeral packed with both curiosity-seekers and her friends—but very few of Lilly's.

People around Eudena were certain they'd known Lilly Doyle Decker. A flashy-looking party girl from the wrong end of town, she'd caught the eye of Beth Ann's dad, Bobby, a wildcatter with a reputation of his own—for kicking ass and taking names. But while parent-hood, a failing heart, and business setbacks had seasoned and matured her father, they'd only made Lilly hungrier for what she felt she'd been missing.

Beth Ann had spent a good portion of her teen years cringing over her mother's reputation—and fending off boys who assumed she had been cut of the same cloth. Still, she had moved home after college, convinced it was her duty to curtail the downward spiral of behavior that took place during the years she'd been away. But as exasperating as Lilly could be, Beth Ann missed the mother who'd been thrilled over her early accomplishments, who'd later pushed her to get out of the wheelchair, who'd grabbed life by the horns and shaken loose all the sweetness she could get.

And who had left behind the riddle of her violent death.

"Did you ever know your mother to make use of First Global Savings Bank in Fort Worth?" Stan Lipscomb had asked when she had stopped by his office the day before.

Beth Ann said she didn't. Other than a modest account she kept at the Eudena Savings and Loan, her finances were handled by a major firm in Dallas. But her mother's attorney had passed Beth Ann an annual renewal statement for a safe deposit box at First Global in Fort Worth.

"What would Mama be keeping there?" she'd asked Lipscomb.

"I thought perhaps you'd know . . . or she might have left a key."

"A key," Beth Ann had echoed, thinking of the one returned to her at the dealership when she'd traded in her mother's car. Since it had hung from the Mercedes fob, she'd mistakenly thought it unlocked the glove box, or maybe the locking console compartment presumably meant to keep valet parking attendants from the driver's stash of Rolexes and diamond pinky rings. "I think I might have it."

Lipscomb had offered to drive to Fort Worth to collect the box's contents, and Beth Ann had considered it. But then it occurred to her that heaven only knew what Mama had squirreled away, out of sight of both her daughter and her attorney. It could be anything from old love letters to nude photos of herself—hopefully alone—from years past. Beth Ann shuddered at the thought of Lipscomb viewing her mother's secrets.

"I'll take care of it," she had told him, though she dreaded the six-hour round trip.

As she sat now in the chapel of Hill's Funeral Home, the name *First Global* threaded through her memory, along with a line from the strange message her mother had thought important enough to make Lipscomb swear on the Bible to deliver. *In truth, the world is yours, should you be bright and bold enough to claim it.*

The world . . . as in First Global's logo, which had been printed on the statement. And what about those other words: "in truth"?

At the sound of whispers, Beth Ann looked up, startled at the realization that Hiram Jessup's service had ended while she'd been lost in thought. As the first few attendees filed past on their way to the door, they eyed her intently. More than likely, they were thinking she had fallen into a pit of despair over memories of her mother's funeral.

Hell's bells. She'd be on everybody's prayer list before day's end.

But for once, she spotted more than pity in their gazes. Perhaps her presence here, combined with Mark bringing her the yellow roses, would breathe new life into the rumor that the two of them were dating.

So let 'em chew it over 'til they choke.

A smile plucked at one corner of Beth Ann's mouth. Maybe she *had* inherited more from Lilly than the wild-woman red hair, after all. Ignoring the furtive stares in her direction, she moved off to the chapel's side and pretended to study a small cluster of floral arrangements.

She waited, watching from the corner of her eye as several of the attendees spoke with Mark and Eli. Big Jim Morrell shook both of their hands, and she heard the rumble of his bass voice as he asked the boy how his favorite junior deputy was doing. Beth Ann recognized Margaret Minton's sausage-plump form and her unmistakable gray curls, too. Among the last to leave, she took Eli with her by the hand, probably back to her home daycare. Mark must have decided to spare the little boy the graveside service and let him spend some time with his new friends instead.

With the other attendees gone, Mark walked to his father's casket. It had been left closed, covered with a huge spray of white flowers, but Mark laid a hand along the exposed mahogany side. He stood perfectly still, except for the bowing of his head and the heaving of his shoulders with a single sigh.

Oh, Jess. Beth Ann wanted to take him in her arms and hold him, but instead, she walked up behind him. As she waited for Mark to notice her presence, she looked at a montage of photos hung on a large easel. All of them predated the crash that had shattered the Jessup family. Beth Ann had to look away from the handsome couple, smiling with their daughter and their son.

"Might as well have buried both my mom and dad with Jordan," Mark said. "There wasn't one picture taken afterward, one major purchase made or trip taken—"

She started toward him. "Mark, you can't—"

"He barely left the damned house. Wouldn't talk to me, accept my letters, or even listen when I contacted his attorney and offered to pay back the money he'd lost in the settlement."

"You didn't mean to hurt your family. You didn't hurt anyone on purpose, Mark. As hard as this is, you're going to have to let the pain go."

"I thought I'd done a decent job of it. But coming back here, seeing the way he was—I didn't just hurt my family, Beth Ann. I killed them, every one."

She took his hand in hers and looked him in the eyes. Those gorgeous chocolate eyes that had rekindled a fire in her she'd imagined had been snuffed out years before.

"You have a son who needs you, Mark. And from everything I've seen, you're a wonderful dad. One of the most caring men I've ever known." She cut herself short, alarmed at the emotion in her words. During her college years, she'd dated—even had a brief affair with one of the grad students. But she had never, even for a moment, felt the way she did now for this man.

Guilt kicked in as she recalled the presence of the envelope inside her handbag. *Don't let this go one inch further. Not until you get the answers you need.*

One hand tightened on her cane, while the other fingered her black skirt.

Yet the gratitude in his eyes short-circuited her caution. "Thanks, Beth Ann. I didn't realize how much I needed to hear that."

"So is everyone heading over to the graveside service?"

Mark shook his head. "I'll go with my father to the cemetery and see this thing through. But he didn't want a big production, so this was really it."

She hesitated before saying, "You look like you could use some company. How about it?"

He made brief eye contact with the dark-suited funeral director, who had entered the room discreetly and stood waiting for a signal.

"Okay, Mr. Hill. I'll be ready in about ten minutes," Mark said before he turned and shook his head at Beth Ann. "Thanks anyway, but you don't have to do that. I'd just as soon go by myself."

She smiled. "Don't be a martyr, Tough Guy. I'll meet you over there."

Half an hour later, she stood in the chill sunshine, along with a cemetery worker, two men from the mortuary—including Mr. Hill—and Hiram Jessup's casket.

But Mark Jessup didn't show up, even after a long wait.

Chapter 16

Mark had meant to go straight to the cemetery, as he'd told Beth Ann, but on the way back to his vehicle he encountered an old "friend."

Or three of them, to be precise. Their two vehicles, the still-muddy tow truck and a newer Accord, had been parked sideways across the front and rear bumper of the sedan Mark had rented while his truck was in for repairs. Otherwise, the funeral home's visitor parking lot lay as empty as the pastureland beyond it and the pale blue sky above.

Mark glanced at the road in time to see the hearse containing his father's casket disappearing in the distance, followed by Beth Ann's new SUV. Mark was anxious to put the photo display back in the car, then follow and conclude the burial. Afterwards, he planned to pick up Eli on his way back to the house.

The last thing he was in the mood for was a confrontation. Yet Gene Calvert leaned against his tow truck's door, his foot resting on the rental's front bumper and his hand clutching a big, steel spanner wrench. Like an echo from a nightmare, two of his old friends flanked his side.

Two of the same small group that had played court to the king of football all through high school, the same group Mark had run into that fatal homecoming night, just after the Red Hawks snapped their losing streak.

Judging from his blue coveralls, Donny Ray Saunders, one of the team's offensive tackles, had gotten so good at following his quarterback's orders, he'd made it official with a job at Calvert's shop. Never the best looking of the Saunders boys, Donny Ray now had the red nose and bloated face of a heavy drinker to go with his coarse features and acne scars. Still in his early thirties, he could pass for a hard fifty.

He took a swig from a longneck, leaned back against the truck, and then, as ever, waited to see which way the wind was blowing.

The third member of the group, Ex—short for Xavier—Walling stood beside and slightly apart from the other two. He looked distinctly out of place with his neat, short haircut, creased charcoal slacks, button-down shirt, and a subdued tie. Always the brightest of the group, he looked as though he'd gone into banking or insurance if his clothes were any indication. Behind his wire-rimmed glasses, his hazel eyes appeared worried.

As well he should be, if he was still running with this crowd.

"Am I interrupting a reunion?" Mark asked as he clicked the remote to open the Ford's door locks and turn off the alarm.

Calvert spit to one side, narrowly missing Donny Ray, who didn't flinch. Judging from the smell of him, the beer in his hand was not his first.

"One of them deputies came out to see me this week," Gene said. "Told me you had some trouble with your pickup."

Donny Ray slid his boss a less-than-subtle smirk and chuckled, then tossed his empty back over the truck's hood. The bottle made a popping sound as it shattered on the pavement.

"That's right," Mark told him as he opened the car's rear door and slid the display board with the photos inside. After closing the door again, he added, "Sorry I couldn't give your shop my business, but I had it towed to Wichita Falls. Oh, wait. You probably know that, since I sent you the bill. You come to pay up, or you want to wait 'til all of the repairs are finished?"

Calvert shifted the spanner wrench in his hand. "Damn shame no witnesses came forward. I guess that anybody coulda done it. God knows, enough people hate you."

Mark glanced down at the dumb-ass's work boots, which were speckled with paint the same shade as the red splashed on his hood and windshield. Deputy Riker had left out that detail when he'd reported back that there was nothing they could do about the vandalism. Then he'd shrugged and added that Mark couldn't have expected a warm welcome in this county.

"I'd debate this with you more, Gene," Mark said, "but I've got to get over to the cemetery."

Ex cleared his throat and said, "I'm real sorry to hear about your dad, Jess." The nickname was a reminder they'd been friends once, before he'd joined the football team and succumbed to the pressure to take sides with Calvert and the others who'd tormented Mark for years.

Mark looked him in the eyes, where he saw the man's reluctance. There was fear, too, white-faced terror. Had Calvert threatened him to get him out here? Or was it the fear that a long-buried secret could come roaring back into his life?

"Now he's finally dead," Calvert went on, "there's nothing holding you here."

This asshole was right, not Lilly Decker when she'd written him. This town deserved its slow death. Teeming with judgmental gossips and hamstrung by a police department that turned a blind eye to thugs like Calvert, Eudena wasn't worth saving.

Except that Beth Ann lives here. Beth Ann and so many others who had inexplicably treated him with kindness.

"I've still got business to attend here," Mark said. "My dad's estate, for one thing."

Calvert scoffed. "*Estate?* That's what you call it? Looks like nothin' but a patch of Jessup trash to me. And you've always been the trashiest—a damned useless piece of shit. Every one of those dead girls was worth ten of you. Especially your sister."

At the mention of Jordan, Mark felt an eerie calm drop over him, a deadly focus he hadn't felt since prison. Without conscious thought, he took one step forward, daring the bastard to say another word about his family.

Calvert slapped the spanner wrench against an open palm as he sneered. "Damn fine piece of ass she was. But I imagine—being a Jessup—that you'd know that."

Ex stepped away from the truck and shook his head. "There's no need to start that kind of bullshit," he told Calvert, even as Mark closed in on the former quarterback.

Calvert's back bumped against the truck's door. Near his left eye, a tic hinted that he knew he'd pushed too far and wished he hadn't, in spite of his greater bulk and the length of steel in his hand. Were they alone, Mark was almost sure Gene would have backed down. But now, with his friends watching, anything could happen. Anything at all.

Common sense threaded its way through the red haze of Mark's fury. *This is idiotic.* He wasn't some punk kid with no responsibilities, and even if he were, this piece of shit wasn't worth bruising his knuckles over.

"If you really want to talk about what's past," Mark told him, "you're gonna have to do it with my lawyers. Is that what you want, Gene? Or how 'bout you, Xavier? You up for the kind of trouble I can afford to dish out?"

"Your blood money doesn't scare me. Neither do your lawyers," Calvert said. But worry flashed over his expression, and his big shoulders tensed.

"You just want to be quick about moving on, Jessup, that's all," he continued. As he stepped away, he gave Mark a half-hearted push in a face-saving attempt to convince his friends he wasn't turning pussy.

It should have stopped right there. And it probably would have, had Donny Ray been smart enough to re-alize everyone was about to get out, male ego intact and disaster averted. But Donny, who'd had one beer too many, blurted, "Just don't forget, when you leave Eudena, be sure'n take your little monkey with you."

Shoving Calvert out of his way, Mark sent a hard left into Donny Ray's midsection. As the mechanic folded at the waist, his head snapped back with the force of Mark's right fist catching his cheekbone. Donny Ray hadn't hit the ground before Calvert jumped in, the steel tool banging down over and over against Mark's back and shoulder. Spinning around, Mark grabbed for Calvert's right arm and at the same time drove a knee hard against his attacker's thigh bone. Unable to catch the larger man's wrist, Mark aimed a blow at Calvert's nose, which shifted with a crunch and spouted blood. Calvert bellowed as Mark raised his fist to strike again, but Xavier grabbed him by the shoulder and pulled him back.

"Stop, man. No more fighting," Ex shouted. "We'll all end up in jail if y'all don't cut it out."

Mark hesitated at the concern in his former friend's voice. But Calvert seized on the diversion, catching the side of Mark's skull with such force that he didn't even feel it when his body hit the ground.

Chapter 17

Beth Ann laid her foot on the accelerator in the hope of shaving minutes from the drive between the cemetery and Hill's Funeral Home. Something had to be wrong. Something terrible.

Her mind spun through possibilities. The dangerous intersection of Travis and Third Avenue, which had so often sparked petitions for the town's first traffic light. Or what if something had happened to Eli, and Mark had been called to meet Mrs. Minton at the hospital? Apprehension squeezed her stomach, and she prayed aloud that the situation was something more innocuous. Maybe a broken fan belt on the car he'd rented or a flat tire or a bad battery.

Panic sparked deep in her stomach as she thought of the vandalism that had forced him to rent a vehicle. Though Mark hadn't mentioned the incident, one of the waitresses from the Blue Coyote Diner was telling anyone who'd listen about Mark Jessup "rescuing" her from a repo and exactly how mad Gene Calvert had been about the way Mark showed him up. Most of the Stillwater Hardware Store crowd—Beth Ann had stopped in to pick up a pair of huge dog bowls for Maia—favored "Mean Gene" as the person who had redecorated Mark's pickup to get even. A few, though, had their money on Larinda Hyatt's father, Billy, who supposedly had been spewing enough threats since Mark's return to Eudena to put the man's position as county tax assessor in jeopardy. If either one—if *any-one*—wanted to find Mark, all he would have to do was show up at the funeral home and wait. Located at the end of a lane on the western edge of town, the place was deserted except during visitations. There would be no witnesses to anything that might take place.

Urged by intuition, Beth Ann pushed the SUV even harder, so that the tires squealed as she turned left onto the lane. With no other vehicles in sight and only a straight stretch ahead, she floored the accelerator and gasped with relief when she spotted the gold Taurus Mark had rented.

"Thank God, thank God," she whispered, assuring herself the problem had only been mechanical and not the crisis her imagination had invented.

Her relief lasted long enough for her to slow down and then turn in to the otherwise empty parking lot. It shattered when she saw the bloodstained heap of man curled beside the Taurus's front tire.

With a cry catching in her throat, she jammed on her brakes and grabbed her cell phone before leaping out. Cane forgotten, she hurtled around the SUV's hood to stare at the form that was inexplicably dressed in Mark's slacks and sport jacket, though the clothing was now torn and filthy.

It *couldn't* be him. It just couldn't—not with that

dark hair so matted and that huge lump rising near his temple. Not, especially, with all that blood staining his face.

Memory transported her to Jackrabbit General's ER, that terrible night when Deputy Stillwater had found her on her mother's bedroom floor. She'd looked the same way, or that was what people had told her. The memory of her pain eclipsed the sunshine, and Beth Ann's weak leg gave out.

The impact of her hands and knees on concrete brought her back to her senses, enough for her to use her undamaged phone to call for help.

"I need an ambulance." She scarcely recognized her thin and shaky voice. "Hill's Funeral Home, at the end of Mockingbird Lane. Better send a deputy, too. Make it fast, Dorothy. Looks like a bad head wound."

After breaking the connection, Beth Ann crawled the last two feet and checked the victim's vitals.

His pulse was fast, his breathing shallow, but it was his moan that got to Beth Ann and blurred her eyes with moisture.

"Damn it, Beth Ann, get your act together," she said. But a tear trickled down her face before dripping onto his cheek.

The brown eyes cracked open, and Mark—she'd moved past knee-jerk denial—looked up and murmured her name weakly.

She swallowed back more tears. It was time to be a nurse, not a frightened woman.

"So you recognize me." She tried for a smile to reassure him. "That's a real good sign, Jess. Help'll be here any minute. Do you know what day it is?"

"Dad's funeral." He pushed against her hands as he struggled to sit up. "I have to go and—ahhh."

The pain must have caught up to him, for Mark sank back down groaning. "Guess today's the day—I find out Calvert's wrench can—can rearrange my schedule."

"He hit you with a *wrench?* That jackass. Once we have you squared away, I'll talk to Sheriff Morrell, see what he can do about that."

"Don't," Mark told her.

"Why on earth not? He could've killed you. And if he's locked up for assault, it's not like he can hurt you again—"

"It's not that. It's—hell, I threw the first punch. Busted his nose and laid out Donny Ray, too."

She winced. "That must've been some fight. Why would you want to get into it with—"

"What about my dad?" The anguish in Mark's voice was palpable. "I'm late—I have to be there for him."

"Your dad's all settled. Don't you worry. I said a real nice prayer as he was buried. Just before I broke about a dozen traffic laws on my way back here."

"What time—how late is it? I promised I'd pick up Eli in a little—"

"Calm down," Beth Ann said. "An ambulance is coming. I'll call Mrs. Minton and let her know you'll be delayed."

He tried to shake his head and pulled a face. "I can't leave Eli. And I don't need an ambulance. I'll be—"

His eyelids closed and his hand clutched the back of his neck. "I think I'm gonna be sick. Everything's—spinning."

"Remember what I told you—no more being a martyr. You've got a heck of a knot on your head, you're bleeding, and you're darned well going to the hospital, even if I have to give you another beating to get you there. Don't think I won't use my cane if I have to."

One eyelid lifted, and he said, "My son's wrong about you. He thinks you're a nice lady."

"I use my cookies and my so-called guard dog to fool kids."

Pain distorted Mark's smile, as did the smear of blood beneath his scar. But Beth Ann was glad to see him at least trying.

"Thanks for coming back to find me. And for . . ."

"Hold that thought, Mark." Beth Ann looked up at the sound of an engine and shortly after, the clunk of a vehicle's door closing. Strangely enough, the noise hadn't come from the road or parking lot, but from the unmown field just behind them. Could it be the landowner, coming to survey it or refill the deer feeder she'd spotted earlier among the swaying golden grasses? With no one else in sight, she stood up and peered over the hood of her SUV, parked parallel to the Taurus.

At the same instant, her vehicle's side window exploded, and a loud crack reached her ear. She blinked, too stupefied for comprehension—only to be knocked off her feet by a blow behind her knees.

She landed hard on Mark's back, then tumbled off and banged her elbow on the asphalt. "What—why?"

She couldn't begin to fathom the reason he had knocked her over.

"Stay down between the cars." He might be injured, but the authority in his voice brooked no argument. Still, his hand grasped her wrist, as if for insurance.

She didn't argue, for she had worked out the connection between the shattering window glass and the bang that she had heard. Someone had shot this way—someone in the field.

"You idiot, you could've *killed* me," she shouted,

rage exploding past her caution. "Gene Calvert, you better get on out of here. Sheriff Morrell's on the way."

"God, Beth Ann, will you be *quiet?*" Mark sounded mad as hell. After a pause, he added, "Are you sure it was Gene? Did you see him?"

She shook her head. "No, but who else? Donny Ray would never have the guts to—"

Another shot cut her off, and small clots of black asphalt exploded not ten feet to their left. Was the shooter moving around in an attempt to hit them?

"We need to crawl inside your car, Mark. Can you make it? We've got to get out of here before he finds a spot where he can shoot us.

"Come on," she urged when he did not move. "We have to hurry."

But his encircling fingers were already slipping loose from her arm as he slumped again, eyes closing.

"Mark?" she asked and shook his shoulder. "Mark, please."

No response—not even a groan, though his breathing was steady and she found a strong pulse. She prayed he had only passed out as a fleeting response to pain—that he wasn't bleeding inside his brain from the earlier blow to his head. If it was that, she'd never wake him, and there was no way she could lift him into the relative safety of the car.

She jumped at a third report—one that brought with it the sensation that she was falling, terror toppling her body down a bottomless black shaft. She hadn't heard this bullet strike, but some sixth sense told her their attacker was moving, still struggling to refine his aim.

Blinking back tears, she bit her lip for focus, then pulled herself to a sitting position and opened the Taurus's passenger door.

"Come on, Mark, you've got to climb in," she begged, to no avail. He wasn't going to wake up, and she couldn't stand to leave him.

An idea sprang to mind, one that had her screaming, "You killed him, you bastard. You son of a bitch—you shot Mark Jessup dead."

Chapter 18

Beth Ann stopped yelling at the sound of a siren drawing near. From the field, a vehicle's door slammed shut, and she heard the harsh rev of an engine.

He's leaving, thank the Lord. Whether her ploy had worked or the shooter simply wanted to escape the authorities didn't matter, as long as they were safe and Mark, who remained unconscious, could get the help he needed.

Still shaking hard, she used the open car door to hoist herself to her feet. By the time she'd managed it, it was too late to see who'd fired at them. The field lay empty and unchanged, save for a track of flattened grasses where a car might have been driven. Or a Red Hawk tow truck, for that matter.

As the county ambulance pulled into the parking lot, Beth Ann waved it over near her SUV and Mark's car. The driver, a tough-looking woman in her mid-thirties, and a gawky, red-haired young man jumped out. Beth Ann told them about the shooting, then filled them in on her impression of Mark's injuries, with occasional interruptions as she glanced around to make certain their attacker wasn't coming back.

Since the county's ambulance attendants had only minimal medical training, she ended up leading the pair through Mark's assessment and helped them ready him for transport.

"I'll meet you over at the General," Beth Ann said, referring to the hospital. Mark's condition could be more thoroughly examined there, and arrangements would be made to move him if he needed surgery.

Not brain surgery, she prayed, so frightened she could barely function. And so distracted, she hadn't heard the sheriff pull up or noticed him until he stood, now back in uniform, at her elbow.

"I understand you called this in." His face was sober as the ambulance doors were closed. "I'll need to talk to you—"

"Where have you been? Your damned nephew tried to kill us," she blurted, too upset to hold back. "Mark Jessup told me Gene Calvert beat him with a wrench. I guess there was some kind of fight, but Mark would never—"

Morrell shook his head. "That Gene always was a hothead. But Jessup's had his moments, too."

"In this decade? Because you and I both know Mark Jessup's come a long way from his Hell on Wheels days. Can you honestly say Gene's changed?" Beth Ann remembered how the football coach had repeatedly benched Calvert for fighting—and how she'd seen his name in the tiny Crime Blotter section of the local weekly last spring—something about a violent altercation with his common-law wife.

Morrell looked hard at her. Beneath the brushy, salt-

and-pepper flattop, his forehead creased, and a frown dragged down the corners of his mouth.

But Beth Ann couldn't care less if he was aggravated by her challenge. As the ambulance pulled into the lane, she kept stealing glances at it, as if its progress might offer her some clue on Mark's condition.

"We cut off his shirt for the assessment." Her voice vibrated with emotion. "Mark has contusions all over his arms and back—Calvert had to've hit him from behind."

Leaning heavily on her cane, which had been retrieved by the young ambulance attendant, Beth Ann closed her eyes against the images of those livid purple knots. And that one near his temple—even the memory of it made her dizzy.

"Maybe you'd better sit down," Morrell said.

"I need to get to the hospital." She started toward her SUV.

"Now hold on just a second, Beth Ann— What the devil happened to your window?"

"That's what I was trying to tell you. Gene came back with a gun."

"Gene did this?" Morrell's brows shot skyward.

"Well, I didn't exactly see him, but who else would it have been? Right after I drove back from the cemetery and found Mark, I heard an engine back in the field there." She pointed out the direction. "I stood up, thinking I could flag down help, and someone shot my SUV—blew that window right out."

"But you didn't *see* this person? Or what about a vehicle?"

She shook her head. "Mark managed to knock me off my feet so I wouldn't get hit by another shot. It was a good thing, too, 'cause there were two more. But I'm *sure* it was Calvert because when I thought to yell at him that he'd killed Mark, he took off pretty fast."

Morrell shrugged. "Anybody might've done that, even if it was just some hunter making a bad shot or some kids messin' with a BB gun."

She stared at him. "You have to be joking, Sheriff. Do you honestly expect anyone to believe this is some kind of an accident with Mark beaten unconscious? Look, I know Gene's your sister's boy, but you can't possibly think you're gonna sweep this under the rug."

Morrell raised his palms in mock surrender. "I know he looks good for it, and I promise you, I'm gonna have a come-to-Jesus meetin' with him and more'n likely throw his ass in jail. But I have to consider all the possibilities here—and especially an unwitnessed shooting. Including the chance the shooter wasn't after Jessup."

"What? But who would—"

"Way I remember it, somebody came close to cracking your skull not two weeks ago. And *you* were the one who popped into view right before the shooting started."

The hearse pulled into the lot, but instead of parking in the covered area on the building's opposite side, the driver stopped and Arlen Hill climbed out of the passenger seat.

"Is there a problem, Sheriff?" the prematurely gray Hill asked. Tall and gaunt as the town undertaker should be, he looked pallid in the late afternoon sunlight.

Jim Morrell nodded. "Mark Jessup's had some trouble. I'll be in to talk to you in a few minutes."

A tic worked Hill's mouth at the dismissal, a rare slip

of his normally impeccable demeanor. But he climbed back into the hearse and had the driver move it to its customary spot.

Beth Ann barely registered the interruption. "Nobody wants to kill *me*. Whoever broke into the Lucky Pull was looking for my mother's money, that's all. Isn't that what you said, that it was probably about that crazy rumor?"

His jowls quivered as his head shook, but his stern look was firm enough. "No, ma'am. I said that was one theory. There *are* others. Including the possibility that you might've been the target."

"But that makes absolutely no sense. Why would anyone—"

"There's a reason the Good Lord put that bit about not coveting in the Commandments. Envy can do ugly things to people. And right now, you're the richest woman in this county. As your mama was before you."

At the thought, Beth Ann tasted bile. She must have looked bad, too, for Morrell insisted on taking her inside the funeral home, where she could sit down.

"Arlen won't mind," he said as he put a big hand on her elbow to support her. "Gives him a perfect chance to eavesdrop and find out what's going on."

Beth Ann made a disgusted sound, exasperated by this town's endless appetite for gossip. Though she had to admit that, were she in Arlen's big black shoes, she would have been at least as curious.

Once she and the sheriff were inside the chapel, Beth Ann averted her gaze from the row of flowers. She didn't want to think about Hiram's lonesome burial—or the photos of his shattered family.

At Morrell's prompting, she gave him a complete account of the way she had found Mark. Since she had already spilled the beans about Gene Calvert, she went ahead and mentioned that Donny Ray had been there, too. She hoped Mark would forgive her for blabbing when he had asked her not to—and that Morrell could be trusted to do what was right.

"Two against one—I see." Morrell looked disgusted. "That's the way it's always had to be for Gene. I never could understand what Scotty saw in that boy."

Beth Ann remembered that back when they'd been dating, Morrell's son—now a state senator as predicted—had hung around with his cousin in high school, but all the football jocks had been tight. Thinking of Donny Ray, who still worked with Calvert, she realized how enduring many of those bonds were.

Had she been wrong in thinking that Jim Morrell, a former football star in a town with an almost maniacal devotion to its team, would not only ignore blood ties, but put justice above the brotherhood of the gridiron? She thought about the way the man had stacked his own department with former football jocks. Aside from Pete, she couldn't think of one who hadn't played ball for the Red Hawks.

"Mark's condition might be serious, even critical. And both of us could've been killed by that shooting." She took the sheriff's arm and beseeched him with her eyes, a shameless play of the protector-of-helpless-women trump card dealt at birth to every rural Texas female. On account of her mama's unsolved murder and her official Tragic Figure status, she probably had an extra two or three at her disposal. "Please, Sheriff, do the right thing by us—and for that little boy of Mark's, too—the one who's probably wearing your Junior Deputy badge right now."

Morrell's face flushed. "By God, Beth Ann, you've got more of Lilly in you than anybody would've reckoned."

Unwilling to push her luck, she fought a smile, though the comparison took some of the edge off her worry.

"Of *course*, I'll take care of this the way I oughta," Morrell grumbled. "And you're testing my goodwill, insinuating that I might do any different. I'll be calling in all my boys on this. I'll have 'em looking for shell casings, taking photos of the crime scene, and interviewing Jessup when he's able. And I can tell you, I'm gonna personally have a heart-to-heart with Eugene P. Calvert, even if I have to hear about it from my sister. But before I do that, how 'bout I run you over to the hospital so you can check in on your new boyfriend?"

"Boyfriend?" she asked.

"Oh, come off it," he said. "It doesn't take a Texas Ranger to figure out that something's going on between you and Mark Jessup. Whole town's talking about them yellow roses, and with you here at the service—"

"Do thirty-three-year-olds even *have* 'boyfriends'?" she asked.

"Maybe not," Morrell said grimly, "but if you think I'm calling him your 'lover,' you can just forget it."

People were speaking; Mark was sure of it. But their words were slick and sinuous, too fluid for him to grasp much meaning, immersed as he was in the heavy haze of pain.

"He's coming around again." Female, that one, and familiar.

"Are you sure?" This voice made nausea—or maybe it was hatred—ball up in his belly.

"There, I saw his eyes move."

The sluggish stream of his blood stirred as Mark recognized the speaker. *Beth Ann.* More than anything, he wanted to look at her, to touch her, to reassure himself she hadn't been shot. But every movement hurt him as he'd never hurt before.

"Good," the male voice grumbled, "because I don't have all night to sit here. Cheryl'll have a regular hissy fit if I don't make it home to dinner. Even if she did make those damned dumplings again."

"You know, Pete," Beth Ann suggested, "if you don't like her cooking, maybe you could take a turn now and again. Mix up a few of your own favorites. Since both of you work full time—"

"No offense, Beth Ann, but if I wanted marital advice from an old maid, I'd tune in to *Oprah* with the rest of you gals."

Deputy Pete Riker, Mark finally realized. As big a jerk as ever.

Beth Ann ignored Riker's provocation and instead asked, "Mark, do you think you could take a little water?"

At her words, his mouth felt dry as the dust he'd swept beneath the empty beds in his father's house. Dry as the desiccated snakeskin he'd found behind the barn. He blinked and recognized her red hair, though her face remained blurred.

Speech, however, was beyond him. He managed to nod his head a few millimeters before pain stove in his skull. Or that was how it felt.

He moaned, gorge rising, and she gently turned his head in time for him to vomit so violently, his ribs throbbed.

"Aw, shit," the man swore. "Damn it all to hell. He's got puke all over me. You did that on purpose."

Mark couldn't tell whether Riker was accusing him

or Beth Ann, but the deputy's anger pulsated in time with the throbbing in his head.

"Maybe you should run on home and clean up, get some dinner, and read a story to those girls of yours instead of sulking in that woodshop," Beth Ann suggested. "I'll make sure you get word when he can talk. Honestly, I don't think he'll be answering any questions before morning—and if you stick around, it could get messy—or messier, I mean."

"Maybe I'll do that. I damned sure don't get paid enough to deal with this. God, this stinks."

Footsteps. Then a door was closed, and none too softly. Mark heard Beth Ann's soft chuckle and felt a little—a very little—better.

"That's quite an aim you've got there," she said. "How about we get you cleaned up, then try a few ice chips. They'll be easy on that stomach."

She came into focus, her smile reassuring as a breath of spring in winter.

"You're all right," he whispered, even more relieved now that he could clearly see her. She still wore the black skirt and light gray blouse she'd had on at his dad's service, though both were rumpled now. Her chestnut hair had fallen untidily around her shoulders, but he liked that. It made him think she would look that way once he made love to her.

And he wanted to—as soon as he could manage. He was putting it, in fact, on the top of his to-do list. Right after moving without pain exploding in his skull and figuring out how he'd come to be in what was clearly a room at the hospital. Judging from the dimness of the window, it was some time after sundown.

"I'm fine," she told him. "Whoever was shooting at us took off when the ambulance showed up."

"Did you see who fired?"

"No, but I told Morrell it was probably Gene. I'm sorry, Mark. I know you asked me not to, but I've never been shot at in my life. I couldn't have kept my mouth shut if I'd tried."

"It's okay. I'm just glad you weren't hurt. If anyone had shot you—" It was a thought he couldn't bear to finish, as if he were imagining something happening to . . .

"*Eli*," he burst out. "Did you call Mrs. Minton?"

As she wiped his mouth, she nodded. "She's keeping him 'til I get by to pick him up. They're watching a Disney movie—he's all right."

" 'Til *you* can get him?" Mark felt as if he was missing something. "But I need to be there—he'll be scared if I don't come."

"Honey, you're not goin' anywhere tonight," Beth Ann said. "Not when you can't even move without spewing on somebody. Now, don't you worry about Eli. Mrs. Minton has him covered for now, and he can stay at my place 'til you're back on your feet. Heaven knows I have the extra room, and he can play with Maia."

"But your house—is everything—?"

"My house is as safe as Fort Knox, if that's what worries you. I had a new security system put in, and you already know about my trained attack dog." Another smile told him she was making light of being conned.

She used a spoon to feed him chips of ice, which felt like heaven on his dry tongue as they melted.

"It *is* all right with you?" she asked. "Me taking Eli overnight? Mrs. Minton doesn't have an extra bedroom."

"Yes, and thank you."

"You could be laid up here a few days, but I expect you'll be stiff and sore for weeks. The docs say there's a concussion, but thank God nothing worse than that. Lots of bumps and bruises where that idiot hit you, but the x-rays didn't pick up any fractures. Do you want me to call someone for you? Eli's mother, maybe?"

"I'd rather you didn't. Rachel . . ." He wanted to put this in a way that didn't sound too critical. "It's easier on both her and Eli if she's not popping in and out of his life. Especially right now, with things so busy for her."

He was beginning to doubt that Rachel would ever play a major role again in Eli's upbringing. She'd met someone in Ohio, she'd told Mark, and they were talking about getting married and starting their own family once they'd both finished their residency.

"What about the Graffs?"

"No need to worry them." He loved Bill and Carol, but he couldn't take the thought of their coming here to hover over him. He especially didn't want them put into the position of defending him when people around here ran him down.

"Think you're ready to try a sip of water?" Beth Ann asked.

"First, you've got to tell me." He attempted a smile. "Did you really aim me at Pete Riker on purpose?"

Beth Ann raised a graceful eyebrow. "A nurse has few enough weapons at her disposal—especially against armed chauvinists."

He tried to laugh and moaned as fresh pain swamped him.

"Oooh, sorry," she said. "I remember all too well how that feels."

When he'd recovered a little, she helped him drink

some water and gave him Tylenol, which she promised would take a little of the edge off his hurt. "Nothing stronger, though," she told him, "not with that concussion."

Mark's stomach threatened mutiny, so he talked to distract himself. "What about Morrell? What did he say about Calvert?"

"The sheriff promised he'd question Gene on the assault. He's investigating the shooting, too, and if he finds—"

"He won't do anything. Calvert's some kind of relation."

"His nephew, yes," she said, "but Sheriff Morrell swore to me—"

"My word against Calvert's?" Bitterness saturated Mark's voice. "It's never gonna happen, Beth Ann."

She sat in the chair beside his bed and crossed her arms over her knees. "I'm not leaving 'til you tell me what this is all about."

"A stupid fight, that's all."

"This isn't junior high, Mark. They could have killed you—could have killed us both."

"I'm sorry, Beth Ann. I never meant to drag you into anything."

"I know that—just the way I knew you took your responsibilities too seriously to disappear before your father's burial. What happened? I heard Calvert was mad about you bailing out the waitress."

"Where did you hear that?"

"You're back in Eudena, Mark. Do you even need to ask?"

He sighed. The lack of privacy was another thing he hadn't missed about this place.

"The thing is," Beth Ann continued, "that only explains why Calvert was upset with you, not why you took the first swing at him. That's what you said earlier, isn't it?"

"It wasn't Calvert I decked first," Mark admitted. "It was Donny Ray."

"You're kidding. Donny Ray's usually too stewed or stupid to do anything but follow—wait a minute. What did he say?" A flush stained her fair skin. "Were they talkin' trash about your daddy at his own funeral?"

"Not my father, no."

"Then who, Mark?"

He tried to shake his head and regretted it immediately. "I'm not getting into this right now. I'm tired, and I'm hurting. I just want to be alone if that's all—"

"I'm sorry, Mark. I need an answer before I go to pick up . . ." Comprehension dawned in her expression, and she shot up from her seat, blue eyes blazing. "It was *Eli*, wasn't it? One of those disgusting animals said—"

"Beth Ann," Mark warned. This was his mess, for *him* to work out. He'd be damned if he would have her fighting his battles for him.

"Boy howdy, I hope you gave them an unholy *thrashing* before that coward, Gene, pulled out his wrench."

"I should've kept my temper in hand. They're idiots, not worth any of this."

"I won't argue with you there, but I can't believe there isn't more to it. It doesn't make sense for Calvert to be *that* upset about your paying another customer's bill. I mean, money's money, and the businesses around here are almost all so cash-strapped. I'm sure you've noticed, more than half the downtown's boarded up."

Mark pressed his lips together. He was throbbing,

hurting in half a dozen or more places. Why couldn't Beth Ann leave it alone?

"This goes back further, doesn't it?" Beth Ann asked. "That night, that last homecoming, they were both there. Gene and Donny Ray, too—only Gene Calvert didn't play in that game."

A vee of concentration etched itself between her eyebrows. "Benched, wasn't he? Something about fighting in the halls a few days earlier."

"It's all water under the bridge. Talking about it won't change anything—"

"But the Red Hawks broke their losing streak that night, with Gene out, beat the Electra Tigers for the first time in a decade," she went on, as if she hadn't heard him. "Everybody was celebrating, but Gene was madder than I've ever seen him. No one could say a word to him without him pushing, swearing—it was like he wasn't happy about the victory if he couldn't be the one to win it."

Mark closed his eyes. Maybe if he pretended to be sleeping, she would leave.

But Beth Ann didn't, or perhaps the current of memory was so strong that it swept her along. "I was leaving. I had to—had to get some stuff before we picked up Larinda, Heidi, and your sister to take them to the celebration over behind Steve Keller's barn. But Gene's friends stuck around to try to cheer him up with some beer they'd sneaked in. Donny Ray, Xavier—and Scotty Morrell . . . You were hanging around, too, I remember . . . But how come? Your sister went home with your parents, so you couldn't have been waiting for her."

He couldn't ignore her any longer. "I thought you'd forgotten."

"I keep remembering more of it." Her eyes brimmed

with emotion. "Since you've come back, I'm getting all these tiny fragments—like shards of a mirror that was broken that night."

"Even if you put it all together, what do you imagine you'll see? Your dead friends, my sister? The way you looked earlier that last night, when we were all so clueless? It *hurts* to see that, Beth Ann. It hurts me so much, I can't afford to waste time looking backward."

"But you *have* looked, Mark, and that's how you've moved forward. Not like me."

He thought about the way she'd stayed in Eudena, the years she'd lived with her mother while so many of their peers had married, started families, and begun new careers in towns with futures. Maybe not knowing had held her back from the life she should have led.

But he felt sick to think of that night, so sick with grief and guilt that he couldn't imagine unlocking the story he'd kept to himself for sixteen years. "I'm sorry," he said. "I can't do this. Not now."

Disappointment flashed over her expression, but she mastered it, then leaned forward and gently touched her lips to his forehead. "You've had a rough day, haven't you? I need to go now and get Eli."

"Thanks, Beth Ann. For everything." Though it hurt to move his eyes, he found her gaze and held it.

"The floor nurse'll be in to check on you, but you just press this button if you need anything tonight. You'll feel better in the morning, Mark. And then we're going to talk about this."

Apprehension tightened in his chest, but he said nothing. Because he owed her the real story. Even if he suspected that the hope of hearing it was the only thing that bound her to him.

Chapter 19

By the grace of the Creator, the One Appointed learned that the authorities were questioning another. No stroke of luck, but a miracle—that was what it was.

It was proof, as well. *Proof my work has been blessed and the letter remains hidden.*

Unless . . . Was it possible the whore's daughter was subtler than imagined? Could she be biding her time, waiting for her chance at revenge?

As the mind of the One Appointed opened—or *was* opened—to this possibility, a vision spun up like one of the twisters that sometimes skipped across the prairie to demolish what it would. It was a vision of Beth Ann Decker's naked body entwined with that of the returned prodigal, Mark Jessup. So detailed was this revelation that the Maker's servant pulled to the road's edge to sit transfixed by their lovemaking, confident this act of voyeurism was no sin. As one of Jessup's hands moved over the pale breast of the whore's daughter, he whispered to his lover, "The authorities can't be trusted. I'm living proof of that."

Beth Ann shook her head, causing red waves to spill across her bosom, and she pushed away the hand that played between her thighs. When she spoke, her words stabbed shock through the One Appointed, for Lilly Decker's voice fell from her lips.

"What makes you think that I'll need the authorities or jail to wreak my vengeanace?" Mockery crackled through her laughter, and the daughter's face changed with each word, until it transformed into her mother's. "I *will* destroy my killer—and everyone and everything that fool has ever loved."

Since garbage collection numbered among the services recently suspended by the nearly bankrupt town, and his neighborhood hadn't come up with the cash to hire a private contractor, Damon had been stuck with the chore of tossing the bagged trash into the bed of his pickup and driving it to the county landfill each week. He wouldn't mind so much except that his parents had decided it was his Christian duty to also take the trash of several neighbors too elderly or infirm to do the job. And the damned dogs had gotten into one of old Mr. Carney's bags again, which as usual stank of moldering pork chop bones and sauerkraut.

After cussing a blue streak—he'd put off the chore so long that it was already pitch dark, and he had to go to work soon—Damon collected a rake, a pair of work gloves, and a new bag from his garage and went back to take care of the mess using the illumination of his truck's headlights. He was nearly through when someone else pulled up, parking in the wrong direction, and flipped on a set of high-beams so he had to shield his eyes to keep from being blinded.

A car door opened, then a second, and Damon saw

a pair of large, male figures silhouetted by the light. His heart skipped a beat, and his grip tightened on the rake handle.

"Practicin' up for your next career, Stillwater?"

The second man laughed, and Damon breathed again. He'd know Deputy Ned Gustavsen's big, full laugh anywhere. Which meant the speaker had to be Pete Riker.

Tall, blond, and good-natured, Gustavsen had always seemed nice enough. But Damon had never liked Pete, for he remembered all too clearly the many times the deputy had pulled him and his friends over in their teen years, whether or not they'd actually been doing anything illegal. Though he'd been friendly and helpful since Damon had joined the department, Damon still couldn't get over the suspicion that the man lived to shake up high-school kids.

"That's what I'm doing," Damon answered, a beat too late. "Figure garbage man might pay better than a starting deputy's salary."

Both men chuckled at that, and their easy camaraderie reminded Damon they were not only friends and coworkers, they were practically related, since the two were married to a pair of sisters.

But their laughter died too soon.

"We thought it'd be the decent thing to come and talk to you first," Pete said, an unmistakable warning in his words. He hooked his thumb into the belt of his jeans, right where his gun would hang if he were on duty.

"What you've been doing," Gustavsen said, "this little 'side investigation' you've been running, well, I won't say it hasn't been, uh, sort of entertaining in its own way—"

"Kind of Hardy Boys," Pete mocked. "Or maybe Nancy Drew."

Damon felt sick with horror at the thought that his fellow deputies were laughing behind his back, thinking he was nothing but a child playing at being a detective. But the sheriff didn't feel that way, he was certain. The thought brought him at least some consolation.

"The trouble is," Gustavsen went on, "when we go to interview folks—"

"As part of the *official* inquiry," Pete added.

"They're getting pretty stirred up. They've already answered all these questions, they say. And they're mad as hell we sent that 'rude Stillwater boy' to ask them."

Damon couldn't help cringing. Maybe, probably, Morrell had been right that his interview technique needed work.

"Anyway," Pete said, "it's got to stop right now. You're interfering with a murder investigation."

Damon nodded, though he wanted to ask why he was beating these two to the punch so often. It wasn't as if he'd started poking around in this case right away. Nor would he have continued, had he seen any signs of professional police work.

But he said nothing, thinking of the unsettling truth he'd stumbled too near, and the tears he had seen shining in his father's eyes.

"I hope we can take that as agreement, Damon," Ned said.

"Otherwise," Pete threatened, "we *will* go to Morrell."

"I understand," Damon told them, "and I mean to try to keep my mind on my own work."

"You do that." There was an audible sneer in Pete's voice as he turned back toward his vehicle. "Or cleaning up other people's garbage is gonna be the only kind of work that you have left."

* * *

Beth Ann's consciousness seemed to float above her own bed, where she watched Mark's hands ply her sleeping body, his every movement igniting pleasure that shimmered on her flesh in phosphorescent waves. His mouth glided along the pale column of her neck, the heat and moisture pulling a moan of sheer frustration from her throat. *Another dream*—another damned dream to leave her aching with a longing that could never be fulfilled. . . .

Beth Ann jolted awake and blinked back tears to focus on the pale shape of Maia by the closed door. Visible in the moonlight leaking through the shades, the Lab stood, watchful and frozen, with a sound between a whine and growl vibrating in her throat. But Beth Ann didn't think the dog had been what she'd heard.

Her gaze flicked to the slow red pulse from the alarm panel, which showed her that the system remained armed. Reassuring, except that something had awakened both her and Maia.

A remembrance soured her stomach, the thought that she had only set the alarm once she'd come home. That she'd grown careless of her safety. When she'd allowed the Winfield brothers access to the place, she had been in too big of a hurry to think of how they might secure it.

When she'd come home this evening, she'd discovered that not only had the alarm been left off, but the back door to the house was unlocked. She'd been unnerved by her own lapse—and infuriated with herself, as well—but everything had seemed in order. Still, as she lay in the darkness, she couldn't help wondering: Had she left some dark spot unchecked?

Could someone have hidden behind the media

room seating or ducked beneath her desk when she had peeked into her study?

There it was again, that sound. High and sharp—a child's cry.

Eli.

Beth Ann sprang from her bed, her hand snatching automatically for her cane, her heart pounding out the staccato code of worry. Had her carelessness not only left her at risk but endangered the child she had promised to keep safe?

"Daddy?" Eli's voice trembled, like a strand of spider's silk in a stiff breeze.

"I'm coming, honey," Beth Ann called as she opened the bedroom door. Maia burst past her and bounded down the hall, where a nightlight guided them both to a guest bedroom on the left.

Eli stood in the doorway, his eyes wide and his jet hair sticking up in tufts. He wore a pair of footed pajamas and an expression of sheer horror.

He looked up to Beth Ann's face. "I want my daddy."

Join the club, kid. Pushing aside the unsettling dreams that had plagued her, Beth Ann squatted to pull the boy into her arms.

Maia, who was becoming more of a love sponge every day, wormed her way between the two of them, her tail fanning with joy at this midnight excitement. The dog smelled good, too, thanks to her unscheduled bath.

"We'll see him tomorrow, sweetie," Beth Ann murmured, "when he's awake and feeling better."

Eli answered, "I had a scary dream where that bad man came to hurt my daddy."

Startled, Beth Ann pulled away to look into his worried face. "What bad man?"

This evening when she'd picked up Eli, she had taken Mrs. Minton's lead and reassured the child that his father had had a little accident. Though Beth Ann wasn't completely comfortable with the white lie, she would rather err on the side of kindness than scare a five-year-old with the brutal truth.

"The bad man by the barn. The one looking in our truck." Eli frowned. "I saw him when I went to play with Stormy."

He had earlier told her about his efforts to befriend the half-wild barn cat. Naming the animal was apparently one step in his program, right behind bribing it with tasty morsels.

But it was the mention of the man that had the fine hairs rising behind Beth Ann's neck. "Did your father know about him?"

Eli's head shook from side to side. "The bad man said I shouldn't tell him. Or he'd take back my star."

"Your star?"

"My junior deputy's star. And he said it real mean."

Her heart thumped hard against her chest wall. "He didn't—did he hurt you, Eli? Did he touch you in any way?"

"No. I stayed away from him. I was scared to get too close."

Thank God. A little of the tension bled out of her neck and shoulders, only to return as another thought occurred. "He told you he'd take the badge *back*, right?" she asked. "Does that mean he gave it to you, Eli? Was the man's name Sheriff Morrell?"

Eli's head shook once more, and his big, dark eyes looked worried. "Not him. It was the bad man. The one that doesn't like me."

"Which man, Eli? Was it somebody you know?"

The boy nodded, then quickly shook his head. "I don't know his name."

"But you've seen him before, haven't you?"

Eli hesitated, and in the dim light, tears gleamed on his face. "I want my daddy."

Beth Ann wanted to scoop him up, but that much lifting was beyond her, so she took him by the hand instead. "You can come to my room. We'll lie down and talk about it."

His eyes shone as he looked at her, intently as an owlet.

"It's all right, Eli."

"Is—is Maia coming with us?"

Beth Ann smiled. "She wouldn't miss it for the world."

Though Beth Ann had been trying to keep the Lab off the furniture, Maia's comforting presence, as she snuggled between the woman and the child, was worth its weight in dog hair. In a few minutes, Eli was covered up, with his head propped on a pillow and his hand stroking the Lab's fur.

Lying on the queen-sized bed's left side, Beth Ann tried to think of how to ask Eli about the man he'd seen behind the Jessup barn, a man who had frightened the child so badly Eli had not mentioned the strange presence. But the hand stroking Maia had fallen still already, and the boy's breaths were stretching into the quiet rhythm of untroubled sleep. Unwilling to provoke more bad dreams, Beth Ann decided she would wait until morning to ask Eli any further questions.

As both boy and dog snored softly, she crept from the bed and took her flashlight, then spent forty minutes checking each closet, nook, and cranny in the Lucky Pull. But even after her return to bed, Beth Ann lay restless, shrouded by the covers, where she watched the alarm system's throbbing heartbeat long into the night.

Two days later . . .

"Sweet Pete says you got kind of snippy with him over at the Jessup funeral."

Cheryl's words startled Beth Ann, who had been driving her courtesy loaner car on autopilot, zoned out by a featureless expanse of prairie and the perfectly straight road that would take them back to Eudena from Fort Worth.

"Here I thought you were sleeping."

"I never sleep in the car," Cheryl insisted. "Especially after I volunteered to keep you company on my off day, out of the kindness of my heart."

Beth Ann smiled. "Then you were drooling and snoring wide awake. And I know you. You volunteered to come because you were dying to see what Mama kept inside that safe deposit box."

"I deny everything." Cheryl gave her mouth a furtive swipe. "And don't think I can't tell when you're changing the subject."

Beth Ann eyed a camel as it looked up from its munching. A few area landowners had resorted to desperate measures to control the overgrowth of scrubby mesquite trees in their fields. The camels seemed to thrive on the thorny growth, but Beth Ann would never get used to the otherworldly sightings, so at odds with the familiar glimpses of jackrabbits and coyotes.

Shrugging, she said, "Guilty as charged. I get a little snippy when he tries to tell me what to do."

"You always take him the wrong way, Beth Ann. He doesn't mean anything by it, except maybe when he starts ragging you over how you voted in the last election."

"It wasn't about the governor's race this time. This time, he was on my case about Mark Jessup. It seems that *somebody* told him about the yellow roses. Any idea who that might've been?"

Beth Ann glanced over at the passenger seat to see Cheryl blushing.

"Sorry. But you know darned well he would've heard it somewhere anyway. It's been a real hot topic all around town. Most've 'em don't like the idea, being you're an angel on this earth and he's the devil that done you wrong. But that little waitress from the Blue Coyote is telling everyone who'll listen that you've landed yourself one sweet catch."

Beth Ann rolled her eyes. "He's not a fish, and we're just . . . acquaintances."

Cheryl's bark of laughter bounced around the car. "Ha. If you two aren't doing the deed already, I'm pretty sure you will be once he gets back on his feet. Pretty slick move, you takin' care of his kid for a few days."

With that reminder, Beth Ann checked the dash clock to make sure they'd be back on time to pick up both Eli and Cheryl's youngest from Mrs. Minton's daycare. No problem, she reassured herself, as long as she didn't get pulled over for speeding again.

Guiltily, she let up on the gas a little, though the open road cried out for acceleration.

Cheryl mused, "Betcha Aimee's wishin' she'd thought of that babysitting angle herself."

"Aimee? With a *human* child?" It was not to be imagined. Especially with the sweetly sensitive Eli.

"She's got Sir Snookums, doesn't she?"

"The rat-dog doesn't count. Despite the color-coordinated outfits she stuffs that poor thing into. Somebody oughta report your sister to the SPCA."

"You're dodging the subject again. You and Mark Jessup. Dish, girlfriend."

"There is no subject. I expect he'll leave town as soon as he feels up to the drive. Nothing to hold him here now. And nothing to prevent me from reverting to Pathetic Spinster status if that's what I want."

Cheryl sobered quickly. "Is it?"

Beth Ann shook her head. "Don't think so. I thought maybe I'd take over Mama's gig and become Eudena's Official Party Girl."

"Don't be sarcastic, Beth Ann."

Beth Ann shrugged. "Like my mother said, the world's mine if I'll claim it. Seems like she was smarter than I ever gave her credit for."

"Probably, but I still don't get why she'd drive clear to Fort Worth to lock up some old newspaper clippings and the owner's manual for that Mercedes she bought."

Beth Ann nodded. All the articles related to the crash. From the original, front-page reports to the obituaries and the coverage of Mark's trial. Two more death notices had also been included: those of Beth Ann's father, only eight weeks after the collision, and Mark's mother, which had come a few months later.

"I guess she didn't want me stumbling across those articles," Beth Ann said. "Probably figured I'd go all Sylvia Plath on her or something if I started reading all that."

The pictures had been even worse. She blinked

back tears at the memory of the twisted wreckage of the Camaro she'd been driving—which she had been spared this long—along with the head shots of the dead girls and her own senior picture. Mark's mug shot, too, was in the folder, looking so young. Hopeless. Lost.

But Cheryl only asked, "Sylvia *who?*"

"Downer poet. Suicide. Patron saint of depressed teenaged girls for generations."

Cheryl stared at her. "Your mama, rest her soul, must've had a screw loose. Anybody who can handle both hospice and Eudena is made of tougher stuff than that."

"Amen. But I tend to agree about that loose screw, at least as far as locking up that owner's manual is concerned. When I went to trade the car, I looked for the thing everywhere."

"It does prove your mother was at Globe Bank not all that long ago. That car was brand new."

"About six months old," Beth Ann amended. "I remember, she traded the Cadillac in on it about the time we moved into the new house. Maybe the Mercedes was some kind of symbol to her. You know how she grew up."

"I do."

Her mother hadn't often spoken of the neglect of her childhood or her alcoholic father, but there were few secrets in Eudena. Especially when this one regularly got into bar fights until he drank himself to death once his wife—Beth Ann's grandmother—ran out on both him and their teenaged daughter.

"Doesn't help to dwell on these things," her mama had always said, often enough over the salt-crusted edge of her margarita glass.

But Beth Ann wondered, was Lilly's history the reason her mother drank and ran around with men she couldn't marry? And had that behavior finally killed her, just as it had the father Lilly refused to talk about?

Could the past, undealt with, strike back with fangs as deadly as the most venomous of serpents? If so, Beth Ann refused to become the third generation in her family to make the same mistake.

Chapter 20

The following day . . .

At the sound of a car door closing, Mark rose from his kitchen chair too quickly—and paid the price in a fresh wave of dizziness. Though he had been released from the hospital the previous morning, he was still unsteady when he stood or turned too quickly, a side effect of his concussion that made it dangerous for him to drive.

Beth Ann had called to say that after taking her new "best bud" to daycare, she was stopping by to see him. "We've got some things to talk about."

Not if I can help it. Because the more Mark thought about it, the more certain he was that nothing positive could come of stirring up old secrets, no matter how grateful he was to her for keeping Eli these past few nights. Calvert had been jailed without bail, since he'd kept spewing threats, and charged with both aggravated assault and resisting arrest, so Mark figured he had nothing else to worry about but tying up loose ends from his dad's estate and heading home to Pittsburgh.

Yet Pennsylvania didn't feel so much like home just now, as Beth Ann let herself in the back door after knocking. Dressed for her day off, she looked good—too damned good—in a pair of jeans that displayed her long legs to their best advantage and a royal blue sweater that flattered her full curves. She wore her hair down, too, and it spilled in sensuous waves over her shoulders.

Mark could have stood forever, taking in the view—as well as the pulse-pounding realization that for the first time ever, the two of them were in a house together and alone. But he locked down his libido and concentrated on the questions he knew she meant to ask him—and the story he'd gone sixteen years without sharing. Apprehension needled his stomach at the thought.

Beth Ann glanced at him, then did a double take. "You'd better sit before you fall down. Want me to bring some coffee to the living room?" She inclined her head toward the freshly brewed pot on the warmer.

"That would be great," he said, "but let me help you."

She shook her head. "Get yourself in there before I have to loan you my cane to make it to the sofa."

Though he grumbled about her bossiness—and the unthinkable image of himself leaning on her cane—Mark complied. She brought his coffee first, then came back with her own mug and lowered herself onto the couch's opposite end.

After an appraising look, she said, "That's one heck of a bruise you've got there on your temple."

"It looks a lot worse than it feels," he told her. Unless he touched the bump, or the ones that marked his arms and upper back, the pain was manageable.

"How's the dizziness?"

"Not bad if I take it slow. But you didn't drive back out here for a checkup."

She blew across the dark surface of her coffee, then shook her head. "No, I didn't," she admitted before reaching for the shoulder bag she'd slung onto the floor and dragging it up to the cushion between them.

He wondered, did she mean it to be a barricade, protection against the wave of lunacy that had prompted him to pull her into his arms before?

"I wanted to say thanks again, for keeping Eli." The words burst out of him, self defense against the memory of tasting her.

A smile warmed her blue eyes. "We had so much fun. It was my pleasure. You're lucky, Mark, to have him. If I'm ever blessed with a child, and he's half as— as . . ."

She shrugged as a flush stole across her features. "I guess you think I'm silly, falling in love with a guy half my height."

"I may be biased, but I think he's always been an easy kid to love. And if it's any consolation, he's nuts about you, too." Mark grinned as he said it.

He was happier still that she'd implied there was at least some chance she could have children. Ever so slightly, the burden of his guilt shifted, making it easier for him to breathe.

"He's crazy about Maia, anyway," Beth Ann said. "He was seriously bummed when I wouldn't let her ride along with us this morning. Seems my highly trained guard dog got into the trash and came down with a case of flatulence that would probably peel the window tinting."

Laughing, Mark said, "Sounds like one of our dog Beau's best tricks."

After she sipped her coffee, Beth Ann's expression sobered. "The thing is, without Maia to distract him, I was finally able to pry some straight answers out of Eli."

"Answers? What do you mean?"

"That first night he spent at my place, Eli woke up because of a bad dream. About a man he was afraid might be coming back to hurt you."

Mark shook his head. "I thought you didn't tell him. He asked about my accident when you brought him by to see me."

And Mark had lied to his son, telling Eli a story about a fall off the back steps of the funeral home. Several times, he'd tried to cobble together some version of the truth that wouldn't frighten the five-year-old, but Mark tasted bile each time he thought about the ignorance that had oozed from Donny Ray's lips.

"Sometime before that fight of yours, Eli saw a man, Mark." Beth Ann looked at him intently. "A man poking around your pickup and trying to look inside the house here."

"What? When was this?" Mark leaned toward her, sitting on the cushion's edge while pain pulsed at the bump on his head.

"Sometime before your dad died, but Eli couldn't say exactly."

"But why wouldn't he tell me this?"

Beth Ann's lips pressed together in a flat line, and moisture glimmered in her eyes.

"Did this bastard hurt my son?" he demanded.

When she shook her head, he breathed again.

"Not that," she said. "He didn't touch Eli. But he scared him pretty badly. He told him if he said anything about it, he would take the little badge back."

"That deputy's badge? Then it was—"

"I'm pretty sure it was Deputy Pete Riker. You remember, from the hospital."

"I know exactly who that son of a bitch is. He's had it in for me since he first pulled me over for speeding when I was fifteen and I swiped my mother's car. But if he's threatened my kid—"

Her head shook. "I don't think he went that far. I don't think he would. Look, Pete's married to my best friend. I agree with you that he can be a horse's ass at times, but she says he can be the sweetest—"

"He's not just an ass, Beth Ann. You should have seen the way he looked at Eli, like he thought the kid was a damned abomination. Riker's no less a racist than Donny Ray, only he's more dangerous. The man's both armed and stone-cold sober."

She shook her head. "Pete's been a deputy for years, Mark, and I can't imagine him doing anything illegal, or at least anything to jeopardize his job. Maybe he was just hunting around, hoping to find some evidence—"

"That I killed your mother? Are you still wondering, Beth Ann?"

"Lord, no." She brushed her bangs from her eyes, her fingers lingering a moment on her forehead. As if his question brought her pain. "Do you honestly think I'd be here if I thought that? That I'd have anything to do with you or Eli?"

She reached into her bag and withdrew a long white envelope before adding, "Can you imagine I would have waited to ask you about *this* instead of taking it to Morrell if I had doubts?"

She passed him the envelope. "What was it about, Mark? I didn't find a letter."

He looked straight back at her but saw no accusation in her eyes. This, from a woman whose mother's death remained a mystery, from a woman whose life he'd changed forever on a dark stretch of rural road.

Grateful beyond measure, he explained, "Your mother wrote to me twice. It took me a good long time to even open the first letter. I figured she was blowing off steam over what I'd done to your life or giving me hell about my company. But when I finally got around to reading the letter, I saw she didn't mention a word about either. She wrote about saving Eudena. I got the idea she cared about this place deeply, even if she wasn't completely honest with me."

"I don't understand. What would either of you have to do with saving this town? And what do you mean, she was dishonest? My mother might have been a lot of things, but she always told it like it was." Beth Ann's smile twisted with pain. "Whether or not people wanted to hear it."

"She led me to believe she was a member of the revitalization committee and she was contacting me on official business. Even dropped in a self-addressed, stamped envelope."

"Oh." Beth Ann's thumb traced the firm line of her jaw. Her gaze dropped, too. "I didn't realize it bothered her so much when they blocked her from joining their snooty little clique. She laughed it off, joked about how that bunch of snobs could go down with the ship for all she gave a damn."

"She might've been upset about the way they treated her," Mark said, "but Eudena mattered to your mother.

The letters that she wrote me . . . I'll send them to you if you'd like, after I get back to my place."

Beth Ann nodded without looking up. "But I still don't understand. What did she think *you* could do?"

"She'd done her homework about my company. And she had an idea about how the two of us could help bring back this place from the brink. Maybe she saw it as a chance for a couple of black sheep to regain Eudena's goodwill."

Beth Ann looked up sharply. "You mean, she thought you could save Eudena with your money? With some of her winnings and your profits together?"

"Something like that," he said, still as amazed by Lilly's suggestion as he'd been the day he'd read it. "At the time, I didn't see it the same way, but I have to admit she had some pretty well-thought-out ideas."

"I don't get it," Beth Ann shot back. "Why *would* she, after the way they treated her? And how on earth could she imagine you would? I mean, you hadn't even lived here for so many years, and—and the memories you do have can't be pleasant."

He managed a smile, though he suspected it looked pained. "A few of them are, Beth Ann. Can't you remember any of it?"

She stared at him for what felt like an eternity, her expression troubled. "Less than I would like."

"I wasn't talking about *that* night."

"I need you to." She paused to take another sip of coffee, but her gaze never left him. "Tell me, Mark, why did you stick around the stadium that evening? After the adults had all gone home."

He hesitated, wondering how to change the subject.

"Mark," she prompted. "*Jess* . . . please."

He thought about the night she'd told him she could never move forward until she understood the things that had brought her to this point. He thought, too, of a time he would have killed to hear her call him Jess.

After a hard swallow, he answered, "I was waiting to see someone."

"Aimee, I suppose."

"No. That was just a one-time thing, before she found somebody new to shock her parents." He released a long sigh. "I was waiting for *you,* Beth Ann."

"Me? But why, Mark?"

"Can't you guess?" He remembered watching her so carefully, waiting for an opening. "Everybody knew that you and Scotty had broken up, and I wanted—I wanted so much to talk to you, to maybe take one more stab at asking you out."

Her eyes glittered, and he imagined he saw the old Beth Ann lurking behind her reconstructed face. She was still beautiful as now, but a pang of sadness swamped him for the girl who had been lost. The girl who could never be the same, no matter what he told her.

"So why *didn't* you?" she all but whispered.

He shook his head, then waited out a throb of pain before answering. "It was just a pipe dream. You were so far out of my league, Beth Ann, with your friends swarming all around you, the way they always were. There was no way to catch you on your own. And no way in hell I'd walk up to you with them there."

"Have you ever wondered—" After setting her mug on the lamp table, she slid closer on the sofa, and her hand settled on his cheek as gently as a butterfly alighting. "—how things might have come out if you had?"

"Only every day of my life." Unable to bear her

touch, he took her hand in his and held it trapped between the two of them. "But I didn't risk it, and then you were gone with your friends. And Scotty started with some shit about me sniffing after you, about how I had no business even looking your way."

"I always liked you," she said. "Maybe I was afraid of you a little, after you started getting so many detentions and tearing around in that truck of yours like a bat out of hell and running with those fast girls. Or maybe I was afraid *for* you. But I never thought you weren't good enough for me."

He released her hand and knotted both of his together. Leaning forward, he balanced the sharp points of his elbows on his knees. "They all started in on me then—Ex and Donny Ray and Gene, too. I guess they figured they were defending Scotty's honor—as if that jerk owned you. Calvert was the worst, of course, but I knew when I was outnumbered, and it was just the usual shit. So I left. Or tried to."

"What do you mean?"

"My damned truck wouldn't start. I was pretty pissed about it. I mean, everybody else was out cruising the streets and celebrating. And there I was, stuck in the parking lot with my hood raised, up to my damned elbows in engine grease. It didn't make it any easier when Gene and his friends brought their party out to watch me about a half an hour later."

"So what happened?" Beth Ann asked him. "Obviously, you got your pickup started. Otherwise, you couldn't have . . ."

He saw her eyes lose focus as the past drifted before them. Was she remembering more now? Did she hear the impact, see the blood and mangled bodies? He did; the sight waited for him always, just behind his eyelids.

Stop this right now. Just quit talking. But somehow, she had lured him past the tipping point, to a place where the long-bottled words spilled free on their own.

"They were sitting in Gene's car, tossing their empties in my direction and shouting out half-assed advice with their insults." He was there again, hearing the vicious words and feeling the tension twisting in his gut, the years of hurt and frustration threatening to split him open. In his memory their name-calling mingled with half a dozen dire predictions for his future: from his teachers and his principal, from Deputy Pete Riker and his own dad. How he'd never applied himself to schoolwork, never followed rules, never fit in with the right kids or kissed the right asses. How his younger sister did right while he screwed up. Too dumb to read his textbooks. Too bad to make it anywhere but collecting trash or making license plates in prison.

God . . . He'd die before he went back to those years—kill to keep from re-experiencing that night. Yet here was Beth Ann, drawing the hateful thorn of memory from him, her only tool the raw need in her expression.

"By the time I finally got the engine going," he went on, "they were pretty wasted, and I was getting madder by the minute."

"So you fought with them?" Beth Ann asked.

He nodded. "That legendary Jessup temper . . ."

"Still, you took on three of them? Or was it four?"

He tried on a smile for size. "Testosterone can't count."

She frowned. "And you'd been drinking, too, right?"

He shook his head. "It's not that I didn't plan to, but I didn't get the chance. Nope, it was pure fury—one of those bottles they were throwing finally hit me, and I pretty much went ballistic. Jumped in with both fists and started pounding. Not that it went on long."

"I guess not, not with those kinds of odds."

"Would have worked out better if I'd figured that out sooner. But you see, the day of my father's funeral wasn't the first time I flattened Gene Calvert's ugly nose."

"You broke his nose that night, too?"

From the look on her face, this was news to Beth Ann, which probably meant it had never gotten around Eudena. Mark wondered how Gene had explained the fracture after the accident. Probably, it wasn't difficult, with everyone's attention on the broken and the dead—and the supposedly intoxicated teenaged driver who had shattered lives uncounted. Anything short of an alien invasion would have gone unnoticed.

"I'm pretty sure I did." Mark remembered the crunch, the shift, the gush of blood—that explosion of rage that had cost so very much.

Beth Ann's gaze intensified. "And those guys just let you walk away from that? I know how they all stuck up for each other—and if they'd been drinking like you said they were—"

"They were drinking, all right." The rest of that night crawled into Mark's throat and wedged there.

She slid even closer, then cupped his knee with her hand. He felt the warmth of it right through the denim. Yet he couldn't say the damned words, not even if she reached inside him and tore them bleeding from the place he kept them locked inside his heart.

Chapter 21

Beth Ann had been many things in her life: daughter, friend, student, patient . . . even, for a time, a lover. But above all else, she was a woman, with a healer's eye and an empathy that let her feel his pain as deeply as her own.

Yet as a nurse, she understood that sometimes, only the most unpleasant interventions could clear the way for true recovery. *But is it mine or his I'm after?* Did she have the right to push?

Hell, yes, she decided as she moved to hug her stomach. She'd damned well bought that right in losses: her friends, her health, her youth. So she swallowed her sympathy—her foolish pity and attraction to the man who'd ruined everything—and let a rush of anger flow into its place.

"So you took off," she accused him. "Drove somewhere and got hammered, maybe with your friends. And then you headed out toward Heidi Brown's place, out on Mustang Road—"

"It wasn't like that, Beth Ann."

"And you smashed into my father's car as I pulled out of her driveway."

"That part's true, God forgive me. But I wasn't drunk. I wasn't . . . I— I was—"

Contempt vied with disappointment to unhinge her. "You did three years for intoxicated manslaughter, and you're telling me you weren't drunk?"

"There was no time." His voice was flat, expressionless, the monotone of someone in a trance. "Not with them behind me. Not with—"

"With who behind you, Mark?" The emptiness in his eyes made her shiver—until a new suspicion slammed the door against compassion. "Don't tell me you were out there racing."

She knew he'd done it on at least a few occasions. He hadn't picked up the nickname Hell on Wheels for nothing. Her tears blurred his face as he turned toward her.

"I wasn't racing either," he said. "I swear it on my life—on my son's life, Beth Ann."

"Then what, Mark? *What?* You had to have been going fast. I'd just pulled out of the Browns' driveway, and—" She froze as headlights filled her vision. *Two pairs of headlights—not one.*

Her hand floated to her mouth. "My God."

"When I punched Calvert behind the stadium, they came after me with broken bottles. Caught me right here with one." He was breathing hard, pointing out the reddish scar beneath his left eye, the one she had assumed had come from broken windshield glass. "They were out of control, Beth Ann, a pack of starved coyotes that had tasted blood. I jumped into my truck and lit off before one of them blinded me, or worse."

"They were—they were chasing you." Her voice

broke with the realization. "Trying to—to run you off the road. I saw it, Mark. I *saw* it."

Tears streamed down her face, and once again, she heard her friends' laughter. Only this time it was interrupted by a shriek.

"Stop, Beth Ann!" Jordan's voice, her last words . . .

Beth Ann fell into Mark's embrace, trembling. He stroked her back, her hair. And it seemed to her that strength flowed through his hands into her body, that it was the only thing keeping her heart from splintering with the shock of memory.

"I'm so, so sorry," Mark repeated again and again. "You pulled out at the wrong moment. If it had been a minute earlier—or thirty seconds later . . ."

But Beth Ann remained trapped in that moment, seeing it and hearing it. Smelling and tasting its sick-sweetness, feeling the brake pedal's surprising give. She felt her forehead wrinkling in confusion, felt herself returning to the present as Mark's lips pressed warm against her temple.

Dragging in a deep breath, she looked into his brown eyes. "If they were chasing you, forcing you out of your lane, and you weren't drinking, tell me, Mark—why were you the one arrested? The only one who went to jail?"

"I think you know that, Beth Ann."

She thought about the boys involved. The sheriff's son and nephew, along with Donny Ray Saunders and Ex Walling, two more starters for the Red Hawks. At the time, all but Donny Ray showed promise of bright futures, just as had the dead and dying cheerleaders from the Chevy.

"Pete Riker *sacrificed* you," she said. "And Jim Morrell

damned well knew it, or just as likely, he ordered it himself."

Though he'd been powerless as a teenager, Mark Jessup now had the money and the know-how to smash the past wide open—and bury State Senator-Elect Scott Morrell's bright future. No wonder Morrell had been reluctant to consider Mark Jessup as a suspect in her mother's murder. Gene Calvert, Donny Ray, and Ex, too, could be damaged if Mark came forward, and both Jim Morrell's and Pete Riker's careers in law enforcement would be over.

"I don't understand it," she said. "Why didn't you say anything about it? How could you let—"

Mark shook his head. "I hardly knew what was happening back then. My sister was dead, and Heidi and Larinda. No one figured you would make it either—and if you did, you'd be either brain-damaged or wheelchair-bound for life. My dad wouldn't spend a single cent on my defense, and the good old boy whose turn it was to play public defender didn't want to hear some bullshit story about a grand conspiracy. For damned sure, he wasn't about to take the time or trouble to do more than plead my case out."

"He was supposed to be your advocate, and he wouldn't even listen?"

"You've got to understand. A cash-strapped rural county like this one pays—or at least at the time they paid—these lawyers the same lowball figure, no matter how much or how little work they put into it. They'd go broke if they put on a real defense for indigent clients or hired an investigator—"

It was wrong. Infuriating. "Who was this so-called lawyer?"

Mark shook his head. "It doesn't really matter. The sheriff's department may have 'lost' the blood-alcohol sample that was taken from me that night, but the prosecution had photos of my truck with beer bottles where somebody—maybe Calvert and his friends or Riker—put 'em. They had photos of your dad's Chevy and the victims. And they had a kid known as a troublemaker, with a history of speeding and an attitude nobody in this town was gonna miss."

"They *sacrificed* you," she repeated. "And you weren't one of the really bad kids. You never hurt anyone before that, not a single person."

He shrugged. "The numbers made sense, I guess. Why ruin the lives of four decent young men when you could pin the whole thing on one loser?"

With fresh tears welling, Beth Ann cupped his face with her hands. And saw a truth she couldn't fight. "You're worth twenty Gene Calverts and a hundred Donny Rays. . . ."

She leaned in to kiss the scar beneath his left eye, then heard his breathing roughen as her lips trailed toward his ear. "A thousand Xaviers and Scottys, and a million lying manure spreaders like Pete Riker and Jim Morrell."

"I've got to say, I like the way you do math." He flushed as he spoke, but it was the rasping of his voice that wound her as tight as an old watch. The past few evenings' fantasies winked through her mind, each image more erotic than the last. Powerless to resist the impulse, she flicked his earlobe with her tongue's tip, then infused his murmured name with the deep ache of her longing. "Jess . . ."

She might as well have struck a fistful of gasoline-

soaked matches; the two of them ignited instanta-
neously.

With an urgent groan, he grabbed her by the shoulders and crushed her lips to his. There was nothing of
sweetness in the way their mouths locked, nothing but
potency, raw hunger, that belied the innocent word
kiss.

She felt consumed by the searing of his tongue
against hers, the blistering of his hands as they cupped
and lifted her breasts. The old house might be drafty,
but her body flamed so hot, she pulled her arms free
of her sweater's sleeves in an attempt to keep herself
from melting.

Quick to notice, he peeled the sweater over her
head, then tossed it away—she didn't see where, as
she was far too busy going for the buttons on his
denim shirt. He grasped her wrists to stop her and
growled the words, "This first," before he devoured her
neck with hot bites that had her breasts burning with
need.

They hadn't long to wait for his attention. He
reached around behind her, unhooked her bra in one
deft move and sent it flying—somewhere east of Dallas, for all she cared. A moment later, his whiskers
abraded her flesh. But that didn't matter either, for his
mouth was suckling, her back arching, and she nearly
flew to pieces as reality surpassed imagination.

He pressed her shoulders downward, until she lay
flat against the bottom cushions. He leaned over then
and gave each breast its due as his hand fumbled with
the button of her Levi's. She made a second play to
undo his shirt, but once more, he resisted, saying, "This
first, Beth Ann. I've dreamed of doing this first."

Her shoes went next, her socks, too, and then the jeans were off, the panties torn, and he was touching her all over, stroking the center of her with his clever fingers, while his tongue laved greedy circles all around her navel. He was kneeling between her knees, his breath hot against her thighs, when he finally paused to look into her face.

"Is this what you want, Beth Ann?"

"Oh, my Lord, if you stop now, you're a dead man."

He grinned at that, then thrust his head down, doing things her grad student lover had never thought of but that Beth Ann had pictured plenty. Yet it occurred to her that her dreams had fallen far short, occurred to her that . . . Her thoughts dissolved into a wordless haze of molten pleasure, its center at his wicked tongue's tip, its rays spreading red heat through her body. As his two fingers pumped inside her, she erupted into cries that shot like flaming cinders toward the heavens.

When the world came back into focus, he was smiling at her. Looking mighty pleased with himself, but she allowed him that. Her heart skipped a beat as she watched him slowly shed his shirt and then slide out of the jeans he'd already unbuttoned to allow room for a huge . . .

Hello, cowboy. Was that all him, in those boxers?

Her eyes met his, and she swallowed, feeling ridiculously apprehensive for someone whose nerve endings had just been turned inside out. But tension re-ignited as her fuse was relit.

His hand sleeked down her bare thigh. "I want you, Beth Ann. I've wanted you since we were both kids. But I'll wait if that's what you—"

She grabbed his arms and pulled him toward her ravenous kiss. No way was she getting this close to life, to living, without experiencing the whole of it. If Mark Jessup headed back for Pittsburgh in the morning, so be it. She'd rather be left with one real, enduring memory than a lifetime of fading fantasies . . . and bedroom solitaire.

His hand was in the pocket of his discarded jeans, and he pulled away from her a second. "Hold on, hold on . . ."

She'd never heard anything sexier than the tearing of that foil packet, never smelled anything so arousing as the scent of lubricated latex.

"Let—let me do that," she whispered, taking the condom from him and kissing along his length—to the sound of his gasp—before she sheathed him. And here she'd worried she might have gotten rusty.

He was shaking as he moved above her. "I should take you to the bedroom."

She smiled up at him. "How 'bout you just take me?"

So he did. And it was hard and fast and desperate as the coupling of two animals in season. Brutal almost, but Beth Ann gave herself up to its rhythm, because at the same time, somehow, the act was tender and suffused with hope, with trust . . .

With blessed friction that had her imploding once more, pleasure crackling through her cells like voltage through downed power lines. And as she came, he followed, desire spilling from him as he shouted out her name.

Tears slanted down her temples, trickled toward her ears. It just felt so damned *good* to be connected—to feel the way that she'd released him. It made her feel powerful and female. It made her feel alive.

He kissed her softly, lingering, and then shifted to pull his weight off her.

"You aren't—are you crying, Beth Ann? Did I—? I hurt you, didn't I? Damn it, I was too rough—"

"It was perfect." But she cried harder as she said it.

Though he kissed and petted and consoled her, she could not make herself stop. She wept for all the years she had spent standing on death's margins, a wall-flower who had merely watched the others dance. She wept as she hugged the others, Jordan Jessup, Heidi Brown, Larinda Hyatt, then finally turned her back to them and stepped into the light.

Chapter 22

Two days later . . .

The One Appointed tore into the thick manila envelope with fingers shaking in anticipation. A sharp intake of breath heralded the wiring diagrams as they slid out of the package.

For all the sin engendered by the modern age, it had its advantages for the righteous. Including the ability to order detailed schematics for almost anything online, even the plans for the alarm system the whore's daughter had put in her palace.

Coming up with the brand name had been child's play, thanks to the huge decals the installation company had thoughtfully displayed not only on its van but on warnings affixed to the windows of the Lucky Pull. Coming up with the model had taken a bit more ingenuity, but thankfully, the Lord had provided—in the form of a salesman too eager for another fat commission to realize that the call from a neighbor wanting to buy a "real high-dollar system like the one my friend Beth Ann Decker picked out" had been a fake. Thanks to the man's greed—one of the Seven Deadly Sins, it might be noted—the One Appointed finally had all that was needed to put an end to this trial.

Everything, that is, except another dark night as well as the opportunity to slip away unnoticed. But there was absolutely no doubt that those, too, would be provided.

Soon enough to put all this unpleasantness to rest, and send not only Beth Ann Decker but her consort off to see the face of God.

"Are you talking to that dog?" Pete Riker yelled over Beth Ann's back gate. He wore his uniform, and she could hear an engine idling in the driveway. Probably, he'd dropped by on his way to work.

"Of course not." Beth Ann felt her face flush. She'd actually been *singing* to Maia as she brushed the Lab, but it was horror, not embarrassment, that caused her discomfort.

"Want to let me in the front?" Pete asked. "I've got your globe fixed for you."

She froze inside, caught between the familiar image of her best friend's husband and what Mark had told her of a deputy who had abused his authority to destroy a young life. She wanted to scream at Pete, to demand an explanation, but Mark's reluctance to speak of that night held her back, as did thoughts of Cheryl.

At last Beth Ann said, "Be right there," and rose from where she'd been sitting. Still ambivalent, she paused to pull a clump of dog-related fuzz free of the brush's metal tines. As the gold-white fur drifted toward the swimming pool, some enterprising sparrows swooped down to snatch it up.

With Maia at her heels, Beth Ann walked toward the front door. When Pete knocked, she took a deep breath to collect herself before opening the door.

"Thanks a lot for fixing that," she managed as he carried the globe's base inside. Outside, she caught a glimpse of his patrol car with its trunk standing open.

"No problem." Pete kept his back to her as he made for the sitting area and set the stand down in its customary place. Straightening, he rubbed his back and pointed out the spot where one of the stand's legs intersected with the wood horizon ring that held the sphere in place. "That's where it was busted—clean through."

"I can't even tell." Beth Ann leaned over her cane to peer at the repair. Anything to keep from meeting Pete's eyes. Swallowing back the bitter taste of anger, she forced herself to add, "You're really good at this stuff. You could probably make a living of it someplace, restoring antiques and expensive furniture."

Pete smiled, clearly pleased. "Someplace, maybe. But not in Hatcher County."

The smile reminded her of times she'd seen him joking instead of arguing with Cheryl, of the careful way he roughhoused with his giggling little girls. Beth Ann could almost hear him sawing a mean fiddle, as he'd done with a little bluegrass band for years—and could still be persuaded to do on rare occasions. Wrong and cruel as it had been, the decision Pete had made on Mustang Road had been the work of a single moment, not his whole life.

But how could she ignore it, knowing that it had cost Mark both his family and his freedom? Yet how could she speak, knowing and loving his family as she did?

"Let me bring in the globe, too," Pete said as he glanced around the room. "Then I'd better get going. Have to keep these mean streets safe from hooligans and stray dogs."

And seventeen-year-olds, she thought bitterly as she watched him go back outside.

Pete returned a minute later, his arms filled with the huge sphere, its relief surface bumpy and its features labeled with painstaking detail. Beth Ann supposed her mother could have taken a first-class trip to Europe for what the handcrafted piece had cost.

"Makes a real statement, don't you think?" her mama had asked anxiously the day it was delivered.

Beth Ann had appeased her by agreeing, though she'd been sorely tempted to reply, *"Yeah, it tells me you can't say no to a certain snooty anorexic."*

"You've got it upside down," she told Pete as he set the globe atop the base with the South Pole pointed toward the ceiling.

"So I do—say, what's this? Looky here." He pointed out what was clearly a seam along the Antarctic Circle. "I didn't see that earlier. Course, I was working on the stand and not the globe."

"I've never seen it, either. But it's just how the thing's made, isn't it?"

Pete shook his head and palmed the globe's south end. "Don't think so; the seam wouldn't be here—hey, look."

He sounded as excited as Eli when the bottom piece shifted beneath his hand.

"Don't break it." Even before the words were out of her mouth, she heard the thing unscrewing. Opening to reveal a small, hidden compartment in the bottom of the Earth.

In truth, the world is yours, Beth Ann recalled, *should you be bright and bold enough to claim it.*

"This is great. You could hide your jewelry in here, or put your—" Pete stopped talking, then reached inside with two fingers. A moment later, he extracted a square of folded paper and handed it to Beth Ann. "That's the only thing in there."

Curious, Beth Ann opened it and tilted her head, as if another angle would make sense of what she saw. "It's nothing but a doodle, that's all. Looks something like a peace sign, but not quite—

"I know," she said an instant later. "It's a Mercedes symbol. You know, I never realized that car was such a huge deal to my mama."

Guilt fluttered in Beth Ann's chest, and she wondered if she'd done wrong, to trade in her mother's pride and joy for practicality and fuel economy. She might have to run from one end of the county to the other for her job, but it wasn't as if she couldn't afford to fill up every few days.

"I heard about her locking up that manual all the way in Fort Worth." Pete shook his head as he spoke, until a scribble in one corner attracted his attention. "Look at this. That's not just a doodle, it's a number."

"You're right." More confused than ever, Beth Ann read the eight digits aloud. Not just any digits, she realized as her mouth went chalk dry. It was a date, *the* date that she had let define her.

The date of the deadly head-on collision out on Mustang Road.

Heartbreaking work, the boxing up of memories. Working since dawn, Mark sorted through his mother's things, which his dad had left untouched all these years, and then made it halfway through the task of packing his father's clothing for donation when he heard the back door slam shut. Closing his eyes, he counted to ten before he mastered the impulse to shout his lungs out at his son and his amazing vanishing act.

Mark told himself that yelling wouldn't do anything but raise his blood pressure anyway. Eli was undoubtedly already out of earshot, his tireless campaign well on its way to convincing Stormy the cat to join the Witness Protection Program.

Which reminded Mark, as he hurried toward the back door—he needed to figure out what to do about that animal. No one would adopt what was essentially a wild cat, and there was no way he was trapping it and hauling the squalling, hissing creature all the way to Pittsburgh next week.

At the thought of his return trip, a pang of regret hit at the same moment the telephone started ringing. Mark hesitated in the kitchen—and spotted movement through the window.

"Well, I'll be damned," he said. Eli was crouching just behind the house, his hand outstretched, his manner unruffled. The gray tabby walked up to him and rubbed her bony back against the boy's palm. Petting herself, in effect.

Still watching, Mark picked up the phone on the fourth ring.

"Hi." Beth Ann's voice. Sexy as ever, but sounding nervous. "Just thought I'd check to see if you're still coming. I need to know how many I should cook for."

"That depends," Mark said. "Do you still want us?"

It was a loaded question, and he knew it. Making love to Beth Ann had meant far more to him than the fulfillment of a cherished fantasy. He wanted more; he wanted *her.* But her tears had left him feeling helpless—and worse yet, *responsible,* especially when she'd been unable to explain why she was crying. He'd instinctively apologized, then flashed forward to an endless series of such incidents. Beth Ann hurting, for whatever reason. His own, knee-jerk pleas for her forgiveness, again and yet again.

He had already learned from Rachel that guilt was no basis for a relationship. Day by day, it undermined, digging away at love's foundations until the whole damned relationship came crashing down into the pit. Better to head back to Pittsburgh, to cut both of their losses before either of them passed the point of no return.

"Of course I want you here, Mark. Both of you."

Her answer sounded so good and honest, he suspected it was already too late to turn back. He should have known it would be, should have guessed that Beth Ann would never give her body without letting go of her heart in the process.

"You said something about other guests?" Safer that way, he thought.

Until she said, "The Rikers."

"After what I told you happened, you mean *Pete* Riker's gonna be there?" Mark was shaking his head, though he knew she couldn't see it. "I don't think so, Beth Ann."

Aside from what had happened sixteen years earlier, that bastard had scared the bejesus out of Eli. And for all Mark knew, Riker was still hoping to put him back in prison.

"Oh, no. Not Pete," Beth Ann said. "I never would have asked *him,* but he has to work Thanksgiving. And anyway, no matter what I think of the rotten things he's done, Cheryl's been my best friend for years, and those three girls are sweethearts. Eli knows the youngest from Mrs. Minton's, Abby, the little blonde. Have you seen her?"

A knot loosened inside Mark. "Are you kidding? The famous Abby is a Riker? Eli talks about her nonstop and draws her pictures every night. I think the kid's in love."

He snorted, trying to contain his laughter. Pete Riker must not know about it, or he'd have probably yanked his daughter out of daycare. The idea that their children's friendship would piss Riker off made Mark's decision that much easier.

"Sure we'll be there," he said. "Wouldn't miss it. Just tell us when to come and what to bring."

She had given him the time and was arguing that he was to bring only himself and Eli when Mark happened to glance out the window.

His son was gone, as was the tabby. But what started Mark's heart pounding was the sunlight gleaming off a small object lying forlorn on a patch of hard-baked clay soil.

It was Eli's silver deputy's badge, the one he insisted upon wearing everywhere.

"I've gotta go," Mark said, trying to control the panic ripping through him. "Eli was outside—I was watching. But I must have looked away a minute. I don't see him anywhere now."

"He's probably just—"

Mark never knew what she was going to say. He was already hanging up the phone, with some paternal instinct urging him to find his young son—before it was too late.

Chapter 23

If he had the nerve, Damon Stillwater would ask his mama to bake a pan of brownies to give to Agnes Miller as a thank you. Because of her complaint about the "insolent questions" he'd asked, Damon had been put back on days, where Sheriff Morrell could "keep a good eye" on him.

Damon knew he'd gotten off darned lucky. Morrell had been tempted to fire him for disobeying a direct order. He'd said as much, three times. But he'd also said he liked the fire in his newest deputy's belly, which put the old man to mind of his younger self, not to mention his supposedly sainted son, Scotty, whose photo hung on the wall behind the sheriff's desk. So instead of getting punished, Damon had been taken under his hero's wing—and allowed access to details on the Lilly Decker killing.

Now Damon sat alone in the conference room, where he pored over the file. He skipped the crime-scene photos, which threatened to bring this morning's bacon and pancakes back for a return engagement, and focused on the accounts of interviews.

Morrell, Gustavsen, and Riker had been more meticulous than he'd imagined. They had interviewed Mrs. Decker's current and past neighbors, a number of purported lovers, and estranged friends resentful of Lilly's "tightness" when it came to sharing her newfound wealth. Damon had always figured money solved a person's troubles, but it seemed, at least in Lilly's case, to have stirred up a host of hard feelings. Though people hated speaking ill of the dead—particularly while being interviewed by law enforcement—struggling business owners, many of whom were members of Eudena's revitalization committee, were clearly upset that Mrs. Decker had chosen to spend her money outside Hatcher County.

But on the surface, none of those interviewed stood out as a suspect. Those few who seemed especially bitter, including Lilly's old running buddy, Gertrude Pederson of Barty's One-Stop, had come up with solid alibis—which had left those investigating to explore the rumor that Lilly Decker had kept money in her house.

Word had traveled far and wide, it seemed, from the town itself to the Mexican encampment, which teemed with poverty and stank of desperation. It was even possible that the tale had caught the ear of out-of-town criminals, dangerous drifters who had started carving Lilly in an attempt to torture her into revealing the whereabouts of the treasure trove behind a wall or underneath some floorboard. There had been attempts to track the movements of known violent felons in the region, but so far, nothing much had come of the effort, nor of attempts to interview the Mexicans, who tended to scatter whenever the authorities approached.

Katie Hill stuck her head inside the doorway and favored Damon with a pretty smile that set up an answering flutter inside his chest. Though the petite brunette had been two years ahead of him in school, here in the grown-up world, that didn't seem like so much of an obstacle.

"Call's come in and I can't reach anyone else to take it," she said nervously. She had been hired only a week before to replace the retiring Dorothy. Pete Riker, whose daughters she sometimes babysat, had recommended her. Katie was still learning the ropes of dispatch and had recently confessed to Damon she was scared to death of screwing up and having to go back to working at her daddy's funeral home for the rest of her life. She'd been the one to paint the cheeks and style the hair of dead folks, a job she hated with all her heart.

"I don't mind. That's what I'm here for." Damon stuck out his chest in an attempt to look manly and experienced, and he flipped shut the murder file.

Katie's big brown eyes looked grateful before she glanced down at the note in her trembling hand. "It's a missing child, on Lost Buffalo. Over at the Jessup place. Did you—do you need a street address? Oh, Lord. I forgot to ask that. Should I call him back? He seemed pretty upset, frantic almost. But I guess I can't blame him. It's a five-year-old boy who's missing, and that's a nasty stretch of prairie. It's chilly, too, this morning, and his father said the little fellow slipped out without his jacket."

"No problem," Damon said, thrilled to have this chance to look heroic. "I know just where that is. I'll hightail it over to coordinate the search."

* * *

The unnatural little freak had seen him, seen him and was about to run squalling to his father. But the kid had made a big mistake, edging back behind the ranch house, out of sight of any of the windows. Far enough from view that with a running start, he had cut the boy off, then grabbed for him with the intention of scaring the living snot out of him, of threatening to eviscerate that cat if word of this morning's "visit" got out.

But the wretched little heathen was faster than he looked. He'd darted away, then made for the dry creek bottom, which was lined with enough low-growing cedars, mesquite, and other brush to hide a hundred brats. There was nothing for it but to try to find him.

The trouble was, the longer this chase went on, the greater the chance there was of getting caught. And though the man had thought at first that a good scare would keep the kid quiet, he changed his mind as he heard someone—Mark Jessup—calling out his son's name. If that sorry bastard found the boy first, the kid would tell him exactly what he'd seen this morning.

If he could talk, that was.

As he released the safety on his weapon, the man gusted out a sigh of resignation. *God forgive me,* he prayed. For all the wrongs he'd done in this world, he had never thought of himself as the kind to kill a child.

Beth Ann was scheduled to visit patients spread out all over the county this morning, but the note of panic in Mark's voice had convinced her to stop out at the Jessup ranch house first.

All the way there she told herself that she would not be needed, that by the time she showed up, Eli would be back inside, drawing racecars while Mark chastised him about running off and scaring him to death. Or maybe she'd pass Mark on the way out to Lost Buffalo as he drove his son to daycare to keep him out of mischief. She told herself a lot of stories, mostly to tamp down the images of Eli's sweet face as he'd handed her a picture or thrown his arms around her neck to hug her.

It was only then she let herself admit that, all joking aside, she really had fallen for the child as completely as she had for his father. *I'm such an idiot. A romantic fool, living inside one of Mama's stories instead of reality. Living in another century, too, if I think for one minute that a man who could easily have his choice of women is going to fall head over heels just because he slept with the one who babysat his son a few times. Deal with it, Beth Ann. We had a few good times, that's all. A little break from our real lives.*

Eli would never be hers, any more than his father. They would go back to Pittsburgh, to a big house and a thriving company. To a place she'd never fit in. Because try as she might, Beth Ann could envision herself nowhere else but here, where she'd attend the dying people and serve as witness to the dying town. She had missed her chance to get out when she came back after college, her return a mostly fruitless effort to keep her mother on the straight and narrow, or at least to save her from herself. Since then, Beth Ann had somehow lost her nerve, internalizing the tragic story—a story built on lies, it turned out—that she had too late tried to cast off.

And what had she gotten for her efforts? A single taste of the sort of life she was missing? And now, the stark terror that this harsh land could have somehow swallowed Eli Jessup.

Still a few miles from the house, she drove past the charred skeletons of acres of scrub trees that had burned in a grass fire during last summer's drought. Ash overlaid the rust of half a dozen dead pump jacks, killed not by the blaze but a drought beneath the surface of the earth.

Beyond the fire-field, the land looked only slightly more hospitable. Thorny mesquite twisted among the brownish grasses as if in pain, and the occasional cedar, a tree that wreaked havoc among those allergic to it every winter, looked no more inviting. Considered nuisance trees by ranchers, both species were often "controlled" but never exterminated, and they had spread over the lost Jessup acreage like a modern-day plague. The only movement that she spotted was a roadrunner sprinting along with a squirming lizard clutched like treasure in its bill.

Was Eli out there somewhere, or was he simply playing, maybe even hiding, among the weather-beaten ranch outbuildings? As she drew close enough to spot them, Beth Ann took inventory of the decaying barn, the well house, and an old shed that had once housed tractors but now served as a garage. So many places a small child could conceal himself—and so many hidden dangers. Containers of weed killer, rotting floorboards, rusted old equipment . . .

Please, God, let him be inside right now, under his father's watchful eye.

She spotted Mark trotting out of the garage, his hands cupped around his mouth. Calling Eli, she was certain. Her heart sank, and she prayed for some other explanation.

Pulling into the driveway, she rolled down the electric window. Before she could frame a question, Mark was asking, "You didn't spot him, did you? Were you looking as you drove up?"

She struggled to hide her alarm. She was used to playing the compassionate but cool-headed professional. This was the time to call on that skill, for Mark's sake. He looked rattled, flushed, with perspiration rolling down his face, though it was no warmer than the mid-fifties.

Shaking her head, she said, "I looked as much as I could, but no, I didn't see him. What's he wearing?"

"I—" Mark put one hand to his forehead. "I can't think—can't remember. Damn it. What kind of father am I if I don't even know what my kid has on?"

"You're a very good father," she said as she grabbed her cane and left the SUV. "Anyone could see that. But I need you to calm down. *Eli* needs you to calm down. Now."

Mark closed his eyes, his face a mask of misery. "I've already called the sheriff's department. I swear, if that boy's playing some sort of game with me—"

"You'll kiss him and hug him and then ground him 'til he's sixteen." She forced a smile as she spoke.

His eyes widened, and he blurted, "Red, white, and blue long-sleeved T-shirt, striped. With a pair of jeans and some white sneakers."

"Shouldn't be too hard to spot," she said. "How do you want to do this? You want me to help you search around the property?"

He shook his head. "I've already looked all over . . . but maybe I missed something. Or maybe I scared him. I can sound a little—um—I get kind of intense when I'm worried like this. I don't mean to, but I—"

"It's all right. Everybody does that." Beth Ann laid a hand on Mark's arm. He wasn't wearing a jacket, but his flesh felt warm, almost fevered. It made her think of the heat the two of them had generated inside the house's living room.

Guiltily, she sent the thought packing. Sex should be the last thing on her mind now.

"The sooner you quit beating yourself up," she said, "the sooner we'll find Eli."

"All right." He drew a deep breath, then eased it out slowly. "Maybe you should look around here. Tell him you've brought Maia for a visit."

"Good thinking." Now that she knew Eli was missing, she wished she *had* brought the Lab. Not that she was under the delusion that Maia was any better suited for tracking than guard duty, but the big dog adored Eli and would doubtless bark with pleasure if she happened upon him on her explorations. "What about you? Will you wait for the deputy?"

He shook his head, sending that rich brown hair across his equally dark eyes. As he shoved the hair away, he answered, "I'm going to take a walk, circle the property about fifty yards out. And you should know I'm taking my dad's old .22 hunting rifle with me."

"You don't think—" She couldn't bring herself to say it, could barely wrap her brain around the bone-jarring idea that evil had set foot here, that it might have taken Eli.

But it wasn't so far-fetched, was it? Since he'd been here, Mark had been insulted and then beaten savagely. Though Gene Calvert was in jail, others still blamed Mark for the crash. Could one of them have taken out that hatred on a little boy? Or could the man

Eli had spotted wandering around here earlier have been someone far more dangerous than Pete Riker? After all, a murderer remained on the loose, the same sick person who had carved up her mother's body.

At the thought of how she'd been killed, Beth Ann's stomach plummeted. They had to find Eli—had to find him right away.

"I don't want to think it." Mark's throat worked, and his muscles tensed. "But I can't discount the possibility. And besides that, not long ago, I killed a big rattler right behind the well house. You be careful where you poke around."

She nodded and tried not to shudder at the thought of snakes. *Ugh.* "All right. And I'll speak to the deputy when he comes."

As Mark went inside to get the rifle, she wondered, would Pete Riker be the one to show up? And if he was, could he push past his animosity toward Mark to do what was needed to find Eli? Pete was a father—maybe an inattentive one at times—but she knew he loved his children and prided himself on his professionalism. Surely, he would put aside personal biases to save a helpless boy.

Beth Ann tried the barn first. Though she left the wide door open, it was dim inside. Looking around, she spotted a few stalls, a number of rusty, old tools hanging along the walls, and a rickety-looking ladder that led up to a swaybacked hayloft. Had Mark already climbed it? Perhaps not, for the ladder looked unlikely to hold a grown man's weight. But a child's—yes, she thought so. Maybe hers as well.

Not that she would go up. She'd come a heck of a long way on physical therapy and sheer stubbornness.

But even if she managed, by some miracle, to climb up there, she'd need a National Guard airlift to haul her down again.

Yelling sounded a lot easier. "Hey, Eli," she called. "Come on out and play with Maia. I have to show you—she's got this great new trick."

The last part was true, anyway. Beth Ann had amused herself by teaching the Lab to balance a biscuit atop her nose, then snap it out of the air upon command. A smart and patient animal, Maia loved the game—or anything else that resulted in her getting more treats.

No sound came back to Beth Ann but the echo of her own voice. Unwilling to give up, she added, "Your daddy's not mad, Eli. You aren't in trouble, promise, but you're kind of scaring us. Please come out now— we'll start a new game. Anything you want."

Once again, no answer. "All right, then. I'm leaving."

She pretended to do just that, waiting just outside the door. But the continued stillness convinced her that he wasn't hiding in the barn.

Moving to the garage and around the well house, she repeated the procedure, with the same lack of success. She was wondering whether to go inside and search the house when she spotted a sheriff department's car coming toward the property. Her stomach clenched as she recognized Damon Stillwater, and she wondered if she would ever again see the young deputy without thinking back to the horrible day he had come to drive her to the Lucky Pull.

Stillwater pulled into the driveway beside Mark's newly repaired truck and shut off his engine before climbing out of the Crown Victoria. He tipped his broad-brimmed hat to Beth Ann, an act so unabashedly old-fashioned that under other circumstances, she surely would have smiled.

"Morning, Miz Decker, ma'am," he said carefully.

Though she didn't need the formality, this was a big improvement over "Poor Beth Ann." She should have threatened to rip lips off years ago.

"Morning, Deputy. I know Mark Jessup called you. His five-year-old son, Eli, is missing."

"Is this unusual?" Damon asked.

"Yes, as far as I know. Mark has mentioned once or twice that he's slipped out to see the barn cat, but Eli's never gone far."

Damon frowned, his expression thoughtful. "Do you know, was he punished when he sneaked out? Could be he's hiding out to save himself a whipping. I know I did the same a time or two myself."

"I can't imagine Mark Jessup whipping Eli. I've spent a lot of time out here—on account of his father—and I've never seen signs that he's anything but a loving dad."

"So where *is* Mr. Jessup?" Damon asked her.

"He said he was walking around the place, about fifty yards out. Every now and then, I hear him calling Eli."

"So what do you think? You know this child. Is he hiding? Lost? Curled up somewhere, sleeping?"

She thought about it, then shook her head. "Not sleeping, I don't think. He's an active little guy, and besides, he wouldn't—what's that?"

She turned toward a rustling sound behind her, but it was only the gray tabby, pouncing on some unfortunate mouse or lizard in the weeds. The cat locked eyes with her, then yowled and tore off behind the garage.

Before she could comment on the animal's jumpiness, a second, louder sound had her whirling around to stare in the direction of the dry creek.

The crack had been a gunshot. She was certain of it.

Drawing his own weapon, Damon yelled, "Get out of sight," and took off running.

Beth Ann shouted after him, "It was probably Mark. He took a rifle in case of snakes or . . ."

She let her voice trail off. The deputy wasn't listening but instead reacting. Which was exactly the sort of action that was going to get somebody killed.

Chapter 24

Though his leg throbbed where he'd gone down to one knee as he had climbed clear of the creek bed, Mark ran blindly, conscious only of the child in his arms and the flow of blood dripping off his elbow. Eli's blood—*Eli's*. He still couldn't grasp that some sick piece of shit had tried to take his son from him—had shot at a five-year-old.

Mark ached to find the bastard, to pump him full of bullets—or better yet, to tear his head off with his bare hands. Stripped of every civilizing layer, Mark was nearly overwhelmed by his raw fury. But even stronger was the panic ripping through him, the desperate need to get Eli to safety.

"It hurts, it hurts." The child's cries were ear-splitting, and he was shaking hard.

Pausing for a moment, Mark crouched behind a gnarled live oak and looked down into his son's face. "I need you to be very brave, son. Can you do that for me?" Mark whispered urgently.

He struggled not to react to the blood dripping from

Eli's split chin. Blood that came not from a gunshot wound, thank God, but the fall that took place when Eli had spotted Mark and started running toward him in the rocky creek bed. The fall that may have saved the child from the bullet that sent fragments of mesquite wood flying a few yards beyond the spot where he'd been moving.

Staring at him gravely, Eli nodded and stopped sobbing. Snuffling, he asked, "Will the bad man get us if he hears?"

Mark measured his words, knowing his reaction could make the difference in his son's recovery from this nightmare. "I'm here now, and I won't let anybody hurt you. You see? I brought Grandpa's gun along to keep us safe."

As Eli glanced down at the .22 Mark held, the boy's eyes grew slightly glassy. "I don't want that man to get us."

He threw his arms around Mark's neck again and squeezed hard. Mark hugged him tight and listened for any sounds of movement. He had to get a bead on where this guy was. So far, Mark hadn't seen him, but that didn't mean the shooter hadn't followed—or hadn't set up in a spot where he could pick off father and son running across the ten yards of open grassland toward the safety of the house. The two of them were close, so close that Mark could hear Beth Ann shouting. But he couldn't trust to chance that he'd lost the gunman by zigzagging among the mesquite trees. With Eli's life in his hands, Mark couldn't afford to make a mistake.

He had promised to keep his son safe, and he damned well meant to do it. But the moment he saw to it, Mark swore he was going hunting—for a human being more evil than the meanest rattler.

He heard someone rapidly approaching: heavy, running footsteps and the sound of a man panting. Eli hunched his shoulders in an attempt to disappear. But Mark peeled away the child's arms and set him behind a rock outcropping.

"Stay quiet," Mark ordered before moving on a collision course with the runner, who seemed to be approaching from the direction of the house.

The opposite direction he would expect the shooter to be coming from. With that split-second realization, Mark raised the muzzle of his rifle just as Deputy Damon Stillwater crashed through the brush, his pistol drawn and his eyes wild.

Instinct made Mark drop the weapon and throw his hands into the air. "It's okay—don't shoot," he told Stillwater. "It's all right."

When the young deputy blanched, a few pink spots of stubborn acne stood out beneath a sheen of sweat. "Was that you?" he yelled, his gun's muzzle pointed straight at Mark's chest. "Was that you firing?"

"Not me. Someone took a potshot at my—"

"That's blood—that's blood on you! Get down. And keep your hands up." Hysteria charged Stillwater's voice, the kind of adrenaline-soaked panic that so often turned deadly.

Rising from his hiding place, Eli shrieked, "Don't you hurt my daddy."

In one horrifying instant, the pistol swung toward the boy. Mark leapt toward Stillwater and struck the deputy's wrist with the heel of his hand.

There was a second crack of gunfire as the weapon discharged, but it was Stillwater who went down to his knees, clutching his injured forearm as he dropped the weapon. "Oh God, oh God, oh God," he repeated as he watched Eli climb into Mark's arms. Tears gleamed in his eyes. "I could have hit him—could have shot a kid."

"You didn't—thank God." Mark stroked his son's trembling back, his own hand shaking just as hard. "But someone else damned near did."

Damon looked up and blinked at Mark. "I think my wrist may be broken."

"It isn't broken." Mark hoped it wasn't, anyway. "You're fine, but you have to pull yourself together right now. Whoever shot at Eli is still out there, so you'll want to pick up your gun. I need you to watch my back while I get my boy inside the house."

Damon rubbed his wrist, then nodded, and Mark saw something switch on in the younger man, some untapped reserve of courage that he had just discovered. After retrieving the pistol, Stillwater straightened his hat and stood.

"I'll take care of it." A promise shone in his green eyes, vanquishing the threat of tears.

Mark had no choice but to believe him. "Ready, Eli? Deputy Stillwater here will watch out for us. He knows you're a junior deputy yourself, so he's bound to protect you."

"That—that's right," Stillwater promised. "I'll—I'll defend you with my life if need be."

A little over-the-top, Mark thought, but the deputy sounded pretty convincing for a guy who'd come damned close to killing them both in his panic. Staring up at Stillwater, Eli wiped away his tears in an effort to look brave, too, and Mark scooped his son up in his arms.

"Wait," Stillwater said. "This shooter—what's he look like?"

"Not sure, I didn't see him," Mark said. "Let's just keep an eye out for anybody else armed."

"Okay." Stillwater nodded. "Yeah."

Mark returned the nod, then turned and started running with Eli toward the house. He changed direction several times, hoping to throw off anyone who might be taking aim.

He spotted Beth Ann near the barn, her cell phone out and her face drained of all color. As he drew closer, she dropped the phone into her pocket and hurried toward him, her gaze glued to Eli.

"He's bleeding," she said. "Is it—he hasn't been . . ."

Panting with a combination of exertion and adrenaline, Mark shook his head. "He tripped and split his chin."

She followed him around the corner of the barn, out of danger, he hoped.

"I heard gunshots," she said. "I just called Sheriff Morrell. He's on his way. That's okay, isn't it? I know you and Morrell have issues . . . over the crash, I mean."

He remembered the sheriff's kindness toward his son and nodded. "Morrell's the least of my worries right now. A bullet came damned close to hitting Eli out there. There's somebody shooting. Maybe the same person who fired on us at Hill's."

"What about the deputy? Did you see Deputy Stillwater?"

He nodded. "I met him out there. He should be here in a minute."

Now that the crisis was over, the days-old bump on Mark's head throbbed, and the bruises on his arms and shoulders echoed a chorus of complaints, along with the knee he'd hit. With a muffled groan, he put Eli down. "You did great, son. Brave and steady."

Eli stared at him with somber eyes, then surprised him by going straight to Beth Ann. Steadying herself with the cane, she squatted to enfold him in a tight hug.

"Here, let me look at that chin," she said, while Mark peered around the corner.

Damon was running toward them, his weapon still in hand. At least he had the muzzle pointed down this time.

"See anybody?" Mark asked.

The deputy shook his head. "Whoever it was probably took off."

"Damned chickenshit feels brave enough to shoot at unarmed people or a little kid," Mark said, "but not brave enough when there's a chance we'll get him.

"Sheriff's coming," he added. "You'll have backup in a minute."

Fear sparked in the younger man's green eyes. "About what went on out there. When I found you. It all happened so fast. I'm really sorry about pointing my gun at your boy."

"Sorry I had to whack your arm, too. But you did fine out there. That's the only part I'm telling your boss."

As Damon nodded, some of the tension visibly melted from his muscles. "What about the shooter? Did you recognize him?"

"I never saw anyone." Mark turned to look at Eli, who stood in silence as Beth Ann looked at his cut. She was speaking softly near the boy's ear, her soothing words and gentle touch reminding Mark of how much his son was missing without a mother in his life. Of how much *he* was missing without a partner he could count on.

The thought threw Mark off kilter for a moment, but there were things they had to know. "How about it, Eli? Do you know who the man was?"

Eli shrugged, his gaze sliding downward to avoid eye contact.

"Was it the same person you saw earlier? The man you talked about with Miz Beth Ann?"

Eli shrugged, then glanced up, trembling and clearly miserable, with tears cascading down his face. "My chin hurts, and I want to go inside now, where the bad man can't get me. I want some SpongeBob Band-Aids and Blue Bunny. And Maia. I want Maia."

Beth Ann looked up, too. "Let me get him cleaned up. I have some butterfly bandages and my nursing bag out in my SUV, and he's had a big scare for a little guy."

"I know, but this is important." Mark felt like a heel for pressing, yet this had to be done. "Did the man have a uniform like Deputy Stillwater's?"

"What?" Damon perked up, his brow wrinkling. "Why would you ask that?"

But Eli's head was shaking. "No, he had on blue pants. Like yours, Dad."

"Jeans, then," Mark said.

Eli nodded. "And a jacket like that, too."

"Then it could be anybody."

Damon repeated, "Why would you ask—?"

"I'm taking him inside now." Beth Ann's jaw had a stubborn set that brooked no argument. "Questions can wait, but if one of you can grab my bag and bring it in—"

"I'll get it," Mark said.

She took Eli by the hand and walked him up to the house.

Mark watched them go inside, then looked at Still-water. "Eli spotted Pete Riker poking around out here a while back. Only Riker scared the kid so bad, my son didn't mention it for days. And he only told Beth Ann because he had a nightmare. That Deputy Riker was coming back to 'get' me."

A flicker of surprise in Damon's expression prompted Mark to add, "Beth Ann kept Eli for me while I was in the hospital."

She wouldn't appreciate it if a rumor started that she'd been sleeping over. This might be the twenty-first century, but Eudena still judged women harshly for the same activities that earned men slaps on the back.

Damon frowned. "I can't imagine Pete would scare your son on purpose. Maybe he came out, uh, in the course of his, um, his investigation. Into, you know, the homicide."

Lilly Decker's, he meant. Mark huffed out a sigh. "I'm sure he'd love to pin that on me. Trouble is, I didn't do it."

The deputy stared at him, then nodded. "That's what the sheriff says, too. And the more I think about it, the less likely it seems to me, too, the idea of you showing up out of the blue and going after Miz Lilly after all these years."

"That's mighty big of you."

Stillwater grimaced at the sarcasm before shrugging. "An investigator's gotta think for himself. Based on the evidence and not emotion."

"So what if the *evidence* points toward Pete Riker?" Mark asked. "Would you think for yourself then, too?"

Stillwater blew out a big breath but didn't answer. Mark hadn't expected any different. The deputy was hardly more than a kid, for one thing, a kid who'd grown up steeped in the tragic legend of dead cheer-leaders and a boy called Hell on Wheels.

Mark excused himself to get the nursing kit for Beth Ann and see to his son. They waited inside for the sher-iff, as if Morrell might bring answers instead of ques-tions, as if he would bring safety instead of more uncertainty.

"How's my number-one junior deputy?" Sheriff Morrell asked as he came in from the backyard.

Eli was sitting on the kitchen counter with slumped shoulders while Beth Ann washed the dried blood off his neck with a warm washcloth. In spite of her and Mark's efforts to engage him, he had hardly said a word in the last twenty minutes. Instead, he kept glanc-ing anxiously toward the window, though Mark had closed the blinds. Even so, the red flash of emergency lights pulsated at the edges of the slats.

The boy shrugged in answer to the sheriff's question and squeezed his father's hand.

"The butterfly bandages will do for the time being." Beth Ann tried not to show her worry, not for Eli's phys-ical but his emotional condition. He looked better since his dad had come back inside, but the boy's un-characteristic stillness troubled her. "He'll need a few stitches, though. Nothing they can't handle over at the county E.R."

Mark started to say something, but Eli interrupted. "Will I get to have a real scar?"

Beth Ann smiled at the spark of animation in his voice. "Maybe a little one."

Eli looked up at Mark. "Just like you, Dad."

Beth Ann felt something pass between Mark and Morrell as their gazes locked. The look was so unfriendly that she would swear she felt the room's temperature drop by ten degrees.

"Yes, Eli," Mark said without breaking eye contact with the sheriff. "Just like me."

Beth Ann shivered, thinking of the story Mark had told her about the night of the collision. Fully accepting that the sheriff had kept it hidden all these years.

At the thought of the accident, a tendril of scent rose from out of the past. Sweet, almost medicinal, with a taste that lingered on her tongue like . . .

"Stop, Beth Ann!" cried Jordan. But the brake pedal squashed under her foot like a marshmallow, and the headlights filled Beth Ann's vision.

She blinked back the threat of tears as a rushing sound filled her ears. By the time the noise diminished, she heard Morrell reassuring Eli that he was doing everything in his power to make sure the bad man didn't trouble his best deputy again.

"I've got practically my whole department out here," he said as he handed the boy his missing badge. "Called in men from every shift and told 'em all to search the area and see what they can turn up."

She forced herself to focus on the present, to shunt aside the ugly past.

"Pete Riker, too?" Mark asked him.

"Sure, Pete's coming. Talked to him myself. And Ted Gustavsen, Jay Hill, and Charlie Colson, too, if that makes you feel any better. Now if you'll excuse me, I'd best go on out and do some supervisin' so I can earn the county's paycheck."

Morrell lost no time in getting back outside, and Eli slid down from the counter, his hand clutching the badge. "Are we going to get my scar now? At the hospital?"

Mark smiled. "Pretty quick, I think. Your clothes are awfully messy, though, so why don't you go in your room and pick out a fresh pair of jeans and a clean shirt. I'll be there in a minute to help you change."

"I can do that." Eli sounded exasperated as he explained to Beth Ann, "I'm *not* a baby. I'm a junior deputy."

"Guess he'll be all right, after all," she said as he left the room.

Mark sighed. "I sure hope so. I swear, Beth Ann, it took years off my life when I heard that gunshot. And then Stillwater came running and damned near blew both our heads off. I don't mind telling you, I've never been so scared in my life."

"I know. I wasn't even there, and I couldn't raise the spit to swallow. I still can't believe anyone would try to hurt a little boy like that. I can't imagine the depravity." To give her hands something to do, Beth Ann grabbed the coffeepot and glanced at Mark. When he nodded his permission, she added, "This hardly seems like Eudena anymore to me, Mark. These kinds of things don't happen here. They just *don't.*"

"But they are happening. First, with your mother, and then with some kind of whacked-out sniper."

She turned from the sink, where she was filling the glass pot with water. "It doesn't make sense. *Why?*"

"And what's the common thread?" Mark asked her. "I can understand why some people here might hate me. Because of the accident, most likely, and the fact that they don't understand my business's objectives. I can even imagine some sicko deciding to punish me by hurting my kid—though whoever the hell did it better hope the sheriff catches him before I do."

"Unless it *is* someone with the sheriff's office. . . ."

Beth Ann said. "I suppose that's possible, considering the cover-up Morrell and Riker were involved in."

They both stood, silent and thoughtful, as Beth Ann poured the water into the machine, then grabbed an open can of coffee from where she knew he kept it in the refrigerator. Once she'd pried off the plastic lid, she asked, "But if it's about the accident, what could that possibly have to do with my mother? I'll admit, she's had her share of detractors, folks who didn't approve of the way she lived or were jealous of her money. You wouldn't believe the calls and the letters and the visits we got. Threats, too. She had to change her number and hire security for a while."

Mark rubbed his forehead. "Maybe there is no common thread. I mean, what happened to your mother was closeup, personal. This—this sniper is shooting from a distance, keeping hidden. Whoever it is, maybe he's not trying to kill, after all. Maybe he just wants me to leave town."

"I wouldn't bet my life on that theory." She added one last scoop to the basket before switching on the coffeemaker.

"Neither would I. And I especially won't take a chance with Eli's safety. The more I think about it, the more I'm inclined to hire someone to finish up my business here. I was going to wait until next week to leave, but proving a point's not worth the chance of him getting hurt or traumatized again. Or worse."

Beth Ann's throat ached, and loss balled up deep inside her. "You're leaving." A statement, not a question. She'd known this day was coming. And of course, Mark had to put his child's safety first. It wasn't as if he'd made her any promises.

The coffeemaker gurgled noisily, its brew's aroma nudging the bare edge of her awareness.

He stepped nearer, then caught her hand in both of his. She cursed, feeling herself shaking.

"Beth Ann," he whispered.

"Don't. Don't look at me that way, Mark." The hunger in his brown eyes only made things harder. "What happened between us, it was nice. No, it was much more that that. It was the most amazing—"

"You called me Jess before."

She dropped her gaze and tried in vain to pull her hand away. "This is too hard. I don't want you to think I'm trying to dig my claws in, to make you feel obligated just because of one—"

He leaned forward and took her mouth in a kiss that made her knees weak. Forgetting everything, from the sheriff and deputies outside to Eli down the hall, she opened her lips to his tongue, opened her body to a wave of pleasure, and opened her soul to the knowledge that this was real and right and . . . this was love. She'd gone and fallen in love for the first time in her life. And it was as magical and as wonderful as anything she'd ever known. As big as the prairie sky and as—

She came back to herself as he cupped her breast and thumbed a nipple. Remembering all those things she had forgotten, she pushed herself away from him. Fear poured into the core of her, an icy flood that chilled her to the marrow.

Love made people stupid. Hadn't she learned that lesson from witnessing her mother's foolishness all these years? How many times had she watched Lilly soar with giddy pleasure at some new relationship, only to crash down into misery when it ended? This hormonal high tide could not be trusted. Especially not with the last thing that she'd remembered from the crash lodged like a secret splinter in her heart.

"Sorry," Mark said. "It's too easy to get carried away when I'm around you. If we were here alone, oh, God, the things I want to do to you . . ."

A sensuous chill rippled through her, and she closed her eyes against the tumble of images his words prompted.

"Look, Beth Ann, I don't want this to end, what's between us. I'm not sure how it'll work out, but I do know one thing. What I feel for you, it's more than lust. More than the best sex I've ever had. I love you, *you,* not just that body, and I want to spend more time together, to see if we can—"

"Daddy?"

Eli was staring at them, looking from one to another, clearly trying to make sense of their proximity to each other. How much had he heard?

Beth Ann sucked in a deep breath. Oxygen—that's what she needed. A lungful of clarity to cool her overheated brain.

Mark backed away from her and cleared his throat. "You'd better comb your hair, champ. It's all sticking up from changing your shirt. Then we'll go and get that scar worked on."

Eli frowned, but after heaving an impatient sigh, he headed for the bathroom.

"You might want to grab another shirt, too," Beth Ann told Mark. "Yours has blood all over it."

The pain in his eyes, as he stared back at her, forced her to look away.

"Beth Ann, you can't just ignore what I said to you. Or was I an idiot not to realize you're sorry we ever made love?" Bitterness edged his voice. "Guess I should've gotten a clue from the way you were bawling."

Her head shook. "I'm *not* sorry. God knows, that's not it. And I—I have feelings for you, too, Mark, or I never would have— Look, we both have a lot on our plate right now. The sheriff's out there, and I'm sure he'll want to talk to you before you take Eli to Jackrabbit General. And I have patients waiting, lots of them. Please, can we discuss this more tomorrow? Or do you plan to leave before then?"

"I'll stay tomorrow, Beth Ann. But whether it's before the turkey or after everybody's sleeping off their pumpkin pie, you and I are damned well going to talk this through."

Chapter 25

Beth Ann was glad no one else had been available to see her patients. Her lateness kept her hopping all through the afternoon and well into the evening as she raced from one end of the county to the other, with only one brief pit stop at the house to meet the Wichita Falls service technician she'd bribed to deliver her SUV—sans broken glass—and pick up her loaner car. Afterward, she'd tended Maia and grabbed a sandwich, which she ate on the fly. Her patients' needs kept her from thinking of her own, and when a fifty-two-year-old woman lost her fight with colon cancer, the family's grief kept her professional and focused. As she raced along a deserted stretch of prairie beneath a star-strewn sky, she understood that in some strange way, the act of dealing with their tears had stanched her own.

Just as it had kept her from thinking of the taste and smell of sloe gin that came roaring back from the past while she'd stood in Mark Jessup's kitchen. Exhausted from the long day, she flashed onto a fresh memory of the sweet, red liqueur, sitting among the bottles Mama and Daddy once had kept on the top shelf of the closet.

The sudden shock of recall jolted Beth Ann hard enough to send her SUV jouncing off the pavement, where the right wheels crackled over a stony stretch of shoulder. With a cry catching in her throat, she wrestled for control, struggling to put the speeding Highlander back onto solid pavement. But the tires had caught in the groove formed by the pavement's drop off into eroded gravel so that when she finally wrestled the SUV back onto the road, it shot across the left lane and beyond, onto the shoulder and then bounced down over clumps of tough prairie grasses.

Inches from an old fencepost, she brought the vehicle to a rattling halt and sat frozen, far too terrified to scream. Too overwhelmed to do anything but shake as more of that lost evening filled her to overflowing.

The sloe gin was the only alcoholic beverage whose taste didn't make her gag. She'd tried all the bottles at one point or another in the last months, thinking it would be cool to casually mention how she'd had some rye or drunk some vodka. But they were all disgusting, even worse than the beer Scotty had tried and tried to coax her into drinking. She began to think he must be right, that she'd never really fit in, not the way she went all queasy and made excuses whenever his big hands squeezed her breasts or crept down toward her panties.

If she were normal, she would like it, he'd said, like practically every other girl on Earth did. He'd hinted that other girls had offered—she suspected her so-called friend, Aimee—since Beth Ann was such a prick tease. If she learned to toss back a few, it would loosen her up, get her in a party mood and she'd stop being so uptight about her dad being sick and getting in her scholarship applications and all that stuff that made her a boring loser. On the night Scotty had wondered aloud how she could be so frigid considering the kind of mother she had, Beth Ann had finally dumped the jerk for good.

Scotty might be history, but Beth Ann was still determined to tease loose her knot of worry, determined enough that she kept gagging down disgusting sips from bottle after bottle whenever her mom was out and Dad was resting. She'd nearly given up her quest when she found the full bottle of cherry Kool-Aid–colored nectar pushed far to the back of the collection.

The stuff wasn't half bad, especially when Beth Ann mixed it with some Sprite, and she'd been so damned relieved, she'd drunk enough to make her dizzy and a little sick. After cheer practice the next day, she'd made such a big deal out of it—working it up to be the next best thing since milk chocolate—that Heidi and Larinda made her promise to sneak the bottle to the party after homecoming. Both admitted they weren't crazy about beer either. And though she'd seemed unsure at first, shy little Jordan Jessup had begged the group to promise she wouldn't be left out when they tried it. A year younger than the others, she'd bought her way into the party by offering to make Jello shots and bring them along for the ride, too.

So after the Hawks came back from a 0-14 first half and beat the Electra Tigers with a vengeance, Beth Ann slipped the bottle into her bag before going to kiss her dad goodbye in his room.

"I'm real sorry I didn't get to see you cheer tonight," he said as he hugged her, his silvery whiskers scratching her cheek. "I meant—I wanted to drive over, but my legs're givin' me a bucketful of grief this evening."

"It's okay, Dad. I understand," she said, barely notic-
ing the swelling or the way the big man struggled to
catch his breath. Congestive heart failure, the doctors
had told him. He'd been struggling with it for three years
now, stuttering toward an ending he had promised Beth
Ann was still a long way down the line. She tried not to
think about it, except to work extra hard at school and
with her cheering because it made him so darned
proud. She pretended that his gushing embarrassed her
to pieces, but the truth was, she ate it all up, banking
each word of praise inside her memory against a day—
still distant, she prayed—when her daddy wouldn't be
there.

"Your mama back yet?" he asked her.

"No." Beth Ann supposed she sounded sulky. Lord
only knew where her mother had gone after the game
and who she was out with this time. Beth Ann was sick
of all the whispers, but she would rather die than men-
tion it to her poor father. "And she promised me she'd let
me take her car this evening. I really hate to call Larinda
after I said I'd take her and the others to the party. I can't
stand letting them down. Again."

Sometimes she'd like to give her mama a good
smack. What an embarrassment.

"I'll tell you what." Her father smiled at her. "You see
my keys there, on the dresser. You're taking my car to-
night."

"The Camaro?" A thrill zinged through her, pinging off
each nerve ending. Her mother's station wagon was a
disgrace, with its wood side panels marred by chips and
dents where Lilly had banged into this or that. Because of
Mama's carelessness—and a fistful of speeding tickets—
Dad refused to let her drive the sports coupe, which had
mostly sat out in the garage in the six months since he

had bought it. Sleek and black as midnight, it was a limited-edition I ROC-Z model, her father's last attempt to recapture the spirit of his legendary hell-raising youth. Never had there been any question of Beth Ann's driving it before, since her dad insisted it was way too much car for an inexperienced teenaged driver to handle.

But now he was smiling indulgently and telling her, "Hell, Beth Ann, I couldn't be there to see you cheer at your senior-year homecoming game—least I can do is find some way to make your evening special. You've been real responsible since you got your license. A sight better than your mama, between you and me."

She felt herself blush, pleasure warming her face and making her tingle to her fingertips. Her "friend" Aimee, who'd gone down on every damned thing but the Titanic, had been crowned homecoming queen tonight, but when Beth Ann drove out to the party, she would be the envy of all her friends. And Mr. Homecoming King, Scotty Morrell, who'd had to hitch a ride in his cousin's crappy pickup, could darned well eat his heart out. She might even kiss Mark Jessup if he showed up, just to watch her ex turn green. As excitement rushed in on her, she hugged her dad and squealed "I love you" until he laughed and started coughing.

When he recovered, he said, "Now, you remember, Beth Ann, that engine's gotta lot of punch to it. You have to promise me that you'll be careful—and take it easy on that gas pedal."

After a final squeeze, she gave her solemn word. But her mind was already busy picturing how she'd look as she and her friends poured out of the Camaro into the Kellers' barnyard, their spirits high and their lips tasting of the sweet, red nectar of sloe gin.

Thanksgiving Day

Mark finally cornered Beth Ann in the kitchen when he carried in the last few pumpkin pie plates. He'd been trying to steal a private word with her all day, but he had barely been able to get her to make eye contact, and she'd come up with pretext after pretext to keep from being alone with him.

As she turned, he realized that she was talking on the phone. "Please, Rosario. You have the new key—it's a good lock—and you have the new alarm code. Come back to work tomorrow. You don't have to wear that silly uniform. Burn the darned thing for all I care. And you can bring your sister, if that would help you to feel safer."

There was a pause; then Beth Ann rolled her eyes. "Yes, I'll pay your sister for her time, too. Thanks, Rosario. You know I could never keep up this house without you."

As she hung up, she shook her head. "My house-keeper thinks the place is haunted. It probably is—by dust bunnies, since she hasn't been coming. Not that I blame her. She was the one who found . . ."

Her gaze went vacant, and Mark knew Beth Ann was reliving the one nightmare she recalled in full.

"Great dessert," he said, too loudly, to distract her. "You must've worked your fingers to the bone on all that delicious food."

She nodded, then turned to fill the sink with sudsy water. She had served the pie on fragile, gold-edged plates—her Mama's best, she'd explained solemnly—with fussy silver forks, none of which looked likely to survive the dishwasher. Fortunately, Cheryl's girls and

Eli had had no accidents, and Mark was happy to deliver what Beth Ann called the "frou-frou ware" intact.

"Is Cheryl coming with the rest?" Beth Ann said over her shoulder. She looked anxious, as if his presence unnerved her no less than her memories.

"No, this is all of it. Besides, Cheryl's conked out on the sofa, and it's my turn to help, anyway, since you two refused to let me wash up the dinner dishes."

"Well, somebody had to watch the kiddos," she said. Avoiding eye contact again.

He shook his head. "They've been playing board games, fussing over Maia, and watching videos in the media room all day—which is what they're doing right now. At least the ones who haven't dropped off yet. My theory is you're just a sexist about men in the kitchen. This is nothing but discrimination."

That got a smile from her. About damned time, he thought.

"Maybe I was trying to keep you from stealing all my culinary secrets. I'd hate for you and Eli to open a big restaurant chain in Pittsburgh and cut me out of the profits."

This kitchen certainly looked like something a gourmet chef would use. Her mother had had all the high-end accoutrements put into it, from coffee brown, deeply spangled granite counters to top-of-the line appliances to enough rich, custom wood cabinets to hide a vast arsenal of cooking gizmos. He spotted Beth Ann's cane leaning against the L-bend in those cabinets, out of the way so she could keep both her hands free. He still detected the scent of turkey, yet he didn't find a single splotch of grease or crumb, though the two women hadn't spent long cleaning up.

Grinning, he threw open the huge, state-of-the-art refrigerator and gestured toward the pie box, which bore a label from Sandi Sawyer's bed and breakfast. As did the containers of leftover cornbread stuffing and candied sweet potatoes. And the turkey, too. "Gotcha. Some culinary secret, faker."

"Huh," said Beth Ann. "Did that so-called, soon-to-be-ex best friend of mine rat me out?"

"Actually, it wasn't Cheryl. An anonymous caller phoned around midnight to tell me you'd been seen loading up your SUV at Mrs. Sawyer's under the cover of darkness. And that you really couldn't cook a lick, if that's what I was counting on to keep my son and me fed."

Beth Ann's laughter echoed through the kitchen. "Did this 'anonymous caller' by any chance have Aimee Gustavsen's patented come-hither drawl?"

"Well, now that you mention it . . ." He was still pissed over Aimee's idiotic effort to cause trouble. Besides that, she'd woken him from a great dream involving a certain gorgeous redhead he was itching to get his hands on again soon.

"I could learn to cook if I wanted to," Beth Ann was quick to point out. "But what the devil's the use of having money if it doesn't get you out of doing stuff you don't like?"

"Can't argue with that." He looked her up and down and was disappointed when she tensed. "I was only going to say you look tired, Beth Ann. I wasn't planning to jump your bones here in the kitchen. Although, I have to confess, the thought has crossed my mind."

About every fifteen seconds . . .

"I'm sorry. Yesterday was . . . awful. I still haven't gotten over hearing those shots and wondering whether you'd been hit, or Eli." Turning from him, she plunged her hands beneath the suds and stared out through a window. It overlooked the backyard pool, which reflected the bruised colors of the twilight sky.

"Lord, I wish the sheriff and his men would catch someone," she said. "They've been striking out on all counts lately. This all seems like one never-ending nightmare."

He moved behind her, placed a hand on each of her hips and breathed in the lightly floral fragrance of her hair, which she'd scraped back and clamped into a hairclip. It was all he could do not to tease loose the soft strands at her neck, to rub their silkiness between his fingers.

"Let me take care of those dishes," he insisted. "You sit right here on the barstool."

A shiver rippled through her, probably because he'd all but blown the suggestion, hot and soft, into her ear. Instead of arguing, she wiped her hands on a linen dishtowel and let him lead her to the island counter, where she took a seat. "I *am* tired," she admitted. "I worked late, and then I was up worrying half the night. And thinking about how this was going to be my first big holiday without Mama."

She shook her head, moisture gleaming at the lower rims of her eyes. "Not that the famous Lilly Decker was all that much fun at holidays. Half the time she just sat chain-smoking and sipping whiskey sours while she moped about how her latest big love couldn't be here. Usually because he was with his wife and family. And when one of her, ah, gentlemen *did* drop by, she'd quit sipping and start tossing back those drinks in earnest. Then there'd be some carryin' on, loud music—it could get a little sloppy. Mama might not've been an educated woman, but the one bit of Latin she understood real well was carpe diem."

Beth Ann smiled at some memory. She clearly missed the woman, for all of Lilly's foibles.

"I wish my dad had seized the day a little better." Mark washed another plate, then rinsed it and placed it in the dish drain. "After Jordan died, the man just plain gave up. I wish I could've been there for him. Maybe there was some way I could have made a difference."

"You did. You forgave him. And you came back here for him and helped him get to know his grandson before he died."

"For all it meant to him."

"It meant a lot," she assured him, "even if he couldn't show it."

"I'd like to think that's true. That this whole trip wasn't wasted."

When he noticed the way her expression closed off, he cursed himself as an idiot. "Except for getting to know you. I'd never count that as a waste."

"Nice save, Mr. Smooth."

He laughed. "It's good to see you smiling. I've been worried about you today. And about us, too."

She gave her head a shake. "There isn't an 'us,' Mark. Just a special memory."

"Why, Beth Ann? Distance doesn't have to end this. Not with phones and e-mail—you do have a computer, don't you?" At her nod, he continued. "And you can come and visit us, get an idea about how you'd like living in the Northeast."

She simply stared at him, the color fading from her face. His heartbeat raced in response to the sight.

"What's wrong? Am I moving too fast for you? Maybe I am, but I don't want to blow this thing between us just because I need to get my son away." He knew he was talking too much, risking too much, but every passing moment weighed on him as a lost chance. "I meant what I said yesterday. Since I was a kid, I've had a thing for you; you know that. But that was just a crush, nothing compared to the way I feel now that I've gotten to know you as a woman. Sure, we have some things to work out, and you need time to decide what you feel. But for my part, I love you, Beth Ann, and that's not going to change whether I'm in Pittsburgh or on Pluto. I'd like to get you clear of Hatcher County, too. I want you with me, Beth Ann."

She sighed. "Your feelings could change, Mark. And they *will* change. When I tell you everything I know about the accident, everything I've remembered."

"Beth Ann, that was years ago. It's all water under the bridge. There's nothing you could tell me that would make one bit of differ—"

"We were drinking that night, Mark, the other girls and I. Passing around a bottle I'd filched from my parents and downing Jello shots as fast as we could. *I* was drinking that night, even though I was behind the wheel."

He winced, but shook his head without a moment's hesitation. "At this point, what does it matter?"

All he wanted was to put that night behind him. Behind *them,* in the hope they could move forward.

"Of course it matters," she insisted. "I was a damned idiot."

"I'll agree it was a stupid thing to do."

"Incredibly stupid, irresponsible, and let's not forget criminal, while we're at it. Don't you see? It was my fault. We were passing the stuff around and laughing, and I got so distracted, I didn't look both ways before pulling out—"

"And I was in the wrong lane, thanks to Calvert and his buddies."

"Jordan saw. She screamed for me to stop, but I must have been impaired because the brake felt like I was mashing down through whipped cream. For all I know, I pushed the gas pedal instead."

Mark closed his eyes and dragged in a deep breath, giving himself a moment to sort out how he felt about this possibility. Yes, anger was flashing through the mixture, and grief, too, at the mention of his sister's cry, which meant that she *had* seen death bearing down on her, that she'd been scared in that last moment. But relief was there, too, in the strange brew of his emotions. Stark gratitude that he was not the only one to blame.

"I'm so sorry." Emotion clotted Beth Ann's voice, and he thought she might be crying.

Some vindictive facet of him thought: *Good for you. Now you know how I felt, how I've felt all these years. How it feels when your apologies mean nothing against the enormity of what you did.*

But that small, mean impulse crumbled like ash against her pain: a raw, fresh wound compared to the scar tissue he'd been living with for so long. After drying his hands, he went to her. She stood and looked into his face. "I'll never be able to tell you how very, very—"

He stopped her by wrapping his arms around her. He stroked her back and whispered, "I know how sorry, Beth Ann. I *know.*"

"You do." She sniffled, then reached for a napkin and used it to blow her nose. "You're the only one who could begin to understand it."

He removed her hair clip, which was poking his shoulder, and smoothed her soft hair as it tumbled free. "When did you remember, Beth Ann?"

"It started yesterday at your house. The rest came

when I was driving home last night. It crushed me like a landslide. I nearly had a wreck."

"No wonder you didn't sleep."

He felt her nod against him.

"I didn't know what I should do, and I was so scared."

"Scared of what?" he asked her.

"Of telling you, for one thing. You've taken all the blame for so long. Calvert's share, and his friends', Jim Morrell's and Pete's. And mine, too, it turns out."

Doubt flickered through his consciousness, eating away at both relief and pity. "There's blame enough to go around—if what you say really happened."

Her head shook. "But it *hasn't* gone around, Mark. That's what needs to be fixed."

"I don't understand what you mean. I don't want anyone else hurt or sued or in jail, Beth Ann. Least of all, the woman I love."

She pushed herself away from his chest to stare up into his face. "How could you possibly still think you love me?"

"I don't think I love you," he said. "I know it. I love you for your gentleness with kids and animals and dying people. I love your smart mouth and that sexy hair and the way you say exactly what's on your mind. And I love your courage, too. I can't think of another woman who'd have been brave enough to tell me what you just did. Do you remember when I said how I was afraid, back in school, that you were too good for me? I still think that, Beth Ann, only now that I've had a taste of you, I'm never backing down."

The words reverberated off the hard surfaces around them, words that Mark could not believe had come out of his mouth. But it was too late to take them back, too late to worry that he'd made a fool of himself or scared her off by coming on too strong. There was nothing left except to wait and see how she reacted.

Clearly stunned, Beth Ann blinked up at him until she finally asked, "You finished?"

His heart sank. "Finished what?"

Mischief sparkled in her blue eyes. "Finished listing all the stuff you love about me. I could go on listening forever."

He laughed before he kissed her, and the joy of it overrode the anguish and the anger her admission had churned up. For he tasted hope on her lips, hope that he could have a lifetime with this woman and that she might learn to feel for him the way he did for her.

As he deepened the kiss, she sucked at his lower lip, which sent a jolt of pure lust through his body and had his hand reaching up to massage one of her full breasts. She moaned deep in her throat and squirmed against him, shifting one leg so that her thigh rubbed up against his stiffness. He was already fumbling with the top button of her jeans when rational thought hit him.

He'd never realized how much he hated rational thought.

Stepping back from her, he dragged in a deep breath.

"No more of that," he told her, "unless you want one of those kids walking in on me tearing off your clothes and doing you right here." He slapped the counter with a palm. Something in the contrast of the hard, cool surface with Beth Ann's soft warmth, along with the odd, refractive qualities of the granite, made the expanse surprisingly appealing.

"That sounds just about perfect," she said dreamily, "except for the part about getting interrupted. And contributing to the delinquency of someone other than yourself."

Lust arced through him at her sultry tone. "Damn it, Beth Ann. I'm going to bust a zipper if you don't stop."

She edged so close they were nearly touching, then threw his earlier words back at him in a whisper. "The things I want to do to you, Mark . . . The things I want to do."

Aching now in earnest, he had to turn away. "Four little kids," he said, mainly to remind himself. "Four little kids in the house and your best friend in the next room."

Her sigh sounded every bit as frustrated as he felt. Served her right, he thought, though he wanted her too badly to take much pleasure in her pain.

"How about a rain check?" he asked and dared another look at her. "In Pittsburgh, Pennsylvania. Pack up your things and come home with us, Beth Ann. Come home and be mine. Again and again and again."

But both the arousal and the playfulness had already ebbed from her expression.

"I can't just run from this—I love you too much." She was staring directly into his eyes, and through some trick of the lighting or emotion, her own burned sapphire-bright. "Too much to let you keep carrying this burden. A lot of people in Eudena *hate* you, possibly enough that one of them is shooting at you and your child. For something that was more my fault than yours. And that's not even counting the parts Gene Calvert and his buddies, Pete Riker, and Jim Morrell played. I can't understand why you'd want to let all of us get off scot free."

"What difference does it make what a few nutcases think if you and I don't live here? Come on, Beth Ann. There's a lot more to this world than this two-bit patch of—"

"This is my *home*, Mark, and the people in it matter. Their opinions matter to you, too, if you'd let yourself admit it."

"You can't honestly be thinking of telling this *memory* of yours to anyone. First of all, how can you be certain that's the way it really happened, that your mind hasn't started inventing details because our involvement's stirred up a lot of troubling emotions?"

"I know it really happened. Do you think I'd *make up* something like this? Being around you has been the key, that's all. It's unlocked what's always been there."

"I'm not so sure about that, Beth Ann. First of all, you had a serious head injury, serious enough to put you in a coma. And even if that weren't true, memory changes over time, with everything shifting to fit a person's hopes or fears or some piece of an old book or movie. Events get jumbled, mixed together. By this time, Gene Calvert recalls a different version of that night than I do. Pete Riker's probably painted himself as a hero. Scotty Morrell might have put it out of his mind completely. And who's to say that what I told you is exactly what took place? I certainly *believe* it is, but I saw this show a while back. It showed these experiments with filmed events—they played those and then interviewed the people involved years later. You can't imagine the ways the different participants described what happened. Every one of them had a different version. And as the years progressed, their stories changed, too."

"This isn't some experiment, and it damned well isn't wishful thinking." Beth Ann frowned, clearly troubled by the fact that he was questioning her story.

"Even if the incident with the drinking really happened the way you described," he said, "this was *six-*

teen years ago. Who would it be helping, reopening those old wounds?"

"You, for one thing. It would make people realize they've misjudged you."

"Don't do me any favors. I still did what I did. I made a choice to run from those guys in a moving vehicle. A choice to speed, to escalate things, just to save myself a beating."

She traced the scar beneath his eye with the warm tip of her finger. "But they could've hurt you terribly, maybe even killed you."

"At the time, I thought the same thing, but now, I can't imagine it really would've gone that far. These guys were kids, not killers. And when I sped off down that dark road, I put other people at risk. I accept my responsibility. As terrible as it is, I've learned to live with it. What I can't live with is the thought of ripping open those old wounds, both mine and the families of the dead girls. Let them rest in peace, Beth Ann. Let all of us—"

"It's not right, Mark, letting this go. Letting Calvert, the sheriff, all of them get away with the things they did. Letting people keep thinking I'm nothing but Eudena's Official Tragic Figure when I'm as responsible for what happened as you or anybody else. And Gene Calvert and his friends didn't beat you up and try to run you out of town for nothing. They know what you know, and they don't want it getting out to hurt them."

"And these are the kind of people you think matter?"

"Of course not, but there are lots of other people in this town. *Good* people who look out for each other's kids, help neighbors when they need it. Some even volunteered to take care of your father when he'd barely spoken to anyone in years."

"Okay, so there are good people in this town, too. But I can't see how any of them would be helped by bringing this all up again. Please, Beth Ann, let this go," he pleaded. "It's not healthy to keep looking backward. The best thing, the only real choice, is to keep moving forward and never mention this again."

"But don't you see? Everything keeps pointing me back to that night. My mother left the clippings in a safe deposit box for me to find, and then there was the date—she kept it hidden in that big globe. It's a message, Mark, a way to tell me the truth is what's important. The truth about the accident."

He shook his head. "I can't imagine that your mother, of all people, would want you wallowing in old pain. From what you've said about her, she lived for the moment. Which seems like a damned good idea. It's bad enough we had to suffer through the past once; let's not live through it all over."

"Did burying the past help with your father?" she demanded. "You came back here to set things right, but it never happened because you both refused to discuss what drove the two of you apart. Neither one of you would face the truth head on."

A rush of anger seared his skin. "*Don't* bring up my father. And don't rake up any more old shit about this crash. I'm tired of being defined by a terrible thing that happened when I was seventeen years old. I've *done* things since then. I've worked, I've gone to college, I've started up and run a company. I've loved a woman, fathered a fine son, and I'm doing my level best to raise him to feel the acceptance I missed out on from my father and this town. I've paid the debt society demanded, and I have moved on with my life. And if you think for one damned minute your dredging up all this garbage will somehow make things better for you, for me, for Heidi's family or Larinda's father, you're living in a dream world."

Her gaze turned deadly cold. "I don't appreciate your talking down to me. And I also don't appreciate the implication that I *haven't* done a thing with my life."

"I wasn't trying to compare us, and I wasn't talking down to you."

"Yes, you were, on both counts. First you try to talk me out of what I remember, and now—"

"Maybe I don't want to see you hurt, Beth Ann. Maybe I think I've paid dues enough for both of us without you sacrificing yourself, too. And I would never diminish what you've done with your life. I've seen up close, with my father, the importance of your work. And while I never could get my relationship with my dad right, you stuck it out with your mom, even though that couldn't have been easy."

"I'm really sorry, Mark. Sorry if I hurt you by bringing up your dad. I still think I'm right about getting the truth out in the open, but that wasn't fighting fair. And if there's going to be some chance for us, I need to learn to do that."

Remembering Rachel's no-holds-barred style of combat, Beth Ann's maturity impressed him. And made him ashamed of the strength of his reaction. "And I'm sorry if I chewed your head off. I just want you to promise me you won't do anything rash."

"Like what?"

"Like talking about this drinking thing with other people."

She grimaced. "So you expect me to carry around this secret? You know, Mark, you've had sixteen years to come to grips with your part in this, but mine is all new to me."

"*If* it's true," he repeated.

In the silence that followed, he felt a wall come up between them.

After an uncomfortable span, she finally asked, "What time do you expect to leave?"

So this is it, he thought. She wasn't going to make that promise, which meant anything could happen. Up to and including some reporter pounding on the door of his townhouse in Pittsburgh on a mission to remind the whole world of his greatest nightmare. Though part of him understood the way Beth Ann felt, the rest cursed her stubbornness—and her naiveté. Did she really believe that ridiculous old saw, *The truth will set you free?*

"I'm not sure," he answered. "Probably late tomorrow. I still have to call some people, work out details about getting the house ready to put on the market and arrange to have my father's last bills forwarded to me in Pennsylvania. And there's some last-minute packing to consider. We may even end up waiting and leaving Saturday."

He vowed to himself that he'd watch Eli like a hawk until that moment.

"Promise me you'll call." She sounded resigned to his leaving, and sad, too. "Promise you'll give me a chance to see the two of you before you go."

It bothered him that she was asking for a promise when she refused to give one, but he could not bear to deny her. "Sure, Beth Ann. I won't forget."

And he wouldn't. Even if it turned out to be their last goodbye.

Chapter 26

By the time he reached the house and tucked his thoroughly worn-out son beneath the covers, Mark was more disturbed and out of sorts than he had felt in years. As he walked the dark rooms, images of Beth Ann, past and present, vied with flashes of his sister screaming and his father dying, with memories of his mother's stricken face when she came to collect him from Jackrabbit General's ER, where a doctor had stitched him up and treated him for shock after the crash. He remembered Sheriff Morrell snapping on the handcuffs, Pete Riker pushing him in the patrol car's backseat. A closing cell door clanged in Mark's memory, a sound that still made him jump when he heard it on a TV show or dreamed it in a nightmare.

There had been so much loss, so much waste. And his relationship with Beth Ann seemed all too likely to end up on the same scrap heap because of her stubborn self-righteousness. With no idea how to fix the situation, Mark went to the family room, picked up the phone, and started dialing.

When a man's voice answered, Mark asked to speak to Aimee Gustavsen. He didn't care that it was almost ten P.M. on Thanksgiving. He was in too foul a mood to observe the niceties, especially considering how late she'd phoned him last night.

Deputy Ted Gustavsen, a former Red Hawks fullback who had graduated a couple of years ahead of Mark's class, hesitated before calling his wife to the phone. Despite his frame of mind, Mark pitied the man; Gustavsen had seemed like a decent enough guy in school, too friendly and good-natured to deserve a woman hell-bent on cheating.

"Hello?"

"Mark Jessup here."

"Just a minute, Mr. Jessup," she said, before covering her phone's mouthpiece and murmuring something to her husband about some urgent matter related to an upcoming closing on a property. Mark heard her moving around, and then she came back on the line.

"So you've changed your mind." A promise of pleasure honeyed her voice, as it had on numerous occasions. "But the thing is, sugar, I don't see how I can get away this evening."

"I haven't changed my mind." Mark knew he sounded harsh, but he didn't particularly care. "I just called to say that if you want that commission, you need to refrain from making anonymous calls regarding Beth Ann Decker."

Aimee started to stammer a denial, but he wasn't having any of it.

"Give me some credit, will you? Listen, Aimee, whatever stupid little high school rivalry's still simmering on your back burner, it's way past time to turn the heat off. And I'll be gone tomorrow or the next day anyway."

"I'm terribly hurt, Mark—" Her pout came through loud and clear "—that you would make such an accusation. Believe me, the last woman I need to compete with is some cripple who's never even had a man in her life."

"You *can't* compete with Beth Ann," he growled, "not in heart or warmth or loyalty."

And not in beauty either, to his thinking, though he had noticed the faint scars on Beth Ann's face and the more pronounced ones that marked the smooth skin of her left leg and her back. He knew that a lot of men would prefer Aimee's flash over Beth Ann's substance, but Mark wasn't looking for a quick, adulterous foray. He was looking for a woman who understood commitment. A woman who was worthy of forever.

"Fortunately," drawled Aimee, "most men can find all those same qualities in a good hound. When they go looking to fill *other* needs, there's simply no one to compare to me, love."

Mark grimaced. She was right. There *was* no comparison to Aimee, especially when it came to ego. He couldn't imagine what he had been thinking to offer her the consolation of handling his real estate dealings. But considering how abrasive he'd been, Aimee's vain words were probably no more than self-defense. At least he hoped she wasn't quite as narcissistic as she sounded.

"Look," she continued, "I understand if you feel sorry for Poor Beth Ann."

"You'd better not let *her* hear you say that." When Mark had last dropped by Stillwater's Hardware to pick up the things he'd need to fix a broken faucet, he'd overheard several old men laughing over the story of Beth Ann threatening the sheriff. On the spot, the geezers had solemnly rechristened her "Rich Beth Ann." Afterward, they'd returned to speculating about the Red Hawks' chances in the play-offs in what might be the school's last year to field a full team, thanks to the decline in its enrollment.

"Oh, *please,*" said Aimee. "I've known Beth Ann since kindergarten, same as you have. You know I'd never do or say a thing to hurt my good friend."

"See that you don't, Aimee, and we'll do business just fine."

After ending the call, Mark cursed himself. He'd accomplished nothing, neither burning off his anxiety over the threat of violence nor his worry over what Beth Ann would do. Despite his exhaustion, it took hours for sleep to find him. And even then his dreams were threaded with dark echoes past and present . . . along with Aimee's promise that she would never hurt her lifelong friend.

"Please don't look at me that way," Beth Ann scolded Maia, who was staring expectantly. "We'll have a good, long walk this afternoon—I promise."

Anxiety had kept her up so late that when she finally dropped off sometime after two, Beth Ann had ended up sleeping straight through her alarm. By the time Maia finally woke her to go out, there was no time for their normal, somewhat leisurely routine. And rushing in the morning always put Beth Ann in a bad mood, especially since she'd come no closer to deciding what to do about the things she had remembered. Should she speak up and lose any shot of happiness with Mark, or keep silent and lose her self-respect?

Unease knotted in her stomach at the thought. Still, she felt guilty when Maia gave her a last, pleading look before slinking from the bedroom. When Beth Ann came downstairs, the Lab waited near the front door, her leash clamped in her strong jaws and her thick tail fanning hopefully.

Sinking onto a lower step as Maia approached, Beth Ann looked into the soulful brown eyes and then hugged the furry neck.

"I'm a rotten mama, aren't I?" Since she couldn't even manage to please an animal who demanded little more than routine, it was probably a good thing she had no children—that she would almost surely never have them. At the thought of Eli, Beth Ann fought an urge to revisit the familiar harbor of self-pity. A memory of Mark's disappointment with her last night returned as well, threatening to push her head beneath the dark waters.

"Damned if I'm drowning in that slop this morning," she vowed, and Maia rewarded her by dropping the leash to lick her cheek.

Laughing as she wiped her face, Beth Ann wondered how she could have lived without the company of such a forgiving creature all these years. As quickly as she could, she fixed herself peanut-butter toast and settled for a cup of instant coffee while waiting for the dog to take care of business in the backyard.

With Maia safely inside, Beth Ann picked up the leash from the floor and hung it back on its hook in the laundry room. While there, she happened to glance at the file of clippings and the Mercedes manual, which she had left on top of the washer.

She should have put that stuff away already. Since Rosario would be here to clean this morning—thank goodness—Beth Ann decided she had better get the morbid articles and photos out of sight. But in her hurry, she dropped the whole damned packet and had to lower herself into an awkward squat to gather the pages.

Holding her breath—mainly to keep from cursing her clumsiness—Beth Ann tried not to look at the pages she was grabbing, tried not to think of how her decision to drink that night could have made the crucial difference. But as damning as the headlines felt, it was another item that snagged her attention: a stapled set of papers that had fallen loose from inside the Mercedes manual.

At first, Beth Ann thought nothing of the receipt for five hundred sixty-nine dollars from a Fort Worth business called Custom Concepts—until she saw the words *secured compartment—rear deck.* On the back of the page, in her mother's childish handwriting, was the notation, *Underneath trunk carpet—if anything happens to me, take to Texas Rangers.*

"Oh, my God." Beth Ann could barely squeeze the words out, her heart was pounding so hard. Her mother had known she was in danger. Had suspected, yet blithely gone on dancing, gambling, and carousing . . .

"Like there's no tomorrow," Beth Ann murmured, quoting one of her mama's favorite lines. Was the risk part of the reason? Had Lilly seen death coming?

Seen it, yet said nothing, though she'd clearly gone to great pains to conceal whatever it was she wanted Beth Ann to give to the authorities. Such great pains that Beth Ann had already traded in the car.

After rising so quickly that she lost her balance and barely caught herself with her cane, Beth Ann hurried to her study and pulled out the paperwork she'd gotten when she'd bought the Highlander. There it was—her salesman's number. Maia looked on anxiously as her mistress dialed and swore when she reached the dealership's answering machine, which explained that the business would reopen at ten o'clock that morning.

With a glance at the small clock on her desktop, Beth Ann cursed anew. Almost two hours, she realized. Two hours to find out whether the Mercedes had been sold yet.

Chapter 27

"So, are you making any progress on the case?"

Damon would have recognized Katie Hill's voice anywhere, but he still glanced up from an ancient computer the sheriff's office shared with the fire department down the hall. Partly, he looked because his eyes were crossing with the monotony of transcribing yet another of Deputy Ted Gustavsen's nearly illegible sets of interview notes. But mainly, Damon did it for the sheer pleasure of looking into Katie's gorgeous brown eyes and feeling the little punch of pleasure that set his heart racing.

"Hi, Katie," he said. "That's a real pretty blouse you've got on. And I like your skirt, too."

The instant the words were out, Damon kicked himself, wondering if she'd think he had commented on the skirt because his gaze was glued to her thighs. Or if he liked the slightly stretchy white blouse because it made the most of her small, pert breasts. Would she think he was some kind of sex fiend? Or maybe she'd believe he was one of those Brokeback boys who noticed women's fashions but didn't give two hoots about the girls inside them.

But his misery was cut short when she smiled and thanked him, her cheeks coloring. He fantasized that she had chosen this morning's outfit in the hope he would notice, that she was slipping in to see him on her break because she felt a little of the same magic that vibrated in his stomach every time they were together.

"From what I'm seeing here," he told her as he tapped a knuckle to the notes, "we're leaning toward the dopers and the petty thieves, interviewing the county's rougher types to see if any of 'em got himself the idea of a fat payday over at the Lucky Pull. This interview's with Gene Calvert, taken over at the jail."

Calvert had denied any involvement, of course, claiming his common-law wife would give him an alibi. But everybody knew the mechanic had her so cowed she would swear to anything.

Calvert had also denied owning a firearm or having any knowledge of who had shot at Beth Ann Decker and Mark Jessup. Since he'd been behind bars when the incident with Jessup's son occurred, it was pretty clear he hadn't done it, but Damon wouldn't count out the man's employee, Donny Ray.

"What about you?" Katie asked. "Do you think it was just some troublemaker or a drifter who killed her? Do you think the rest of us are safe? My mama—she's been really nervous, checking all the locks and going on about some sex-crazed killer out to get Eudena's women."

Damon could barely suppress a smile at the idea that Katie would be interested in his take on the Decker killing. Heaven only knew nobody else was. From his own home, where he didn't dare bring up the subject, to work, where despite the sheriff's leniency, he was being assigned more and more clerical duties, Damon's theorizing had been systematically shut down.

"You can tell your mother I don't think she needs to worry," he said, rapidly warming to the forbidden topic. "I still think Lilly Decker's killer must be someone who knew her well. Whoever broke into the Lucky Pull and assaulted Beth Ann later was easily frightened off. But the—uh—the manner of Mrs. Decker's death was so violent, so personal, and so clearly connected to the victim's—her um—her sexuality, that I can't help thinking her assailant was somehow threatened by the way Mrs. Decker lived her li—"

The sound of a throat clearing had Damon's head whipping toward the open doorway, which was currently filled by a doleful-looking Sheriff Morrell. *Oh, holy shit.* Damon hoped like hell a puddle wasn't spreading under the rickety, straight-backed office chair where he was sitting.

"You finished printing that report yet?" Morrell's deep rumble was the throaty growl of an old lion.

"No, sir. But I'm on it, sir."

"Good. You bring it to me in my office, won't you? Within the next ten minutes."

Damon promised that he would, though with his typing skills, the timing would be a near thing.

"We'll talk then," Morrell said ominously before nodding at Katie. "Miss Hill."

"I was—I was just going back," she said. "My break's nearly over anyway, and Deputy Gustavsen won't like it if I show up late to relieve him."

Damon heard Morrell's heavy footsteps retreating

toward his office down the hallway. Damon didn't look, though. He was too busy trying to push his usual fifteen words a minute up to fifty.

"Sorry, Damon," Katie whispered. "I hope I didn't get you into trouble."

"I'll forgive you," he said, backing up the cursor to correct a typo, "as long as you'll have dinner with me tomorrow night at the China Lotus."

"Okay, Damon," she said brightly. "But didn't you hear? The China Lotus has closed down. The Chens are leaving town to go cook someplace in Dallas."

"The Blue Coyote, then." Since the DQ—which gave Damon deep-fat fryer flashbacks—was the only other choice. . . .

Katie smiled and nodded. "Why don't you call me about the details later, after we get off?"

With a goofy smile plastered on his face, he finished his transcription in record time. By the time he changed the ink cartridge on the sorry printer and got it to spit out the pages, however, a glance at his watch showed that close to twenty minutes had whizzed past. A choking sensation lodged in his throat, and he hesitated at Sheriff Morrell's office door, only to hear a woman speaking inside.

"He told me all about it, Sheriff." Tartly feminine, the voice was familiar, yet Damon could not immediately place it. "I know what went on with Gene Calvert, Donny Ray, Xavier, and your boy, and I know about the cover-up."

Beth Ann Decker, Damon realized, but what the devil did she mean about a cover-up? One part of him—the part that always scolded in his father's voice—warned Damon that if he wanted to remain a Hatcher County deputy, he should immediately move away from the door and go back to type another transcript. But the curious part, the one that for so long routinely exasperated his parents, his former teachers, and his employers, rooted Damon to the spot. Pretending to reposition mixed-up pages from his transcript, he listened in on the conversation in the office.

"I don't know what that Jessup boy's been fillin' your head with." Morrell sounded breezy, unconcerned by her charge. "But we don't have ourselves some kind of Watergate conspiracy right here in Hatcher County."

"Mark Jessup never should've gone to jail—or at least, not alone."

"Well, Beth Ann, I can't think what you would *really* know about it, other than hearsay from a convicted felon who everybody in Eudena knows is hot to get you in bed. If you weren't so shook up, what with your mama passing the way she did and that other break-in, I'd expect you to have better sense than to fall for some smooth-talking—"

"Don't patronize me, Sheriff. What Mark told me just plain *fits,* on a lot of levels. But though I think it's reprehensible, I'm not here to call you on what you did sixteen years ago."

"I've been damned tolerant lately." If Morrell had sounded like a lion earlier, he was a grizzly this time, all snarls. "First, you showed up at a house of worship on the Sabbath, accusing me of ignorin' Mark Jessup as a murder suspect. And now you're saying I set him up to cover for my boy and his friends."

"What about *me?*" she demanded, clearly unafraid of Morrell's bluster. "Were you covering for me, too?"

If there was an answer, Damon didn't hear it.

"Well?" Beth Ann pressed, and though Damon wished she'd stop, he had to hand it to her. There weren't many grown men in Hatcher County, let alone ladies, who'd go toe-to-toe with Jim Morrell the way she was. There was something damned scary about that man when he got riled.

"Just tell me what you're getting at." Annoyance filtered through Morrell's resignation. "Whatever fool idea you've come up with, I might just as well hear about it, since I'm sure you won't give me any peace until we talk this through."

"You know I haven't been able to remember much of anything about the crash."

"Understandable, what with the way it busted you up." Morrell's anger softened yet one more degree. "I still remember that night, Beth Ann. I still have nightmares about the things I saw after Riker called me out there. You might think a fellow in my line of business gets used to seeing hard things. But when it involves young people like that accident . . . there's no forgetting those poor, shattered girls—or the way it felt to tell their mamas and their daddies. My heart about broke that night. Broke into a million pieces."

"I know," she said, compassion touching her words. "Certain deaths hit me that way, too, even though in my job, they're expected, sometimes even welcomed."

After a pause, she spoke again. "Things are coming back to me, Sheriff. Bits and pieces that happened just before the accident. But the memory that most concerns me has to do with drinking. *My* drinking in particular."

"It was a long time ago."

"Not to me, it isn't," she said. "It's fresh and raw to my mind—and it hurts like anything. I've been worrying all night and riding around all day with it chewing at my insides. I have to know if it's true, Sheriff."

Morrell's sigh followed another hesitation. "You've got enough on your plate for any three people right now. You ought to let this go. Or make yourself an appointment with Pastor Timmons for some counseling. He can pray it out of you if anybody can."

"How do you know your office isn't where my prayers have led me?"

"Then maybe one of them head-shrinker fellas, if you don't want to see the preacher. I know you haven't been real steady in your church attendance lately."

"You're suggesting I need a psychiatrist?" Dark amusement weighted the question.

"Well, I don't know about that, Beth Ann, but in my experience, a lot of young people these days go for those doctors with the fancy degrees hung on their walls. I hear they've got a few in Wichita Falls. Counselors, too, maybe. Those are different, aren't they?"

"Those are different," she confirmed. "But I don't need any happy pills or couch talk, Sheriff. All I need are answers to a few short questions. Did you find a bottle of sloe gin in my car?"

"How am I supposed to remember such a thing? I've slept a time or two since then, you know."

"You've already told me, you remember everything about that night. Because three young girls were dead—and your son and nephew were involved."

"We all figured it for four girls dead that night." Morrell's voice was barely audible. "No way anybody thought that you could live. Or that you'd ever be sitting here with me, able to walk and talk and nag the living daylights out of a man."

"So you didn't see much point of speaking ill of the dead, did you? You found my bottle and the little plastic cups from Jordan's Jello shots, but you and Pete Riker and the others never said a word about it. And you never ordered blood tests on any of us girls."

"Are you asking me if I regret it? Because I don't, Beth Ann. Not for one damned minute. Their families and your parents, too—"

"Your decision smashed what was left of the Jessup family into pieces. And put a young man into prison without a single person to stand by him. He was only seventeen years old then, and his sister had been killed, too. Yet you hung him with the whole thing."

"There are times in this life, young lady, when a man has to make the best decision he can under the circumstances."

As Morrell's volume rose, Katie stuck her head out of the dispatch office and Deputy Ted Gustavsen popped out of the break room, holding a half-eaten square of coffeecake in one huge hand. Even the fire chief emerged from his office at the other end of the short hallway. All three of them looked at Damon for an explanation, but Morrell wasn't finished.

"A *real* man doesn't have hours to make this choice or a committee there to offer its advice. All he can do is act, knowing the critics will come later, goddamn Monday morning quarterbacks who've never had the intestinal fortitude to make a tough call in their lives. *Don't* you second-guess what I did, young lady. Someone had to pay the price, and someone had to make the call that night."

As if drawn by a magnetic force, the listeners in the hall drew nearer, careful not to make a sound.

"If I had been you, maybe I would have done the same," Beth Ann said. "I don't know, and I'll never know, but I can tell you that in the long run, no one was really spared by your decision. I've had to live with pity, and now I'll have to deal with knowing I was probably at fault, too. Gene Calvert is in jail because of this, and Donny Ray's a hopeless drunk. Maybe Xavier and Scotty are okay. I can't say, but I'll bet if you asked them, they'd tell you it's changed their lives—or maybe it *will* change Scotty's down the line in his career, if some opponent or reporter dredges this up. And as for you and Pete, only the two of you can say how much it's hurt you. But if you're honest with yourself, you'll know there's been a cost."

"You need to leave now, Beth Ann, or so help me I will throw your ass in my jail."

"I'm already there," she told him. "And you're shackled right beside me."

The listeners scattered as Beth Ann Decker strode out of Morrell's office. Later, everyone agreed that she walked straighter than usual, with more confidence, her cane's tip barely tapping the pale green tile as she left.

For his part, Jim Morrell closed and locked his office door. None of the witnesses had the nerve to knock, so after glancing at each other with half embarrassed, half concerned looks, each one drifted back to his or her own duties.

As Damon transcribed another interview, he tried not to think about the rumored flask inside the sheriff's desk drawer, tried not to picture the man he had so long looked up to falling into weakness. But thanks to Beth Ann's accusations, he couldn't stop thinking of the stories floating around town that Evelyn Morrell had grown tired of her husband drinking himself to sleep most nights.

Though he'd always been quick to defend his boss

whenever he had heard such whispers, Damon now found himself wondering, as he corrected typo after typo, if those tales might amount to more than just loose talk. And if Mark Jessup was the reason the sheriff needed bottled help to fall asleep.

In the sheriff/fire department's parking area, Beth Ann found the large white envelope tucked behind the windshield wiper of her SUV. Too keyed up over her confrontation with Morrell to feel anything but irritation, she jerked the distraction free and climbed into her vehicle to start it.

"Stubborn old man," she said of Morrell. If he hadn't made her so damned mad, she might have gone ahead and talked to him about the hidden compartment in her mother's car. Though she still had no idea what was in it, the salesman—who was clearly thrilled to have this bit of intrigue to enliven his day—had told her the Mercedes had been sold. He'd then promised to contact the buyer to arrange a time, which he'd vowed to share with Beth Ann, for the new owner to bring in the sedan for some free maintenance.

With her SUV's engine idling, Beth Ann glanced down to see her name in block letters written across the envelope's front and circled in black marker with a flourish.

"What now?" she grumbled before tossing it onto the passenger seat. Unable to deal with one more aggravation, she headed toward the home of her last patient for the day.

She should have gone to Mr. Johnston's first, but during the long drive back to Eudena from the ranch house of her previous patient, Beth Ann had gone from worrying about the contents of the trunk safe to obsessing again over her recovered memory. By the time she had finally rolled back into Eudena proper, the compulsion to demand an explanation of the sheriff had taken root so deeply, her Highlander had all but steered itself toward the department.

Though Mark had been dead set against her talking to the sheriff, and Morrell clearly hadn't enjoyed it, Beth Ann felt better, freer, for having everything out in the open. Sure, there might be repercussions, but she would worry later about those.

With her mood lifting, she parked in front of her patient's aging bungalow. But as she reached for her cane, Beth Ann's gaze latched on to the mysterious envelope, and a thought slashed through her consciousness. Might it be from Mark, a quick goodbye that he had stuck onto her windshield as he was leaving town with Eli? Sick with fear that she could have missed her last chance to see them, she ripped into the envelope, her hurry tearing a corner of the single page inside.

It was a photocopy of a bid, a bid to purchase a large chunk of acreage on Lost Buffalo Road. The old Jessup acreage, she was certain, and Mark Jessup was listed as the bidder. Across the bottom, in the same black-marker block lettering that graced the envelope's outside, a single question had been written: *STILL THINK HE DIDN'T KILL HER?*

The shock of the message detonated deep inside her, wave after wave that raised goose bumps on her skin and left her nauseated. Who would send her such a sickening, anonymous message? Though she flipped the paper several times and shook out the envelope, she found no clue, and the squared-off print, she thought, could have belonged to almost anyone.

Including the sniper who appeared hell-bent on

punishing Mark Jessup with a bullet. Had the shooter fabricated this bid in an attempt to drive a wedge between her and his intended victim? But why bother with such a thing, if he really intended to kill Mark?

Maybe killing him had never been this person's goal. Running him out of Hatcher County might suffice. If so, whoever had sent this didn't know he had won already.

Assuming that the sender really was a *he*. . . .

"Aimee Lynn Baker Johnson Gustavsen," Beth Ann said as if it were a string of curse words. Her so-called lifelong "friend," who'd been drooling over Mark Jessup since before he had arrived. The same woman who had obviously been insulted when Mark made it clear that he preferred Beth Ann to a few no-strings, sweaty rounds with the former homecoming queen of Hatcher County High.

Aimee must have found it incredibly disappointing that she had lured home the "bad boy" of her fantasies only to find he had turned into a responsible and family-oriented man. Worse yet, he'd begun pursuing a scarred, pathetic also-ran, a woman no man in Eudena wanted.

Beth Ann's heart darkened, clouding with a far more frightening suspicion. What if Mark had seduced her, had even told her he loved her, in order to . . . what? To disguise the fact that his involvement with her mother had gone much further than his letter declining her request to get involved in saving his hometown?

Beth Ann shuddered, her stomach knotting, before she shook her head.

"No way," she muttered, still unable to reconcile Mark's tenderness and passion with the idea that he could have hurt anyone, let alone butchered her mother. Besides, Beth Ann would have been smart enough to know if he'd been playing on her spinster status . . . wouldn't she?

"Damn right, I would have known," she muttered as she climbed out of the SUV and hauled her nursing bag up the sidewalk. But as she hobbled toward the front door, her limp deepened step by step.

The greatest challenge was convincing the Companion that the time for watching was beyond them, that both of them were called upon to do the work of God.

The One Appointed would have much preferred, as in the whore's case, to attend to this blood sacrifice alone, but the Companion had played a part from the beginning, had, in truth, set this long ordeal into motion. So perhaps it was fitting that the one tempted into sin would play a role in its redemption, that the innocent would be protected by the labors of the guilty.

All this and much more had been poured into the mind of the One Appointed as the whore's daughter had earlier come out of the sheriff's office building, grimness written into her face and determination in her stride. She had paused to pick up the envelope placed there only a few minutes earlier, then climbed inside her vehicle and driven off to tend the dying . . .

Never guessing that before this day was over, she would beat her patients in their headlong race to the grave.

"Please, Dad," Eli pleaded as Mark packed one of the last boxes into the back of the extended-cab pickup. "Stormy's nice now, see? And Beau would like her, too. For sure he would. I know it."

Their two-year-old Lab, a proven wuss, would probably be scared to death of the gray tabby, but there was no arguing that Eli had managed to bring about a transformation in the cat's behavior. Stormy was rubbing against the boy's hand as he squatted, occasionally daring to stroke the black-and-gray-striped head. Even from where Mark stood, some six feet distant, he could hear the rumble of the cat's purr.

"This is Stormy's home," he said. "And I told you, Mrs. Gustavsen promised she'll come by and feed her 'til the place sells."

But Mark wondered, would Aimee follow through? Try as he might, he couldn't picture the blonde strutting on her catch-me, do-me heels into the barn to get the cat food or make sure the animal had water.

"Can't we bring her with us? I'll pick up my toys every single day. Every single *second* if you'll let me keep her." Eli's face was earnest, even if his promise didn't fool his father for a moment.

Mark shook his head. "She would never be happy as a housecat. And you know we can't let her run where we live."

Their townhouse was in an up-and-coming urban neighborhood that was still a little dicey around the edges, in spite of its ongoing revival. Mark couldn't even let Eli play in the yard without supervision, and an outdoor cat would get squashed flat within minutes by the traffic.

"We should just stay here then. I like my friends and Mrs. Minton. I like Miz Beth Ann lots, too. And I know she really likes you."

"I care about her too, Eli."

Eli looked up sharply, his big, dark eyes appraising and the late afternoon sun glinting off his junior deputy's badge. "Like in a love way?"

"Maybe," Mark said after a hesitation. Though there

was no doubt in his mind as to his feelings, he had to answer carefully, for he was far from certain that his relationship with Beth Ann had any sort of chance. And if either distance or their differences dashed his hopes to pieces, it would be hard enough dealing with his own pain without worrying about Eli's disappointment.

Eli pursed his mouth and nodded. "Then I think we should stay here. If it might be a love thing, it's important," he said with the kind of earnestness only a five-year-old could manage. "She could maybe marry you and be my other mom."

Mark's heart sank. This was exactly the sort of leap he hadn't wanted his son taking. He shook his head and said, "I'm sorry. You know we can't stay, champ. But I'll tell you what. I'll talk to Miss Beth Ann before we leave, and I'll ask her to look after Stormy. You know she'll do a good job. Just look at how she spoils Maia."

He smiled at the thought of how she'd fixed the big dog a "Thanksgiving feast" that included slices of the bird of honor with all its trimmings. Maia had rewarded her by promptly barfing on the living room's white carpet.

Eli stood, his small fists clenched in defiance. Thrusting out his chin, he shouted, "I'm not scared of that bad man. I'm staying right here in Eudena."

With that, he turned and ran inside the house. Aggravated beyond all reason, Mark counted to ten before he followed. But by then, his stubborn son had hidden. Though he'd thought that he knew every nook and cranny of the old place, Mark flat-out couldn't find the little turkey, and no amount of bribes or threats could coax Eli out.

Chapter 28

A doorbell, a fuel can, a garage door opener, and a junior-high-school student's knowledge of the explosive properties of natural gas: these and the Lord's grace were all the ingredients one needed to do murder. Well, these and enough rawhide to lure a large dog behind a closed door, where it would be out of the way.

The schematics for the alarm turned out to be unnecessary. God had provided for the One Appointed and reassured the Companion of His blessing, in the form of a pair of Mexican women—housecleaners, from their mops and buckets—who lingered long near the front door but couldn't seem to figure out how to set the system before leaving. Once the two finally quit arguing and drove off in their rusted minivan, the alarm's status was quickly confirmed by a glance through a side window. After removing the hinge pieces on the back gate to allow access, the One Appointed used a glass cutter and a suction cup on one of the rear windows that overlooked the heart-shaped pool.

"We can't let people see us here." The Companion sounded nervous. "They're going to know it's not an accident."

The One Appointed smiled, all worry veiled by grace. "Of course it won't be an accident. It is God's will brought to fruition, a blessing for us all."

In the driveway of the old Jessup place, Damon sat inside his dusty pickup, his hands shaking so hard, he could barely read the document he had pulled from the department mail only thirty minutes earlier. He'd frowned down at it a moment, registering the blocky print and lack of a return address, which could mean powdered death or a letter bomb, according to the postal service warning memos. But the envelope's postmark said Eudena, which wasn't exactly a hotbed of terrorism, and the envelope was addressed to him, so Damon had torn into it and then stared at the copy of the real estate bid bearing Mark Jessup's name.

BLOOD MONEY CAN BUY ANYTHING, screamed the black block letters, *EVEN MORRELL'S SILENCE!*

Damon would never forget the gut-punch of suspicion, nor the impulse that had made him slip out past Morrell's closed door and drive away from the department. Had it been his first step toward betrayal of the man he had so long admired? And would his half-formed plan to question Jessup prove to be the second?

There was still time to back out of this driveway. Time to return to the office and knock emphatically at Big Jim Morrell's door. Talk to him about the message . . . a message sent specifically to *DEPUTY STILLWATER*.

But Damon wondered, why had it been mailed to him? Had the sender noted his tenacity, his refusal to quit digging in spite of community complaints and warnings from his boss? He remembered Morrell arguing with Beth Ann and denying a conspiracy, recalled her mentioning Pete Riker's name as well. Could dishonesty in the department run even deeper? And if Morrell came into possession of the contents of this envelope, would they quietly disappear? And what of the messenger? Would he vanish, too?

Damon shuddered, not imagining himself killed but somehow discredited and dismissed with the sort of recommendation that would make it impossible for him to work in law enforcement anywhere.

"Shit, shit, shit," he said, paralyzed with indecision. Morrell had been Hatcher County's sheriff since long before Damon had come into this world. No one had bothered to run against him for years, and despite the grievances of his soon-to-be ex-wife, Damon had never heard any whisper of professional wrongdoing.

But still . . .

It was Mark Jessup who finally made Damon's mind up for him by coming outside carrying a box. His son walked behind him at a snail's pace, his small face scrunched like a storm cloud. On spotting Damon, the father's expression shifted from frustration to curiosity and concern. After setting the box on his truck's tailgate, Jessup headed straight for Damon's pickup as the child followed, picking up his pace considerably.

Damon heaved a sigh and slid out of his vehicle. A lump formed in his throat to see Eli light up at the sight of his badge and uniform.

"You caught that bad man, didn't you?" the boy asked. Looking at his father, he added, "Now we won't hafta go away. We can stay forever."

"I'm sorry," Damon said. "This is about another matter."

"Then what?" Mark's gaze flicked to the envelope but didn't linger. "We were about to go say goodbye to Beth Ann before we head out. I told the sheriff we were leaving town, and I gave him some phone numbers and an address where he can reach me."

I could leave right now, thought Damon. *Wish the Jessups a safe trip home and go back to headquarters. Keep my head down. Keep my job. Maybe get my own place and get serious about a woman.* Katie's pretty face flashed through his mind.

But not even that temptation could keep him from doing the right thing. "I—uh—I need to talk to you," he said. "Please."

Jessup paled. "Has something happened to Beth Ann?"

"It's nothing like that," Damon reassured him. "I just—I have to talk to you, that's all. Inside. Inside would be better."

He didn't want to get into it out here, where anyone might happen by and see them talking.

Jessup nodded, looking more curious than ever. "All right. I'll unlock the house."

Eli cheered and raced to the back door ahead of them.

"It's just for now," his father told him. "Only ten minutes, maybe less."

Jessup unlocked the door and let them inside. Once they reached the kitchen, he turned to his son. "Why don't you go back in Hiram's bedroom and look in that box of knickknacks in the corner of the closet. You can pick out one more of those ceramic frogs to take home with us."

"What about two? Can't I take two? In case I have a tie between the best ones?"

Colleen Thompson

"Two—if you promise you'll stay in the house and get here on the double when I call you. Otherwise, no deal. Plus there'll be no stops for french fries on the trip home."

"Not even once?"

"Not once."

Eli crossed his heart before disappearing down the back hallway, and Jessup gave Damon a hard look. "Whatever you've come here to say, it's just cost me a couple more coyote-ugly knickknacks. So let's get to it before Eli starts negotiating for a three- or four-way tie."

Damon pulled out a round-backed kitchen chair and sat down without invitation. Mainly because his legs didn't feel up to supporting him. Unable to speak, he pulled the paper from the envelope and laid it on the table.

Mark flipped on the overhead light and took the seat across from Damon. After pulling the paper toward him, Jessup stared down at it for some time before swearing under his breath.

Finally, Damon found his voice. "Is this right?"

"That I bribed Morrell? Of course not. Why the hell would I do that?"

"What about this bid? Is that part true?"

Jessup shrugged. "Well, it was true as of a couple of days ago. Before someone shot at my kid. Since then, I've been thinking of withdrawing it. I'm not sure Hatcher County deserves any kind of favors. Or would even welcome them, from me."

"Favors? What do you mean? What does buying back your family's land have to do with favors for this county?"

"Why do you think I'd be buying it? To live on?"

Considering the reception Jessup had been given,

304

Damon had to admit that seemed unlikely. Unless Jessup's relationship with Beth Ann was more serious than anyone imagined. "I don't know. Why'd you want it?" He felt a smile tip up one corner of his mouth. "To build us a nice toxic waste dump?"

Jessup laughed. "How 'bout a nuclear testing facility?"

Damon grinned in relief at the reaction.

"Actually," Mark said with a shrug, "it's neither. I've been looking to expand my business, which is high-tech and as environmentally friendly as anyone could want. And I started thinking this might be the place to do it. In honor of Lilly Decker, who had the vision and the guts to write me to suggest it."

Damon's heart pounded against his sternum. "You were in touch with Lilly Decker?"

Could he have been right about Mark Jessup from the start? Damon wondered, was he sitting, even joking with a murderer?

Jessup answered with a shrug. "If you can call it that. She wrote back in the beginning of September, pretty persuasively, as I recall. About our so-called 'duty' to save our hometown. And I wrote back to tell her hell, no, only I put it more politely."

"And then what happened?" There had to be more. Otherwise, why would he have killed her?

"She tried once more, but I didn't bother to respond. Then, a week or two afterward, Aimee Baker—I mean Aimee Gustavsen—dug up my office number and called to let me know about my father."

"What about Mrs. Decker? Did she let things rest? Or did she keep bothering you about her idea for a plant here? Did she find out you were coming home and meet you to confront you? Or was it blackmail? Did she threaten you unless you went along with her plan?"

Jessup laughed. "You're watching *way* too much TV, Deputy. As far as Lilly Decker goes, the woman took the hint, and I put her letters out of my mind. I had more than enough to think of with my father dying."

"I'm sorry about that, by the way. It's got to be a real hard thing to lose your daddy the way you did. And I'm sorry, too, you've had so much trouble since you came back." Damon spoke automatically as he struggled to deal with an embarrassment so keen, his ears burned with it. He'd been an idiot, allowing his fantasies of busting this case wide open to color his judgment. Any fool could see that someone in this town had it in for Jessup, that someone was going through a hell of a lot of effort either to kill the guy or run him out of town. Someone who'd have access to information regarding real estate transactions in the county.

Nodding, Jessup sobered. "Apparently, whoever sent that paper's not content with taking potshots at my kid and me. Now this person's out to get you on my case, too."

Damon's mind raced through the possibilities. Including the conversation he had listened in on earlier.

"Which brings me to a question," Mark said. "Why did you come out here to speak to me instead of your boss?"

Damon looked down at the tabletop. There was a faint scorch mark on the maple, where someone had once set an overly hot platter or a pan. He stared at the burn to avoid eye contact.

"Deputy?" Jessup prompted, and when Damon looked up, the man's expression spoke of both patience and the capacity for understanding.

"I overheard something this morning." Damon had to force the words out. "Beth Ann Decker talking to Morrell about a cover-up. It was about that night, the accident. The one you were involved in."

Standing, Mark swore, then muttered, "Why did she have to go and do that?"

"She seemed to think you weren't the only one at fault," said Damon, thinking the explanation might calm him.

But Jessup started pacing and raked a hand through his dark hair. "I could've just left town. Let 'em hate me from afar again. But dredging things up this way—I can't see how it helps anybody."

He stopped in his tracks to stare at Damon. "And I especially can't see how this translates into your thinking I've bribed Morrell to keep quiet over Lilly Decker's murder."

Damon shrugged. "Okay, I admit it. Whoever sent this note probably picked me because he thinks I'm a dumb kid who would fall for anything."

"Or maybe the culprit thinks you're the only one in the department with guts enough to defy the boss. Probably heard you'd been running around town stirring up hard feelings with a lot of questions."

"You know about that, too?"

"This *is* Eudena." Jessup flashed a grin, though bitterness singed the edges of his humor. "You can't help hearing everybody's business, even when you're the resident pariah."

Damon frowned, then allowed, "Guess it's a little better thinking this guy figures me for ballsy and not stupid."

"That would be my pick, too," Jessup told him, "but I'm not so sure this guy's a guy."

Damon looked up sharply. "What? You have a

woman in mind? Someone with a particular grudge against you?"

Jessup gave a nod. "Unfortunately, I do. And she'd certainly have access to that bid you're holding."

"Then name her," Damon told him, thinking that since he was already acting outside the scope of his current assignment, he might as well question two suspects as one.

After he and Jessup wrapped up their conversation, Damon left the house and climbed back into the cab. With the beginnings of a headache pounding at his temples, Damon started the old pickup and backed out onto Lost Buffalo Road. As he headed in the direction of downtown Eudena, he glanced up at his rearview mirror to check for any traffic.

But it was not a vehicle that had him tapping his brake pedal. It was the glimpse of a lone figure crossing the road and trotting toward the cover of the mesquite trees closest to the Jessup house.

Bent low, he or she—Damon couldn't be certain from this distance—was carrying either a shotgun or a rifle. It might be deer season, but this was no deer hunter wearing the required safety orange, or even an illegal poacher.

Both the gun-wielder's furtiveness and location pointed to a more troubling possibility. This was the sniper, the same sniper who had shot at Eli Jessup only days before.

Eager as he was to get to both Gustavsen's Realty and the city hall, Damon pulled the truck to the roadside and reached for his radio. After identifying himself, he told Katie, "We've got another situation out on Lost Buffalo. . . ."

Chapter 29

As Mark strapped Eli into his car seat, the boy frowned. "Are we going to see Maia first? Will we get to see Miz Beth Ann like you said?"

Mark wished he hadn't made that promise. Though he disagreed with her about going to the sheriff, at the same time he admired the incredible courage it had taken. It was just one more thing to love about her, one more thing to miss. Because in his heart he knew that Beth Ann's future lay in Eudena, that she wouldn't put aside the life she'd made to join him, any more than he would come back to the place where he'd known such heartbreak.

The thought of seeing her again, knowing he would leave behind a woman he would always love, made Mark want nothing more than to slip out of this town unnoticed, to drive away as evening faded into a black expanse broken only by the passing headlights of other travelers. He needed the broad prairie emptiness to settle over him, to anesthetize him like a draught of whiskey against the pain he felt.

But Mark wouldn't do it, for he wasn't in the habit of breaking promises to his son. And as difficult as it would be to say goodbye, he'd made a promise to Beth Ann, too, and he would honor it.

"Sure, Eli," he finally answered in a voice rough with emotion. "We'll go and say a quick goodbye. And then how 'bout we stop at the Dairy Queen on our way out of town. We'll pick you up one of those meals with the toy in it."

Mark's mood darkened another shade at the realization that he had descended to the level of bribing his own kid with junk food.

At the sound of a loud crack, Mark jerked back so suddenly, he banged his head against the door frame. Recognizing the noise as a gunshot, he yelled, "Get down, Eli," and slammed the truck door closed in the hope it would offer some protection.

Mark glanced over his shoulder before darting around the hood to the driver's side door. He opened it, intent on ducking inside and driving both of them to safety, but he heard someone shouting.

"Wait. I've got him. I've got the shooter."

Mark froze. It sounded like Stillwater, from the trees to his left.

"Deputy?" Mark called back.

He heard voices, rough and low, but only seconds later, Stillwater emerged from behind the screen of the mesquite, half guiding and half pushing a handcuffed man in front of him. A man Mark didn't know, though it was difficult to be certain since the prisoner kept his head down and was dressed head to toe in desert camouflage. His upper right sleeve had a slashlike tear, and blood was dripping from it. Damon must have winged him with that shot Mark had heard, but at the moment the deputy was reciting the man's rights.

"Here's your sniper," Deputy Stillwater announced once he'd finished.

At their approach, Eli bailed out of the car.

"It's the bad man." Excitement pitched the boy's voice higher. "The one I saw when I got my scar. You got him. You really got him."

The man glared at Eli. "Shut up. Just shut up, you freak of nature."

Wild blue eyes turned to stare at Mark. "Wish I'd put a bullet through his heart so you could know how it felt. So you'd find out what it means to have a child murdered."

As the voice cracked, Mark knew him. Larinda's father, Billy Hyatt, looking far grayer and craggier than Mark remembered from the trial, as if the man had aged thirty years instead of just sixteen. As the county's tax assessor, he would have been the person Aimee consulted to find out who owned the property Mark wished to buy. Had he then contacted the owner with some excuse to get a copy of the bid before sending Stillwater the anonymous message?

"Get back in the truck, Eli." No need for his son to hear any more of this ugliness than he had already.

"Now we're safe here for sure," Eli exclaimed before Mark sent him a look that had him scrambling back inside the pickup. As curious as the boy was bound to be, he'd probably crack the window to eavesdrop, but Mark still felt better getting him out of Hyatt's line of vision.

"What happened to your daughter was a terrible accident, one that I regret with all my heart," Mark said.

"But you tried to shoot a five-year-old. And you tried to kill a woman at the funeral home."

Hyatt shook his head. "I'd never hurt Poor Beth Ann. It was you I wanted. But that girl lied to me, she *lied*. She tricked me into thinking I had killed you. I don't understand it. I never would have let Larinda go anywhere with that girl if I'd figured she'd grow up to be such a liar."

The man sounded near tears, wounded by the desperate falsehood of a woman under fire.

The deputy shook his head. "You maybe want to save it for now, Mr. Hyatt? Talk to a lawyer first before you say more."

With a glance at Mark, Stillwater added, "At least until we get you in a room with a recorder. Otherwise, it's not admissible . . . for later."

"Do you have backup coming?" Mark asked him.

Damon shook his head. "No reason to call backup now. Everything's under control here. Glad I spotted this fella. Man had a rifle on him—it's still out there."

Mark blew out a long breath. If Stillwater hadn't seen Hyatt, would Eli be dead now? Or would the boy have had to watch as his father was gunned down?

"Thank you," Mark said simply. "Thank you. Do you need any help with him?"

Stillwater glanced at Hyatt. "Don't think so. I'll collect that gun of his, and then we'll go back to my truck and call the sheriff's office. I'll have someone meet us at the hospital, where we'll have Mr. Hyatt's arm looked at before he's transported back to the sheriff's office. I will need you to drop by and make a statement, get the complaint against this fella sorted out before you leave town."

Mark nodded. "I'll be by as soon as I see . . . as soon as I see Beth Ann."

For in the backwash of relief, his heart was flooded with a need to hold her, to talk to the only person who could understand what he felt at learning the depth of Hyatt's rage. Even more, Mark ached to hold her close and to tell Beth Ann he *did* understand the way the past weighed on her—and to do all that he could to convince her that the best chance they stood of shouldering that burden was together.

Home sounded so damned good now.

Beth Ann had run late at Len Johnston's since, for some reason or another, the home health care aide hadn't bothered to show up earlier, maybe hadn't shown for days, judging from the man's condition. He was in dire need of a bath and a change of bedding, and though those tasks weren't technically her job and the work made her back throb in protest, Beth Ann couldn't very well leave the frail, eighty-three-year-old wife to deal with the situation on her own.

Once she finally left, she phoned Cheryl with the intention of griping big-time about the AWOL aide. Beth Ann had to settle for voice mail, though, because Cheryl wasn't in her office. Probably, she was out tooling around in that slick new ride she'd bought—if Pete hadn't beaten her to the car keys. The couple hadn't purchased a vehicle in eons, and they were like a pair of toddlers squabbling over the same toy.

Shaking her head at the thought, Beth Ann pocketed her phone. She still had plenty of paperwork that needed her attention, but instead of heading toward the cramped rat hole the hospital district called an office, she made straight for home. No reason she couldn't fill out her reports sitting in her favorite chair, with her legs propped up, a big turkey sandwich at her elbow, and maybe some Nora Jones tunes, fine and mellow on the stereo.

But as relaxing as that scenario sounded, her mind worried at the question of whether Mark had left already, forgetting his promise to get in touch before he did so.

He wouldn't do that to me. He's not that kind of man.

It was one of the things she loved best about him, that he chose to do the right thing, no matter how hard it might be on him. As it might be if he had heard she'd gone to see the sheriff.

Beth Ann hadn't missed the quick dispersal of eavesdroppers outside Morrell's office, any one of whom could have begun a rumor that had made its way to Mark. Or what if the sheriff had stopped by to see Mark after she'd left? Could he have urged Mark to make tracks back to Yankee territory as soon as possible?

Even if the sheriff had insisted, Beth Ann still couldn't believe Mark wouldn't try to contact her before he left. Unless something was wrong, she realized, her stomach going cold as she thought about the sniper.

As she hung a right onto Mill Pond Bend, Beth Ann decided to phone Mark as soon as she got to the house and find out if her worries had any basis in reality.

After passing a parked car on the street, she pushed the security code on her garage door opener, then waited for the door to rise before she pulled her SUV inside. Unable to get her mind off the thought that something terrible had happened, she hurried to unlock the connecting door and reached toward the keypad to disengage the Lucky Pull's alarm. But in the space of a heartbeat, three realizations struck her: The alarm wasn't turned on, as she had left it; the dog's muffled barking meant that she was shut up somewhere, since she hadn't rushed out with an effusive greeting; and there was a pungent, rotten-egg stench strong enough to take her breath away.

It came to her at once that she hadn't practiced the procedure to arm the new system with Rosario, and the housekeeper's grasp of English could be spotty. Since she'd seemed leery of Maia the day she'd picked up the new key, Rosario might have shut the dog up somewhere, too. But there was a frantic edge to the Lab's barking that punched up Beth Ann's pulse rate—along with the realization that she was smelling natural gas.

Could Rosario or her sister have accidentally turned on the stove's gas jet without noticing while she'd cleaned? It seemed unlikely, but the reason for the leak hardly mattered to Beth Ann at the moment. What counted was getting out of this house and calling the gas company before she accidentally sparked off an explosion.

But she wasn't leaving Maia behind to asphyxiate. With that thought in mind, Beth Ann hurried in the direction of the frantic barking.

Chapter 30

As Mark turned right onto Mill Pond Bend, he heard what sounded like a clap of thunder, though only wispy clouds floated in the dimming sky. Eli—who was growing more cheerful by the minute—distracted him from the thought, laughing and pointing out the white duck giving his friend a piggyback ride in the water.

Her friend, Mark could have corrected, since the ducks were clearly working on increasing the local duckling population. But instead of seizing the moment for an impromptu lesson on such matters, or even wondering why the birds were getting amorous out of season, he felt his face heat as he asked, "Hey, isn't that a turtle over there?"

As a car passed on its way out of the neighborhood, Eli did a double-take. "That's only an old rock, Dad, and how come you're getting all red?"

"Guess I'd better get my eyes checked," Mark said as he began the turn into Beth Ann's driveway.

Began but never finished, for the sight of shattered glass had him slamming on his brakes.

"The bad man was here, too." Fear raised Eli's voice an octave. "He busted out the windows."

As Mark stared at the dust and smoke billowing through the broken glass, a dark-haired teenaged boy in jeans and a Cowboys sweatshirt burst out of the house next door, his eyes wild as he, too, gaped at the Lucky Pull.

Mark threw his truck into park and jumped out. He looked toward the house next door and saw that several of its windows had cracked, as well.

Explosion, Mark thought. What he'd taken for a thunderclap had been something far more frightening.

"What happened?" the boy yelled to him. "It sounded like a crash, or . . . oh, shit. It's on fire."

Eli climbed out of his car seat, slipped out the open driver's side door, and clung tightly to his father's hand. "Where's Miz Beth Ann? Where's Maia?"

Ignoring him for the moment, Mark told the older boy, "I'm going to see if Beth Ann's in there. But I need you to take my son to your house and call for help— sheriff, fire, ambulance, the whole works, in case she's home and hurt."

The teenager went dead white as he stared toward the Lucky Pull's rear. "Oh, man. I'm pretty sure she *is* home. I heard her garage door go down just before the boom."

Since Beth Ann's garage was nearest the property line, Mark believed him.

Snapping out of his daze, the teen tried to run past him. "We have to get her out of there. She could be hurt bad, and look at that black smoke."

Mark intercepted him and shouted in his face. "You take my son inside where it's safe. Then call for help and get your parents."

"I'll call them, too—they're out now."

Mark squeezed his son's hand before peeling it off and passing it to the older boy. "I'm trusting you with my son's life."

"Daddy, I don't want to go. I want Miz Beth Ann and Maia." Big tears ran down Eli's face.

"I'm Matthias," the teen said as he swept the boy up in his arms. "Everything's gonna be all right. Come and help me make that call."

As Matthias started off with Eli, Mark saw flames flickering through the side windows and black smoke pouring from the back side of the mansion. He raced to the front, which didn't appear to be as heavily involved, and shouted Beth Ann's name through a window that looked into the smoke-charged living room.

Struggling not to cough, Mark screamed above the shifting, groaning, and crackling, ignoring the warbling shriek of an alarm. "Beth Ann. Where are you?"

He listened for a voice, a cry—any kind of answer. No human sound reached him, but he thought he detected frantic barking.

Instinct told him the Lab would be with Beth Ann, but where were they in the house? With the storm of sound and smoke, it was impossible to judge. But he couldn't afford to wait for help, not with conditions growing more dangerous by the second.

Fear ripped through him at the thought that Beth Ann could have been killed by the blast. God, no— fate couldn't be so cruel.

Pulling off his jacket, Mark wrapped the denim around his right fist, then used both his protected hand and booted foot to smash out enough of the remaining window glass to allow him to climb through. Once inside, he immediately tripped over a low table, but his fall turned out to be a blessing since it put him beneath the thickest smoke.

He could breathe well enough, at least for the moment, but his eyes were watering so badly, Mark could barely see a thing. Worse yet, he could no longer hear Maia. Had her barking been drowned out by the cacophony around him? Or had the big Lab, with her mistress, already fallen victim to the flames?

Chapter 31

"He'll get her out. He'll save her."

On hearing the relief in those words, the One Appointed glared an accusation at the Companion. *Betrayer!* Never again could such disloyalty be permitted.

"He *can't* get her out—she knows. We're turning around now."

The Companion's head shook. "No. We can't. Place'll burn for sure—all that gasoline we poured, plus the explosion. The evidence will burn, too."

"The letter isn't in there. The whore's daughter found it and showed it to the sheriff, showed it to her lover—"

"You can't know that. I told you, you can't—"

"I have seen it. I have been shown. Better they should all die, to protect the innocent."

"How will it protect anyone if we're caught here?"

The One Appointed opened the glove box and slipped a handgun from its padded case. "Where *is* your faith? Have you not felt His pleasure? Have you not heard the Lord's voice saying we cannot fail in this, not so long as we serve Him in all His fearful glory. And we will not fail in courage, either. . . . There can be no turning back."

The letter from her mother saved her life, that same, odd message that had frustrated and confused Beth Ann when Mama's lawyer, Mr. Lipscomb, gave it to her after the funeral. Stepping past Maia and inside the office, Beth Ann had meant to grab the file folder where she'd placed it, along with the contents of the safe deposit box and the doodled note that had been hidden in the globe.

Beth Ann's action had been more instinctive than well-reasoned; she had only time to think, *important papers,* and edge inside before a blast shoved her forward and a wall of sound rolled over her. She was knocked to the floor as debris pelted her like hailstones. Mixed in with the burst of noise, she heard a sharp yelp, but she didn't know whether it had come from her or from Maia, who had been at her side.

For a while—she had no sense of how long—Beth Ann lay insensible, too stunned to think or move. The world had fallen silent, but warm wetness broke through her shock. *Blood,* she finally realized, once her thoughts took shape. *I'm bleeding?*

But as she reached toward her face, she felt Maia. Sweet Maia, lapping at her cheek to rouse her. Beth Ann opened her eyes, or tried to, but they weren't cooperating. Something in the air—she registered a charred taste—had her coughing, and when she wiped at her face and eyes, they felt chalky, gritty with thick dust.

She blinked and tried once more to look around her. Through a pale haze, she saw the yellow Lab's face close to hers. Wild with excitement, the dog pawed at her and appeared to bark, but all Beth Ann heard was the cataclysmic ringing in her own ears.

Recalling the gas odor, she understood. *Explosion. I could have been blown up—still could die if there's a fire.*

As her vision cleared a little more, she saw that chairs had been knocked over and items from her desk and bookshelves were strewn about the floor. But she could make out only the hazy lower strata of the room, for above her, dark smoke charged the air.

House burning. Have to get out.

File forgotten, Beth Ann felt for her cane. But she couldn't find the thing, couldn't find much, with the absurd exception of a mariachi duck. Hurling it aside in disgust, she righted the nearest chair and used it to pull herself into a stoop.

With the change in position, she hacked and choked until she dropped down again, where she found her purse and slung the strap around her neck and shoulder. Still on the floor, she struggled on hands and knees toward the door, her crawling slowed by the throbbing strain of her old injuries, along with what felt like a bruised hip.

Frantic, Maia grabbed both the purse strap and a clump of material from Beth Ann's top and pulled with her strong jaws, but the dog only succeeded in dropping her mistress flat onto her belly.

"Damn it," Beth Ann shouted in frustration—and heard the dim echo of her words despite the loud ringing in her ears. Maia barked near her face, and this time Beth Ann caught some bit of that sound, too.

Yet she couldn't hear the shattering of glass or the collapse of a wall inside the house. Nor did she make out her own name as it was shouted, only a room away.

Chapter 32

Damon hadn't quite made it to the hospital with his prisoner when a call came over the radio.

"Deputy Stillwater—Damon." Normal protocol was left behind in the rush of Katie's panic. "It's the sheriff. I was worried when he wouldn't answer. No one else was here, so I jimmied his lock and found him passed out cold behind his desk."

Oh, shit. New to the job and clearly shaken, Katie must have forgotten that people all around town were listening on their scanners. Doubtless, some of them were remembering Evelyn Morrell's complaints about her husband.

"Call an ambulance," Damon told Katie. Maybe it was the old man's heart; a cardiac scare could be forgiven. "Check to see if he's still breathing."

"Oh, no, it's not that," Katie blurted. "I think he'll just need a little time, hot, black coffee, and some clean pants—"

Damon made a sharp turn, changing course. "Katie,

wait until I get there. And not another word about this on the radio."

"*Oh!* Oh, God." She sounded horrified at her lapse. "All right. I'll see you."

In the passenger seat beside him, his handcuffed passenger, Billy Hyatt, straightened, his eyes sullen and suspicious. "What's this? I thought we were heading to the emergency room about my arm."

Damon didn't answer, and he didn't get far before Katie called over the radio again, her voice shakier than ever.

"Rescue Unit Two, Deputy Stillwater, all personnel. A call just came in. There's a report of a fire and explosion at 107 East Mill Pond Bend. Any volunteers listening to scanners, please respond. Respond now—hurry. Caller says there are two people trapped inside the house."

The Lucky Pull, Damon thought as he changed course once more and careened around a corner, his concentration so fierce that he barely registered his prisoner's pleas and screams.

"Aren't you taking me to jail?" Hyatt stared at him with scared eyes as they blasted through a stop sign. "I think I ought to go to jail now. I want to call my wife and have her get me a lawyer."

"Shut up," Damon told him. "You'll see the inside of a cell soon enough and long enough to suit you. This is just a little detour."

Dazed, blinded, and dripping with sweat, Mark had lost track of where he was. He'd thought he was crawling in the direction where he'd last heard barking, but terror and adrenaline spawned confusion. Though he fought to form a mental image of the lower story's layout, he couldn't make the picture come together. His sense of left and right—never strong because of his dyslexia—fled completely, and he was breathless from coughing and shouting Beth Ann's name.

I could die in here, he realized for the first time, and he thought of Eli, left with some teenager they didn't even know. Yet Mark couldn't make himself give up on Beth Ann, and even if he did, he was no longer sure of the way back to the place he'd come inside.

Desperate to reorient himself, Mark reached up, his hand fumbling with some piece of furniture—maybe a lamp table? But in his hurry, he ended up flipping it and bringing something heavy down atop his head.

Chapter 33

Beth Ann thought of changing direction and making for the window, but Maia barked furiously and stubbornly blocked the way, no matter how many times her mistress pushed her. Since the door was closer anyway, Beth Ann half crawled, half dragged herself in that direction.

She came across the cane, lying in the doorway. She grasped the stick, though creeping along as she was would be awkward with it, and she didn't dare stand.

Maia bounded over her and barked again, but Beth Ann saw not only smoke, but the orange pulse of flame in that direction. Reaching out, she tried to snag the dog's collar. . . .

Her hand slapped instead against a sprawled, but clearly human body.

Maia was lapping at the face—Mark's face, Beth Ann realized with a cry. Oh, God, not Mark—had he tried to save her? Had he died because of her?

But she felt him move as his hand reached to his head, and faintly, she heard him moan.

"Mark," she screamed. "Wake up, Mark. We have to get out right now. This way—through the office window. Hurry."

He coughed, then said, "Beth Ann. I was—was scared the fire got you."

"Come on." She pulled at his arm, and after a moment, he responded.

They helped each other back inside the office. This time, Maia, who must have heard Mark outside the room, followed, and Beth Ann closed the office door behind them to block as much heat and smoke as possible.

Though there was much to say, neither could spare the breath for anything but making their way to the window, which Mark quickly opened.

He helped Beth Ann out first and allowed Maia to follow before joining her on a strip of grass near the back deck leading to the pool. Still on hands and knees, Beth Ann sucked in draught after draught of air before looking up to see a face she knew well.

"We need help," she cried—only a split second before realizing that the person she had every reason to expect would bring salvation was instead holding a gun on her and Mark.

"Don't you move, whore's daughter."

Still blinded by soot, Mark couldn't see the speaker, but he heard the icy malevolence radiating from the voice. *Her* voice, he quickly realized, but it sounded strange and unfamiliar.

He started to get up, but Beth Ann grabbed his arm.

"She's got a *gun,* Mark," she cried. "She's pointing it at you. Please, stop this—can't you see we need help?"

"I'll shoot him first if you won't be still."

"Put the gun down, Ginny," a man's voice ordered. "This has gone too far."

Mark risked wiping his eyes against the sleeve of his shirt, then blinked until he saw blurred figures. The female, an older woman with an old-fashioned, blond dome of hair, swung her pistol to point it at the heavy-set man beside her.

"I've told you," she shrieked, "I'll tolerate no more betrayal. Bad enough that you've lain with a whore, let alone played me false for her daughter."

"Ginny, stop this," he said, and at once, Mark recognized him. He was Earl Stillwater, owner of the local hardware store. Was this wild-eyed creature his wife—and Damon Stillwater's mother?

"You're the one who told me to think of our children and their innocence," she shrieked at her husband. "The one who lent me strength when mine faltered, the one who mentioned how a person might get the plans for anyone's alarm system."

"I was scared, yes, but it's gone too far, involved too many people. Can't you see how crazy this is?" Earl Stillwater persisted. "If this stops now, we can get you in a hospital. Ginny, darling, *you* can still be saved."

"What therefore God hath joined together—" The shot cracked, louder than the fire. As Earl Stillwater dropped to the deck, his forehead perforated, the woman calmly finished, "Let no man—*or woman*—put asunder."

"What are you *doing?*" Beth Ann screamed at her, and the gun's muzzle turned her way.

"What I should have done the moment I found out." Exhaustion hollowed Ginny's voice.

Mark made a wild lunge, shoving Beth Ann aside as

he sprang forward, intent on overpowering the crazed woman.

He felt the bullet's punch to his chest before he heard it, felt the strength flow from his body . . .

And then felt nothing but unimaginable pain as he struggled to draw breath.

Something tore away inside Beth Ann as she rolled Mark over and saw the frothy blood gurgling from a right-side chest puncture and the glassiness of shock veiling his eyes as his mouth gaped. *Lung shot,* she knew instantly. *It's got to be a sucking chest wound.*

Not caring whether Ginny Stillwater killed her, too, Beth Ann leaned over him and pressed her palms against the oozing hole in a desperate attempt and seal it and keep his lungs from totally collapsing. Beside her, Maia whined and lay close beside Mark's body.

"Mama, no," a man screamed.

A glance told Beth Ann it was Damon Stillwater, in uniform. His gun drawn, he was sobbing as he shouted, "What have you done, Mama? What have you done to my father?"

"Put the gun down, Ginny," Beth Ann pleaded as she felt Mark draw a ragged breath. "We'll get them both help. We can make this better."

"I've been a good and godly wife," Ginny told her son as her pistol's muzzle wavered. "I've been the help-mate that the Lord intended. But he wanted that woman—nothing but that whore, with her false words and her false breasts—and then her hell-spawned money to tempt him yet again."

"You killed my mother," Beth Ann said, mostly to herself, though the knowledge seemed remote, with

Mark laboring for each breath beneath the weak seal of her palms.

Widening his stance, Damon said, "Drop the weapon, Mama. You're sick. We'll get you to a doctor."

She was sick, Beth Ann realized. But right now, nothing mattered except stopping her while there was still a chance to save Mark.

A glance told her that Earl Stillwater was already beyond that possibility.

Resolutely, Ginny Stillwater pointed the gun back toward Beth Ann. "She has to die. She has the proof about the accident—and she showed it to her lover."

"I love you, Mark. I love you," Beth Ann whispered, tears cascading down her face.

"Poor Beth Ann, you'll walk on two good legs in heaven," Ginny promised. "The Lord's voice hath decreed it."

A third shot exploded, but instead of dying, Beth Ann gaped at the realization that Deputy Damon Stillwater had put a bullet through his mother's heart.

Chapter 34

Three days later . . .

"If it isn't Miz MacGyver," Mark said with a wry smile. "I heard you saved me with a plastic bag from Barty's One-Stop and a roll of duct tape. How come you didn't tell me?"

Beth Ann only stared at him as tears welled in her eyes. It seemed only yesterday that she and Cheryl, who'd arrived at Jackrabbit General just as the helicopter took off, had driven hell-for-leather from Eudena clear to Dallas, where he'd been air-lifted to the nearest Level One trauma center. For five long hours, Beth Ann had prayed and prayed, yet she had been certain she would arrive to find him dead.

Instead, he'd been in recovery after surgery. Since then, she had stayed at his side. But she'd had to make an exception for today's trip, a nearly intolerable commute to Wichita Falls in a rental car, since Cheryl had had to leave last night to take care of her kids and check on Eli, who was camping out with Mrs. Minton.

All the way back to the Dallas hospital, Beth Ann had imagined some setback would snatch Mark from her: a sudden fever or a staph infection, though she knew the chances were remote.

As she had after each leave-taking since the shooting, she feasted her eyes on him. He looked much better this afternoon, she decided, his color good, his breathing nearly normal as he lay back among the white-cased pillows. But how would he feel once she told him what she'd learned today?

"I did tell you how I rigged that seal for your chest." She hugged her own arms as the images returned to haunt her. "Several times, since you kept asking. It's just that you were too drugged up to remember."

"Come on, Beth Ann." Mark reached up and brushed moisture from her face. "It's okay to lighten up now. I'll be fine, I promise. The doctors said they'll be turning me loose in just a few more days."

She captured his hand and kissed his knuckles, where she tasted her own tears.

"Besides," he added, "proficiency with duct tape gives you automatic admission to the Hot Babe Hall of Fame."

In spite of her anxiety, she smiled and rolled her eyes. "Only a true guy would think that. Now, can I get you anything? Some water? Or do you need more pain medication?"

He looked up into her face. "All I needed was that smile. That's all I'll ever need."

"It's yours, Mark," she vowed, "whenever and wherever you want it. Even at your place in Pittsburgh."

If he still wanted her once she shared the news about Earl Stillwater and her mother.

"My place," Mark said, "is wherever you are, Beth Ann. And if that's in Eudena, so be it."

"But I thought you said you'd never—"

"I'm going to build a plant there, in honor of all the good that still lives in our hometown. Good I never would have seen without you."

Beth Ann couldn't help herself. Fresh tears spilled.

"In return, I'm asking only two things," he said.

She nodded. "Anything you want."

His gaze softened as he studied her. "I want you to take a little time off, see some of the country with me, some of the world outside Hatcher County. The Grand Canyon, Hawaii, Paris, Venice—I don't care. Wherever you and Eli want to go."

"Such a hardship," she said, allowing herself to imagine the three of them together, traveling almost as a family. "However will I cope?"

"You haven't heard the hard part yet. I want you to marry me, Beth Ann. Please. It's all—*you're* all—I've ever wanted in this world."

"That and a good, stout roll of duct tape."

He winced as laughter strained his healing wound, now bound with higher-tech materials. Sobering abruptly, he said, "Don't mess with me, woman. Just tell me that you love me and say you'll be my wife."

She sighed. "I do love you, more than anything. When I saw you lying there, the blood bubbling out of you—I thought my life was over. I knew I couldn't go on breathing if you didn't. I—"

"Shh, Beth Ann. It's over. Please don't cry again."

Pressing her lips together, she struggled to regroup. "Before this goes one bit further, there's something I need you to know. And then maybe—maybe you won't be so eager to get married."

Mark used the remote to incline his bed more, his dark eyes growing somber. "What is it? What did you find out?"

She had told him this morning that she was driving to the dealership in Wichita Falls, to pick up the envelope the auto salesman had retrieved from her mother's old Mercedes. The sedan's hidden trunk compartment had been locked, but Beth Ann knew at once the combination.

Her mother had used the date of the collision sixteen years before. Secreted inside, she'd left two letters, only one of them in her handwriting.

"There was something from Earl Stillwater." Beth Ann sat next to Mark, where the bedrail had been lowered. "A letter written to my mother a few weeks after the accident. *Our* accident. And he—he said—"

Mark gingerly reached over her shoulder and pulled her closer to his good side. "Go ahead. Just tell me."

"He begged for her forgiveness. He never meant for anyone to get hurt—anyone, that is, except my—my father."

Mark looked at her, his confusion obvious.

"He and my—my mother were having an affair. They talked about—" Beth Ann had to stop to catch her breath. "They talked about running away together. To Mama, it was just talk—she swore it in the letter she left, but Earl Stillwater took it seriously. He sabotaged my father's car. My dad was dying anyway, Earl figured. Why not get the insurance right away so he and my mother could use the money for a fresh start somewhere new?"

"Son of a bitch cut your brake line, didn't he?" Mark guessed. "That's why it gave when you pushed down on it."

Beth Ann nodded. "I think that's right. He didn't say exactly in his letter. He just begged Mama's forgiveness and told her he understood why she'd chosen to stay with me, since I'd been hurt so badly."

"That selfish bastard," Mark said. "And your mother *knew* he did it. Knew it all these years and yet said nothing."

"I don't think she knew until she got his message." Beth Ann told him. "In her letter, she claims that when she found out, she was terrified she'd be implicated and no one would believe her because of the way she—the way she was with men. She said what she most feared was being sent to prison, where she couldn't help me through my rehabilitation."

Mark went silent, leaving Beth Ann to imagine his fury at the years he'd spent behind bars, partly because of her mother's decision.

Beth Ann endured the stillness for as long as she could before saying, "She was wrong, I understand that. An irresponsible adulteress, but she'd never be part of a conspiracy to murder."

"Only to a conspiracy to send me to jail."

"You're right. She should have spoken up for you instead of hiding Earl's letter all these years. She was weak and wrong and selfish, and I wouldn't blame you if you hate her. But she was still my mother, Mark, and in spite of all of it, I loved her. I still love her, and I'll miss her all my life."

Beside her, she felt Mark's head shake.

"I'm angry. I admit it," he said. "But I can't really hate her, either. In the end, Lilly Decker was the first to reach out to me from Eudena. And God help her, she paid for her sins, and paid horribly."

Beth Ann nodded. "Yes, she did. After the accident, she broke off all contact with Earl, but when she won that jackpot, he showed up again, insisting there was no reason they couldn't be together now that money was no object. Mama told him she'd kept his letter, and she used it to blackmail him into staying clear of her. The only problem was that Ginny Stillwater somehow found out about the whole thing."

"How?"

"I don't know. Maybe she followed her husband, or caught on to his behavior somehow and then kept after him until he told her everything. But when he did, she went off the deep end and killed Mama."

"The woman was insane. I've never seen anyone so completely unhinged."

Beth Ann nodded. "She was a sick woman, sick with lupus, which sometimes affects the brain. I think that, combined with the shock, caused a psychotic break. She really thought that God was speaking to her, telling her to do such horrible things."

"A damned shame her own son had to be the one to kill her. Poor Damon. He's a good kid, but this kind of thing—I'm not sure how he'll come through it. I know he's a deputy, but still, he's not so much older than I was, back when all hell broke loose."

Beth Ann squeezed Mark's hand, awed by his capacity to think of someone else in spite of all he'd been through. She could look for a thousand years and never find another such man. How could she have imagined for a moment that his feelings for her would change when he learned of her mother's secret?

"It'll be much harder for Damon if this comes out," she said, "about his father, that is, what he did to that car and why."

Mark perked up. "You said *if*."

She drew in a deep breath and moved to get the envelope, which she had laid beside her purse on the bedside chair. After removing the two letters, she handed both to him.

"It's completely up to you, Mark," she said. "I've been thinking a lot about what you asked me earlier. About who it would help to bring the accident up again at this point. Earl and Ginny Stillwater are both dead, and Morrell's been disgraced. Gene Calvert is locked up, along with Billy Hyatt."

Mark nodded. "Almost everyone who's had a hand in this has paid a steep price. And those who didn't will have to live with themselves—and there's a cost to that, too. Maybe a higher one than we know."

"So who's left but the innocent to suffer if we share this?" Beth Ann asked him, then began to tick them off. "Larinda's mother, who's already dealing with her husband's arrest; Heidi Brown's family; and especially poor Damon and his sister. But still, you've taken all the heat for that head-on for so long."

"I can handle it," he told her as he tore the pair of letters into pieces. "I can handle anything, just as long as I have you."

Carefully she sat back down beside him, her heart overflowing with all the things she'd given up the hope of having, all the things she'd found in him.

As she put her arms around him, she said, "Forever, then, Jess," and sealed her promise with a kiss as firm as bedrock and a love that stretched eternal as the unblinking prairie sky.

Coming in December 2007

THE SALT MAIDEN

by

COLLEEN THOMPSON

CHAPTER ONE

Long before the ancient Aztecs and Egyptians ever dreamed of making mummies, nature had perfected her technique. First, take a body—a human's, for example—and protect it from the ravages of predators and weather. Then find a quick way to strip the corpse's tissues of all water content.

Dry winds do a fine job, providing the unfortunate's final resting place is cold enough to discourage hungry insects. But even in a hot locale—let's say the arid country of West Texas—certain natural compounds serve the purpose quite well.

One of the most effective substances is common salt, including the white crystals surrounding a body in a cavern so far beneath the desert's surface, the coyotes and the turkey vultures never sense its presence. And neither do the searchers, whether they use horses, SUVs, or small planes in their hunt for one missing woman amid the hundreds of square miles where rattlesnakes outnumber humans and scorpions have outlasted every species since the dinosaurs. Could she speak, our modern mummy might beg the searchers to look longer and look deeper. But of course, she's been beyond that for some time.

Dana Vanover stopped dead in the middle of the hallway of Texas Children's Hospital in Houston. Her head was already shaking as her mother turned.

"I'm not doing this," Dana told her. "I'm sorry for these people, Mom. Truly sorry their daughter's condition is so serious. But I don't want to get to know them. I don't want to feel…"

Her mother arched an elegantly-sculpted blond brow and folded arms both tanned and toned from tennis. Her latest cosmetic procedures might have smoothed the lines from her face, but they did nothing to erase the disapproval. "Feel what, Dana? Sympathy for the only grandchild I'll—?"

"She's really not your grandchild, or my niece either. Angie saw to that when she put her up for adoption. Nikki belongs to the Harrisons. We were never meant to know about her. And we never would have if she weren't in such bad shape."

Tears welled in her mother's green eyes. "They've asked for our help. To save that dear child's life."

Though Isabel had only learned of the "dear child" when a private investigator had landed on her doorstep three weeks earlier, here she stood, playing the Queen of Empathy, though she had never shown more than ill-disguised revulsion for her own two daughters' illnesses. Had Nikki Harrison and her parents really won Isabel over during her first, brief visit to the cancer center, or was she merely trying on the role of distraught grandmother to see how well it suited?

"We've both been tested," Dana told her, "and if the match had been good, I would have gladly donated bone marrow for a transplant. But it's not a possibility, and I can't afford to get any more involved in this—"

"You used to be such a caring girl. And you still do so much good. For animals, at least. "

Dana braced herself against the implication that she thought more about her canine and feline patients than people. "I told you, I *am* sorry. But I can't bleed for everybody, Mom. I don't have the energy right now. I have a veterinary clinic operating at a loss, thanks to the time I took off after surgery. And I still have a ton of wedding gifts to send back, along with some pretty damned awkward notes to go with them—"

"You haven't finished that *yet?*" Her mothers eyes shot wide. "Oh, Dana. It's been more than three months now. What on earth are people going to *think?*"

Dana didn't have an answer. She felt guilty enough without the woman hammering the nail deeper.

After passng a nurse's station, her mother paused to check the room numbers on a sign before she turned a corner. Dana followed in her wake, helpless as a leaf drawn by the current. But not as unprotesting.

"I'm sorry, Mom. Sorry *I* won't be giving you a grandchild. Sorry I hven't been able to write your friends to tell them, 'Here's your Waterford dust-catcher back, thanks anyway. Rat bastard fiancé thought the whole hysterectomy-at-thirty-one thing was too much of a downer.'" She wanted to deck the sniveling coward every time she thought about how Alex had dumped her by text message and then ducked the resulting shit-storm with a quick transfer to the New York office of his brokerage firm. "And I'm especially sorry I can't get sucked into another of my big sister's dramas right now."

"Finding Angie is the least we can do to save that sweet child. And her parents—when you see how hard they're praying for a miracle, how totally devoted they are to—"

Still following, Dana cut her off. "There's no guarantee Angie's going to be a match, even if we did know where to find her. She still hasn't cashed those checks, right?"

Dana and her sister each received a modest monthly stipend from a trust fund set up after their father's death. Neither would come into the full amount until she turned thirty-five. For Angie, that was less than a year away. Then she'd be free to blow two-point-four million dollars on her various addictions. Until then, however, she depended on the monthly payments. But Dana wasn't too worried that Angie had put off cashing the last two mailed to her. It probably meant she'd drifted into a relationship with a man content to pay the bills for as long as the ride lasted. Or possibly, she was so into one of her commissioned weavings that she'd temporarily forgotten about drugs—or even food. Or maybe she'd hooked up with some commune and given over all her cares to Jesus. Where Angie was concerned, almost anything could happen—except another rescue from her sister. That ship had sailed—and sunk—already.

"She hasn't cashed them," Isabel confirmed, "and when I called, the sheriff told me no one's seen her in at least two months. But she can't have gone far. He found her car out by the house where she was living. Apparently, the engine's gone bad. Something about a cracked block, maybe?"

Dana felt the first frission of unease then. "What about her loom?"

"He says as far as he can tell, all her things are still there. And I asked especially about the loom."

It's not my problem, not my problem, not my problem. Dana repeated the words until they blended like a mantra. Angie had sworn at her for rushing to the rescue at the last place, had skipped out of town and vanished the time before that. *And if I have to fight with her now, on top of everything else…*Dana rubbed her temples, but she couldn't hold back her concern.

Troubled though she might be, Angie wouldn't leave her loom behind. Not that one thing, not ever. Once, during a rare, calm visit while Angie was in rehab, she had described it to Dana as her only constant: the shuttle that married the varied strands of warp to weft and wove scant snatches of peace out of her chaos. She could become almost poetic when she talked about it. Angelina Morningstar, she called her weaver self, the artist. Other people called her that, too, and during her more stable periods, "Angelina" made good money selling work inspired by years' worth of cultural anthroplogy courses that had never quite translated into a degree.

"Maybe you should fly out there and check on her." Dana's suggestion slipped out before she could stop herself, though she already suspected it was a lost cause.

Her mother paused before a closed door. "Heaven knows I've tried enough times. But you know very well she'll head for the hills if she hears I'm within a hundred miles. Besides, Jerome has put his foot down this time."

Although her mother's husband of six years loved nothing more than seeing his name listed among the big-time benefactors of well-publicized charitable endeavors, the real estate developer had never approved of his wife "enabling" Angie's irresponsible behavior. But Dana suspected Isabel was using him as an excuse, that she would far rather send her younger daughter as an emissary and throw money at the trouble than risk yet another heartbreak. It was tough to fault her mother, since Dana wished that she could do the same thing, that the buck didn't always stop, inevitably, with her.

"I'm *not* doing it this time," she insisted. "And I'm not

going to make the Harrison family's tragedy mine."

Her mother raised her knuckles toward the door and paused to give her a look from the intersection of Shrewd and Appraising. "Come inside for just a minute. We'll need to wash and put on masks and gowns. Then we can meet the Harrisons. Do that much for me, and I swear I'll never bring up this subject again."

Not my problem, not my problem, not my problem, went the mantra. But the moment Nikki Harrison looked up at her through Angie's brown eyes, Dana's resolution shattered, along with her vow to stay out of her sister's life and get her own on track.